The Texas Tradition Series: *Number Thirty*

James Ward Lee, *Editor*

Fast Copy

a novel by
Dan Jenkins

Foreword by Sally Jenkins

Afterword by Jeff Guinn

TCU Press
Fort Worth

*This book is a work of fiction. Names, characters, places and incidents are
either the product of the author's imagination or are used fictitiously. Any
resemblance to actual events or locales or persons, living or dead, is
entirely coincidental.*

Library of Congress Cataloging in Publication Data

Jenkins, Dan
    Fast copy / by Dan Jenkins ; foreword by Sally Jenkins
        p.cm. — (The Texas tradition series ; no. 30)
        ISBN 0-87565-240-9 (pbk. ; alk. paper)
    1. Newspaper publishing—Fiction. 2. Women journalists—Fiction. 3.
Police corruption—Fiction. 4. Depressions—Fiction. 5. Texas—Fiction. I.
Title. II. Series

PS3560.E48 F37 2001
813'.54—dc21
2001027299

Acknowledgments and Permissions at the end of the book on page 403

Foreword

DAN JENKINS has always considered Texas to be a seat of world history, practically on a par with Rome and Constantinople. While it's not uncommon for authors to exhibit a literary fascination with the place they were born, I would suggest that his love for and preoccupation with his birthplace exceeds even that of Faulkner's with his Mississippi or Shakespeare's with his England. In *Fast Copy* it achieves full expression. What you hold here in your hands is a novel of atmosphere and a work of historical fiction, but mainly, it is a book about home.

I love this book because it is the only father-daughter story he ever wrote, and I am his daughter, and it's set around our hometown. I love it too, because it is his sole attempt to excavate and place on paper the vivid images of his childhood in Depression-era Texas, ones that I listened to him describe when I was a girl and he was my daddy, driving me around Fort Worth. There, he'd point, was his old grade school, where he was with a gang who busted out all the windows throwing rocks at them. There was the grocery store where he stood lookout for an adolescent instance of burglary when his friends were trying to acquire doughnuts. There was Paschal High, where he ruled the radiators. Mostly, I love this book because like him I am a writer and it is an example of where good writing really comes from: it comes from ineradicable memories that seep down inside a person's consciousness and disappear for decades, only to reappear later in the form of good material that, if you aren't afraid to use it, if you can give it meaning and story context, becomes art. *Fast Copy* is my father's most serious book, and, in places, it is far and away his most evocative, and perhaps even (he'll kill me for using the word but it's true) his most outright artistic.

Fast Copy is also a book he might never have written, and had he not, it is also the one book he would have regretted not writing. At the end of his career, after all the best sellers are counted up and all of the notoriously profane Jenkins-invented rules of drinking and dining and talking and screwing have passed into common usage, it is the book that will signal readers what his deeper, more buried intentions were. His books, contrary to popular assumptions, do have deeper intent, although he has long been resigned to misinterpretation. "Comedy," he once told me, "has always been under-appreciated." The price for writing funny was not to be taken seriously. He has been willing to pay it—mostly.

The majority of his books are, as he calls them, "romantic comedies," or comedies of manners, ostensibly lighter-than-air works of fiction but with scathing undercurrents on the subjects of sex and race. It is a pertinent fact that in every book he has ever written the women are routinely smarter than the men, and the good guys always win in the end. His plots follow a specific construct: he sets a traditional male world in motion and then creates irreverent outsiders to come along and upset things. Nobody dies, except for the readers who die laughing at themselves (which of course is the whole point).

Fast Copy differs. It is an anomaly in several ways; there are dead bodies everywhere, it is not a romantic comedy or a comedy of manners, it is not set in the modern era or a sports arena, and while there are screamingly funny things in the pages, it is not always especially funny.

He wrote it purely for himself. Nobody else wanted him to write it. Absolutely nobody. His readers, his publishers, and his agent urged him to return to the sports novel form. He ignored them and instead wrote the book, that I, for one, had always wished he would. He wrote about a time when his home state seemed to be the most important place in the world, when the Texas Centennial brought Billy Rose and Casa Mañana to town, and a Texas Ranger named Frank Hamer chased Bonnie and Clyde, and Sam Baugh was throwing footballs on the practice field over at TCU, and Fort Worth-bred golfers Ben Hogan and Byron Nelson were sauntering down fairways, and newspapers were vital to a town.

My father's second great love, apart from Texas, is journalism. For him, they are indivisible. One day his grandmother found an old typewriter in the attic and put it on the kitchen table for him to play with, and he started teaching himself to type on it by retyping the stories in the local newspaper. He was around ten or eleven. He would retype the sports stories and the war stories.

Then one day he started rewriting them, trying to improve them. He got his first newspaper job when he was still in high school, and he spent a dozen years on daily newspapers in Fort Worth and Dallas, so the newsroom setting to *Fast Copy* is more authentic and came more naturally to him than anything in his sports novels. He was once asked how he made the leap from journalism to fiction. He answered, "I didn't go anywhere, I just put another piece of paper in the typewriter. Like most journalists, I think, I'd always wanted to try a novel. I'd written some non-fiction books, so I was a 'published author.' I knew I ought to write about what I knew. I'd never been to war, but I'd been in a lot of locker rooms and press boxes, so I wrote *Semi-Tough*, a novel about football. It got me out of the box, so I wrote *Dead Solid Perfect*, a novel about golf. And I've kept at it, with other novels about magazines, newspapers, Hollywood. Stuff I've experienced."

But *Fast Copy* is also the longest and most elaborately plotted of all of his books. More happens in it. He did not have a clear idea of the plot before he started. I can remember sitting on the floor of his den, helping him sort through the old front pages from Depression-era newspapers. "I know how it's going to start and how it's going to end," he likes to say, "but I like to surprise myself along the way. A new character I hadn't planned on always seems to jump in along about the fifth or sixth chapter. That's part of the fun. Otherwise, it would just be carpentry."

At a certain point, he left behind research, and the collaboration between his own memory and writer's sensibility took over. There are pages and pages of things in this book that he included to please no one but the author, from descriptions of famous college football teams to expositions on journalistic ethics. In the epilogue, the main character gives a dissertation that is one of my favorite things he has ever written. It is a piece of dialogue for character, but it happens to sum up many of his own feelings about writing, journalism, and the 1930s Texas he was reared in.

On rereading it, it strikes me that perhaps, after all, this book was not strictly, entirely for him.

It may have been a little bit for his children, too.

—Sally Jenkins
New York City
January 2001

For every ink-stained wretch

who knows what it's like to wait

for the deadline muse.

Is it true what they say about Dixie?

Does the sun really shine all the time?

—From the song that was

No. 1 on Your Hit Parade

in June 1936

———

PART ONE

Just So Glad to Be Back Home

One

———

BETSY THROCKMORTON stared out of the train window at the amoeba. That's what she thought the heat looked like as it came up off the ground in Texas in that blistering summer of 1935. Microscopic bugs. Things that wriggled and crinkled and seemed eager to attack an innocent person's neck or shoulders or poor old armpit. When the Texas heat got to stirring around with the Texas dust, you could almost reach out and grab a handful if you wanted to, not that anybody ever did—there was always so much of it inside your clothes you could damn near make biscuits, air conditioning being what it was at the time.

The train was one of the new stainless-steel zephyrs. Flashes of eerie light bounced off the cars as the zephyr rolled across the dry, lumpy prairie in bright sunshine.

It amused Betsy to think how the sight of the zephyr might be causing dogs to howl and scoot for cover, and old Model A's to cough and jerk, and may have even scared a few human beings so bad they had gone out and done something drastic, like buy a Goddamn newspaper to see if Buck Rogers was real and had come down here to fuck with Texas.

The Sunshine Special, as the train was called, was moving through some scrubby flatlands that were generously known as North Central Texas. This was a dignified name for a harsh and inconsiderate land that could show you a blue norther, a black tornado, a brown dust storm, and melt a dinosaur into a sweat stain, all in one day.

A half-hour out of Fort Worth now. Betsy realized the city must be getting closer as she looked out beyond the amoeba and saw a grain elevator, tall and fat, the color of sandpaper, ribs bulging as it rose up out of the mesquite and weeds and scorpions.

A grain elevator could sometimes look like a giant ship

sailing on dirt, or even a small town, but that's when you were a little kid, prone to daydreaming. To Betsy, this one just looked like a big old grain elevator, a reminder of how those things often grazed like cattle on the Texas landscape.

Fort Worth had grain elevators like New York City had skyscrapers. Betsy's old hometown of Claybelle, twenty-five miles south and slightly west of Fort Worth, only had one grain elevator. Bewley Mill was Claybelle's skyscraper.

Counting the time it would take to drive to Claybelle from the T&P station in downtown Fort Worth, figuring in the stops for freight trains, chugholes, and armadillos, Betsy guessed she was now only a couple of hours from the place where she had been born and raised.

Back for good? That would be partly up to her husband, somewhat up to her daddy, and a whole lot up to Texas.

Betsy was aware that living in Texas again wasn't going to be easy, not as easy as the people around Claybelle would think. They thought of it as God's country, of course. The people who never left small towns, in Texas or anywhere else, always called it God's country, as if they knew for a fact that God took a dim view of bright lights, dark saloons, jazz, theater, swanky restaurants, tabloids, foreigners, and interesting conversations with interesting people. God, they were certain, was partial to the big sky, the solitude of the land—all that tumbleweed shit.

After nine years up East, a good bit of New York City had stuck to Betsy Throckmorton. More of it than the Texas dust, she was happy to admit.

But this trip was no lark, no visit as in the past, no casual experiment. The newspaper was going to be hers, the radio station was going to be Ted's. Ben Throckmorton had guaranteed it, and Betsy's daddy didn't make empty promises. If Ben shook your hand, it was a done deal.

Betsy knew how fortunate she was. Not everybody's daddy owned a thriving daily newspaper and a profitable radio station in the middle of the Depression.

Most people in the country were down and out, trying to get by on hope, prayer, handouts, the kindness of relatives, and radio jokes. And those who may have been suffering the worst were the ones who had made money and lived high in the flamboyant Twenties but had suddenly lost everything they owned, and their pride along with it, when Wall Street had gone down on itself in 1929.

Ben Throckmorton hadn't been one of those. The stock market was for thieves and suckers, he had said all along. Ben hadn't invested in anything but his own hard work in building up his newspaper and radio station. He had not only survived the Wall Street crash, he was one of the few Americans who was even prospering in these Depression Thirties, a personal condition for which he made no apologies whatsoever.

The question of why Ben had now decided to turn over his empire to his only daughter and this Eastern fellow she had married a little over a year ago could be answered by anyone who knew him well. He wanted to get Betsy back to Texas. She was his favorite person.

When Betsy had eloped with Ted Winton, Ben hadn't been caught by total surprise, but he wasn't sure that she had known what she was doing. Still, he had tried to accept the news cheerfully. Cheerful was his style, except when it came to finding his golf ball in a sand trap or seeing TCU lose a football game.

Betsy had said to Ben on the phone, "Think of it this way, Daddy. You haven't lost a daughter, you've gained a Yale man."

"Honey, if one of those is what you want, I'm happy."

"You don't sound happy."

"Well, I reckon it could be worse," Ben had said. "He could have a hyphen in his name."

Betsy was eager to take over the paper. Eager to prove that a woman could handle it. Eager to kick ass editorially. Eager to introduce the world to the second coming of Herbert Bayard Swope.

As a kid, she had spent more time in the newsroom of the *Claybelle Times-Standard* than a molded sandwich. By the time she was twelve, she had taught herself how to use a typewriter. She would sit at desks and copy stories out of the paper, pretending to be a reporter, a *writer*. Before long, she was rewriting the leads to improve them. That's when Ben might have guessed he had an ink-stained wretch on his hands.

Betsy had loved hanging around the paper, learning about layouts and makeup, learning to read the lead type backwards in the makeup forms, learning to write a 2-36 that would count. She had never learned how to run a linotype machine—only guys named Les and Squirrely could do that —but she had been fascinated to watch the writers wait for the deadline muse and then bang away at their machines. She had caught the disease. And now she was coming back after four years of college in New York and five years on the magazine in New York, and bringing with her some vigorous opinions about what a good newspaper ought to be.

To start with, she had told her daddy, it might be a slight improvement to run more stories about world affairs than how to put up peach preserves. She was determined to be an aggressive, innovative editor. She understood that most people didn't care for the press in general, but screw the people. The people needed a free press whether they wanted one or not.

Ted Winton was a journalist, too. He had worked on the same magazine with Betsy. He wasn't going to give up writing—he planned to free-lance articles in his spare time—but he was intrigued with the awesome power of radio, though he didn't suspect that running KVAT could be all that difficult for a man of his inherent good taste, him a Yale man.

Betsy was confident that together she and Ted could enlighten Claybelle a little. Maybe, as she said, let everybody in on the news that Benito Mussolini wasn't the guy waiting in line to fight Barney Ross for the welterweight championship of the world.

Ben Throckmorton wasn't opposed to enlightenment. He just hoped it didn't fuck up revenue.

Now in the dark wood and maroon-upholstered compartment of the train, a private compartment, Betsy looked out at a large billboard as it went past the window.

A pretty blond lady held a mixing bowl and a tablespoon, her hair worn in the short-bob fingerwave fashion of yesterday. She seemed to be saying that everybody should buy Gladiola flour.

Betsy felt better about her own hairdo for a moment. She

didn't look like a lady advertising Gladiola flour, although she may have looked like somebody who had been overly impressed with Ginger Rogers in *The Gay Divorcée*.

She was letting her own light brown hair grow out longer and was keeping it in a smooth shoulder-length pageboy, brushed over to one side and often held back with a barrette, as it was today.

Betsy was a slender but curvy young woman of twenty-seven. Her deep brown eyes invited conversation. She always looked alert. She laughed easily and often, an honest, husky, likable laugh, but she probably laughed too often when laughter wasn't called for—a journalistic affliction.

She was that rare type of girl who looked as good in one of her husband's baggy shirts or sweaters as she did in something fashionable, such as the pale green short-sleeve silk dress she was wearing.

Betsy had never had to work at looking good—she woke up pretty. And with those big dark brown eyes and her long soft hair and her Claudette Colbert cheekbones and her smooth creamy skin, she was almost as pretty as her husband.

Ted was still back in the club car talking to Johnson, Leland, and Lawton, three Texas businessmen, robust gentlemen who could have passed for grownup triplets with their Stetsons, string ties, Western suits, and toothpicks.

Betsy had been with Ted in the club car earlier. She had spent much of the trip in the club car, seeing as how the air conditioning there at least strived for the temperature of a damp basement, whereas the air conditioning in the private compartment only aspired to a chilled humidity.

Johnson was the tallest and oldest of the three. He had introduced himself and the others by saying, "I'm Johnson. This here's Leland. That there's Lawton."

They had sat down with Betsy and Ted to share a bowl of peanuts. One of the men had taken a handful of peanuts and poured them into a bottle of Dr Pepper.

Betsy had attempted conversation, saying that the club car was the coolest place on the train.

The only place you could adequately cool off these days, she said, was in a picture show.

"I don't need the flu that bad," Johnson said.

He sounded like Ben Throckmorton.

Betsy smiled and said, "My daddy prefers a good ceiling fan over air conditioning. He says a picture show is a pneumonia parlor."

"I ain't ever seen a picture show that made sense," Johnson said.

Leland and Lawton nodded in solemn agreement.

Betsy smiled again, looked at Ted, and did a reasonably good imitation of her daddy.

She drawled:

"It ain't worth pneumonia for me to watch a Northwest Mounted Policeman sit on a horse and sing a song."

"Movies," Leland said, shaking his head.

Back in her own voice, Betsy said, "Actually, it doesn't bother me so much when the Mountie sings. It's when the fur trapper sings back—that's when you're in trouble."

Nobody laughed.

Lawton said, "I seen a movie one time where a man on a horse chased a man in a automobile and caught him! I'm derned if he didn't. Right there on the screen."

"Well, you liable to see anything in Hollywood," Leland said.

"Horse caught a car," said Lawton. "I think it was a '32 Ford. Something like that. Man on the horse roped the driver. Jerked him right out from behind the wheel."

Johnson, Leland, and Lawton were from Waco and thereabouts. Cotton belt. They said they were on their way back from a weekend of watching the St. Louis Cardinals try to play baseball. It was an annual trip. Three games at Sportsman's Park, then back to the old business grind.

"Cardinals is everybody's team," Lawton said. "Everybody west."

Too bad about the Cardinals, Ted said. It looked as if they weren't going to repeat as the National League champions. Quite an entertaining team, though.

"Naw, Dizzy got hisself a sore arm in July," Johnson said. "Ducky's hittin' singles, but he can't do it alone. Pepper ain't hit squat."

"You can stick a fork in 'em," Leland said.

"Yeah, they done," Lawton agreed.

"Balloon heads," Leland said with a sigh. "You win you a World Series, you get a balloon head. We seen 'em play the Pirates twice, Cubs once. Arky Vaughan hit everything they throwed. Bill Lee ain't throwed nothin' they could hit."

Lawton stretched and popped his neck and said, "Baseball's a game of slumps. There ain't much else to it."

"Tell you what they done," said Johnson. "They done got me ready for football. I'm ready to see 'em pump air in the old pig bladders."

Betsy brightened as the topic changed to football. She mentioned that Ted had played football in college, for Yale.

The men all stared at Ted.

"Where is it Yale's at?" Lawton wondered. "Just north of the outdoors, ain't it?"

Johnson answered before Ted could. "Aw, it's up there around Boston or New England. I forget which."

"New Abshire," Leland said. "It's New Abshire or Rhode Hampton."

The men weren't that dumb. Betsy knew it if Ted didn't. She hoped her husband wouldn't wind up buying a set of encyclopedias from one of them.

"You played the game yourself?" Lawton said to Ted.

"For Yale, yes."

"Halfback," Betsy added.

The men exchanged looks as Ted politely reminded them that college football had originated in the East, that all of the rules and nearly every wrinkle in coaching strategy in football today had been developed in the East, and that up until the last ten or fifteen years most of the greatest players had come from the East.

"You ain't even been cut up," Lawton observed.

"I what . . . ?"

Lawton grinned. "I'll tell you what. Feastin' my eyes on a soft old boy like you, I'd have to say football's in a little better hands now that it's found its way down here to Texas."

Ted's looks were deceptive. He had curly black hair, a fair complexion, a sweet smile, as some described it, and a fetish for clean fingernails. On this day his oxblood shoes were polished to a high sheen and his red and blue striped tie was carefully knotted at the collar of his clean white shirt. A well-muscled body was hidden beneath his shirt and gray slacks, and there was something else Johnson, Leland, and Lawton might have noticed if they had cared to: Ted's broad neck, the trait of any football player, even the wiriest halfback.

In the autumn of '27, Ted's senior season at Yale, he had been a sixty-minute halfback on Coach Tad Jones's greatest team. Though he had primarily been a crisp blocker and sure tackler, Ted had become a surprisingly fierce ballcarrier on one particular Saturday that year. It had been Ted more than any other Bulldog who had helped Bruce Caldwell, the All-American in the backfield, lead Yale to a 10-to-6 victory over Army in the biggest game of the season. Yale had gone on to win the National Championship of college football in '27, as chosen by *Illustrated Football*. The esteemed sportswriter Grantland Rice had neglected to give Ted a nickname, but Ted had been an authentic football hero nonetheless.

Betsy had considered pointing all this out to Johnson, Leland, and Lawton but hadn't gone to the trouble. She had long since learned that Texans seldom liked to let facts interfere with their opinions.

Betsy had only mashed out her cigarette in an ashtray and risen to leave. "I think I'll go back to my book."

"I ain't much for books," Lawton said. "They real thick. Most of 'em."

It was all Betsy could do to keep from repeating something she had once heard a Texan say with immense pride: "What I don't know, I don't ask."

Now back in the private compartment, Betsy lit another Lucky from the dark green pack on the table in front of her. She exhaled through her nostrils like the bitchy ladies in the picture shows, and enjoyed her own company.

Funny how football had been such a big influence on her life.

She wouldn't have wanted to trade places with a triple-threat quarterback in this world, but she supposed if there was such a thing as reincarnation, she would rather come back as a football star than any number of female things she could think of offhand: mother of six, carhop, crippled seamstress, fat person, holy roller.

Football was partly responsible for her and Ted being together. Those football feats of Ted's—and Yale's—had more than likely been responsible for Ted landing his job at *Time,* which was where they had met in the first place.

They had each been hired personally by Henry Luce, the direct, fast-talking, no-nonsense gentleman who had founded The Weekly Newsmagazine in 1923.

Ted had joined the magazine first. Henry Luce had offered him the job in the spring of '28, before Ted had even graduated from Yale. Ted had applied for a job on the edit staff. He hadn't expected to be hired as a writer immediately. He thought he might be asked to join the research staff first.

"You're from Bridgehampton," Luce had said at their meeting. "Long Island kid."

"Yes, sir. I played high school football. That's what got me to Yale. My father owns a grocery store in Bridge. My mother teaches English at Bridgehampton High. I guess that's how I got interested in writing."

"We practice journalism here, not writing," Luce said.

"Yes, sir, I understand. There's definitely a difference in the two things."

Ted had felt confident going into the interview. He had known Luce was a Yale man, and someone had told him Luce had seen that Yale-Army game in '27.

"Sales," Luce said.

"I beg your pardon?"

"That's the big ball game."

Luce opened a copy of a current issue of *Time* and pointed to a page.

"You know what this is?" Luce asked.

"An ad?"

"It's a *full-page* ad, Ted. In the magazine game, this is known as a touchdown!"

Ted had been hired as an ad salesman at *Time,* Luce believing that Ted's reputation as a Yale football player would bring in some business.

For Ted, ad sales had largely meant going to extravagant lunches in fancy hotel dining rooms with clients who dropped the names of their wealthy fathers-in-law. It wasn't day labor, but it wasn't journalism either.

Ted had been rescued from this fate soon enough, about a year later, by Stillwell Padgam-Norris, one of *Time*'s most valued editors. Stillwell Padgam-Norris wore bow ties, constantly toyed with a lock of sandy hair which kept falling over one eye, and possessed an English accent that seemed to come and go. He might have looked more at home on the staff of *The New Yorker*, the other magazine which had offices in the building on West 43rd Street, except it had never entered his mind to try to work at *The New Yorker*, he said. He knew most of those overblown talents personally, and *The New Yorker* was doomed to failure.

It was "Still" Norris, as he liked to be called, who convinced "Harry" Luce, as *he* liked to be called, that Ted should move into editorial. Still Norris felt he had observed in Ted a "concern" for society, for the world, and he also liked Ted's knack for writing memos in backward sentences.

Ted had become a "catchall" writer at *Time*, one who worked in all sections of "the book," as Still Norris referred to it, and one who gradually learned to master the use of Still Norris's pet phrase—"by week's end," the valued editor's major contribution to journalism.

Betsy was hired as a researcher in the spring of '30, only a month after receiving her degree in English from the Barnard College for Women. She had always suspected—but could never confirm—that her daddy had made a phone call to somebody important, like Amon Carter in Fort Worth, the influential publisher of the *Star-Telegram,* and that Amon Carter had made a phone call to somebody else important, and that this was how she had wound up sitting in Henry Luce's office one afternoon, cagily overdoing her Southern accent.

Betsy's interview with Henry Luce couldn't have lasted more than five minutes. She'd hardly had time to take in all the photos on Luce's walls—the handsome Luce in the company of Chiang Kai-shek, Jack Dempsey, Charles Lindbergh, Calvin Coolidge, Knute Rockne, and other newsmakers—before the interview ended.

"Our writers entertain, our editors inform, our researchers keep us accurate," Luce had said rapidly.

"I can do that," Betsy had said, straight from Dixie.

"Which one?"

"All three."

She had been hired on the spot. Maybe the phone calls had made the difference, but so what? She had been more than qualified for a job on the *Time* staff. Her? An ink-stained wretch? Raised on the music of the press run at the *Claybelle Times-Standard?* And she was pleased to discover in less than a year that she was more qualified to be in journalism than most people on the magazine's staff, starting with that old clean-up hitter, Still Norris, and followed by all of the other yacht-club commodores who masqueraded as editors.

That spring, Ben Throckmorton had offered to send his daughter to Europe for the summer as a graduation present. Betsy had turned down the trip to snap up the offer at *Time.*

"Daddy, Europe sounds great, but I can't pass up this opportunity," she had said.

With pride, Ben had said, "Of course you can't, honey—with your genes and all."

She *did* accept a graduation present of another kind. She allowed Ben to pay the first year's lease on a one-bedroom apartment in the Ansonia Hotel, which, as she said, was a way to go to Europe without sailing.

The Ansonia was an overwrought fortress in the Seventies up on Broadway, a building of soaring towers and ornate balconies, reeking with turn-of-the-century splendor. Most of the residents of the Ansonia looked like seedy royalty, artists, musicians, and authors of thirty-pound philosophy books.

Ben approved of the Ansonia. It looked safe. "An oboe never killed anybody," he said.

This apartment was a vast improvement over the one where she had lived during her last two years of college, a decaying hovel at 93rd and Amsterdam that she shared with Millicent Saunders, her best friend at Barnard.

Millie Saunders, a cute lippy redhead from Pittsburgh, had adopted Betsy, and Betsy had adopted Millie, the moment they met and discovered that they laughed, drank, smoked, and cussed more than any other two women on the campus.

"Got a light, sailor?"

That was the first thing Millie had said to Betsy.

Millie's father, Pete, was a self-made man on the order of

Ben Throckmorton. Pete Saunders sold auto parts, lots of them; and Pete and Sheila, Millie's mother, liked to "destroy money," as Pete loved putting it.

Millie's parents had once hired a Negro maid for the sole purpose of teaching the family how to do the Charleston.

Pete and Sheila, both flashy dressers, would come to New York often and take the girls out on the town, to speakeasies like Leon & Eddie's, the Vendome, the Tree Club, Gallant's, and Texas Guinan's, where Pete was on the priority list of the owner, a raucous blonde from Waco, Texas, named Mary Louise Cecelle Guinan.

Pete had been known to dance on a table with Texas Guinan, and Sheila had been known to dance on a table with a trombone player. It was easy to see where Millie got her spunk.

The experiment of Prohibition had been perpetrated on the United States in 1920, and it had been so successful, predictably, that by 1926—Betsy and Millie's first year in college— there were only 100,000 speakeasies in Manhattan alone.

A row of canopies and step-down joints on 52nd Street between Sixth and Fifth Avenue was known, quite affectionately, as "the wettest block in America."

Betsy and Millie would go into the speaks with Millie's folks and leave with membership cards for themselves.

Pete Saunders would arrange it. Pete would introduce the girls to Charley, the owner or manager of a joint, and suggest that the girls be given a membership card.

He would be shaking hands with Charley at the time.

"How old are they?" Charley would ask.

Pete would laugh. "They're both a hundred."

Charley would look down at his palm and the girls would get their cards.

Betsy to Millie on one of those nights: "You know what I admire most about your daddy? He has no threshold for inconvenience."

Pete and Sheila had also introduced the girls to the classy white-trade nightclubs in Harlem. There, Betsy and Millie would revel in the low-down syncopated jazz sounds that were creeping upstream from New Orleans.

Up in Harlem, where canaries sang while hepcats played

the mothbox, hides, plumbing, and licorice sticks, they had listened to the rhythms of Fletcher Henderson at the Cotton Club, Duke Ellington at Barron's Cabaret, Bennie Carter at the Alhambra Ballroom. On many a night they had wound up at their two favorite hot spots, which were in the same block on Seventh Avenue at 132nd Street.

At the Lafayette, they would sway and groove to "The Empress of the Blues," Bessie Smith. Millie's father, flashing a double sawbuck, would make a request. Bessie would take the twenty, stick it in the pocket of the carpenter's apron she wore beneath her long white-fringed dress, and belt out "Give Me That Old Slow Drag." Two doors away, in a low-ceilinged rendezvous called Connie's Inn, the girls would kick out to a group led by a cornet player known as Father Dip to the other musicians and Satchmo to the customers, as Louie Armstrong would "take it on home" with "Alabamy Bound."

A professor made the observation in class one day that jazz was immoral; that it combined nervousness and lawlessness with a savage animalism; that it was nothing more than an attempt by a joyless industrial civilization to arouse the fatigue-poisoned minds and drudgery-jaded bodies that inhabited it.

"Gosh, I'm fatigue-poisoned," Betsy would say to Millie. "What do you want to do tonight?"

"Oh, I don't care," Millie would reply. "I've been feeling so drudgery-jaded lately, I think I'm in the mood for something immoral."

They began going to the speaks and nightclubs on their own, to hear nervous music, drink lawless whiskey, smoke savage cigarettes, and laugh immorally.

"You know the best thing about college?" Millie said one night. "It's the last time you're above the law."

Lucky for them that in all those nights in the speaks, somebody hadn't rolled a pineapple under a table trying to snuff out Big Frenchy De Mange, the only actual gangster, to their knowledge, who had ever bought them drinks.

They understood that their parents *did* expect them to graduate, but they refused to cut back on their nightlife, even after they were grownup juniors and were living in the wretched hovel at 93rd and Amsterdam.

At some vague, distant point in the future, they assumed, a diploma would come floating down from heaven.

"Busy?" Betsy would say.

"No. You busy?"

"No."

"Want to go to class?"

Ben Throckmorton had seen the wretched hovel once, which was enough. He had come to New York for a publishers' meeting and had dropped in on the girls the day before they had been expecting him.

Ben had been welcomed to a sight of peeling paint on the walls, faded flowers, unmade beds, debris everywhere—books, newspapers, clothing, "race" records, overflowing ashtrays, empty bottles of bootleg whiskey, and dirty dishes in the sink and elsewhere.

"My contract clearly stipulates that you aren't supposed to be here till tomorrow," Betsy had said.

"I guess I could buy you a washing machine," Ben had muttered after looking around.

"Thank you, Mr. Throckmorton, but we already have a cocktail shaker," Millie had said.

Betsy had said of the hovel, "It's not so small, Daddy. It holds three—me, Millie, and Raskolnikov."

Betsy thought of Ted back in the club car with the rural intellectuals. What were they discussing now, pathos and humor in the American novel?

She had been stricken with Ted from the moment she had seen him up close in a hallway at *Time*. Here was an ex-football hero so good-looking he needed to wear a keep-off sign to protect him from the office wrens.

That Ted had been a football star had impressed her all the more, for Betsy had been brought up a football fan by her daddy. Ben was something more than a football fan, actually. Around Claybelle he was known as Football Silly.

While at Barnard, Betsy had seldom missed a college game on Saturday, somewhere. Up at Yale or West Point, over to Princeton, Baker Field occasionally, the Polo Grounds—somewhere. She had given some thought to staying in Texas and going to college—to TCU in Fort Worth or SMU in Dallas

—because she had grown up on Southwest Conference football, but Ben would have suffered two strokes and a brain hemorrhage if she hadn't gone East to get the hot-shit, thickbook education he could well afford and wanted her to have.

Betsy grew to like Barnard after the traumas of her first semester, that awkward period when she'd had to get used to sharing cramped spaces with other girls, some of whom might have been able to play a little football themselves.

"Arm yourself and wait" had been Millie's advice regarding two or three of their dormmates.

Betsy lived in Fisk Hall her first two years at Barnard. It was the oldest residence on the campus. Fisk sheltered about a hundred young ladies. The din up and down the hallways, the bathwater that ranged from cold to brown, and the wholesale theft, Betsy assumed, were all designed to prepare young ladies for the afterlife of adulthood.

Ben called his daughter often that first year to see how she was getting along with her studies.

"Great," she would say. "Today I discovered the dessert spoon."

Betsy had wanted to lavish all of her football interest on the Columbia Lions, they being neighbors in Morningside Heights—across the street, in fact—but in those days the Lions didn't look as if they could hold their own against a squad of amputees. They might defeat a Union now and then, but they would get tied by a Johns Hopkins, and they would lose with remarkable ease to any Yale that came along.

Conversationally, Betsy referred to her football neighbors as "the severely average Columbia Lions."

She badly wanted to settle on a New York team that she could support wholeheartedly, but a team that made sense, and one that might win a game intentionally as opposed to accidentally.

Fordham and NYU had winning teams then, but they weren't serious possibilities. Fordham was up in the Bronx, and there were all these priests creeping around in the trees. Coming from Texas, Betsy had never known a Catholic who admitted it publicly. She was pretty sure that Catholics didn't kidnap small children in the middle of the night, beat them with crucifixes, and poke lighted candles at them until they could speak Latin fluently, but she wasn't altogether certain. NYU? The Violets had a great back named Ken Strong, but NYU was down in Greenwich Village; and somehow Greenwich Village didn't have the ring to it of a South Bend, an Ann Arbor, a Tuscaloosa, or a Palo Alto.

She had finally chosen Yale. After all, Yale had practically invented college football. Walter Camp and all that. All-Americans outnumbering stock portfolios. National Championships stacked up like investment bankers. A mammoth stadium. Yale dominated the New York sports pages. If Boston was Harvard's town, New York was Yale's—and she didn't know where this left Princeton.

"Yale is the team of the discerning New Yorker," Betsy had announced to Millie one evening.

"I prefer Yale," Millie had agreed. "More guys."

The day Betsy had summoned up the courage to introduce herself to Ted Winton in a hallway at *Time,* she had said, "Hi, I'm Betsy Throckmorton. I saw you throw that block on Chris Cagle."

"My only time in a newsreel." Ted grinned shyly.

"I was there!" Betsy said. "You got the block, and Bruce Caldwell ran thirty-two yards. Big play. It set up your field goal. Yale's, I mean."

"We got our share of the breaks."

"I *knew* that game would be for the National Championship! Two great teams. You guys had four All-Americans— Caldwell, Webster, Quarrier, Charlesworth. Army had two— Cagle and Sprague."

"I'm sorry, did you say your name was Graham McNamee?"

"I'm kind of a football nut," Betsy had explained.

Betsy had instigated similar conversations with Ted for over a year, long after the magazine had moved into its new offices on the fiftieth and fifty-first floors of the Chrysler Building.

By then she was convinced that Ted had dismissed her as some sort of tomboy nutcake who had been raised by Football Silly.

Ben Throckmorton had introduced his daughter to the glamour, the excitement, the drama, the color—the *importance*—of college football when she was thirteen. That's when

Ben had taken Betsy to Fair Park Stadium in Dallas to see a post-season game between Texas A&M and Centre College.

Betsy had never forgotten how nervous and excited her daddy had been that day, the day of the Dixie Classic, when the Texas Aggies, champions of the Southwest Conference, had taken on the incorrigible Praying Colonels.

The Praying Colonels of Centre College had been slipping up on national acclaim for four years, and in 1921 they had captured the whole country's attention. Here was an obscure little school located in Danville, Kentucky, but it had not only won all ten of its games, it had gone up to Cambridge and put an end to mighty Harvard's twenty-five-game winning streak. A player for Centre named Bo McMillin was doing for his school what Jim Thorpe had done for Carlisle, another little-known college, in an earlier chapter of American football history.

"Who's Jim Thorpe?" Betsy had asked her daddy.

"Don't matter," Ben had said. "Man you got to watch out for this afternoon is Bo McMillin. I'm sorry to say he's from Fort Worth. Somebody paid him to run off to Kentucky."

Ben was obviously going to pull for the Texas Aggies. State pride.

Ben expressed disgust as he watched Centre's stars—McMillin, Red Roberts, Red Weaver, Bill James—signing autographs before the game. He was further exercised by the sight of Bo McMillin escorting his wife, whom he had married that very morning, onto the playing field before the opening kickoff.

Texas A&M's Corps of Cadets, a great swatch of khaki in the grandstands across the way, had joined Ben Throckmorton in jeering this flagrant act of overconfidence.

Betsy had been enthralled by the uniforms—the Centre players in their black jerseys with gold stripes around their chests and gold numerals, and A&M's players in their gray jerseys with a wide maroon stripe around their chests, maroon numerals, khaki pants, and brown leather helmets.

"I want a football suit," Betsy said to her daddy.

"Girls don't play football," Ben had said. "Girls watch football."

"That's not fair!"

The game was the kind the sportswriters would call colossal, gigantic, and otherwise stupendous. The Aggies kept Bo McMillin bottled up, and meanwhile an Aggie named Puny Wilson ran wild, largely on deceitful end-around plays.

"Why do they call him Puny?" Betsy asked.

"Because he ain't," Ben said. "Puny's a pretty good-size boy."

Betsy thought this over. "So if he was a little scrawny guy they'd call him Blubber?"

"No, if he was a big old fat boy they'd call him Blubber. If he was a little old scrawny boy they'd probably call him Dogbone."

"But he's average so they call him Puny?"

"I guess he used to be puny, I don't really know."

Betsy thought about it some more. "Why don't they call him Average?"

"Just root for A&M," said Ben.

Ben liked to maintain later that he had seen it happen. This was the legendary game in which Texas A&M's Twelfth Man tradition had been born. In the fourth quarter of the hard-hitting game, Dana X. Bible, Texas A&M's coach, had sent a plea to a promising sophomore sitting in the stands with the Corps of Cadets. Injuries were depleting the squad. The coach wanted the kid to come down to the bench, slip into a uniform, and be ready to go in the game if called upon. The kid had done so. He hadn't been used, but from that day forward, the A&M Corps of Cadets had remained on its feet throughout every moment of every Aggie game—ready if needed, each cadet eager to be another Twelfth Man.

"I saw it," Ben would say when reminiscing about the game. "The kid came down out of the stands and . . ."

Which was bullshit.

Nobody knew about it until later when the A&M coach told a reporter.

In the closing minutes, after it became clear that the Aggies were going to pull off a big upset, Betsy said, "I want to be an Aggie."

"Can't," Ben said. "It's a military school. Men only."

"That's not fair!"

She stomped her foot, the spoiled little bitch.

When the final whistle sounded, the cadets in the stands sailed their campaign hats into the air, charged onto the field, and carried their heroes off on their shoulders.

Ben Throckmorton shed a tear of pride. He wasn't an Aggie, just a Texan.

He pointed at the scoreboard sitting on a platform at the open end of Fair Park Stadium.

It read: Texas A&M 22, Centre College 14.

"Remember this day," Ben said to his daughter. "What you saw here today was the biggest news story since the Armistice."

Betsy had seen right away that football involved the conflict of storybooks—the knights wore a different kind of armor, that's all.

Nothing aroused emotions like a football game. She liked it when bands played tunes that made her want to march or sing. She liked to watch cheerleaders have fits. She liked it when homecoming queens and campus sweethearts were given bouquets, kissed by game captains, and paraded around the stadium in convertibles. Almost nobody liked halftimes except Betsy, and people who needed to go to the bathroom.

And then it would be back to the playing field, where the knights in armor would hurl their bodies this way and that—diving, plunging, darting, passing, catching, kicking, blocking, bashing into each other.

Betsy recognized that college football was a game of causes, beliefs, loyalties. At stake were campus pride, civic pride, state pride.

It was a game in which the athlete could suffer monumental embarrassment and crushing heartbreak, or achieve the most incredible lasting glory.

She had heard her daddy say that great games, like great ideas, never went away.

Football was more than chess with human beings. It was the supreme test of bravery in sports, as close as man could come to war without death.

For Betsy, the game wasn't quite the inoperable tumor that it was for Football Silly, but it was a keen interest.

Ted opened the door to the private compartment.

Betsy gestured toward the view that was still available through the windows of the train—more vacant land, hardly a tree in sight, a rotted fence, a dilapidated farmhouse, a gravel road looking for a way out of the brush, the amoeba hovering.

"Tell the truth, Ted. What do you like best about Texas—the palm trees or the waterfalls?"

"Who's Joel Hunt?" he asked.

"Why?"

"Those chaps in the club car have never heard of Albie Booth. One of them said if Albie Booth *was* a football player, he couldn't piss a drop compared to Joel Hunt."

Betsy grinned. "It's a good thing you didn't mention Ducky Pond."

"I mentioned Ducky Pond," said Ted. "They're still laughing."

"Joel Hunt was a great halfback at Texas A and M. His last season was '27, same as you."

"I can't keep the Texas schools straight. There's Texas A and M . . . Texas University—"

"Texas Christian," Betsy said. "That's TCU. Don't get TCU mixed up with anybody. Daddy bleeds purple."

"Which ones are the Aggies?"

"A and M."

"Funny name. Who was Agatha?"

"*Agricultural* and *mechanical*," Betsy said with a look. "Soldiers are what they are, mostly. Texas A and M is a big military school, like West Point. More Aggies were killed in France than West Pointers."

She had no idea whether this was a fact but said it as if it had been taught in her high school.

"I know who Joel Hunt is," Ted said, bending down to give his wife a kiss. "He scored a touchdown in the East-West game. I heard it on the radio."

"That was a big day for Daddy. SMU's Gerald Mann scored a touchdown, too. TCU's Rags Mathews played a great game on defense. We won."

"The West, you mean?"

"Of course."

"That's because I wasn't invited to play for the East." Ted took the seat across from Betsy, shoving aside some books, magazines, newspapers—the residue of a long journey.

"It was a big scandal, too," Betsy came back quickly. "They all wrote about it for days—Rice, Runyon, Lardner, everybody."

Ted surrendered with a grin.

Betsy then poked around in her large brown leather bag for a fresh pack of Luckies. She came across an object, a chunk of wood. She held it up to Ted.

"Journalists like to remember where they've been," she said.

Betsy rolled the chunk of wood around in her fingers, and they both started to laugh at something nobody would have understood unless they had worked on that story.

Two

IN BETSY'S day, a female researcher at *Time* lived a happier life when she was assigned to work with a male staff writer who could actually write or, failing that, was attractive or, if nothing else, was single.

Since Ted was all of this, it led to some frustrating months for Betsy when their relationship had only been casual, much too distant to suit her. She was dying to get to know him better, even if she did not yet yearn to do what Millie said would be fun: tie him down and lick his whole body.

Betsy and Ted would see each other in the hall or copy room or art department and pass along a news flash from the world of college football—Bernie Bierman was leaving Tulane to coach at Minnesota—or laugh about an editor who had lost the contents page behind his radiator again.

But then they would go their separate ways: Ted to his cubicle where a Remington sat on a clean desk in front of a swivel chair, and Betsy to her cubicle where she would be buried among two telephones, a pile of reference books, two dozen out-of-town newspapers, a Smith-Corona with a cranky ribbon reverse, four smoldering ashtrays, and no window.

A researcher never had a window.

Researchers were expected to know how to write and report stories if called upon, but their job for the most part was to check the facts in stories that were written by the staff writers and edited by men like Still Norris, of which there were eight or ten, all of them dripping with Princeton ivy or speaking in quaint Harvard stammers. One editor harbored the dark secret that he had gone to Lehigh, and another flatly denied, unless drunk, that he had been anywhere near the Valparaiso campus.

It was a rule long established—by whom, no one knew— that a factual mistake that might appear in the magazine was never the fault of a writer or editor. It was the researcher's fault. This explained why it never bothered Betsy, or any of the other researchers, to disturb someone on the phone in the dead of night to ask if his nickname was "Oklahoma Face," or ask a woman getting ready to jump out of her apartment window to please verify that Dayton, Ohio, was in flames, or inquire of a professor if he was the same Nobel scientist who had proved that algebra caused spinal meningitis.

There were three other women among the nine researchers on the staff. Mabe Forrest, the doughnut queen, had led Smith College in home runs and RBI's. Tincy Courtney from Larchmont frequently suffered from shopper's limp when she wasn't having her hair done on office hours. And Lynne Burger, as unmarried as the others but now pushing forty, was determined to get elevator operators and mailroom boys into the Guild.

The five male researchers were all the same person—young men who had chosen the wrong profession but didn't know it yet. One of them was ideally suited for wine-tasting, two could have posed for clothing ads, and the other two should have been grinding it out on the old treadmill of the stock market. None of them could find the elevator without assistance.

The researchers were supposed to be under the direct control of their chief, a woman named Hazel Hanrahan, whose hair was worn in bangs, who wore bulky sweaters, Scottish plaid skirts, and ballet shoes, and could name all of the European capitals. But Hazel could only be relied upon for advice or direction when trapped in the presence of an editor. The rest of the time she was either talking on the phone to her suicidal daughter, a struggling actress, or her suicidal son, who also wanted to be an actress.

Now and then a researcher would be sprung from the office to interview a subject in person, but any notes the reporter might type up, regardless of how clever or illuminating, would be thrown in the wastebasket by an editor. A *Time* editor knew everything there was to know about everything, by virtue of the fact that he was, though God knows how it happened in many cases, a *Time* editor. Occasionally, the

Times or *Herald-Tribune* might tell him something he didn't know, if he bothered to read a paper on his commuter train, which he rarely bothered to do, being a *Time* editor and knowing everything to begin with. All of them had hopes of improving their position on the masthead, of becoming an assistant managing editor someday, so it *did* help that they had all been pedestrian writers themselves, had no ear whatsoever, no savvy, and were no earthly threat to anyone above them. Their lives mostly revolved around their weekends in Connecticut or Westchester—and their profit-sharing statements.

Time was a nice comfortable slick-paper place to work, a swell calling card and all that, but the job was beginning to get to Betsy. She was wondering if she would ever be promoted to staff writer, and if so, what grand assortment of nitwits would be handling her copy, and would it be worth the agony merely to be able to say she worked for the publication that Still Norris endearingly called "the flagship." Complaining to Millie one night, she said, "I'm not in journalism, I'm a Goddamn telephone jockey!"

Betsy was dating. She was going out with keen and earnest young men Millie dragged around from Lord & Taylor, where Millie had become an assistant buyer in Better Dresses, or the keen and earnest young men one normally tripped over in speakeasies and luncheonettes.

The keen and earnest young men would seldom have a sense of humor, or even a sense of purpose, other than to make social or financial connections. Betsy would shed them quickly, after one or two dates. Even quicker if they began to reminisce about their fun-filled days at Amherst or Sewanee, or started to talk about sailing.

Her list of all-stars had included the severely average Page Sumner, the doggedly mediocre Fieldon Wells, the supremely uninquisitive Rick Fesler, the intrepidly forgettable Jason Morris, and the fiendishly ordinary Mark Singleton.

All the while, Betsy lusted after Ted from afar.

It wasn't easy for her to watch him get involved with a couple of secretaries in the office. First with Nina Fought, sly kitten, who preferred editors. Then with Janice Bowen, slinky temptress, whose goal, as everyone knew, was to knock off the entire masthead.

Betsy's powers of concentration alone kept Ted from being joined at the hip to either one, though it may have been his lack of stamina.

There were moments when she was tempted to become a Nina or Janice herself—pounce on him in a bar one night after whispering, "Okay, kiddo, you know it's going to happen someday, I know it's going to happen someday, so why don't we drop the act and hit the old mattress?"—but a lady didn't do that sort of thing.

"Pounce!" Millie advised her one evening. "*I* won't tell anybody you're a slut."

Such was the state of Betsy's social life before the "Crime of the Century," as the tabloids called it, imposed a more intimate friendship upon her and Ted.

Tabloids had been flourishing since the birth of the *New York Daily News* in 1919, and they usually found a way to come up with a "Crime of the Century" four times a year, but this one had truly stunned the whole country.

It was the Lindbergh kidnapping.

Charles Lindbergh was an authentic aviation hero, a shaggy-haired symbol of everything courageous in the American spirit, and when a kidnapper climbed up a ladder to the second-story nursery of the Lindbergh home near Princeton, New Jersey, and stole away with Lucky Lindy's twenty-month-old baby, it was as though the kidnapping son of a bitch had violated every home in the United States.

Stillwell Padgam-Norris said the kidnapping was a malodorous act, if ever he'd seen one. Andrew Cheshire, another of *Time*'s valued editors, who could often be seen in the halls with a tennis racquet, said he had never been quite so discomforted by anything. It was *Time*'s managing editor, Lafester Cleed, a plump, drawling Tennessean with bushy hair, ever nostalgic about his days at W&L, who said the magazine should put its own people "in the field" on this one. Still Norris quite agreed—he never *disagreed* with a superior—whereupon he assigned Ted to the story as the writer and Betsy as the writer's trusty sidekick in that spring of 1932.

For six weeks, Betsy and Ted watched 50,000 police officers and volunteers search the Sourland Mountains, eighteen miles from Trenton, for the Lindbergh baby. They stayed at an inn called the Mountain Vista, which largely had a vista of the four hundred other newspaper and radio reporters who were covering the story.

They interviewed everyone possible—police, FBI agents, shopkeepers, volunteers—but mostly they swapped information with the other newshounds, which is how it is when reporters gather in droves on big stories.

A *Time* editor would never acknowledge it, but this was the true meaning of "group journalism."

When Charles Lindbergh paid the kidnapper a $50,000 ransom, Betsy and Ted and everyone else in the country hoped it would result in the child's being returned safely, but then, exactly seventy-three days from the night of the kidnapping, the battered body of Charles Augustus Lindbergh Jr. was found in a thicket only five miles from the house—and America was hit even harder by the tragedy.

Still Norris chose to think that *Time* had led the fight to persuade Congress to pass an urgent "Lindbergh Law," which Congress did, a law permitting J. Edgar Hoover's G-men to chase snatchers across state lines. Ted dealt with the issue numerous times in the magazine, but Betsy, for one, thought Ted's stories would have carried more bite if Still Norris hadn't inserted so many of his own words in the copy. Words such as depravedness, peccability, Gothicistic, fulsome, *élan*, and encroacher, among others, prompted Betsy at one point to accuse the editor of a crime more vile than the kidnapping.

"Are we writing for English teachers or what?" she asked him one day as she sat with him and watched him approving her check marks on copy.

"I tend to go along with Harry's view," the editor literally hummed. "If we please ourselves, we will undeniably please the reader."

"Harry said that?" Betsy smiled. "Why, that funny old Gothicistic encroacher."

The editor must not have heard her, or perhaps he didn't get it, which was no upset in either case. He went on butchering a sentence with his blue pencil.

Everybody covering the story had been ordered by their editors to try to track down a tall wooden ladder the kidnapper had used to enter the house. It might bear fingerprints, clues of some kind.

Still Norris had shrewdly said to Betsy, "It's my guess if you find the ladder you'll find the loathsome creature who did this."

"Will he be standing there holding it?" she had asked.

The ladder had never been found.

Two years passed before Bruno Richard Hauptmann was arrested and charged with the kidnapping and murder. Part of the ransom money had been traced to the Bronx apartment of Hauptmann, an ex-convict from Germany, a man with a bony face and shifty eye.

Shortly after Hauptmann's arrest, on a September night in '34, Betsy and Ted went for drinks to a favorite bar of Betsy's on 44th Street, a newspaper dive called Charley, Al, and Sally's, one of those places that served cheap hooch and a mystery stew that would only taste good if you had just returned from a six-month assignment in the Congo.

Once a speakeasy, Charley, Al, and Sally's catered to the tabloid set, guys and occasional gals who could write punchy leads and teasing headlines about torch murders and love nests, sugar daddies and thrill killers.

Betsy loved the joint, and every gossipy backyard-snooping gutter-urchin cynical gin-guzzling degenerate reporter who hung out there.

Tabloids were a good thing, Betsy had believed. They were as American as jazz. Just as necessary. In only a few short years they had taken her profession out of the hands of the club secretaries, tweed jackets, and fraternal handshakes and breathed new life into it. They were newspapers *of* the people, not *above* the people, as somebody had said. Maybe this wasn't altogether for the best, but it didn't make tabloids a national drug habit either. Wasn't it better for people to read a tabloid than no paper at all?

Anyhow, she loved Charley, Al, and Sally's even before she found the Lindbergh ladder in there.

The ladder had been chopped into four hundred pieces of wood and crammed into a burlap sack, and it sat on the floor at the feet of Marty Walsh, a radio technician for Mutual. Weary-looking man, slouch hat, wrinkled blue suit, loose tie, gin drinker. He was at the stand-up bar in the front of the room, drinking with two other weary-looking middle-aged men, Rauch of the *Evening Graphic* and Hitch of the *Daily Mirror*.

"Hey, Betsy, how's the newshen?" Marty Walsh had said as Betsy and Ted entered. "What are you hatching these days?"

Saluting the comrades, Betsy said, "Same old thing—gripping human drama and the grainy details of life."

Marty Walsh ordered drinks all around as the men went on with their conversation.

"Peaches Browning," Rauch was saying. "That was my best," and he quoted: " 'She was only a fifteen-year-old schoolgirl but her dream of love had already turned into a hideous, revolting nightmare.' Not bad, huh?"

Hitch only looked at him.

"It's great!" Rauch answered himself. "I should have got the Pulitzer, but they give it to Skeets Miller. Louisville guy. What'd he do? Climbed down in some cave, I don't know."

Hitch said, "Floyd Collins was '25. Peaches was '26."

"Whatever." Rauch shrugged, and everybody took a drink. "Who beat me in '26, the *Hartford Courant*? Another toilet backed up in a schoolhouse?"

"A highway didn't get paved," Hitch said.

Marty Walsh nodded at the burlap sack and asked Betsy if she wanted to buy a souvenir. He was selling pieces of the Lindbergh ladder for five dollars each.

"What do you *mean* this is the ladder?" Betsy said with astonishment.

"We got there first," Marty Walsh said. "I took it."

"You *took* it? You stole evidence?"

"I had it dusted. No prints."

Betsy and Ted looked at Rauch and Hitch, to whom it was old news, then at each other, then at the burlap sack.

Marty Walsh reached down in the sack and came up with a chunk of wood an inch thick, an inch wide. He handed it to Betsy.

"You've had this for *two* years?" Betsy said.

Marty Walsh shrugged.

Betsy burst into laughter. "Marty Walsh, accomplice."

"What, the guy flew in the window?" Marty Walsh said. "A guy on stilts kidnaps a baby? A pole-vaulter? If there had been any prints, I'd have given it to the cops after we scooped everybody. They've got the Kraut who did it, so what's all the commotion? You want a souvenir? It's five bucks."

Betsy bought a chunk of the ladder.

She and Ted then moved to a table in the rear of Charley, Al, and Sally's, back among the red-checkered tablecloths and the pictures on the walls of prizefighters, musicians, politicians, Yankees, Giants, gangsters. A poster-size photo of Al Capone adorned the back wall. It had been autographed by a newspaper wit, and said:

"When I sell hooch, they call it bootlegging. When you serve it, they call it hospitality. Your friend, Al."

Ted said that Betsy wanting a piece of the Lindbergh ladder was ghoulish.

"I couldn't resist," she said.

"What about a little piece of the baby's clothing? Would you like that?"

She bristled and said, "It's just a memento. Come on! The ladder's Goddamn funny and you know it!"

He manufactured a smile.

Betsy laughed and said, "The whole world's been looking for this for two years! I can't wait to tell Still Norris the Lindbergh ladder is two blocks from our vigilant office."

Betsy put the chunk of wood back in her brown leather bag. She said, "You know what it really reminds me of? The Lindbergh story was when I landed on you."

"You made an impression."

"I landed on you. It was the start of everything."

On the seat beside him in the compartment Ted rummaged through the magazines and newspapers, wondering if there was an article he had only read once.

"We went to lunch," he said, settling on a copy of *Vanity Fair*. The cover featured a caricature of FDR riding a horse into the sky.

"We went to lunch a *lot*," Betsy said.

"We went to Charley, Al, and Sally's."

"We *lived* at Charley, Al, and Sally's."

"We didn't have a real date for a year."

"You were working up to it."

Ted tossed the magazine aside, looked at his watch, and stood up. He reached up to the overhead racks and started to lift down some luggage to get ready for their arrival—suitcases of Betsy's made out of heavy, shiny, burnt-orange leather.

"I hope Millie's serious about coming down for Christmas," Betsy said. "I already miss her."

At their farewell party at Charley, Al, and Sally's, Millie had instructed Betsy and Ted to find her a rich Texan and be quick about it. Cattle or oil, she wasn't choosy. And preferably married. "The other woman has more fun," she had said.

Millie had moaned about her life. Who was she ever going to find that was interesting around the aisles of Lord & Taylor —Franklin Pangborn?

"The right guy will come along," Betsy had promised. "You live in a great city, full of guys. You're gorgeous, smart, witty . . . impatient, aggressive, vulgar."

"I'd rather be Bonnie Parker," Millie had said.

"You'd be dead."

"Yeah, but I would have traveled—met people."

Ted grappled with a large suitcase.

Betsy said, "The porters will do that, sweetie. Go find us a Coke or something. All this lush scenery is making me thirsty."

A henpecked look from Ted.

Betsy responded to it with an exaggerated Southern accent. "Then y'all come on over and we'll make some fudge."

That trip to the Coast. How many debts did she owe to football?

In the autumn of '33, the severely average Columbia Lions had suddenly and unexpectedly begun to win football games, and it hadn't taken long for the Columbia Lions to replace the Yale Bulldogs in her heart.

Almost overnight, Columbia had become the team of the discerning New Yorker.

Betsy wasn't alone. All of sports-minded Manhattan was having a flash fever over the Lions.

One day outside the Chrysler Building, while Betsy and Ted were having a hot dog on the sidewalk, Betsy said, "How 'bout those Columbia Lions? We have a great team this year."

"*We* . . . ?"

Seeing Betsy so worked up over Coach Lou Little and the Columbia Lions, Ted did a nice thing. He got his hands on two hard-to-come-by tickets for Columbia's last home game. He took Betsy up to Baker Field at 218th Street and Broadway, where, outlined against a blue-gray sky of apartment buildings and factories, they watched the Lions maul the Lafayette Leopards, 46 to 6.

Betsy thoroughly enjoyed the cold afternoon, despite the score, despite Ted's criticism of Columbia's uniforms.

"Too many stripes," he said. "I mean, down the sleeves, around the socks. What *are* your colors, light blue or navy blue?"

"I like them," Betsy said. "They'll look good in the Rose Bowl."

There had already been talk of Columbia being invited to the Rose Bowl, most of it generated by the Eastern press, principally by Damon Runyon, who was using his syndicated column to taunt the West Coast.

"Invite Columbia and let's try an experiment," Runyon had written. "Let's see what happens when students compete against animals."

Ted had a suspicion that if the Columbia Lions *were* invited, it would only be for one reason. The Rose Bowl committee would be trying to make amends to the state of New York for what it had done to Colgate a year before. In '32, Colgate had been undefeated, untied, unscored on, and . . .

"Uninvited," Betsy completed it. "They took Pitt instead."

"Maybe Colgate was lucky. Southern Cal murdered Pitt."

"I know. Thirty-five to nothing. It wasn't even USC's best team. I say the Trojans were stronger in '31. Gus Shaver, Erny Pinckert, Orv Mohler, Ray Sparling, Johnny Baker . . ."

"I give," Ted said.

After the game, as Ted was dropping Betsy off in a cab at

the Ansonia, he surprised her by telling her he wanted to take her for drinks at "21" and dinner at the Stork Club. She should slip out of her sweaters and jodhpurs and into something appropriate.

Earlier in '33, Prohibition had been repealed and some of the reliable old speakeasies—Jack & Charley's, the Stork Rest, Elmer's—had become "21," the Stork Club, and El Morocco—chic cafes—giving newspapers a term they loved to fondle almost daily: cafe society.

At the Stork that night, where Betsy was a standout in her sexiest bare-shouldered bright blue evening gown, she couldn't stop beaming. There she was, this girl from Claybelle, Texas, sitting only two tables from Barbara Hutton, the Woolworth heiress, who was with an arrogant-looking man whom Ted identified as Alexis Mdivani, a Russian prince if you trusted the word of gossip columnists.

Other swells surrounded Betsy and Ted, at times oomphing in conga lines, at other times trying to learn the sugarfoot, but mostly looking bored with each other as they slumped in their seats or propped their chins on their hands and sipped their highballs.

"My word, she's a chunky little thing," Betsy whispered to Ted, unable to keep her eyes off Barbara Hutton.

"I liked her quote in the *Daily News* the other day," he said. " 'Why do they hate me? There are other girls as rich . . . richer . . . almost as rich.' "

Betsy howled at this and gave Ted a hug at the table and thanked him for the most wonderful night of her life.

"This is the most white trash I've ever seen under one roof," she said.

Two weeks later the Columbia Lions were indeed invited to go to Pasadena to play the Stanford Indians in the Rose Bowl on New Year's Day. Betsy was ecstatic. A New York City team was going to the Rose Bowl for the first time ever. When might it happen again?

"I can't believe my school is going to the Rose Bowl," she said to her daddy on the phone by way of telling him what she wanted for Christmas—a lower berth single room with bath on the Burlington Zephyr to Los Angeles by way of San

Francisco. The round-trip ticket was only $214.30, not including meals.

"You went to Barnard," Ben Throckmorton reminded his daughter.

"That counts!" Betsy said defiantly.

Millie Saunders asked her parents for the same Christmas present. Millie cared little for football, but she said if Betsy went off on an exotic trip like this without her, it would haunt her the rest of her days.

Betsy grew even more ecstatic when Ted was assigned to cover the game, more specifically to write what Lafester Cleed called a "scene piece," or what Still Norris called a "prose pictorial," on the New Yorkers who were going out to the Coast for the game.

"I'll give you a yarn," Betsy had remarked to Ted, doing her best impression of Jean Harlow.

The trip from New York to Los Angeles only took five days on the Burlington Zephyr.

Betsy, Millie, and Ted boarded the train at Pennsylvania Station on Christmas Eve. They exchanged presents in the dining car. By prior agreement, Betsy and Millie gave each other a carton of Luckies. Betsy gave Ted a sleeveless sweater. Ted gave Betsy a Columbia helmet for a desk ornament. Ted and Millie only exchanged funny cards. Ted's to her said get well soon. Hers to him included an I.O.U. for a French job whenever Betsy would permit it. Afterwards, they stayed up until dawn with other revelers in the club car, getting so gasolined they must have sung "It's Only a Paper Moon" thirty times to the accompaniment of Wilburt de Paris and His Saratogans, the jazz band on board.

They slept most of Christmas Day and night. Chicago to Denver. During the seven-hour stopover in Denver, Ted took the girls to dinner at the Brown Palace Hotel. The stopover in Salt Lake City came between midnight and 5 A.M., a disappointment to Millie. "Darn, no Mormon Tabernacle Choir," she said, sipping from the flask she carried in a garter above her left knee.

By the time they reached San Francisco for a twelve-hour stopover, Millie had befriended a dwarf on board, Hal Boyd, a

Hollywood press agent who told anyone slowing down to a walk that Janet Gaynor and Joe E. Brown were among his clients. He insisted on showing them San Francisco, saying, "I know Frisco like the back lot at Warners."

Hal Boyd took them to breakfast at the St. Francis Hotel. He guided them onto four different cable cars that went up instead of down, or down instead of up, or turned instead of going straight, but they saw Fisherman's Wharf—"Nice smell," Betsy commented—the mansions on Nob Hill, and Alcatraz, though in the fog it was difficult to tell exactly what was sitting out there in the Bay.

"That's Al Capone's window," Hal Boyd said, pointing into the fog.

For dinner, the press agent steered them to John's Grill, a rustic cafe-saloon near the *Chronicle* and *Examiner,* where they drank too many martinis, it having been said by a waiter that the martini was invented in San Francisco.

They ate pot roast at a table Hal Boyd pronounced a landmark. Ambrose Bierce, he said, had sat at this table and held court in the days after William Randolph Hearst had made him the first Page One columnist in America, on the *Examiner.*

"Bierce disappeared, you know," Hal Boyd mentioned during dinner.

"You're kidding?" Betsy said, feigning shock.

"I know what happened," Millie said. "He got on a cable car with you."

The train ride from San Francisco to Los Angeles took ten hours. They arrived in L.A. at noon on December 30, two days before the game. Hal Boyd had arranged for them to tour Paramount that afternoon. They saw cowboys, Indians, pirates, Mounties, but no movie stars they recognized, unless the pudgy fellow sitting at the counter in the diner outside the Paramount gates was Jack Oakie.

Betsy, Millie, and Ted had wanted to go to dinner at the Cocoanut Grove, but Hal Boyd had said no, the Cocoanut Grove was passé now. He dragged them to Clara Bow's It Club instead.

Hal Boyd had seemed to shrink before their very eyes, and Millie had indicated to Betsy with more than one glance that she would like to see the press agent embalmed, but they agreed later that it had been worth it to go to the It Club.

They didn't see Clara Bow, but never again in this life did Betsy, for one, expect to see so many astounding young women dressed like trapeze artists, wearing high heels, and carrying feather boas. ·

Hal Boyd had insisted on driving them to their hotel in Pasadena, the Huntington, although Millie had made it clear to him that there was a history of several contagious diseases in her family.

The drive over and through the Hollywood hills to the San Gabriel foothills seemed to take an eternity, but this was due to the rain. It would rain for the next three days, eighteen inches in all, a record rainfall for Southern California. The heavy, continuous rain left nothing much for anyone to do while they waited for the football game. They played cards, listened to the radio, dined, danced—all in the hotel—but the rain had little to do with the fact that this was when Betsy finally got Ted Winton into bed.

She invited him to her room under the pretense of wanting to show him some research. "Where is it?" he asked. "Under here somewhere," she said, turning back the covers on her bed with a look that said, in effect, "Tonight's the night, you lucky stiff."

The rain caused floods that washed away scores of homes two miles from the Rose Bowl. Most of the roads to the stadium were impassable. The Pasadena fire department worked all of New Year's morning to pump water off the playing field. And it kept raining. All of which encouraged thousands to stay away from the game, Millie among them, of course.

But Betsy Throckmorton and Ted Winton were among the lonely 35,000 who huddled under umbrellas, rain slickers, and homemade canopies to watch the twentieth annual Rose Bowl game in a stadium that would have held over 90,000 people.

"We look like we're waiting to be rescued," Betsy said as she glanced around at all the empty seats.

Betsy concluded that Damon Runyon had been right as she watched the two teams slog through their warm-up drills before the kickoff. It was definitely going to be a case of students against animals.

The Stanford Indians looked bigger than rhinos in their red jerseys with white numerals, khaki pants, and black leather helmets, and many of their names were straight out of Big Little Books: Bobby ("Bulldozer") Grayson, "Horse" Reynolds, "Bones" Hamilton, "Monk" Moscrip, Bill Corbus, "the Baby-Faced Assassin." The Columbia Lions were not only smaller, they didn't even have nicknames. And as for their uniforms —powder blue jerseys, white numerals, dark blue stripes down the sleeves, light blue helmets—she remarked to Ted, "You're right, we look like ushers."

The first twenty minutes of the game were about as exciting as watching gravy thicken, but in the middle of the second quarter Betsy suddenly leaped to her feet and let out a rebel yell, for Columbia completed a long pass down to Stanford's seventeen-yard line.

And on the next play, almost before Betsy stopped yelling and punching the drizzle with her fist, something else happened. The Lions lined up in a single-wing formation with an unbalanced line, strong to the right. On the snap, Columbia's inspirational little quarterback, Cliff Montgomery, took the ball and spun around. Halfway through the spin, he sneaked the ball to a halfback, Al Barabas. Completing the spin, he pretended to hand the ball to his other halfback, Ed Brominski. He also pretended to keep the ball himself, tucked deep under his chest. Montgomery and Brominski both churned into the Stanford line, each acting as if he had the ball. Half of the Stanford team tackled Montgomery and the other half tackled Brominski—but Al Barabas had the football. And Al Barabas was all alone and free to go prancing seventeen yards around his own left end for a touchdown.

"Suckered 'em!" Betsy had shouted, nudging Ted in the ribs as the play, old KF-79, had unfolded.

The extra point made the score 7 to 0, Columbia, and although Stanford spent the rest of the afternoon wallowing around inside Columbia's ten-yard line, this was the final score of the game. Columbia had somehow pulled off a staggering upset that would be remembered as long as the football was oblong.

In the piece he filed to *Time,* Ted wrote that Al Barabas had enjoyed enough time on KF-79 to stop for a cup of coffee, buy a paper, read Little Orphan Annie, take a screen test, phone home, and then lope into the end zone, at which point it had looked as if he held up the football to the Stanford Indians and said, "Wanna buy a duck?"

Still Norris didn't tamper much with this story of Ted's, only to change the reference from Little Orphan Annie to Flash Gordon.

When Ted had later asked the editor to explain what had seemed to be a pointless change, Still Norris said, "I rather think a football player would be more inclined to read something masculine, don't you?"

There were occasions when a staff writer could only throw up his arms and walk away from a *Time* editor.

Back at the hotel on that New Year's Day, Betsy and Ted had trudged into the lobby and found Millie sitting on a piano with a cocktail in her hand, singing "Roar, Lion, Roar," and whooping it up with other joyous New Yorkers, acting as if she had gone to the game.

They had only waved at Millie and dashed up to their rooms to bathe. They had then made love even more quickly in Ted's room.

It was while they were snuggling under the covers, resting up to derive further pleasures from one another, that Betsy had said, "I like a man who takes his time."

Ted had raised his head up from her breasts and stared at the brazen harlot, and then realized that Betsy had done her best impression of Mae West.

The Sunshine Special had almost come to a complete stop as Ted returned to the private compartment with a lukewarm Coke. The train was now on the outskirts of Fort Worth, unhooking a car, lurching forward, then backward.

Betsy was standing up at the windows when Ted came in.

She turned to him with an uncharacteristic look of distress and spoke in a soft voice.

"God, Ted, have you looked out at this?"

Three

THE HOBO camp was strung out along a river bottom. A crude stretch of dugouts and tin sheds, shacks built of packing boxes and scrap metal. Junk-heap cars and junk-heap trucks were being used as shelters—as homes. Betsy was looking squarely into a jungle of poverty and degradation. She had seen nothing like it in New York, though homeless people were pitching tents in Central Park and along an embankment off Riverside Drive. Everyone in the camp looked ragged and dirty. How many of them were there, hundreds? Men, women, children of all ages, most of them white but a few of them Negroes. Some of the people were staring wistfully at the train in silence, despair etched into their faces.

Struck by the sight, Betsy fell back on her cynicism—the journalist's ammo. "You call this a country club, Ted?" she murmured. "It looks like they'll let anybody in."

One of the hobos, a gaunt unshaven man in his thirties, held up a hand-lettered sign that said, WORK IS WHAT I WANT —NOT CHARITY. An older black man wearing a tattered Army jacket over an undershirt and motheaten wool trousers on this hot day—he must have owned nothing else—clutched a sign that said, MY CHILDRENS NEED MILK AND WOMAN NEEDS SHOES AND DRESSES. Leaning against the fender of a rusty jalopy, a younger white man pointed to the sign he had made, which said, STARVED, STALLED, AND STRANDED. A frail young woman, Betsy's age maybe, held hands with a little girl of about seven. Both were caked in dirt. They smiled feebly at the passengers on the train.

"Transients," said Ted.

"Yeah, right," Betsy said knowingly.

Stillwell Padgam-Norris had edited the word into a *Time* story which had pointed out that there were 10,000 homeless people a month traveling across Texas. Not poor, starving, jobless people. Transients.

Betsy said, "I wish the idiot could see *these* transients. He envisions them singing happy little union songs and doing tricks with their yo-yos while they skip along the highways. Damn this Depression."

"It's not just the economy." Ted sighed. "Nature isn't helping things."

True enough. Ted had written about the fact that many of the homes and farms in the middle of the country were in ruin; how for too many years too many rain gullies had been carved out of the land and too many forests had been chopped down, and now there was a serious problem with soil erosion. Dust storms were commonplace.

Betsy was familiar with dust storms. Claybelle was on the eastern edge of flat, windy, wide-open West Texas, and dust storms had been a fact of life for years. They could strike suddenly, out of nowhere. Clouds would rise up from the ground, darken and fatten, and come rolling in off the prairie. The brown dust came from Oklahoma, the gray dust from Kansas, the red dust from New Mexico or Colorado.

Betsy had burning memories of scampering into the house and helping jam the cracks of doors and windows with wet towels and rags and covering her face with a wet cloth. A bad dust storm could paralyze traffic, close schools, kill livestock. "Dust pneumonia" had become a common disease among Texas children. Ben Throckmorton had seen a dust storm so Goddamn bad, birds were afraid to fly.

What had made matters worse by 1935 was a searing drought of the year before along with one of the great physical disasters in American history, which occurred on May 11, 1934.

On that date, after a long period of scorching heat in the middle of the country, a dust cloud 1,000 miles wide remarkably lifted up what was later calculated to be 300,000,000 tons of fertile soil and carried it across 1,500 miles of land. New York and other Eastern cities had been darkened at midday by dirt from far west of the Mississippi River.

Betsy and Millie had been together in Manhattan on that

bright, sunny day, down on the street on their way to a gabby lunch, when the dust cloud arrived. They looked up, and—

"Busy?" Millie asked.

"No. You busy?"

"No."

"Good, let's get the hell out of here!"

When they were safely inside a bar, Millie had said, "What do you think, Betsy? Is God trying to tell us we drink too much?"

One of Betsy's last chores at *Time* had been to check a cover story, a "take-out" as it was known to Still Norris, on the nation's economic condition. The story was written by a talented man named Phil Jessup, who couldn't be bothered by anything the editors did to his copy—he was more concerned with the novel he was writing. "It's *their* music," Phil Jessup would say. "I try never to read the magazine myself."

Betsy became better acquainted with the Depression by working on the story, which told her that factory gates were closed all across the industrial belt from Chicago to New York, that half the automobile plants in Michigan were shut down, that nobody was working in the iron beds or copper mountains or Southern textile factories, that ranchers were turning cattle loose to graze on the open range because it didn't pay to send them to the stockyards in Chicago, Kansas City, or Fort Worth, and that passenger and freight cars by the hundreds were rusting idly on railway sidings. Fifteen million Americans were out of work in 1935, and they had 30 million other mouths to feed. One-seventh of the population, 5 million families, were being supported by public relief or private charity.

She learned that things might never again be as cheap as they were today. Eggs were down to nineteen cents a dozen, gasoline was eighteen cents a gallon, cigarettes were fifteen cents a pack, a box of cornflakes was eight cents, a dental filling cost a dollar, a ticket to a movie was ten cents, a hamburger was a nickel.

The story touched on the fact that there were thousands of people with college degrees who were delivering groceries, pumping gas, doing yardwork, or selling apples on street corners; and it described the long lines of jobless Americans in every city who waited for daily handouts of dried bread and watery soup. But Still Norris deleted the paragraph about the instances of people actually fighting over the garbage that would be thrown out the back doors of restaurants.

"You're taking that *out?*" Betsy had said as the editor drew a blue line through a sentence.

In rough copy, a *Time* story could sometimes look like modern art after an editor's blue pencil was finished with it.

"Yes, I am," Still Norris had said. "I hardly think it's in the interest of our subscribers to make them sick at their stomachs."

"It's true," Betsy had said. "You can see it in a newsreel."

"Oh, I have no doubt." The editor had smiled agreeably, resuming his zigzag marks with the blue pencil.

Long before Betsy had checked that article, she was keenly aware that for her the Depression was more of a news story than a hardship—and she was more deeply grateful for this than anybody may have known.

Her daddy knew—what with her genes and all.

And yet Ben Throckmorton was among those people who could well afford to pay $49.95, and up, for a fine console radio. He owned four, two that were bigger than chiffoniers. He also was driving a new burgundy Packard sedan with white sidewalls, fog lights, and leather seats. The car had cost $2,100.

In a letter home, Betsy had teasingly asked her daddy if it gave him a lot of pleasure to drive that car around Claybelle, or in and out of Fort Worth and Dallas, while people were standing in breadlines.

Ben had called her on the phone to say that it didn't look to him as if his lavishly raised daughter had missed any meals lately, and that furthermore, a man like himself, who had worked harder than a Goddamn one-armed plumber to make a success of his newspaper and radio station, could do whatever he pleased with his money, including give as much of it to his daughter as she ever asked for, without complaint. If he felt like it, he said, he might even go out and buy himself one of those new twenty-dollar golf shirts tomorrow, the kind you slipped on over your head, "and anybody who don't like it can go play with hisself."

He told Betsy there was another way to look at it. His buying a new automobile had provided four months' work for a dozen other people, and this had allowed *them* to go out and buy goods, so in his own way he was helping President Franklin D. Roosevelt bring back prosperity.

"And don't gimme no more crap about my car," Betsy had said to him, doing one of her impressions.

When she had last spoken to her daddy on the phone, before she and Ted had left for Texas, he had insisted on telling her all of the Hoover jokes that had reached Claybelle.

There was nothing anyone could do about Herbert Hoover now but make jokes. He was the Republican President who had been occupying the White House when the stock market had crashed in '29. He was a man held in total scorn by the vast majority of Americans, as if he was singlehandedly to blame for every bloated belly on every starving child.

"What's a Hoover blanket?" Ben asked Betsy.

"I've heard it, Daddy."

"That's a newspaper you cover up with when you're sleepin' on a park bench. You seen a Hoover flag?"

"I've heard it."

"A Hoover flag is when you turn your empty pockets inside out—you're flyin' that old Hoover flag."

"Daddy—"

"What's a Hoover hog?"

"Daddy, these jokes—"

"Jackrabbit."

Ben's laughter turned into a wheeze. He smoked as much as Betsy, although there were those who said this wasn't humanly possible.

"You got any Hoover wagons up there in the big city? That's a car that don't run without a mule pullin' it."

"Uh-huh."

"Hoovervilles," he had said.

"Uh-huh."

"Some folks call 'em Hoovervilles. Most folks call 'em hobo jungles."

Betsy said, "We don't call them anything, but there are people living in tents and huts in Central Park."

"Right there in Central Park?" Ben had said, acting surprised. "Damn, that must play hell with everybody's horseback riding."

Betsy waved at the hobos as the Sunshine Special pulled away from the encampment. Then, as the Fort Worth skyline came more clearly into view, she felt a strange pang of excitement. Fort Worth didn't have much of a skyline compared to Manhattan, or even Dallas, but if you had grown up in Claybelle, it had always looked like a burgeoning metropolis.

They were coming in from the northeast, and downtown Fort Worth was spread across a ridge west of the river bottom.

Betsy pointed out the lacy old Victorian homes on Samuels Avenue, the city's first ritzy neighborhood. Above them, the Tarrant County courthouse, a red granite relic dating back to the 1890s. From the courthouse, North Main crossed the Trinity River over the Paddock Viaduct and led to LaGrave Field, the Texas League ballpark, and then out to the stockyards, meat-packing plants, and indoor rodeo coliseum.

"We used to win the Dixie Series all the time," Betsy said.

"Which we is this?"

"The Fort Worth Cats. You've never heard of Big Boy Kraft —Clarence Kraft?"

"Not yet."

"He was our Babe Ruth."

"I'm a Giants fan," Ted said. "The Giants are the team of the discerning New Yorker."

"He was our Mel Ott, then—only he didn't bat funny."

"People who say Mel Ott bats funny have been found dead floating in rivers."

Ted assumed a batting stance. Lifting his front leg, he rocked back and took an imaginary swing in the slugging style of Mel Ott.

"You've never been to the Polo Grounds?" he said.

"For football, sure."

Rising from a two-story base of green marble, the W. T. Waggoner Building towered over the city's three best hotels —the Texas, the Blackstone, the Westbrook. Twenty stories high, the Waggoner had been the tallest building west of the Mississippi when it had been completed in 1920. Oil money had built it.

That's where Betsy could find Millie a rich oilman, but Millie wouldn't like him. His big talk would drive her to opium. Money equaled smart to a Texas oilman.

"After they get lucky and hit oil over in East Texas, or out in West Texas—Caddo, Desdemona, Antelope, some little town like that—they move to Fort Worth so their daughters can be debutantes."

Ted said, "Fort Worth's the third-largest city in Texas. The population's over a hundred and fifty thousand now. I looked it up."

"We helped win the war."

"We did?"

"The Thirty-sixth Division trained here. Out on Camp Bowie Boulevard—west, that way. Ten minutes from downtown."

"Goodbye Broadway, hello France."

"We're ten million strong," Betsy sang. "Goodbye sweethearts, wives, and mothers, it won't take us long." With a laugh, she added, "Mary Pickford says hi to all the boys in khaki."

The train approached the T&P station at the opposite end of town from the courthouse, the south end.

The terminal building, sixteen stories tall, had been designed by that individual in the late Twenties who went running around the country putting eagles, Egyptians, and Indian heads on the terra-cotta friezes of cast-concrete and buff-brick buildings.

The huge cream-colored terminal had become the pride of the city. Its dining room on the ground floor was carpeted and walled in by marble statues. Its big newsstand in the rotunda bordered on the exotic, offering stacks of out-of-state newspapers and mysterious magazines that couldn't be found anywhere else in town. Stars of stage and screen, generals, statesmen, sports heroes, all came through the T&P station and posed for photographs on the rear platforms of trains.

Unfortunately, the terminal had done nothing to improve the neighborhood where it had been built. In the days of the cattle drives, this south end of town had been known as Hell's Half Acre. Fort Worth had lured such frequent visitors as Sam Bass, Luke Short, Butch Cassidy, the Sundance Kid, Deaf Charley Hanks, and Blackjack Tom Ketcham, men who fancied a town which offered—by actual count—411 saloons as opposed to eight churches. But even though that era was long past, the neighborhood was still dominated by beer joints, pool halls, pawnshops, flophouses, and whore-lady hotels.

Betsy could see the neighborhood as she stood and lowered a window, the train slowly creeping toward the railway sheds that adjoined the terminal building.

She ventured the guess that a man could still catch the drip down here somewhere.

And now she heard music. Live music.

A cowboy band, with horns added to the guitars, fiddles, and banjos, was playing a Western swing version of "Is It True What They Say About Dixie?" and voices were singing.

> *Do the sweet magnolias blossom*
> *Round every cottage door?*
> *Do the folks down there eat possum*
> *Till they can't eat no more?*
> *Is it true what they . . .*

"Jesus," said Betsy. "I guess André Kostelanetz and Lily Pons weren't available."

She ripped open a fresh pack of Luckies, stubbing out a short cigarette, lighting a new one.

She straightened her pale green dress and picked up a copy of *Liberty* to fan herself.

Ted slung his dark blue jacket over his arm and opened the door of the compartment.

They found Johnson, Leland, and Lawton in the passageway.

"Cowtown," this-here's-Leland said.

"Where the West begins," said that-there's-Lawton.

Johnson said he had a soft spot in his heart for Fort Worth. "Met me a redheaded woman here that I ain't forgot till this day." He whispered the rest of it to Ted. "She was built like a frog. Big old titties and no ass."

This-here's-Leland said, "We got us a three-hour wait before we head on to Waco. Man could drive quicker."

"Not if I was ridin' with him," that-there's-Lawton said.

"Best of luck," Ted said. "Sorry about the Cardinals."

Johnson said, "Aw, I 'magine the Cardinals ain't in no worse slump than most folks nowadays."

Betsy and Ted stepped down off the Zephyr.

> *Is that dream by the stream so sublime?*
> *Do they laugh, do they love, like they*
> *   say in every song?*
> *If it's true, that's where I belong.*

Ben Throckmorton moved away from a group of friends to catch his daughter in his arms. A long tight hug and kisses on the cheek.

Ben was looking fit. A man six feet in height, in his middle fifties, he wasn't carrying too much excess weight around. It must have been the golf. His face was tan, leathery, sharp-featured, but his normal expression was that of a kind, generous man, which he was most ways to most people. Today he wore a well-tailored three-piece dark gray suit and a small white Stetson, a hat no rancher would wear but a businessman would.

Off to the side were five men and one woman, all of them known to Betsy except for the stranger who looked something like Tom Mix. The familiar faces smiled and waved at Betsy but kept their distance.

Ben shook Ted's hand firmly as he clung to Betsy.

"My bribe worked," Ben said. "You brought her back."

"It was two against one," Ted responded pleasantly.

"Daddy, the band," said Betsy. "Honestly."

"That's Booty and Them Others," Ben said.

"*Who?*"

"The pride of KVAT."

The musicians tipped their hats to Betsy. There were seven in all. Booty Pettigrew, the one holding the clarinet, was the leader. His stomach wanted to burst out of his shirt. His square face was dotted with red blotches. Slits for eyes. Booty had drank some gin in his day.

To her daddy Betsy said, "Booty and Them Others—that's their name?"

"Honey, you ever heard of the Light Crust Dough Boys from Burrus Mill?"

"They're on WBAP," Ted said. He had done some homework.

"Real popular, is what they are," Ben said. "But Booty and Them Others make the Light Crust Dough Boys sound like there's chickens loose in the yard. I've got 'em on KVAT every weekday at noon. Booty don't get nothin' but cards and letters."

Ben motioned for Booty to come say hello.

Booty sauntered over, clarinet in hand.

Ben said, "Honey . . . Ted, I want y'all to meet Mr. Mail. This here's Mr. *Fan* Mail!"

"Hidy," said Booty.

"Thanks for the welcome," Betsy said.

"Very nice," Ted added.

Booty signaled to his boys that it was time to haul.

"We play out at Crystal Springs most weekends," Booty said to Betsy. "Come on out."

Crystal Springs was a popular nightspot, a combination dance hall and swimming pavilion on the western rim of Fort Worth that was gaining a certain amount of fame as the place where Bob Wills invented Western swing.

Walking away, Booty said, "We only play two kinds of music out there, country *and* Western."

Time now for Betsy to greet the other members of the welcoming committee. She went first to Leatha Wardlaw, a thin, smartly dressed woman—fortyish—whose blond hairdo might have been influenced by Alice Faye.

"Betsy, I'll bet you are so glad to be back *home!*"

Betsy and Leatha carefully touched cheeks.

Frankly, Betsy had never known how much she cared for Leatha Wardlaw, though she had known her for fifteen years, which was as long as Leatha had been trying to marry Ben Throckmorton. Leatha had been a friend of Betsy's mother, Elizabeth, and she had attached herself to Ben immediately upon Elizabeth's death. Betsy's mother had died from a kidney infection when Betsy was twelve. Elizabeth had been only thirty-five.

There was an air of independence about Leatha. She made a decent income for herself at Leatha's Creations, her dress shop on the square in Claybelle. Betsy had always known her to be nice, pleasant, never judgmental or demanding, always outwardly serene. Jesus, was Leatha serene. She had always lived in her modest little two-bedroom house a block off the square, keeping a beautiful yard, presiding over the largest and prettiest magnolia tree in Claybelle—"Leatha's magnolia," as it was known. Leatha seemed always to be on a committee in town. She thought of herself as a force in the community, but essentially she was Ben's constant companion, his hostess, his woman. Most people thought Ben and Leatha made a good couple and wondered why they had never married.

The reason, if anybody had bothered to ask Ben, was that he liked his life the way it was. He could work as many hours as he felt necessary, or play as much golf as he wanted to, and not have to take any shit about it. Besides, no woman was ever going to mean as much to him as Elizabeth had, or as much as his daughter did now.

"Leatha, you look wonderful, as always," Betsy said as she and Leatha held hands.

Betsy introduced Ted.

"My heavens, aren't you the handsomest thing!" Leatha gushed.

Leatha turned back to Betsy. "Florence and Warren can't wait to see you. They've been cooking for a week!"

Florence and Warren Richards were the black couple who lived in the servants' quarters, a garage apartment, through the porte cochere and behind the big two-story redbrick rectangular house where Betsy had grown up. Betsy had practically been raised by Florence and Warren. Pampered and spoiled would be better words. She hadn't needed to be told that Florence and Warren had been cooking for a week. Of course they had.

Betsy politely hugged the banker, O. L. Beaton, though she held no special fondness for the flabby self-important blowhard; but he was Anna Sue's daddy, and Betsy and Anna Sue

Beaton had known each other since they had played dolls together.

O. L. apologized for Anna Sue not being at the train. She was in Dallas.

"Is she living there again?"

"Buyin' it. She thought she bought it all last month, but she didn't, so she had to go back today and buy the rest of it."

Anna Sue was back living at home, Betsy was informed.

"Tell her I'll call her."

"Do that," the banker said. "You've always been her link to the big world out there. By dang, Betsy, it don't look like them New York Jews done you any harm."

Glancing at Ted, he said, "I knew this little girl when she was so skinny she could cook naked in a deer camp!"

Betsy hugged Buck Blanchard, who owned B's Cafe on the square in Claybelle. B's served the best chicken and dumplings in North America, although it was no fault of Buck, who spent most daylight hours on a golf course. Buck allowed that his wife, Joylene, was fine, real fine, doin' good, which meant that she was still running the register at B's and trying to keep up with his gambling debts.

Betsy shook hands with Ray Fletcher, the managing editor of the *Claybelle Times-Standard,* an unexcitable hands-in-his-pockets man in his fifties. Betsy had always looked at Ray and seen a furniture salesman. Ray believed the only obligation of a daily newspaper was to come out every day.

She also shook hands with Big 'Un Darly, the sports editor of the *Claybelle Times-Standard,* an old high school classmate of Betsy's whose nickname dated back to his years when Big 'Un had been the biggest, slowest, and most awkward fullback in the history of the Claybelle Yellow Jackets.

Ben Throckmorton now introduced Betsy and Ted to the stranger. He was a broad-shouldered, thin-waisted man of six-two with striking blue eyes and an ironbound jaw. Cowboy-handsome. A man in his thirties, he wore a starched white shirt, black string tie, pressed khakis, boots, and gray Stetson. His hat was tilted down to eyebrow level. A sparkling silver badge was pinned to his left breast pocket, and an eye-filling bone-handled nickel-plated .45 was strapped to his right hip. He was Captain Lank Allred of the Texas Rangers.

Betsy had wanted to say, "Hi there, Straight Shooter, I eat Ralston's every morning," but thought better of it. A Texas Ranger didn't like to be made sport of, and Betsy hadn't been away so long that she had forgotten this.

Ben said that Lank Allred was making quite a name for himself these days. He was catching bank robbers right and left, and Lank had been with Captain Frank Hamer of the Rangers and the other lawmen when they had ambushed Clyde Barrow and Bonnie Parker on the little country road over near Shreveport. Talk about Lank Allred and you weren't talking about a traffic cop.

"We got us a crime spree around here, is what we got," Ben said. "Derned if some people don't look up to all those John Dillingers."

The Texas Ranger had been at the T&P station by chance, there to nail up two posters from the roll of posters he was carrying under his arm.

Ben took a poster from Lank and unfurled it to show Betsy and Ted. The poster read:

REWARD
$5,000 FOR DEAD
BANK ROBBERS

Not One Cent for
Live Ones!

———

The Texas Bankers Assn.

"I'll be headin' on," the Ranger said, retrieving the poster. "Got to put the rest of these up around town."

"Has it been much of a deterrent?" Betsy asked.

"A who?"

"The reward," she said. "Has it stopped anyone from trying to rob a bank?"

"Some, I reckon. It's only been in effect for a month or so."

Betsy said, "It wouldn't have stopped Bonnie and Clyde, I don't imagine."

Lank Allred said, "Tell me about 'em. Some folks think they

was about half romantic, but them two sadists, they even lowered the standards of the crime profession."

"That must have been quite an ambush."

"It was a spellin' bee."

"Didn't they count fifty bullets in their bodies?"

Lank Allred said, "Yeah, I hated to bust a blister on a woman, especially one sittin' down, but it was either them or us."

He tipped his Stetson to Betsy and wiggled the tube of posters like a baton. "We're gonna put a stop to robbin' banks," he said. "You can write that down in your diary right now today."

And the Texas Ranger walked away.

The group made its way through the high-ceilinged lobby of the T&P terminal building, their heels clicking on the tile floor, their voices echoing through the marble-columned room.

"What have the Yellow Jackets got this year?" Betsy asked Big 'Un Darly.

"Worst schedule in the world," the sports editor said. "We open with Paschal. Then we don't play nobody but Masonic Home, Breckenridge, and Sunset. We'll lose four games before District starts."

"Who's Paschal?"

"They went and changed the name of Central High to R. L. Paschal, don't ask me why. Dick Tracy couldn't tell you who R. L. Paschal was."

"Are we any good?"

"Could have been, but we'll all be cripple by the time District starts. Remember Slop? Sloppy Herster?"

"I haven't been gone *that* long."

"His little brother's playin' quarterback this year. Eugene."

"Whatever happened to Slop—Huntsville?"

"He's around. Him and Tommy Jack Lucas. They beautify the curbs and gutters."

Big 'Un Darly weighed in at 250 pounds. He walked with a splayfooted gait and his trousers were too short. His lower lip protruded from a mouth that curved down at the corners, giving him a look of continual displeasure. His habit of pouring cream gravy on everything he ate, including a slice of watermelon, hadn't endeared him to many people; but he loved football, all sports, and he worked sixteen hours a day at his job. It was unfortunate that his daily column was virtually unreadable, but Ben said this was sometimes the price you had to pay for loyalty on the part of an employee.

Outside the terminal, as Betsy and Ted's luggage was being loaded into Ben's Packard, Ray Fletcher asked Betsy when she was coming into the office to take charge.

Betsy said, "I don't know, Ray. I'll come by and meet everybody, of course, say hello. But Ted and I want to get settled before we start to work. Middle of September, I should think. Tell the troops to relax. I may want to do some shifting around, but nobody's going to be out of a job."

"She's not gonna do anything drastic," Ben said. "I'm still holding the cheese."

"*You*," Betsy said, whirling on her daddy with a glare. "You are going to get lost on the golf course!"

Ben Throckmorton laughed. He opened the right-hand door of the Packard for Leatha Wardlaw.

"Come on, you two, hop in the back," Ben said to Betsy and Ted. "Let's go to Claybelle, Texas."

Four

AT THE wheel of the burgundy Packard, Ben Throckmorton, the old tour guide, went zipping through the streets of downtown Fort Worth with occasional indecision, flirting with dark green streetcars and blinking yellows. It was around four in the afternoon but still bright and hot. Betsy rolled down the window on her side—to hell with her hair.

The car now slammed to a stop in the shade of a downtown building. Betsy and Ted slid around on the hand-crushed tan leather of the back seat.

"There it is, Ted," said Ben. "Seventh Street. This is our Great White Way. All the best department stores, restaurants, nightlife, picture shows. Folks come up here from Claybelle when they want to play big shot. *Star-Telegram*'s there on the corner. Biggest paper in Texas—over 160,000 daily. Amon Carter's a good friend of mine. My box is next to his at the TCU games. Across from the Electric Building, that's the Cotton Exchange. Hollywood Theater. Worth. Palace."

Ted said, "I've seen Amon Carter's name in *Time*."

"Yes, you have," said Ben, pulling away and circling Burnett Park, a city block of trees and lawn. "Amon does a lot for this town. I'll tell you how strong he is. I sat right there on his front porch out on Broad Street and met Franklin D. Roosevelt!"

"There are quite a few wealthy people in Fort Worth, I gather," Ted said.

Ben was lighting a cigarette as he headed out West Seventh Street. "Not as many as act like it. Most of 'em are only good at spendin' Daddy's money and hangin' around the Fort Worth Club. Big hat, no cattle."

An enormous Montgomery Ward came up on their right—a fine tourist attraction, Ben said—and the Triple-X Drive-In came up on their left. Young girls in tight shorts and cadet

caps were hopping cars on roller skates. A Fort Worth girl—
Lanette something—had gone down to the state contest in
Galveston last year and won Fairest Carhop.

"Made us all proud," Betsy said.

Ben turned south on University Drive, cruised down a hill,
wove through a wooded area, crossed a river, and started up
another hill. It wasn't too much out of the way to show Ted
the TCU campus.

Betsy's daddy wasn't a TCU graduate—he hadn't gone to
college anywhere—but Texas Christian University was his
adopted alma mater because the Horned Frogs, as they were
eccentrically named, had become a football powerhouse. The
Horned Frogs had been undefeated in '29, Cy Leland's year,
and undefeated again in '32, Johnny Vaught's year, and it
was a damn shame they weren't getting more national recognition, Ben said.

"On their name alone," Betsy suggested.

"We're apt to be a little bit of hell this year," Ben raved on
as the hot wind blew his cigarette ashes toward Leatha. "Got
a great line. Darrell Lester's back. He's our All-American
center. Jimmy Lawrence is only the best halfback in the country, is all. Whoosh—he's gone!" Ben made a gesture with his
cigarette hand, and more ashes flew at Leatha. "Wait till you
see our quarterback, Ted. You'll be hearing about Mr. Slingin'
Sam Baugh. Arm like a deer rifle. Wham!" Another gesture.
"That's six! Sam can do it all, throw that football, run, punt,
play defense. We operate out of a double-wing, Ted. Do a lot
of razzle-dazzle. Honey, you seen Williamson, the pre-season
poll?"

"The *Herald Trib* ran it."

"How 'bout that? Rice Owls number one. Southwest Conference team's never been rated that high before. Well, the Owls
went up there and beat Purdue last year. Same day Texas
beat Notre Dame in South Bend. Made the North take notice.
Rice'll be good again. They've got everybody back. Bill Wallace and them. They'll be great. So will SMU, if Bobby Wilson
don't get hurt. But we're gonna whip both their asses. When
the Frogs get done with 'em, they'll be lucky if they can shit
marbles."

Blushing, Leatha looked around at Ted. "Ben gets excited about football."

Ted winked at Leatha.

The buff-brick buildings of TCU's campus came up on their right, scattered across a bald hill. The campus could have used Leatha's magnolia, and any shrubs or hedges somebody might care to donate. Ben drove around behind the campus to the football stadium, which was down a slope near a creek bed. It was a fine concrete stadium, only five years old, envied by most other colleges in Texas. It held 30,000. Ben was proud of it.

"That's a nice-size press box," Ted said, trying to pay the stadium a compliment.

"What's Yale hold?" Ben asked.

"Seventy-one thousand," Betsy answered with relish.

"Well, this ain't bad for Texas," Ben said. "When we learn how to proselyte down here, we'll get bigger stadiums."

Ben started back toward town.

"Where are you going, dear?" Leatha said.

"Forgot to show 'em the Frontier Centennial."

"They haven't built it yet."

The sun was still bearing down as Ben, halfway back to town, stopped the Packard at a barren patch of land where a park seemed to be taking shape. Workers were planting shrubs, trees, laying sod, pouring cement for pathways.

He insisted that everyone get out of the car and follow him.

Next year, in 1936, Ben explained, the State of Texas would be celebrating its hundred-year anniversary, but when a Texas Centennial Commission had designated Fair Park in Dallas as the official site for the celebration, Amon Carter got hot. Amon wouldn't go to Dallas for a business meeting without carrying his lunch in a paper bag. The rivalry between the two cities dated all the way back to 1886, when Dallas put on the first State Fair of Texas. Fort Worth counterpunched by building an indoor coliseum out at the stockyards and inaugurating the annual fat stock show and world championship indoor rodeo. And now Amon Carter had decided that next year Fort Worth would stage an extravaganza of its own that would beat anything the shitheels in Dallas could offer.

He had hired Billy Rose, the Broadway producer, to put the whole thing together and bring in the famous personalities. Amon had even thought up a slogan that would attract thousands of folks to what would be a world's fair, Fort Worth-style. The slogan was "Dallas for Culture, Fort Worth for Fun!"

"It's gonna be the dangdest thing you ever saw," Ben said. "The Casa Mañana will be over there. That's what Billy Rose is calling it. World's biggest open-air supper club. It's gonna have a revolving stage, big old pools of water, fountains, Lord knows what all. Billy Rose has already signed up Paul Whiteman for the revue. Straight ahead, that's where the Pioneer Palace will be. *Big* saloon. Vaudeville shows, comedians, jazz bands, striptease ladies, shit, I'm tellin' you. Jumbo will be down there. A theatrical circus like the one up in New York. Actor sits on a elephant and sings a song, something like that. There'll be an arena for a Wild West show, carnival midway, exhibits of all kinds. Sally Rand's Nude Ranch will be around here somewhere. It all starts next July, but Amon says, hell, if folks like it, we'll do it every year."

Leatha Wardlaw said, "Fort Worth is very excited, Ted—and so is Claybelle. We tend to identify with Fort Worth."

"Yep," said Ben, looking around. "I dare say in a few months, we'll be seeing our share of them tall showgirls with feathers in their heads."

Betsy was dabbing at her neck with a handkerchief when she heard the yell.

"Betsy! Betsy Throckmorton!"

She turned around with the others to see the two debonair fellows coming toward them.

Slop Herster was huskier than Tommy Jack Lucas. Slop was wearing a grimy sleeveless undershirt and soiled corduroys and lace-up construction boots. Tommy Jack wore no shirt at all with his soiled corduroys and lace-up construction boots. Slop's hair still grew in different jagged directions, as it had in high school. Tommy Jack's wool baseball cap was frayed and dirty. They were both drenched with sweat. Their body odor would have clogged up the sinus on a giraffe.

"Betsy, you remember me?" Slop said. "I caught the pass against Corsicana."

"Sure, Slop. How you doing?"

Betsy quickly noted that Slop still had the maniacal gaze which had so distinguished him from other Claybelle punks and street fighters, and that Tommy Jack still looked mystified by everything that life on earth had to offer.

"I guess you remember Tommy Jack, too."

"I do indeed."

Tommy Jack said, "We heard you was comin' back from New York, Betsy. What happened—Jews run you off up there?"

"Naw, it was the niggers," Slop said through a laugh.

Betsy said, "Uh . . . this is my husband, Ted, and you know Daddy and Leatha, of course."

Slop took off his cotton work gloves so he could test the strength of an Easterner's handshake. Ted smiled at Slop as he withstood the pressure of Slop's grip.

"You boys been workin' here long?" Ben Throckmorton asked.

"Off and on," said Slop. "They don't pay squat."

"Squat beats turds," Tommy Jack said.

Leatha pretended to study a newly planted shrub.

Slop said, "Betsy, I'd have give odds on you marryin' Bobby Walker. Y'all was close as puppy dogs in high school."

"Is this the Bob Walker who never got his high school letter jacket returned?" Ted inquired.

"Uh-huh."

"Y'all was thick," Tommy Jack said.

"Yes, we were," Betsy said. "Bob's a great guy. He's working in Dallas now."

"Sportswriter, ain't he?"

Slop was cleaning his fingernails with an icepick he had taken out of his belt.

"A good one, too," Betsy said. "Writes a column. Covers all the big stuff around."

"He's good," Ben confirmed. "Goes off on a smart-aleck tangent now and then, but he's good."

"Slop's little brother's playin' quarterback this year," Tommy Jack said. "Put his picture in the paper."

"We'll do that," Betsy said.

"Better hurry," Slop sneered. "Paschal's liable to kill him."

"Eugene's a good athlete," Tommy Jack said.

"My ass," said Slop. "He ain't got a gut in his body."

"We have to be going," Ben said. "You fellows take care."

"We'll see you around Claybelle," Slop said. "Lookin' good, Betsy."

Slop and Tommy Jack watched Betsy as she walked away with Ted, Ben, and Leatha, their eyes on her only, on her trim ankles and her cute ass in the pale green dress.

Slop said, "That there's what I call lap moss. Grade-A."

"Tell me I ain't got a bone," Tommy Jack said, feeling around on his crotch.

"That right there," Slop went on, "that's lap moss like you don't find too often. Remember how she used to get them tan legs in the summer?"

"Fuck," said Tommy Jack, looking pained, tortured by the memory of Betsy Throckmorton in a bathing suit at the swimming pool of the Shadowlawn Country Club in Claybelle. "You know old Popeye's arm? That's what I got down here in my pants. Damned old lap moss give it to me. But I guess there ain't no *bad* lap moss, is there?"

"Naw," Slop agreed, spitting through his teeth. "Niggers is all."

It was still daylight as the Packard purred along a two-lane farm road, nearing Claybelle, and Ted Winton was saying, "Ben, I don't think you know what a good writer your daughter is. She didn't just type up research at the magazine, she wrote stories. They were good enough to be published."

"Not by those editors," Betsy said.

"Well, it's in her blood," Ben said. "You get newspapers in your blood, ain't no doctor can cut it out."

"You can play that on the piano." Leatha was looking out at the pastures and hills that were lusher than anything surrounding Fort Worth.

Smiling, Ben said, "When she was nine years old she put out her own paper. Remember that, honey?"

Betsy said, "I broke the big story on Anna Sue Beaton's lemonade stand. There were raisins in her oatmeal cookies."

"What was the name of your paper?" Ted asked.

"*The Wildflower Cricket*," Betsy said proudly. "No ads. All editorial."

Leatha looked around to inform Ted that Ben's house was on Wildflower Drive, the most desirable address in Claybelle, the street where all of the best families lived. Wonderful old trees on Wildflower Drive and marvelous homes—Italian Renaissance, Georgian Revival, Mediterranean, Tudor. What she didn't say was that some of the old ranchers and cotton farmers had done good, and even better, if they had managed to get in on the West Texas oil boom of '17.

Betsy explained the basic editorial position of *The Wildflower Cricket*. A good oatmeal cookie didn't need raisins in it. For that matter, nothing needed raisins in it.

"This hasn't come up before," said Ted. "What's wrong with raisins?"

"They're bugs," Betsy stated flatly. "Some people would try to have you believe they're grapes, but I've never fallen for *that* myth. They're bugs, and they've been crawling into food ever since Anna Sue Beaton invented them."

Leatha faced the back seat again. "Betsy, you campaigned for us to enter the war. I've heard your father laugh about it."

"I did!" Betsy confessed with satisfaction. "*The Wildflower Cricket* said we were going to have to fight the Germans sooner or later, so why not now?"

"How could you have thought something like that when you were only nine years old?" said Ted.

"I saw pictures in the paper. All you had to do was look at a picture of a German. You knew he couldn't be up to any good. They had spikes on their helmets! Show me a guy with a spike on top of his helmet and I'll show you somebody you're going to have to lick in a war."

A long tunnel of overhanging trees with two-story homes on both sides of the street—quite nice, but not as nice as those on Wildflower Drive—led into the square.

The square was two blocks long and two blocks wide. Old pecans and oaks stood among patches of lawn. Cinder pathways and park benches were woven through the trees. The square had always been a cozy, inviting place to hang out. Betsy was delighted to see that the square looked the same as it had in all of those days and nights when she and Bob

Walker had held hands there, sneaking kisses and feels, bequeathing their undying love to each other for the rest of their days and eternities. Ted and Bob Walker would like one another and become good friends, she was certain.

In the center of the square was a tall bronze statue on a granite base, the figure slowly being tarnished to a sickly green by age and weather. It was a statue of General Riley Jefferson Clay, a Confederate hero, after whom the town was named.

One day soon, Ben would corner Ted and tell him how Riley Jefferson Clay had fought with Major General John Bell Hood, "Lee's grenadier," the commander of the Texas Brigade, in all of the bloodiest battles of the Civil War—Shiloh, First and Second Manassas, Chancellorsville, Antietam, Gettysburg, Chickamauga. The Texas Brigade had been the fightingest unit in the Confederacy, Ben would brag. Clay had been Hood's bravest, most daring officer. Ben would tell Ted how Clay, with his curved sword in one hand and his Colt .44 in the other, had led the tough batch of rebels who had twice taken Bloody Lane at Antietam and almost held it.

He would tell Ted how it was Clay and Colonel Bill Oates of the 15th Alabama who had led the advance up Little Round Top at Gettysburg and had come within a hair of securing it, which would have turned the tide of the whole conflict, no doubt about it. And how it was Clay at Chickamauga, after Hood had been wounded, who had ridden at the head of the column that charged through the Yankee forces and routed Philip Sheridan's cavalry. Clay had left an arm on the field at Chickamauga but had fought on till the end of the war. He had then returned to Texas and farmed cotton. The town of Claybelle had sprouted up around him. Ben would be proud to say that the Throckmorton home on Wildflower Drive was built on land that had once been part of Clay's plantation.

And Ben would be even prouder to say that John Bell Hood's blood ran through Betsy's veins. Betsy's mother, Elizabeth, was a Hood, the daughter of the general's youngest brother, Clinton, a mule trader from Kentucky. Betsy's mother had been born in a covered wagon in Indian Territory, now Oklahoma, when Clinton and his wife had been making their way to Texas. That was back in 1885. Betsy's great-uncle, the general, had died in 1879. When Betsy's mother had passed away in 1920, three old Civil War veterans, remnants of the Texas Brigade, men shriveling up in their seventies, had come to the funeral, the way Shriners turn up at funerals, and they had been wearing their mended gray tunics with fading yellow trim and their old forage caps.

Ben would tell all this to Ted later. At the moment, he only pointed at the statue and said, "Right there's a fightin' son of a bitch."

Ben drove around the square twice, slowly, not only for Ted's benefit but for Betsy's.

The buildings surrounding the square were of varying sizes and constructed of various materials: brick, wood frame, sandstone, stucco—a rural Monopoly board. Betsy was encouraged to see that the six-story Dixie Hotel's white stucco exterior had been freshly painted and there were no letters burned out on its blue neon sign. New owners, Ben said. Two sissies from Dallas.

Flanked by Stubblefield's Jewelers and Guarantee Shoe Store, B's Cafe was in the middle of a block. Two signs were in the window. One said NO HELP WANTED. The other said GO, YELLOW JACKETS!

O. L. Beaton's Fidelity Bank, a two-story building of red brick, occupied a corner of the square. On the opposite corner was the modernistic Tivoli, presently running a double feature: *Chinatown Squad* with Lyle Talbot and *Broadway Gondolier* with Dick Powell and Joan Blondell. Between the bank and the picture show were Belk's Five 'n' Dime, Allied Loans, and Thompson's Pharmacy, which was more celebrated for its soda fountain and comic books than it was for its supply of Bisodol, Sal Hepatica, and Campana Italian Balm.

There was more to downtown Claybelle, Ben hastened to say, than what Ted could see around the square. On all of the side streets and back streets there were law offices, meat and produce markets, hardware stores, auto stores, a bicycle shop, the post office. "Whatever you need," Ben said.

Prominent on the square, covering an entire block, was the three-story brown-brick Times-Standard Building, KVAT's signal tower rising from the flat roof. The second- and third-story arched windows were set in arcaded rows and looked as if they had been cleaned for Betsy and Ted's arrival.

Ben stopped in front of the building on the second turn around the square.

"You want to run up and say hello real quick?" Betsy was asked.

"I'd rather have a bath."

Ben put the Packard in gear and wondered if Leatha wanted to pick up her own car.

"It's at your house," Leatha reminded the driver. "We should probably get there before—"

Leatha caught herself but had given something away.

"You're having a party for us!" Betsy said, raising her voice. It was an accusation.

"Sez who?" Ben said to the rearview mirror.

"Listen to you," Betsy said. "Sez me!"

Ben said, "Now, damn it, honey, there's folks who want to see you and meet Ted."

"What if I don't want to see them?"

"You'll want to see one of 'em."

"Who?" said Betsy, meaning Name one, I dare you.

"Bob Walker."

Ben couldn't help looking pleased with himself.

Five

A ROUND dinner table was the secret to a happy life. Ben Throckmorton said it first. Betsy hadn't appreciated how profound the statement was until she had grown older and had suffered the imprisonment of the long dinner table. At a round dinner table, you at least had a fighting chance to talk to each of the guests, to participate in as many different conversations as you liked—shop around for a good one—whereas at a long dinner table you could get trapped by the person on your immediate left or right, the man or woman who never took a breath and could pin you to your chair and slowly drain your blood with a riveting tale about home decorating, the insurance business, an automobile's idiosyncrasies, or some amusing child who didn't sound the least bit clever and probably ought to be drowned.

At the dinner party that night, with the ceiling fan going in the dining-room bay and doors opened onto the full terrace and cast-iron balustrade that stretched across the front of the house, Betsy would have been protected even if she had been sentenced to a long table. Her daddy was on one side and the empty chair was reserved for Bob Walker, who was late, but Ted wasn't as lucky. He was directly across from Betsy, between Anna Sue Beaton and Olive Cooper, the coach's wife.

While Anna Sue was a gorgeous blue-eyed blonde, fashionable down to her pedicure, her regal carriage and haughty glances were betrayed almost every time she opened her mouth. Every other sentence, if not painfully stupid, seemed to come out with a complaining whine to it. Olive Cooper, meanwhile, was a chatty overweight woman who was trying to hide her bulk in a long dress she must have made herself out of several yards of blue-and-green-striped awning.

Betsy and Ted traded glances more than once when Anna Sue prattled on about her day. She had been to the Highland Park Shopping Village in Dallas. It was a wonderful plaza near Dallas Country Club, on the good side of town, of course. North. Which was the *only* side of town in Dallas. South was Oak Cliff. All those Baptists and no liquor, not even a decent cleaners. West was warehouses. East was colored people. The Highland Park Village had these terrific specialty stores, far better than anything in Fort Worth. It was only the second shopping plaza of its kind in the whole United States. The Country Club Plaza in Kansas City had been the first, and, in fact, Anna Sue had been to the Country Club Plaza in Kansas City when her father had attended a bankers' convention there, but the Highland Park Village was superior in every way.

Ted expressed his gratitude to Anna Sue for filling him in on this history of modern American shopping plazas.

Olive Cooper had let Ted know that she was a major force behind Dub Cooper's coaching success.

For fourteen years, Dub Cooper had been a molder of men at Claybelle High. It was true that he had only coached one District winner in all this time, but the Yellow Jackets had never failed to be in contention. A break here and a break there and they could have won District four or five times, even State. The material had been there, only Dub, in her opinion, had been too stubborn to listen to her advice about prayer. Prayer was a weapon.

Yes, they might be rich now if the Yellow Jackets had won State. Families of the boys took care of the coaches who won State Championships in Texas. Some were set for life.

Why, when Claybelle had only won District in '25—Betsy and Anna Sue's senior year—the fathers of the boys had got together and bought Dub a set of tires for the Ford and a suit of clothes. It had been a touching thing, and Dub had cried at the team banquet when the gifts were presented.

Olive said, "Anybody who says a football coach don't have a heart just hasn't never been on the inside of the game."

She reached down in her dress—her awning—and showed Ted a charm that hung around her neck on a chain, a thumb-sized gold-plated football on which the letter C, for Claybelle, was upraised in yellow enamel. Everybody connected with the team had been given one of the gold footballs when the Jackets had won District in '25.

"Sometimes I wonder if it's all been worth it, but then I look at this," Olive said lovingly.

Leatha Wardlaw was at the dinner table, as were four other people, the Beatons and the Websters.

O. L. Beaton's wife, Bernice, a frail and unhappy-looking woman whose prematurely gray hair was worn in a bun, had let Ted know upon introduction that she bore the curse of migraines. Always had, Betsy remembered—and small wonder, being married to that lard-ass loudmouth.

The Websters, Florine and Shady, were unknown to Betsy, but she thought she might like them, particularly Florine, a beautiful woman of forty-two, auburn-haired, tanned, friendly. Florine was a smash in her white coatdress, the sleeves pushed up, gold bracelets jangling on her arms.

Shady Webster was a short, gabby, fidgety man, full of opinions, most of them not serious. He was studiously casual in a red slipover shirt that laced up with a white cord, a Hollywood shirt, white duck trousers, and saddle oxfords. With darting eyes, he lipped off at will and drank heavily but seemed to be able to hold it.

Betsy had heard from Olive Cooper during the cocktail hour that Shady and Florine hadn't been all that socially acceptable until Shady had hit oil in West Texas three years ago. He had been a house builder who specialized in roofs that leaked and foundations that crumbled. The Websters had no children, but Olive said they couldn't wait to buy a two-and-a-half-story mansion on Wildflower Drive as soon as they took rich, the old Sweeney house, the one with the tall white columns.

"Livin' in that house don't make 'em royalty," Olive had said.

Betsy learned that the Websters were originally from Fort Worth, that Shady was a regular golfing buddy of Ben's, a zealous supporter of TCU football, and that Florine was a close friend of Leatha's.

Florine and Shady had overheard part of Anna Sue's monologue about the Highland Park Shopping Village.

"I wouldn't piss on Dallas," Shady had interjected once. "Last time I looked, that's where SMU was."

Florine had mentioned that she would sooner shop at The Fair in Fort Worth as drive to Dallas.

"Fewer Jews," Shady had said.

"That wasn't the reason I had in mind," Florine had said coldly.

"Here's the deal," Shady said to Ted. "Take all the Jews out of Dallas, all the niggers out of Houston, all the spicks out of San Antonio, and all the whores out of Fort Worth, and Claybelle's a pretty good size town."

Shady roared laughing at his joke. Betsy and Florine looked relieved that Florence and Warren had been out of the room, not that they hadn't heard worse.

Florence and Warren had been waiting outside the house on the terrace to greet Betsy when she arrived: Warren, now getting a little gray around the temples, at parade rest in his white jacket; Florence, a fleshy woman, popping her chewing gum, in her black dress and white apron. Betsy had dashed from the car, and the three of them had hugged and kissed and cried and laughed. "Four eleven forty-four," Betsy had said, and Warren had said, "Dixie queen. Still the best number." It was the policy number he bet five days a week. "Gypsy witch," Betsy said to Florence. "Seven six seven six seven," Florence said. "I dreamed about a rabbit last night. I believe I'll have me a winner for sure." Warren and Florence each bet a nickel a day on policy. Warren had once won forty dollars— on the Dixie queen.

Florence and Warren had outdone themselves on dinner. They had fixed a choice of salad: cottage cheese and pear, or lettuce, tomato, and crumbled crackers with ketchup. Then had come the crispy fried chicken, breaded pork chops, mashed potatoes with brown gravy, green beans cooked in salt pork, their special hoppin' john, which was black-eyed peas and rice with hot sauce, pinto beans cooked in salt pork, mustard greens cooked with fatback—pot likker—cheese grits, and corn on the cob.

It was when everybody was having the homemade straw-berry shortcake that Anna Sue brought up the Depression.

"It made me sick to look at it," she said. "I was coming back from Dallas on the back road, over by the Santa Fe depot, and there they were! Right there on those vacant lots, as if real people aren't living two blocks away. Stringing up clothes-lines, letting their dirty little kids run loose. It turned my stomach, is what it did."

Dub Cooper, the coach, said, "Who you talkin' about, Anna Sue, them hobos?"

"Whatever you call 'em," Anna Sue whined. "Those *people*."

It was hard to un-know certain high school friends. Betsy and Anna Sue had kept up largely through Anna Sue's ef-forts. Anna Sue was one of those individuals who corre-sponded faithfully at special times of the year—birthdays, holidays. She wrote in a neat, tiny script and could turn a simple birthday card into a letter so long and boring it would slam Betsy's eyes shut faster than a page of Proust.

Anna Sue had enrolled at SMU the same fall that Betsy had gone to Barnard, but she had dropped out of college after two years to marry Jerry Sturgeon, a singer and tap dancer. Jerry Sturgeon had thought Anna Sue was rich. She had thought he was going to be a Broadway star. The marriage had lasted less than a year, much to the relief of O. L. and Bernice, who hadn't been all that thrilled to see their son-in-law peddle sheet music by singing and dancing at Grant's variety store during lunch hours in downtown Dallas.

Jerry Sturgeon had moved to California, determined to break into motion pictures, but Anna Sue had refused to leave the security of Texas. As far as anyone knew, Jerry had yet to make it in Hollywood. The only break he'd had—Anna Sue had sent Betsy the photograph—was when he and a girl in an aviator cap and boots had won a long-distance dance contest by doing the tango from Santa Barbara to Los Angeles.

Anna Sue's second marriage had only lasted five weeks. She had fallen in love with a stunt flier, a carefree rogue named Soupy Kennerdine, who had won her heart on Sunday after-noons at Meacham Field, the Fort Worth airport, in his World

War Jenny by doing loops, tailspins, and Immelmann rolls, and skywriting "Whitley's Drug" in the skies above.

Anna Sue had been married to the flier less than a month when he threatened her with divorce unless she became a part of his act. His idea had been to fasten her to the top wing of his Jenny with cables, in a standing position, so that she could bat a paddle ball as he flew low past the crowd.

O. L. had gone after Soupy Kennerdine with a shotgun. The stunt flier had left town with buckshot in the fuselage of his Jenny.

Anna Sue's father had bankrolled her in two business ventures that Betsy knew of. First in an antique shop which functioned more as a tea room, and then a specialty store that sold nothing but Holeproof hosiery in pure silk. Both ventures had failed. Anna Sue blamed the failures on Claybelle's lack of taste. O. L. blamed the failures, at least in part, on the owner's absenteeism.

Anna Sue was back living at home with her parents, working as a receptionist at her father's bank, but mostly looking for another husband.

"Might be some good football players mixed in with them hobos," Dub Cooper said to Anna Sue. "You didn't see any orphans runnin' around, did you?"

"Did I do what?"

A burly, balding man who had shed his checkered coat, yanked his tie loose, and rolled up his sleeves so he could get at the food better with his gnarled hands, the coach said, "Ain't no wonder them Masonic Home Masons do good every year. They got them orphans. State finals in '32. Semifinals last year. I'd like to have me some orphans. Orphans is mean. They'll hitchee. 'Cause they orphans."

Anna Sue said, "I don't know what in the world you're talking about, Coach Cooper. How would I know who's an orphan and who's not?"

"Orphans has got freckles and they wiry. That's as a general rule."

Dub and Olive would be leaving the party that night with as much leftover food as they could carry. In their little one-bedroom house over near Bewley Mill, the Coopers were supporting Dub's out-of-work brother, Volney, Olive's sister, Ida

Brite, and Ida Brite's asthmatic nine-year-old, Dorrance, who sometimes sounded like dueling train whistles in his sleep. Volney and Ida Brite and Dorrance slept on the screened-in porch when it was warm, but when cold weather came, it could get a little "close" around the house, what with Volney in the living room, Ida Brite in the dining room, and Dorrance wheezing on a pallet in the kitchen.

Ben Throckmorton, now smoking a Chesterfield, said, "Every town has hobos. We might as well have ours."

"It's getting where you can't stay home," Leatha Wardlaw said. "Three times a day I go to the back door and it's some dirty old man who wants a glass of icewater. I have about run out of fruit jars."

"What gets me are the ones who come to the *front* door," O. L. Beaton said. "Can you believe that? Come to a man's front door? Like I'm gonna have a job for somebody who stinks that bad."

Florine Webster felt sorry for the hobos. There were people in this world who couldn't help it because they were hungry. She had taken to making up a platter of potato patties twice a week, and she would give everybody who came to her door a cold potato pattie. It wasn't much, but they all seemed to be grateful.

"I like a potato pattie if it's got onions in it," Dub Cooper said. "You put onions in yours, Florine?"

Olive elbowed her husband. "She's talkin' about feeding the *needy*, dimwit."

Dub said, "Look at my guards and tackles and tell me I ain't the neediest sumbitch in town."

O. L. Beaton stifled a belch, patted his stomach, and said he didn't like the idea of a bunch of vagrants being in Claybelle. "Whoever owns those vacant lots ought to run 'em off."

"Those are my lots," Ben Throckmorton admitted, clearing his throat.

This was news to everyone, including Betsy.

"I told the Salvation Army it was all right by me if some of those folks wanted to use the property for a while. I know most of 'em are uneducated, and some of 'em are lazy, but what are we supposed to do—let 'em crawl off and die? They can't find work. They've lost their homes. They're stuck."

O. L. shook his head. "God damn, Ben, you're a soft-hearted scogie. Most of them people ain't thinkin' about nothin' but what they can steal next. There's honest work around if people want to look for it hard enough."

Ted was compelled to speak up. "If that's true around here, Mr. Beaton, it's the only place I know of. People are starving to death all over the country."

Florine said, "Ted, some of us are a little more compassionate than O. L. There are relief stations in town where people can get free food and coffee. I volunteer two days a week at the Santa Fe station."

"They can get a free lunch at the Mission, over there off the square," Olive said. "That nice young pastor feeds everybody he can."

"Yeah, he sure does," said the coach. "All you got to do is let the loud sumbitch preach you a sermon."

"Wouldn't hurt *you* none," Olive barked.

The coach looked around the table. "Well, let me say this. If I thought the dumbass could help me win a football game, I'd be there ever day, but God and football ain't got nothin' to do with one another."

"You don't know that," Olive said.

"I don't, do I? I only been at it fourteen Goddamn years— and you know what? I ain't seen an invocation score a touchdown *yet.*"

Florence and Warren brought coffee. Leatha asked to have hers on the terrace. Olive, Bernice, and Anna Sue joined Leatha outside. Betsy and Florine stayed at the table with the men.

"Maybe you gentlemen can tell me something," Ted said. "Why Hoover jokes? This isn't Hoover's Depression, not totally. Why doesn't anyone blame Coolidge and Mellon?"

O. L. said, "Andrew Mellon was a fine Treasury Secretary."

"Oh, he was wonderful," Ted said. "He was so wonderful he had to resign before Congress impeached him."

"Congress." The banker smirked. "I got some ideas about what you can do with Congress."

Ted said, "You know, when you look back on what happened to the stock market, I think it's obvious that Coolidge and Mellon could have prevented the crash, and they certainly could have kept it from being so severe. They knew most of those holding companies and investment trusts were phonies. It seems to me they were more interested in helping the upper five percent pay even fewer taxes than they already were. What do we read now? They were 'blinded' by the growth of the Twenties? I don't buy that."

Betsy put cream and sugar in her coffee and cream only in Ted's.

"The grand old stock market," Ted said. "How high was up? If you had bought a share of General Electric in 1921 for a hundred dollars, it was worth over sixteen hundred dollars by 1928! I'm sorry, but this defied logic. It was a dream world. But the people in Washington kept saying everything was fundamentally sound. This only encouraged more people to speculate. They weren't investors, they were speculators. Buy on your word, pay for it with the gain. It was a can't-lose bet. A way to hit a home run without leaving the dugout."

Ben Throckmorton said, "We know what stopped it, of course. Paper."

"Exactly," said Ted. "Paper that didn't happen to be money. All it took was for a few stocks to go down instead of up, a few margin calls, and brokers realized their 'investors' couldn't come up with the money—not without going to the pawnshop."

In the lament of a stock market victim, Betsy said, "How can I owe you fifty thousand dollars? I've never *had* fifty thousand dollars!"

"Dummies," O. L. Beaton said. "I don't waste any sympathy on dummies."

"Bankers," Shady Webster said sourly, glancing at O. L. "I only know one thing about bankers. Your interest is workin' while I'm sleepin'."

O. L. took that as a compliment and was still laughing when Betsy said, "Ted covered the crash, for *Time*."

He had. Ted had been sent down to Wall Street at noon on the Thursday of October 24, 1929. The market had been shaky for a week, falling and rising, but things had gone crazy on that Thursday. Institutions had started to unload, and stocks had begun to drop at the rate of ten, twenty, thirty points an hour.

Ted had stood in the gallery of the New York Stock Exchange and watched a thousand men tearing at their collars, perspiring with fear, racing about, being swamped with phone calls, cables, hysterical cries to sell. A wild day but nothing compared to what lay ahead.

The market had rallied a bit on Friday, and again on Monday, and all of the "smart" people issued statements to the press saying Wall Street had regained its "composure."

It was John D. Rockefeller himself who said on Monday, October 28, that he had supreme confidence in the economy— he was going on a buying spree.

"I wonder how many people *he* busted?" Betsy said through an exhale.

The following day was Black Tuesday, October 29. Armageddon.

Ted had dashed back and forth between the Exchange and two banks. He watched exhausted runners collapse on the marble floors of bank buildings. Down on the floor of the Exchange, he had seen brokers red-eyed and wan by midday. A distress sale was on. Brokers fainted. Brokers went mad, wallowing in ticker tape. Word spread on the radio about the panic. Thousands of people gathered on the streets around the Exchange. The city dispatched four hundred policemen to Wall Street to keep order.

In the lobby of the National City Bank, Ted had run into a classmate from Yale, a fellow named Barton Cox. He had lost a fortune on margin, a fortune he didn't personally have, but Barton Cox had only shrugged and said, "It's one of life's rich emotional experiences, old boy."

What was he going to do?

Barton Cox said, "As I see it, I have two choices. I shall either throw myself on the mercy of Grandfather or find a rather tall window ledge."

Window ledges had been crowded. The president of Union Cigar leaped out of a hotel window after seeing the stock of his company, in only three hours, drop from $113 to $4.

In that single day, stocks lost a value of $30 billion.

Andrew Mellon—"Your man," Ted said, looking at O. L. Beaton, but pleasantly—had only sat back and pronounced the crash a *wholesome* opportunity for the country, a chance to slice away "fat," liquidate labor, stocks, farmers, real estate.

Ted continued: "I don't argue that the government has made matters worse—price-fixing, the NRA, bureaucratic bog, complicated regulations—but it was the crash that got us into this Depression, and it was pure greed on the part of the rich that caused the crash."

"You know what's amazing?" Betsy said. "Newspaper editors vote every year on the biggest stories, okay? Guess what they said was the biggest story of '29? Not the stock market crash. They said it was Admiral Byrd flying to the South Pole!"

"I voted for the crash," Ben said.

Ted wasn't finished. "With all due respect, Ben, this Depression has never been covered properly. Bankruptcies and foreclosures are a big part of it, but they're nothing compared to the millions of people who are out of a job, have no place to live. It's scary to think about how their ill health is going to affect the future."

"Most hobos are born," the banker said as Betsy looked at sweat forming maps of small continents on his blue shirt.

"I'm serious," Ted said. "The malnutrition and undernourishment of these people can mar the human race. Their poor health . . . insanity . . . tuberculosis . . . these things may affect generations."

O. L. Beaton, with a sly grin for Shady Webster, said, "Can I ask you a question, Ted?"

"Sure."

"Are they lots of Bolsheviks up East?"

It was a half-hour later. Everyone had moved out on the terrace. Betsy was smoking and only pretending to listen to Shady Webster's long, drawn-out joke about a priest, a rabbi, and a shoeshine boy trying to get into heaven when Warren came outside to tell her she was wanted on the phone.

It was Bob Walker. He was calling to apologize for missing

the party. He had felt the need to sub a column. This was the opening day of Southwest Conference football practice, and just as he had been walking out of the office the SMU beat reporter had called in to say that Harry Shuford, one of SMU's best players, had injured his knee. A columnist had to be topical, Bob said. Readers of the *Dallas Journal* expected it of him. He expected it of himself.

Bob was an oddity among Texas sportswriters, a columnist who never took the games or heroes too seriously. He had a natural gift for seeing the absurd or pretentious side of things, though he knew sports well. He had been an oddity in his college days at the University of Texas in Austin, where his leads and headlines in the *Daily Texan* had confused and perplexed his journalism professors but had resulted in job offers from papers in Dallas, Houston, and San Antonio after he had graduated. The professors couldn't get jobs on newspapers. How could Bob?

When a University of Texas pitcher named Jimmy Austin had thrown a no-hitter against the Arkansas Razorbacks one afternoon, Bob's headline had said: WHY DON'T WE NAME THE STATE CAPITAL AFTER HIM?

The State Championship game of Texas high school football had been played at Memorial Stadium in Austin one year, and Bob had covered it for the *Daily Texan*. He had watched two Amarillo Sandies named Red McKee and Spud McCully trample the Goose Creek Ganders. His lead had read:

> It didn't take long for Amarillo's Red McKee and Spud McCully to McMincemeat of a football team yesterday afternoon.

Bob's lead on the Texas–Texas A&M game of 1928 was regarded by one of his journalism professors as a classic example of bad taste, but it was still quoted in Texas newspaper circles. That season, Coach Dana X. Bible of Texas A&M had fielded a mediocre team, and the University of Texas had defeated the Aggies, 19 to 0, in their traditional Thanksgiving Day game. Bob's story had begun:

The University of Texas and Texas A&M played another storybook game yesterday, and the Longhorns had a lot of fun reading about Ali Bible and the Forty Sieves.

"You've chosen an SMU football player over me, is that it?" Betsy said to Bob on the phone.

"He's a vital cog in their juggernaut. How's married life? Don't tell me. You cook, Ted does the dishes. He washes, you iron."

"I want to *see* you, damn it."

Bob said he was anxious to see her, too, but it might be a couple of weeks. He was going off on a pre-season tour of Southwest Conference football camps, and after this he had an important baseball series coming up, Beaumont and Galveston. The pennant might hang on it.

He said, "Listen, babe, I wanted you to hear it from me first. It's no big thing with Anna Sue."

"What's no big thing?"

"She hasn't mentioned it?"

"Mentioned what?"

"I've sort of been, like, kind of, you know . . . going out with her lately."

Betsy said, "There must be something wrong with our connection. I thought you said Anna Sue Beaton."

"Like I said, it's just something to do."

"I broke you up once in high school. Do I have to do it again? Jesus, Bob. Your taste!"

"She's not exactly ugly."

"Nope."

"She knows how to pretend she likes sports."

"I suppose."

"She knows how to stay up late."

"Of course."

"You know, she's just somebody to date, go out with occasionally, somebody to—"

"Fuck," said Betsy. "I understand."

A pause, and Bob said, "There's something I've always been curious about. Did you get into journalism so you could talk like a waterfront whore?"

He said he would call her for lunch when she least expected it. They hung up, and Betsy went straight to Anna Sue on the terrace.

"Betsy, I'll bet you are so glad to be back home!"

"That's what everybody keeps saying. When were you going to get around to telling me about you and Bob?"

Looking embarrassed, Anna Sue said, "I was working up the courage. Y'all are so close and all."

"God, Anna Sue, I'm a married lady now."

"Who told you I was dating Bob? Did Eva Jane McKnight write you a letter?—I will *kill* her!"

"I just spoke to Bob on the phone. He's not going to make it tonight. Eva Jane McKnight? I haven't thought about her since we were seniors."

"Bob called here?"

"I just talked to him. Didn't Eva Jane marry a lawyer and move to Austin and have babies and things?"

"Bob called here and didn't ask to talk to *me?*"

"He was on a deadline."

"Deadlines, deadlines!" Anna Sue frowned. "People are always on a *deadline*."

"It's part of the deal."

Betsy lit a Lucky. Anna Sue took one and confided, "Eva Jane's back here now with her two kids. Divorced. Remember the Pemberton house on the road to Shadowlawn? She bought it. She's doing it over, and she is spending money, let me tell you."

"Got a good settlement, huh?"

"It's better than that," Anna Sue said with a look.

"What do you mean?"

"I couldn't meet you at the train today because I was in Dallas with Eva Jane. It's better if she has a friend with her when she's having lunch in public with . . . this person. Eva Jane looks good. I mean she looks *real good*. If she didn't have those two kids, I'll bet she could go to Hollywood. Seriously. She knows everything about clothes and makeup. But do you want to talk about brats? Her two boys destroy *everything* they touch. And loud? I've told Eva Jane, do *not* bring those children to my house!"

"Who's the guy?" Betsy asked, not really caring.

"It is very sticky," Anna Sue said, lowering her voice and turning her shoulder to the others on the terrace. "It is making me a nervous wreck."

"He's here?"

"Hmmm."

Betsy scanned the terrace. It could only be one person.

"Shady Webster?"

"Hmmm."

"I don't know him at all."

"He's nice, Betsy, and let me tell you, he *spends* with both hands."

"How long has it been going on?"

"Over a year. I've been to New Orleans with them twice—and Hot Springs. He not only bought her the Pemberton home, he gave her a cabin on Eagle Mountain Lake. Near the Fort Worth Boat Club. They go there all the time, can you imagine? They walk in like nobody should think anything about it, and Shady and Florine are known in Fort Worth society now. He swears he'll get a divorce and marry her if she'll get rid of her rotten kids. She has two boys, six and eight. She's tried to get Bubba Dean to take 'em. That's her ex. But Bubba Dean knows what little shits they are, excuse my language. I am telling you, those kids can screw up a one-car funeral. She thinks she's found a boarding school for them in California."

"Is money that important to Eva Jane? She'd give up her children?"

"Betsy, there's money and there's *oil* money. You've been gone too long."

Betsy smiled at something.

"What?" said Anna Sue.

"I was thinking about Millie. My friend in New York? Shady Webster sounds like the man she's been looking for."

"Nobody is going to pry Shady Webster away from Eva Jane McKnight, believe me," Anna Sue said with conviction. "She has him wrapped up like a tamale. I wish he would hurry up and get a divorce. Every time I go somewhere with them I think Florine's going to walk in with a butcher knife and stab all three of us."

"I think I like Florine a lot. Does she have any idea he's fooling around?"

"None," said Anna Sue. "I mean, I don't think so. I'm not sure. Eva Jane doesn't think so. Betsy, don't breathe this to anybody. If Leatha finds out, she would like nothing better than to tell Florine."

"I'm not going to tell anybody, Anna Sue. I'll probably forget it by tomorrow. How serious is it with you and Bob?"

"*I* could be serious. I was serious about him in high school till you broke us up."

"It was destiny."

"All he does is work. I never know what's on his mind. He's always *thinking* about something he has to write. He's there. I'm here. I drive to Dallas a lot more than he comes here. Some romance."

"The sex is good, I'm sure."

"You should know."

There *was* the odd instance when Anna Sue could hold her own.

"Can I tell you something, Betsy? I'm glad you went away to college, I really am. If you had stayed home, you and Bob would have gotten married. He wouldn't be available now."

"I'm not sure about that," Betsy said. "Half the time, I never knew whether we were friends or lovers. It seemed to change back and forth. Most of the time, honestly, all we did was laugh and make fun of everything. We even made fun of sex! He still would have gone to school in Austin, and I would never have gone to the University of Texas. I would have gone to TCU. We would have drifted apart eventually.

"Oh, we tried to keep it going after I went to New York. My first year up there we wrote these terribly witty letters to each other every week. That finally stopped. Even those two summers when I came home, when we were together, I think we could both feel the distance growing between us. We talked about it. We were starting to think about our careers. Nothing was going to affect our friendship, but love could go to the sideline for a while. I knew by then I was going to live in New York after college. I was a Manhattan lover. I was going to find a job and stay there. A newspaper, a magazine, book publishing, *something.* I guess I thought Daddy could pull some strings if I couldn't get a job on my own.

"Bob wasn't ready to take on New York. He said he would go to New York the day he was offered a *good* job up there. He figured he would have to make a reputation for himself down here before that happened. He's still confident he'll get to the 'big league' someday, but he doesn't know how many years it's going to take. Two people in love, I don't think you can keep them apart. That's why Bob and I couldn't have been lovers so much as we were loving friends. Besides, we always laughed too much to be lovers. If none of this was true, I wouldn't have fallen for Ted."

"That's what's so crappy," Anna Sue said with a frown.

"What is?"

"You two are so damn close. Here you are, Betsy, married to that gorgeous man over there, and I feel like I have to ask your permission to go out with Bob Walker!"

Six

ONE OF the problems with leaving New York to live someplace else, almost *anywhere* else, as Betsy had suspected beforehand, was in having to explain almost everything you might be inclined to talk about.

You didn't have to explain anything to New Yorkers. They knew about it. And you didn't have to entertain them, either. Not unless you felt like it—and it better be good.

But Betsy knew that in Texas everything would have to be explained, most often to the point of ruining every punch line of every story, and that people would *expect* to be entertained. You had lived in New York and they hadn't. You had been around and they hadn't. So you had by God better entertain them, unless of course you wanted them to think you were a stuck-up bitch.

Betsy had been reminded of this a little later at the party after everyone had moved back indoors, into the living room, and had settled in with cognac and more coffee, and the subject of bank robbers had come up.

Shady Webster started it by saying he had seen one of those posters that were being tacked up all over North Central Texas. "Damn fine idea," Shady said to O. L. "You bankers finally got smart. Shoot the sons of bitches, and this bullshit will come to a screechin' halt."

"We got us a epidemic, no doubt about it," O. L. said. "Must be three or four a week somewhere in Texas. Right around here, they've hit the bank in Waxahachie, two in Dallas, one in Fort Worth, another one in Cleburne."

"Don't forget Midlothian," Olive Cooper said. "That's where they killed one of the robbers."

"Who did?" Ted asked.

"Texas Rangers," Shady Webster said. "Rangers had a tip.

They were waitin' for 'em. Splattered that sumbitch like paint on a fence."

"Rangers don't take any shit," Dub Cooper said.

"Will you kindly watch your *mouth?*" Olive shook a fist at her husband.

"Doo-doo," Dub said, twisting his lip at the corner. "Rangers don't take no doo-doo."

O. L. Beaton sniffed his cognac and said, "When you've got yourself an epidemic, you better find yourself a cure. I'm proud to say I'm on the board of the Texas Bankers Association. Fact of the matter is, a bunch of low-life scum are using the Depression as an excuse for lawlessness. What the Texas Bankers Association is saying, by offering these rewards, is that the only *good* bank robber is a *dead* bank robber."

Ben Throckmorton took pleasure in announcing that his daughter and Ted weren't unfamiliar with bank robbers. They had covered the John Dillinger story.

Dillinger's name grabbed everyone's attention. It was time to entertain.

Betsy began by doing an impression of J. Edgar Hoover. "The criminal army in America is on the march," Hoover had said in a national radio address. "Crime today is sapping the moral and spiritual strength of every American."

Hoover had sent his G-men out to do something about it, and 1934 had been a good year for the Feds, Betsy reminded everyone.

"President Hoover?" Anna Sue asked.

Helping Betsy out, Florine said, "J. Edgar Hoover, Anna Sue. The head of the FBI."

Betsy said, "Dillinger would have had to kill fifty people and rob forty banks if you believed everybody who claimed they saw him, but he did kill three cops for sure. A reporter in Indianapolis got a great quote from a friend of Dillinger's. The guy said, 'Johnny goes out and robs banks and things, but he's just like everybody else, aside from that.' "

"He came through Claybelle once," Olive said. "I kept our doors locked for a week."

Dub said, "He didn't never come through Claybelle. You'd be a hell of a reporter, woman. That was Bonnie and Clyde."

"Same thing." Olive shrugged.

Betsy explained that she and Ted were assigned to the story after the Feds got Dillinger in Chicago.

"John Dillinger is dead?" Anna Sue said with a startled expression.

Betsy caught the look from Florine.

A man of patience, Ted explained to Anna Sue that a trap had been set for Dillinger and he had been shot down as he walked out of a little third-rate movie house in Chicago, the Biograph. Melvin Purvis, an FBI agent, had been tipped off to the badman's whereabouts by Anna Sage, "the lady in red," who hadn't spent a lot of time in the Social Register. When Dillinger reached an alley outside the theater, a G-man stepped from behind a telephone pole, revolver in hand, and said, "Hello, Johnny." Dillinger had instinctively gone for his gun, a .38 he carried in his trouser pocket, but before Dillinger could get to his gun, another G-man had moved up behind him and pressed a pistol in his back and fired three shots. Two bullets went through his heart and the other one came out under his left eye.

Betsy said to Ben, "Nobody wrote it better than Jack Lait, Daddy. Did you ever see his lead?"

"Chicago fellow?"

"His old connections paid off for him. He was the only reporter who was an eyewitness." She quoted Jack Lait's lead: " 'John Dillinger, ace badman of the world, got his last night —two slugs through his heart and one through his head.' "

Florine Webster smiled at Betsy as she said, "You and Ted honeymooned with John Dillinger, didn't you?"

"I don't think I would put it *that* way, Florine," said Leatha, trying to appear offended in Betsy's behalf.

"I would," Betsy said good-naturedly. "We were going to get married anyhow. The more I thought about it, the more I didn't want to come back here and dress up like Marie Antoinette and have the ceremony in an Episcopal church I'd never seen before. We found a justice of the peace in North Shore. The vows took—what?—six minutes? Then we did a very romantic thing."

"What?" asked Anna Sue eagerly.

"We went to a hospital to look at John Dillinger's body."

Ted said, "It was my job to look at the body. I was the writer. Betsy was the researcher. A fellow named Chet Weatherford with the FBI agreed to let me see the body. Betsy insisted on coming along. I thought it was unnecessary, but I couldn't talk her out of it."

"I wanted to see his whatyoucallit."

Leatha wasn't sure she heard this right. Neither was Olive. Neither was Anna Sue.

"His who?" Leatha said.

"His what?" said Olive.

"His deal," Betsy answered.

"His grandeur," Florine clarified.

Betsy said, "If you think I was going to pass up an opportunity like that, ha! Now I know what it looks like. You're not going to con *me* at some carnival, telling me this loaf of pumpernickel is John Dillinger's dick."

"How big was it?" Dub Cooper wanted to know.

"What do *you* care?" Olive said.

"Hell, he was Public Enemy Number One!"

O. L. Beaton said, "I bet it ain't bigger than Rudolph Valentino's. I saw his at a carnival last year."

"About like this," Betsy said to Dub Cooper.

"That little? You're shittin' me."

Dillinger's body had been lying on a table in the basement of the Alexian Brothers' Hospital in Chicago. A sheet covered the body from the waist to the knees. Betsy had been surprised to see that his feet were so dainty, his arms so skinny. His hair had been dyed jet black to throw off the Feds, but he still had his mustache. Ego.

Betsy had lifted the sheet while Chet Weatherford was talking to a hospital attendant.

"I'd like to know how all them dicks get in carnivals," Shady Webster said. "That's the big mystery to me."

Betsy didn't go into what happened later in the evening. How she and Ted spent their wedding night at the Ambassador Hotel, dined in the Pump Room, drank champagne, danced to the music of Ray Noble's orchestra and Connie Boswell's lazy vocals—or how they had made love until Ted lapsed into a near-coma and Betsy had propped herself up in bed and smoked a cigarette and had said to herself with amusement, "Ted Winton got his last night—two on his back and one standing up."

Florence and Warren brought in a fresh pot of coffee and a large plate of sugar cookies. Betsy knelt on the floor and poured coffee for everyone as she and Ted kept talking about their experiences at *Time*.

Still Norris, their editor, refused to acknowledge that Betsy was ever any help in improving Ted's stories, even though there were instances when she would practically write half of them, and her research would be responsible for *all* of them.

Ted had tried to see that Betsy received the credit she deserved, but Still Norris would only give Betsy credit for being a "bright girl" because, in the final analysis, it was a *Time* editor who made a story work, not the writer or the researcher. "Give me the lumber and I will build the house," the editor would say. The editors *were* masters at inserting that essential second graf which made the story seem more important than it actually was. "Never before until last week ..." "Haunted by this myth until last Friday, the American people ..."

Most of Ted's pieces had been written from files and clips. The files were the tons of copy that poured into the office every day over Western Union and Postal Telegraph, coming from the magazine's "stringers," as Henry Luce named them— newspapermen in other cities who were kept on a retainer to furnish information stolen from other papers, which meant it was inaccurate or useless or both.

Ted had written the "Happy Jack" Hamilton story after the Feds had taken "Happy Jack" alive in Indiana. He had written the "Pretty Boy" Floyd story after the G-men had trailed Floyd to a farmhouse in Ohio and cut him in half with machine guns. From Betsy's research, Ted had written the Bonnie and Clyde story, surprising Still Norris with a number of facts: that Bonnie had liked to puff on cigars, that Clyde was slightly effeminate, that they were despised by other bandits because they tended to kill haphazardly and bungled most of their stickups.

Betsy said, "Fort Worth made them famous—after they

killed that motorcycle cop and wounded another one on Easter Sunday. Bonnie did all the shooting."

"Out there on the highway to Lake Worth is where it happened," Shady Webster said.

"They were a grand couple," Betsy said. "The cops only stopped them to get their autographs."

Betsy told her favorite story about her favorite *Time* editor. In November of '34, Ted had gone back out to Chicago, without Betsy, to do a story on the demise of Lester Gillis, alias "Baby Face Nelson." Nelson had been driving through a street in suburban Chicago, minding his own business, when two Feds, recognizing him, had opened fire. Nelson had returned the fire. In the bloody gun battle that lasted three minutes, the two Feds and Nelson had all been killed.

Recreating the action as best he could, Ted had written a story he had been reasonably satisfied with—until he picked up the magazine later. Betsy had lost a violent argument in the office between checker and editor on closing night, and in the interest of accuracy throughout the story, Still Norris had changed the gangster's name to "Baby Face Gillis."

"I don't get it," Anna Sue said, running a comb through her hair.

Betsy closed her eyes with tiredness and for a moment felt deeply, *deeply* concerned about Bob Walker.

Leatha was the last to leave. Ben walked her out to her car in the circular drive and came back inside to sit at the butcher-block table in the big country kitchen and have a piece of cold fried chicken with Betsy and Ted, Florence and Warren.

Warren was saying, "Mr. Wintons, you done seen you some bad folks in your day."

"I mean!" Florence said. "But they can't whup a G-man. G-man gets 'em all."

"Do you know why they're called G-men?" Ted said to the couple.

"I reckon I don't," Warren said.

"Chet Weatherford, my friend in the FBI, was the man who caught Machine Gun Kelly two years ago. Chet and three other agents caught him in a boardinghouse in Oklahoma City. When they kicked in the door, Machine Gun Kelly threw up his hands and said, 'Don't shoot, G-men, don't shoot!' Chet said, 'G-men? What's that?' Kelly said, 'It's short for Government, ain't it?' "

Ben nibbled on a chicken wing as he said to Betsy, "You didn't tell the crowd about Ma Barker—how you could have got yourself killed."

Betsy said, "By who, the FBI? There must have been fifty of them down there."

"Whom," Ted said.

"Anyhow, I had a very nice bulletproof vest. Very chic. From Abercrombie."

Ma Barker and her four crazy sons—Dock, Freddie, Herman, and Floyd—had been the most active and elusive of all the famous bandits. A stocky big-bellied woman who wore cloche hats, frilly dresses, and white stockings, Ma read the Bible regularly, never missed church on Sundays, but then she and her sons would kill and rob during the week—"to get what's mine," she had said in the letters she enjoyed writing to newspapers. Her real name was Arizona Clark Barker.

When Chet Weatherford invited Ted to go down to Oklawaha, Florida, to watch the Feds get Ma and her gang—to be the Jack Lait on this one—Betsy had insisted on going along. It might be the only chance she would ever have to see an ambush, she had said, and she was, after all, the researcher.

"It was great," Betsy said. "The gang was in this little bungalow, way back in the trees. The Feds had it completely surrounded. We hid behind trees. The Feds opened fire after Chet hollered, 'FBI!' I was a little disappointed. I thought they should have waited for Ma to say, 'Come get me, coppers!' "

"Six hours," said Ted. "It went on for six hours, these loud bursts of fire, from machine guns, shotguns, pistols. It was rather incredible."

"I'd have brought a thermos if I'd known it was going to take so long," Betsy said. "We didn't see it, we were on the front side of the house, but Freddie Barker tried to run out the back door. He was killed instantly. The other brothers weren't there. When we went inside the house, we found Ma and one of her boyfriends. I thought from the position of her

body and the pistol in her hand that she'd killed herself—
she'd always said she wouldn't be taken alive—but the
G-men took the credit. I'd have liked to see the ballistics test,
but they never revealed it."

Betsy had been immensely pleased with the story Ted had
written for the magazine, a story Betsy had all but rewritten,
which had something to do with how pleased she was.

What had basically been her lead had read: "That swell
American mother, Ma Barker, won't be going to church this
Sunday—or any other Sundays in the future. Last week, as
Ma and her boys were having a prayer meeting in their little
home down in the Florida glades, some G-men invited them-
selves over and brought along their machine guns."

But that wasn't what had run in *Time*. After Still Norris
had put his deft pencil to the copy, the story had begun:

"Arizona Clark Barker, known as Ma to many, along with
one of her four sons, Freddie, and another man who had yet
to be identified by week's end . . ."

Which was as far as Betsy had ever been able to read it.

This had been the worst of all editing atrocities, and it had
put Betsy and Ted in more of a mood to accept Ben's offer last
spring.

Ben had always hoped he could lure his daughter back to
Texas. He had gone to New York in May, and over dinner at
the Savoy Plaza Hotel on Fifth Avenue he had said to Betsy
that the newspaper and radio station were going to be her
responsibility someday eventually, so why not now? She could
be the editor-in-chief of the *Times-Standard,* Ted could run
KVAT.

It had been part of Ben's sales pitch to say, "I know you're
in love with New York, but we're almost a city. Our population's up to 52,000. The paper gets into eighty percent of the
homes. That's better than good—it's shithouse rosy. And
KVAT is a darn good little station, considering it's not in Fort
Worth. I've got a swap deal with WBAP so I can get the shows
I like on the NBC feed."

"Daddy, are you sure you're ready to retire?" Betsy had
asked that night.

"Honey, I didn't say I was going to an old-age home. I said
I was making you the editor."

"It would have to be my newspaper, Daddy."

"I'm real proud of you, honey. You been up here working in New York City and all, but you ain't no Richard Harding Davis yet."

Betsy had said, " 'The Germans flowed into Brussels like a river of steel, gray and ghostlike.' My paper, Daddy. Put up or shut up."

"I would think I might be called in on a decision now and then."

"Of course you would," Ted had said reassuringly.

"It's our station, too," Betsy had said. "I mean it, Daddy. No interference."

Ben had looked at Ted like a man in need of sympathy.

"We play a lot of music on KVAT, Ted. People like it. People like their favorite programs. *Vic and Sade* at three-thirty every afternoon. *Amos 'n' Andy* at seven every night. I don't need me no H. V. Kaltenborn around the clock."

Ted had looked at Betsy and said, "It all sounds good. I think I'm ready to get out of the gore business. What about you?"

And so the deal had been done. And now Betsy and Ted were in Texas on a warm August night in 1935, sitting in the kitchen of Betsy's childhood home, on a lovely old street, in a quiet little town, having no way of knowing that their adventures in crime were far from over.

PART TWO

Don't Write Me Nothin' That Rhymes

Seven

IF YOU start in Fort Worth on a map of Texas, as Ben Throckmorton did, and draw a line thirty-five miles east to Dallas, and then eighty miles south to Waco, and then eighty miles back north to Fort Worth, you have something of a geographical triangle. This was the territory to which Claybelle belonged in scenery, spirit, and attitude. It was within these boundaries, through all of the other little towns set among flat pastures, knobby hills, and trees warped by time or wind, that the *Claybelle Times-Standard* reached out for its circulation and KVAT sought a listening audience. Ted referred to the triangle as his new "communal surroundings," a term too flattering for Betsy—she called it the dunce cap.

Three weeks had passed since they had arrived. They had dropped by the *Times-Standard* but only to say hidy and look around. Most of their days had been spent getting familiar with the people and accents and sights that were going to be a part of their lives from now on.

They had taken strolls around the square and along the side streets and back streets of Claybelle, and they had bought two automobiles at Thurman Gonder's used car lot— a light yellow '33 Dodge convertible for Betsy with chrome headlights and the spare tires mounted on the sides, and a '32 blue Terraplane four-door for Ted.

Ben had told Betsy that Thurman Gonder, a former Texas League baseball player, would give them a good deal on the cars.

Eating a doughnut with his mouth open and spilling coffee down his shirtfront, Thurman Gonder had written down the price of the two cars on a slip of paper and shoved it across his desk to Betsy, as if the price were a secret.

Betsy had drawn a line through Thurman Gonder's figure and had written down her own, cutting the price by $200.

"Dang, who hollered bunt?" Thurman Gonder said.

The used car salesman had regaled them with the story of his trip to New York City a year ago. Thurman and his wife, Miriam, had stayed at the Plaza Hotel, but he had hired a bodyguard to stand outside their hotel room, and two other bodyguards to patrol the halls directly above and below them, and they had not left their room after sundown. That was how you handled New York City.

He had said, "We was gonna go to the theater and all such as that till I seen what I saw when we took a taxi from the train station to the hotel. Lord God-a-mighty, I thought I was in a foreign country! I even seen Chinamen!"

Betsy said to Thurman Gonder that he had been wise to hire bodyguards in that neighborhood. Cutthroats were known to hole up in places like Bergdorf's and Tiffany's.

"We went in that jungle," Thurman Gonder said.

"The what?"

"There in the hotel."

"The Palm Court?"

"Ever what they call it. Eighty cents for a orange juice and coffee. Money funnel's what they got up there in New York. Just get off the train and ask somebody where the funnel is— pour your money down it."

Betsy suggested that it might be best if Thurman Gonder never went back to New York City.

"You don't have to worry none about that," he said. "I don't need to go to China neither, not now."

It had been decided that Betsy and Ted would occupy the entire upstairs of the old homestead, a redbrick house with a glazed green tile roof. It was no match for the Tudor Revivals and Spanish Colonials on Wildflower Drive, but it had character, for it was, as Leatha was always so eager to point out, "the Throckmorton home."

The upstairs had been remodeled for Betsy and Ted. A wall had been knocked down. The wall had separated the old master bedroom from Betsy's childhood room. This created a new bedroom—sitting room with a fireplace. A door opened onto a terraced porch roof that ran across the front of the house overlooking the terrace below.

Ben had added an air conditioner to the furnishings in the upstairs master bedroom. The air conditioner stood five feet high and was three feet wide. It was finished in wood veneer. It rumbled like a distant storm but cooled wonderfully. It was Betsy's favorite piece of furniture, for the weather was still boiling hot in early September.

What had once been a nursery for Betsy and a guest room upstairs had been converted into studies for Betsy and Ted. The whole second floor was carpeted. It was all quite cozy and nice. Ben had spared no cost to make his daughter and son-in-law comfortable.

The big change downstairs had occurred with the screened-in porch on the back of the house. Part of the porch had been walled off and was now a bath off Ben's combination bedroom, den, and office-at-home, which was also cozy and nice, as Ben well knew.

This was a large room with a beamed ceiling and ceiling fan, an arched fireplace, a big thick Oriental rug that covered most of a pegged floor. There was a floor-to-ceiling bookshelf, a rolltop desk, two couches of heavy brown leather, and a red leather easy chair with ottoman next to a console radio resting on thick legs in a corner. Three dark oil paintings in gilt frames hung on the paneled walls. A portrait of a beautiful woman in her twenties—Betsy's mother, Elizabeth. A Russell. A Remington. Ben's brown leather golf bag, crammed with a mixture of hickory and steel-shafted clubs, usually rested in a corner. On top of the radio was a framed photograph of TCU's 1929 football team, and on a bookshelf was a framed photograph of TCU's 1932 football team. A big picture window at the rear of the room gave Ben a sweeping view of Warren's well-kept back lawn, all the way down to the boat dock and the six-acre lake, a dark body of water that had been dammed off from the Brazos River. There was only one natural lake in Texas, and this wasn't it, and you could only call it a lake if you were interested in fishing for a perch from a rowboat.

Hanging on a coatstand were Ben's old khaki tunic and overseas cap from the World War, mementoes from the four months he had spent with the 36th Division in France as a combat correspondent.

Ben was forty years old when he had gone off to cover the war in 1918. He had already been an editor and publisher for twelve years, but he was going to do *something* in that war, even if he was too old to fight in it.

It was in 1906 that Ben had borrowed the money to buy two country weeklies, the *Times* and the *Standard,* and merge them into his own daily newspaper. He had known nothing about journalism. It was purely a financial opportunity. He had gambled that Claybelle was ready to support a daily paper. He had guessed right, just as he had guessed right in later years when he gambled on the radio station.

Betsy, her mother, and Warren and Florence had seen Ben off to the Great War. Ben had boarded a troop train in Fort Worth that was bound for Newport News, Virginia.

At the station, Elizabeth had said, "Watch out for those madamoiselles."

Ben had said, "Why would I need a madamoiselle when I've got me a Gibson Girl back home?"

Betsy's mother had been precisely that: stately, artful, always superbly dressed in her peek-a-boo shirtwaists, rakishly short skirts, and satin-brimmed afternoon hats. Above all else, Elizabeth was disturbingly beautiful.

Betsy had never forgotten how her mother hadn't cried on the train platform. She had only smiled and waved at Ben, leaving him with a vision of a Gibson Girl to take to France. Elizabeth had cried later on, in the privacy of her bedroom.

In Newport News, Ben and a group of other reporters, men from Dallas, Houston, Tulsa, Oklahoma City, and six units of the 36th Division, had sailed for France on an Italian cattle boat. Ben had landed in Brest on the last day of July. For two months, living in a barracks, he had filed human interest dispatches while the T-patchers had undergone combat training. Each day, the reporters would put their stories in a bundle and give it to an Army messenger. After that, it was up to electricity.

In the third week of October in 1918, the 36th had finally been called into action. Day and night for the next six weeks, up till the end of the war, the 36th had fought in the Meuse-Argonne.

Elizabeth had kept a scrapbook of Ben's stories and letters

and postcards home. The scrapbook now lay on a table in Ben's bedroom-office-den. Betsy had often leafed through it as a young girl enamored of journalism, dreaming of a time when she might see her own byline on datelines as romantic as those seemed to be.

Ben's dispatches told the story of a war that had been fought by younger men.

Report by Ben Throckmorton

WITH THE AMERICAN ARMY NORTHWEST OF VERDUN, Oct. 4.—The Americans are advancing through the Germans' strongest lines of resistance in an area between the Meuse River and the Argonne Forest, and the 36th is now in the thick of things, having relieved General Pershing's battered 2nd Division.

Report by Ben Throckmorton

WITH THE AMERICAN ARMY NORTHWEST OF VERDUN, Oct. 10—This is the story of Maj. Edwin G. Hutchings of Austin, Texas, who led his men of the 141st Infantry into the Argonne Forest and fought from shell hole to shell hole, knocking out one machine-gun nest after another, until a German artillery barrage ended his brave young life at the age of 28.

Report by Ben Throckmorton

WITH THE AMERICAN FORCES NEAR VERDUN, Nov. 2.—The Germans are giving way everywhere to the pressure from the Americans. American aviators are dropping Red Cross emergency rations to the boys of the 36th, who are in the front lines and are pursuing the Germans at such a rapid pace they have outdistanced supply wagons.

Report by Ben Throckmorton

PARIS, Nov. 15.—On the crisp, foggy morning of Nov. 11, I stood near a battery east of the Meuse and watched a doughboy hold his handkerchief in the air as he looked at his watch. Ropes were tied to the lanyards of four big guns, each rope manned by some 200 soldiers. At eleven a.m., the handkerchief fell, the men pulled on the ropes, and the guns cursed out the last shots of the war. It grew quiet for a moment or two, and then I started to hear laughter and singing, and these sounds were coming from the Germans, too. This was how the Great War ended.

Once or twice a year, in quiet moments alone, Ben himself would browse through the scrapbook. Not to admire the words he had written, but to remind himself that he had once left Claybelle, Texas, and witnessed history.

Actually, he wished he had covered the Civil War.

B's Cafe was a starting point for all of Betsy and Ted's strolls around town.

Wynelle Stubbs still worked as a waitress in B's, and Wynelle was still testy, still unimpressed with most things and most individuals of the human-being variety. A thin woman who wore thick glasses, now in her forties, Wynelle looked something like a homeroom teacher who had encountered innumerble difficulties in her life.

Buck Blanchard didn't see why she had to take this out on some of his customers, but Wynelle's speed and efficiency couldn't be replaced. Wynelle was an unofficial assistant manager. She worked behind the counter or out on the floor—wherever it was busy or wherever a tip loomed. Four of five days a week, she would work a double shift, and she would open or close the place if Buck or Joylene asked it of her. She would cuss and complain and maybe flick her cigarette ashes in somebody's cream gravy, but she would do it.

Booths and tables ran along one wall of B's, from the front windows to the kitchen in back. A parallel lunch counter ran along the other wall. The kitchen was run by Edgar and Wilma, who had worked at B's as long as Wynelle, which was as far back as Betsy could remember. Edgar specialized in breakfast and lunch and Wilma specialized in dinner, and they rarely spoke to each other, seeing as how they were married.

Their first time in B's, Betsy and Ted had sat at the counter, where they could visit with Wynelle and Joylene, whose chair behind the register was at the front end of the establishment, by the windows facing the square.

Joylene Blanchard's hair was the color of crude oil, and there had been a frown on her face ever since she got fat.

"There's ten dollars missin' from this register," Joylene was saying as Betsy and Ted walked in.

"Guess what golfer took it," Wynelle said.

"I'm gonna divorce him one of these days," Joylene vowed.

Wynelle said, "Hell, you couldn't get him off the golf course long enough to drag him in a courtroom."

Wynelle was wiping off the counter when she looked up and saw Betsy.

"You can't take the high school out of nobody," was Wynelle's greeting.

The waitress then glanced at Ted. "This it?" she asked Betsy.

Betsy and Ted drank a cup of coffee with the ladies.

Wynelle grilled Ted about his background, and when she found out how big Long Island was, she said *National Geographic* "ought to be told about that deal."

Joylene said to Betsy, "I hope you're gonna do something with that rag of your daddy's. If it didn't have *Mutt and Jeff,* I'd never pick it up."

"I hope to make the paper a little livelier," Betsy said.

"What are you gonna put in it, *news?*" Wynelle said. "Only news I'd care to read is that Wynelle Stubbs left town."

Joylene hushed everyone as she turned up the radio that was sitting by the register. Time for *Road of Life.* Suddenly an urgent female voice came out of the radio saying, "Dr. Brent, call surgery . . . Dr. Brent, call surgery."

Betsy and Ted left the cafe and started across the street toward the square, but they had to hurry to get out of the way of a top-down jalopy loaded with cheerleaders from Claybelle High.

The first football game of the season was a week off, but in Claybelle, as in any other Texas town or city, they started getting ready early.

The car skidded to a stop in front of B's and out jumped the pep squad, three girls in yellow sweaters and brown skirts and brown-and-white saddle oxfords, and three undernourished boys in yellow sweaters, brown slacks, and brown-and-white saddle oxfords.

"Kick 'em in the stomach,
Hit 'em in the head!
Come on, Jackets,
Kill 'em till they're dead!"

"Same old yell," Betsy said. "We were cuter, though."

"Wait a second," Ted said with surprise. "You were a cheer-leader?"

"Would you rather be married to a cadet sponsor? Dumb."

They sat down on a bench in the square and Betsy revealed that she had been a cheerleader her last two years in high school. She and Eva Jane McKnight had both been cheerlead-ers their last two years. Laura Mueller had been the third girl their junior year. Patsy Thornton had been the third girl their senior year. Laura and Patsy had both married beneath them, according to Anna Sue Beaton.

It had been a big deal to be a cheerleader, Betsy explained. You had to be elected by a vote of the student body after all of the candidates had led yells on stage at assembly. If you were elected as a junior, it was almost a foregone conclusion that you'd be re-elected as a senior, unless, of course, you happened to develop a case of acne in between. Such cases had been known of. Billie Renée Cowden, for one.

The Claybelle pep squad had dressed differently in Betsy's years. The girls had worn beanies, sashes around their waists, longer skirts, and long satin cloaks.

Anna Sue Beaton had never forgiven the school for not elect-ing her a cheerleader. She'd had to settle for cadet sponsor.

"How did one get to be a cadet sponsor?" Ted asked.

"Flirt with a colonel in the ROTC. There was gossip that Anna Sue carried it beyond flirting, but I never believed it."

"We don't have girl cheerleaders in the East."

Betsy said, "I know. It's terrible. Girls don't get to do any-thing up there but sell chrysanthemums."

"Why do you think this is?"

"I've thought about it a lot," Betsy said. "I think it has something to do with the Civil War. In the South, all avail-able boys were expected to go to war. Football is war, so to speak. So all available boys are expected to go out for football, which means you have to have girl cheerleaders."

"There were boy cheerleaders a minute ago."

"They have asthma. It's okay for a boy to be a cheerleader if he has asthma."

The jalopy carrying the cheerleaders had driven around to Thompson's Pharmacy and the kids had stormed the drugstore to make life miserable for Bertha Thompson, a birdlike woman in her sixties. Bertha would not be a happy person as she sat behind *her* register and tried to listen to *her* radio.

The ruckus around the soda fountain and amid the stacks of comic books would no doubt distract Bertha from the plight of Helen Trent, who, when life mocked her and broke her hopes and dashed her against the rocks of despair, fought back bravely, successfully, to prove what so many women longed to prove in their own lives—that the romance of youth could extend into middle life and even beyond. Sitting in her apartment on Hollywood's Palm Drive, Helen would be facing another crisis in her love life, having been caught in another trap set by the beautiful but evil Fay Granville.

There on the bench in the square, Ted asked what bleak fate must have enveloped all of the sad young ladies who had been denied the status of cheerleader or cadet sponsor in Claybelle High.

"Well," Betsy thought, now smoking, "they could be a sophomore favorite, a junior favorite, or a senior favorite, except I was all of those."

"They had nothing, in other words."

"They had lots of things. There was something for everybody—if you weren't a crud."

"A *crud?*"

"You met Fred Astaire and Noel Coward the day we arrived?"

"Cruds?"

"Classic. But Slop and Tommy Jack could get by because they were on the football team."

"A girl crud didn't have it so easy, I gather."

"No, they didn't," Betsy admitted. "I can tell you it was pretty rough sailing for Dalilla Roper and Evelyn Miellmier."

No one to go out with, other than cruds. And cruds always had to sit in the middle when riding in cars.

"I think Still Norris had to sit in the middle," Betsy mused. "That's why he butchers copy."

"Beware of people who had to sit in the middle, that's your advice?"

"Many become mass murderers."

Betsy went into all of the activities that were available to those students who were less fortunate than cheerleaders, cadet sponsors, class favorites, or athletes.

They could be officers in the YMCA or the YWCA. They could be in the Home Economics Club and learn to make pie crust. They could be Meliorists. Nobody knew what the Meliorists did, but they wore glasses and carried tin lunch boxes. People who were smart had passes to go home for lunch so they could not go home at all but go to the soda fountain at Thompson's or the lunch counter at B's, or hide in the bushes and smoke, as had often been the case with Betsy.

They could join Los Hidalgos if they had a fondness for Spanish. They could be in the Dramatics Club. This was if the boys were named Dorcas and the girls were named Helga. They could be in the Parabola Club if they were math nuts. They could be a member of The Brushes if they appreciated art as much as Bob Walker had.

Bob had been taken into the art club because Old Lady Ziegler had liked his drawings of soldiers and football players, but he had been kicked out of the art club because the teacher had lacked a sense of humor. Assigned to make a sculpture out of soap, Bob had carved a nice set of tits and a lady's ass out of a bar of Woodbury.

"And what is this supposed to be?" Old Lady Ziegler had asked.

"It's for the skin you love to touch," Bob had said.

He had been sent to the principal's office, where Old Man Byers was supposed to punish him, but Old Man Byers had only laughed, primarily because Bob Walker was Claybelle's best quarterback.

Betsy continued. The less fortunate students could be in the Natural Sciences Society if they wore thicker glasses than the Meliorists. They could be in the band, which was one of the neatest deals around. The band got to travel. The band went to Fort Worth and marched in the Armistice Day parade, and went to Dallas and marched in the State Fair parade, and went to Tyler and marched in the Rose Festival parade.

They could be in the Choral Club if their mamas wanted to make them a white vestment out of a bedsheet. And finally, they could be in Alpha Chi, the national honor society, in which case they were either Marguerite Whitehouse, who always waddled around with an armload of books, or Elmer Otis Kinkel, who did all of the homework for the eleven starters on the football team under the constant threat of having his head shaved and painted yellow and brown.

"The cruds revolted one year," Betsy said.

"I'm not surprised."

"My senior year, somebody called a meeting—we never found out who. All of a sudden, two hundred cruds were in the lunchroom one afternoon, yelling, making speeches. People we'd never seen before were standing up on tables and shouting, saying if they all got together they could run the school—elect cheerleaders, favorites, everything. Bob Walker named it. On page one of *The Yellow Jacket:* 'The Great Crud Revolt of 1926.' "

"How could there be students you hadn't seen before?"

"Well, it's a big school, but I think tradition had more to do with it than anything. The best neighborhoods in Claybelle are on the west side of town. So we always hung out in front of the radiator at the west end of the main hall. I don't think I ever had a class on the east side of the building."

The cruds had celebrated what they thought was a victory later in the spring of that year when L. M. Spragins, one of their own, was elected junior favorite. In actual fact, however, the west-siders had stuffed the ballot box for L. M. Spragins, who was a retarded epileptic. Moreover, when the yearbook had come out in May, L. M. was featured in the snapshot section. Someone had taken a picture of L. M. threshing around in a flower bed, having one of his fits, outside of Old Lady Vaughn's homeroom. Bob Walker had sneaked the picture into the yearbook.

Let the cruds revolt again, Bob said.

Shadowlawn Country Club's golf course was considered something of a freak. It consisted of only eleven holes. A wealthy cotton farmer named Jack Wilkinson had built the club and designed the course in 1922. His logic had been that a round of golf didn't have to be nine holes or eighteen holes just because somebody back in Scotland had said so.

The founder had died in 1927 and the members had taken over the club, Ben Throckmorton among them. They someday hoped to have an eighteen-hole golf course that wouldn't cause as much laughter among out-of-town guests, but the widow lady in Dallas who owned the farmland surrounding the course was asking a fortune for it. It was the hope of the members that when the widow lady died her heirs might be sympathetic toward golfers.

Betsy explained all this to Ted on the day that she took him out to the club for lunch.

The clubhouse at Shadowlawn was a two-story wood-frame house. Thick round white columns on the wraparound porch supported a gabled roof with flaring eaves. Members could sit in rocking chairs on one side of the porch and look at the swimming pool. They could sit on the other side and look at two asphalt tennis courts. They could sit in front and look at the putting green, a little patch of grainy Bermuda set within the circular drive.

Betsy and Ted went out on the porch after lunch, and that's where they noticed Shady Webster sunning himself in a reclining chair by the swimming pool. It was a weekday and Shady was all alone at the pool.

They walked down to say hello to the oilman.

"They like 'em tan," Shady said by way of explaining his presence.

His presence was further explained a moment later when Eva Jane McKnight showed up with her two boys, Billy V. and Robbie D., eight and six.

As Anna Sue had promised, Eva Jane was a hot number, a willowy girl with a sexy walk, shadowed lids, and thick dark hair tumbling down to her shoulders. In a white bathing suit, Eva Jane's deep tan from a whole summer in the sun made Betsy feel anemic.

Eva Jane yelped at the sight of Betsy. They hugged, for this was their first encounter since Betsy's return from New York.

"It's grand to see you, Betsy. I'm so happy you're back in

town. What fun! I'm back. You're back. We'll have each other to talk to. Believe me, there aren't too many others around. I want to hear about New York. What are they wearing? Where are they going? Everything."

Betsy introduced Ted while he was being jarred off balance by the flying tackles of Billy V. and Robbie D.

"Y'all get the hell out of here!" Eva Jane snarled at her sons. "Go bother somebody else!"

Billy V. gave his mother the finger.

Eva Jane drew back a fist. "You hear me?"

Robbie D. spit at his mother's foot.

"I said git!"

The kids went racing onto the golf course in their swim trunks.

Eva Jane and Shady exchanged casual hellos as if they were mere acquaintances.

Shady suggested he buy everyone a cool drink. Swell idea, Eva Jane said. Shady jogged into the clubhouse and came back with a rum collins for everyone, and the four of them took a table under an umbrella.

Eva Jane talked non-stop. She said that if Betsy went to Neiman's she should ask for a saleslady named Clara, that she was leaning toward Swedish modern in the bedroom of the Pemberton house she was doing over, that Anna Sue was wasting away in Claybelle, that she, Eva Jane, hadn't divorced Bubba Dean Norwood a minute too soon—he wasn't a lawyer, he was an ambulance chaser—and that she hoped Betsy would do something about the *Times-Standard,* specifically about Carolyn Moseley's so-called society column.

"As a reader, Betsy, I can't tell you how putrid her column is. She has the same names in there all the time. All she cares about is who comes to the tea dances out here on Sunday. Does she even *know* where Fort Worth and Dallas *are?*"

Shady Webster got around to saying he was drilling in Caddo lime out near Strawn. It was prolific, but you might have to go a little deeper than normal.

"What does it cost to drill an oil well?" Ted asked.

"About thirty thousand the way I do it," Shady said. "All you really need's a driller, a roughneck, and cable tools. But I got four goin' at once right now, and I'm afraid my partners are gonna have to come up with more cheese. I ain't rollin' all them dice by myself."

"I hope Daddy's not one of your partners," Betsy said. "I plan to spend his money on the paper."

"Ben?" Shady said with a grin. "Ben Throckmorton wouldn't bet on a big dog to whip a little dog."

Shady's partners were silent. They wanted it that way, he said.

"But you'll hear 'em holler if I make the ocean."

"What does that mean?" Ted asked.

"It means we've done hit saltwater instead of dinosaurs."

Betsy and Ted left Shady and Eva Jane to themselves. But as they walked away, Betsy had slyly glanced back and seen Eva Jane drape her shapely tan leg over Shady's hairy white leg and kiss him in his ear.

On yet another day of wandering around town, Betsy and Ted had wound up at the Star of Hope Mission a block off the square. They had been drawn there by the sight of a line of transients waiting to get in the door for a free meal.

They had edged past the line and entered the mission to find nothing more than a stark room, a space which had been vacated by a previous tenant. Though it was now supposed to be a place of worship, Betsy thought it had retained most of its auto supply store ambiance.

There were a half-dozen rows of folding chairs where men of all ages were either eating off tin plates or dozing.

Along a blank wall was a plywood tabletop supported by two sawhorses. Behind it, Olive Cooper and another Claybelle woman, unknown to Betsy, were dishing up pinto beans for the hungries.

Betsy and Ted waved at Olive and stood in the back of the room and looked at Reverend Jimmy Don Tankersley standing at a podium. The reverend was a fat tousle-haired young man, drenched with sweat, his gray pin-striped suit too small for him and shining like satin.

"Jaysus never got drunk, never!" the preacher squawked. "Jaysus wouldn't take a drink if you tied him down! Jaysus was never out of work, not him! He held down two, three jobs at a time. He was a plumber when he wasn't workin' as a carpenter. Sure, he was a plumber, even when there wasn't no plumbin' over there in Jayzeeland. He was shuttin' off the tears of folks what wanted they souls saved! If Jaysus was here today, his heart would be oh-so-heavy, friends. He would look at you sinners and he'd be hurt, deep hurt, the same as I'm hurt. He'd see what I see and he'd know why you're hungry. You're hungry 'cause you've drank whiskey and shot pool and known blond-headed women and drove with your tops down! Forgive 'em, Lord, they ignernt."

Reverend Jimmy Don Tankersley paused to glower at the group.

"I didn't hear me no amens," he bellowed. "Are your bellies too full now, is that it?"

From the audience could be heard two or three scattered amens—and a loud one from Olive Cooper.

Betsy and Ted were approached by a young hobo, a particularly lost-looking young man, nineteen or twenty. Dingy coveralls and barefoot.

"Can anybody get food?" he asked them. "Just walk up?"

"I'm sure it's okay," Betsy said. "What's your name?"

"Charley."

"Charley . . . ?"

"Atkins is my other name."

Ted asked Charley where he was from.

"Hollis, Oklahoma."

"How long have you been in Claybelle?"

"Been stuck here two weeks. Come here with my mama and daddy. We're headin' for California."

"Have you looked for work?"

"Aw, yeah, all around, but there ain't any. I could have painted a house the other day, but I didn't have no money to buy a ladder. Lady said she'd furnish the paint but I had to get the brushes and a ladder. Folks are nice around here, though. A woman gimme a big old potato pattie the other day. It was real good."

Ted wondered about Charley's dad, could he work?

"He was gassed in the war. That's why we're tryin' to get to California. Mama says it'll be good for his health. Mama says we wouldn't be so bad off if Daddy could get his bonus from the war, but he's havin' a hard time gettin' it. We're gonna make out all right. Mama's got some money saved, but she's hangin' on to it for emergencies. Guess I better get me some of them beans."

Charley moved away.

Betsy and Ted waved goodbye to Olive as they were leaving.

Before they reached the door, they heard Reverend Jimmy Don Tankersley holler at two men holding out plates to Olive.

"You men drink whiskey? Tell the truth!"

"No, sir, Reverend, I sure wouldn't never do that," said a thin, ragged hobo. "God don't like it."

"He sure don't," said the other hobo.

"I believe 'em, Jaysus!" the preacher shouted, his eyes blazing at the ceiling. "Let 'em eat!"

Outside the mission, Betsy and Ted were startled to find Sloppy Herster and Tommy Jack Lucas waiting in the line to get in the front door.

"Hey, Betsy," Slop called. "They got beans in there today? This is bean day, ain't it?"

Tommy Jack said, "We only come when they got beans. Pigs wouldn't eat the damned old stew."

"Olive's in there," Betsy reported.

"Aw, shit," said Slop—and they stepped out of the line.

Slop and Tommy Jack walked up to the square with Betsy and Ted.

Betsy, having nothing better to say to them, asked Slop how his brother, Eugene, was doing in football practice.

"Won't hit," Slop said.

"He'll hit," Tommy Jack disagreed.

"My dick," Slop said.

Tommy Jack blew his nose on the sidewalk, wiped his hand on his dungarees, and said, "Guess what, Betsy? We're gettin' a new offense. Dub's puttin' in the Y-formation. It's like the offense Rusty Russell runs up there at Masonic Home. It's kind of intricate, but Dub says if them orphans can run it, there ain't no reason why the Yellow Jackets can't."

"Shit for brains is what Dub's got," Slop said. "He better go back to the single wing and hope Eugene don't have to tackle nobody on defense."

"Eugene'll tackle."

"Tackle a fart if it ain't too loud."

"You don't give your brother no credit at all. You're down on Coach, too, and I don't see why. He was a great player at Texas."

"Bullshit."

"He was!"

"Bullshit, batshit, and owlshit!"

"He didn't play at Texas, did he?"

"He played some."

"Dub Cooper played down there with Rats Watson and Hook McCullough and Slippery Elam. I've heard him talk about it his whole life!"

"Got in their way, is all."

"You don't know fuck, Slop. That's what I think sometimes."

"The fuck I don't. It's you don't know fuck about fuck-all—and if you want your ass whipped, you've come to the right place."

"I didn't say nothin' about wantin' my ass whipped. We was talkin' about Coach."

"Awright, then. If you want to talk about it, shut the fuck up!"

"That's what I'm doin'."

"Okay, by God."

"Okay."

Slop spit through his teeth.

"Fuckin' dickhead," he said.

Betsy and Ted left them to their intellectual discussion.

They walked up the street and stopped in to say hello to Leatha, but Leatha quickly put her finger to her lips, and from her radio came the news that Young Widder Brown, the most beautiful woman in Simpsonville, was a woman as real as her friends who listened to her, and that hers was the dramatic story of a very human mother's duty to her two fatherless children, in conflict with the dictates of her heart.

Leatha went on record that afternoon as saying that Ellen Brown would be a lot better off if she would give in and marry Dr. Anthony Loring. Leatha was sure of it.

Eight

THOSE TWO old high school sweethearts, Betsy Throckmorton and Bob Walker, finally caught up with each other on a Friday night in September.

Bob had called Betsy two days earlier from Austin to say that the sports editor and columnist of the *Dallas Journal* was up to his ass in incoherent Texas Longhorns but he would soon be up to his ass in incoherent TCU Horned Frogs. Fort Worth was the last stop on his tour of Southwest Conference football camps. Anna Sue was going to drive up to Fort Worth that evening, he had said, so why didn't Betsy and what's-his-name come along? The four of them could make a night of it.

Betsy had thought it sounded good.

"We could go to the Venetian Room at the Blackstone or the Den at the Texas," Anna Sue had said when Betsy had gone to the Fidelity Bank to see her and plan the evening. "Bert Noyd's orchestra is at the Blackstone. It's not bad if you like slow stuff. We could go to the Pirates' Cave. It's fun—down in a cellar on Seventh Street. Maybe not. It'll be drunk and loud. The Clover Club's a possibility—well, not really, come to think of it. It's mostly men and very few wives, if you know what I mean. I know! I'll tell Bob we'll meet him for drinks at Lola's Oasis, then we'll go out to the Casino. Jack Amlung and his band will be at the Casino. I love Glenda Petty. She's a local girl, but she sounds like Lee Wiley."

Anna Sue went to Fort Worth early in her Pierce-Arrow runabout. She wanted to get in some shopping. Betsy and Ted took the Dodge convertible and got to Lola's around sundown.

Lola's was a couple of miles northwest of downtown Fort Worth on what most residents referred to as the Jacksboro Highway but churchgoers referred to as The Sin Strip. It was said that if a person couldn't find whatever he or she was looking for on any given night on the Jacksboro Highway—

jazz, Western swing, gambling, whore-ladies, fistfights, gang-land killings, home cooking, reefer—somebody would have it for you by the next day.

On their way to Lola's, Betsy and Ted drove past Pug's Beer & Dancing Nitely, The Four Deuces, The Four Sixes, The Four Aces, Bonnie's Lodge, Pauline's Tip-Top Tavern, Dottie's Paradise, Jimmy's Lounge, The Ringside Club, Betty's Tittle Tattle, The Crap Shoot, The Do Drop Inn, and a dozen hot-pillow motels.

Lola's advertised itself as "the coolest spot in Fort Worth." The reason was that half of it didn't have a roof. Beyond the indoor bar, dining room, and dance floor there was an outdoor dance floor, bandstand, and tables. Tornadoes, dust storms, and northers permitting, you could dine and dance under the stars at Lola's.

They parked the Dodge among Cadillacs, Essexes, trucks, motorcycles, Packards, and squad cars, and entered the road-house. They walked past the stand-up bar, where mechanics were talking to cowhands, where whore-ladies were discuss-ing the economy with businessmen, and where married cou-ples were splitting up and falling in love with other people.

They took a table outdoors to have a drink as they waited for Bob and Anna Sue. Anna Sue would be late, Betsy pre-dicted. She wouldn't leave downtown until the stores closed, which would get her caught in going-home traffic.

"I have the perfect funeral planned for her. She should be cremated and her ashes mixed with sequins and sprinkled over the first floor of Neiman's."

A waitress came to take their drink order. Her name was Shirley. She was a pretty woman of, say, thirty-two, if you liked rawboned cowgirls. Heavy makeup, orange hair, tight britches.

Betsy ordered a Scotch and water, Ted a Scotch and soda.

"Y'all can't be from around here," Shirley said.

"I am originally, he's not," Betsy said.

"I don't drink Scotch myself," Shirley confided. "Never ac-quired the taste. Tastes like iodine to me. Guess I never had enough sores on my lip."

Betsy, with a look at the bandstand, asked Shirley what sort of entertainment Lola's featured—blues, Western, what?

"Them niggers come in around nine," Shirley said.

Betsy and Ted finished one drink and were starting on another when Anna Sue glided onto the patio in her new flowered "crazyjamas," pink and green, a purchase at The Fair that afternoon. Anna Sue's hair had been done—de-waved, similar to Betsy's—and she had evidently taken lessons from Eva Jane on the use of sultry eye makeup.

Knowing Anna Sue, Betsy was inwardly amused at the trouble she had gone to for Bob Walker's benefit. Anna Sue had wanted to be a knockout in contrast to Betsy. She did look stunning, if a little advanced for the crowd in Lola's.

Shirley followed Anna Sue to the table to get her drink order. As Ted pulled out a chair for Anna Sue, Shirley said, "We don't serve breakfast, hon."

Shirley laughed to signify that she had made a joke, and said, "That the newest thing?"

Anna Sue coolly ordered a bourbon and Coke.

When Shirley returned with the drink, she said, "I guess I'd know more about what's goin' on in the world if I ever got my butt out of here for more than a day at a time."

"Who's Lola?" Betsy asked her.

"Who *was* she, you mean. Lola Brinson died a year ago. Her daughter runs the place now. Rhonda will be in later—after she strangles her kids and poisons G. T. Lola was somethin' else. Big old thing. Had these bazooms. But she could *move* the whiskey, I'm tellin' you. Best friend I ever had."

"How did she die?"

"Acute gunshot wound is what I called it. Two old boys come in here late one night to rob her. Lola kept money tucked down in here for stickups, but for some reason, she didn't want to get robbed that night, so they shot her. For a piss-ant eighty dollars, they shot her. Never caught the bastards either. They weren't anybody like Bonnie and Clyde, they were just nobodies. Hell, Bonnie and Clyde were good customers. Never caused any trouble. I waited on 'em lots of times. Tipped real big, too. Naw, they were just low-lifes. I'll tell you what. They better hope they never get caught. They'll never see a courtroom. Every policeman in this town was a friend of Lola Brinson."

"Sounds like a good lady," Betsy said.

"Yeah, she was," Shirley said, "but, like they say, she died with her tits on."

A big grin came over Betsy as she saw Bob Walker coming toward their table. She flew from her chair and met him halfway across the dance floor.

Bob Walker swept her up in his arms. They hugged and kissed, and for a long moment Bob clung to her familiar female body.

"Divorce final yet?"

"I won't ask how your life is," Betsy laughed. "I'm sitting with it."

Bob was a fraction taller than Ted, around six feet, but thinner. His thick brown hair didn't seem to know where it was supposed to be parted. His face was a little sunburned from his travels, from dozing on the sideline at so many football workouts. He had a strong chin and nice teeth. He had a store-bought smile for strangers—journalism required it—but the steady glint in his gray eyes often betrayed his unrelenting cynicism, and he smoked as many Luckies as Betsy.

Now lighting one, he bent over and gave Anna Sue a kiss, which she turned into a longer kiss than he had intended.

"Sorry I'm late," he said. "I had to drop off a column at Western Union downtown. What are you wearing, Anna Sue?"

A glare.

Getting the message, he said, "It looks good. Pants, aren't they?"

"I wouldn't expect a sportswriter to know anything about fashion," Anna Sue said. "They are called crazyjamas. They are being worn in New York."

"Who wears 'em? All those debutramps?"

"I'll debutramp you!" Anna Sue pinched Bob on the arm.

"You must be Red Grange," Bob said, extending a hand to Ted.

"It's a pleasure to meet you, Bob. I've certainly heard a great deal about you."

"It's all true, except for some of it. Listen, I didn't mean to call you Red Grange. I know you were the Four Horsemen." Bob looked at Betsy. "Was he all four or just three?"

"Two."

The waitress swung past the table carrying a tray of drinks for other customers. Bob stopped her with a gesture. "Scotch on ice," he said, "and sprinkle the infield."

"I got you covered, baby," said Shirley, and kept moving.

Bob looked at Betsy and said, "I'll get right to the point. You have my letter jacket and I want it back."

"We *do* have it," Ted said. "I found it in a closet one day. It reminded me of how small we all were in high school."

"I don't intend to wear it," Bob said. "I want it for the archives. You haven't seen a little gold football around anywhere, have you?"

"I gave it back to you," Betsy said.

"Oh, that's right. It was Maxine Chilner who never gave it back."

"Who?" Betsy said, tickled at the name.

"Maxine Chilner. I dated her my freshman year at Texas."

"You were going with me then!"

"You were in New York."

"So? We were still going together."

Bob shrugged. "I cheated."

"You bastard!"

"It wasn't my freshman year. It was my sophomore year."

"We were still going together!"

"It was my junior year."

Anna Sue said, "I have a question. What does it matter, for God's sake?"

"You're right, it doesn't matter," Bob said. "It was only gold-plated, it wasn't valuable. I think I wrote a column about Sam Baugh today, but I'm not sure. I've seen six football teams in eleven days. They all practice offense and defense. The coaches all chew tobacco and hate publicity—except when they win. Oh, well. All columns are good when you're done. Maybe Western Union will garble it and give it a deeper meaning."

"Don't write me nothin' that rhymes," Betsy said, imitating her daddy.

Ben Throckmorton was the avowed enemy of what he called "prissy writing." By that, he meant writing that in his opinion was too strained, too flowery, too brainy, too experimental, too precious. He lumped all such authors into one category—pretentious prissies—and whenever he came across them in books, magazines, or newspapers, he tossed their work into a wastebasket, saying to himself, "Don't write me nothin' that rhymes."

It wasn't a bad philosophy if you were running a paper, which was why Betsy tended to agree with it.

The drinks came and Bob said to Ted, "What do you think about the station? Radio's a different world, isn't it?"

"Actually," Ted said, "I've only looked around. I've been doing some studying, analyzing. We haven't started to work. We've been getting settled. I can't actually say I've gotten my feet wet."

Bob turned to Betsy. "Feet wet—can I have that? Would he mind?"

"Is this how it's going to be the rest of the night?" Betsy asked.

"No," Bob said convincingly.

Back to Ted, he said, "Ben's got a lock. He's a member of the club. All the stations in Fort Worth and Dallas trade off on programs. WBAP and KFJZ in Fort Worth, WFAA and KRLD in Dallas. They team up to do remotes. Saves money. A popular show comes along, they'll all carry it. Big football game, they all have it. They swap feeds, save on the overhead. Ben's a good friend of Amon Carter. Not a bad friend to have. It means Ben can get any show he wants from WBAP. Sweet deal."

"I've been finding all that out," Ted said.

"Know how Ben got the license for his station?"

"I don't believe I do."

"He wrote a postcard."

"He took a risk," Betsy put in.

"What risk?" Bob said with a grin. "It's a locomotive. Want some advice on how to run KVAT, Ted? Give the guy a raise who knows how to put all the plugs in the sockets and take up golf."

"I've been thinking of one or two things that could be improved."

"Don't fool with it, Ted. Don't even listen to it, except for football or *Vic and Sade*." Bob lifted his glass to Betsy. "Well, babe, here's to Edna Merle Reece."

The name alone drew a laugh from Betsy. She said, "Who was the guy who always jumped out of his car before it stopped?"

"Opened the door and dragged his foot?"

"Uh-huh."

"Wanted to be the first guy in B's?"

"Uh-huh."

"Two-tone."

Betsy collapsed.

"God, he could sweat."

Anna Sue said, "Who?"

"Wendell Whitten," Bob said. "Two-tone."

Ted said, "We had a fellow . . . "

But Bob was talking to Betsy. "What do you hear from Johnnie Mae Bussey?"

"She's fine," Betsy said. "She and Almarine Mims are taking tap dance."

"Almarine Mims wasn't bad-looking."

"Almarine Mims was a stool pigeon! She told on you if you smoked."

"I thought that was Vanabel Griffin."

"Her, too. Almarine Mims and Vanabel Griffin were the campus police!"

Anna Sue broke in to say, "I am sorry, but I do not remember Wendell Whitten. Did he play ball?"

"Wendell?" said Bob. "No, he was too busy trying to get that big one on his chin. You know who I miss, babe? I miss old Doyle Laymance."

Betsy fought off another collapse, and said, "Whur goan, baugh?" It was an imitation of Doyle Laymance asking the question "Where are you going, boy?"

In Claybelle High, Betsy and Bob had learned to speak fluent Laymance, and now they did.

"Whur at old baugh gee dat?" Betsy asked.

"Heen Dows."

"He livid Dows?"

"Yeah, he oar air in Dows. He go Ford Earth some, but he livid Dows."

"He ever gee mar?"

"He mar. He mar Naomi Cuthrell."

Betsy was jolted back into English. *"Naomi Cuthrell* married *Doyle Laymance?"*

"Long time ago."

"That's not possible. Naomi was cute, smart . . . Did Doyle suddenly get smarter?"

"No, just wider."

Bob said he hadn't seen them in two years, but they were still in Dallas. Doyle had played football at SMU, and some Mustang degenerate alumnus had put him in the dry cleaning business after he had somehow graduated. Naomi had gone to SMU and she had fallen in love with Doyle after he made all-conference his senior year. Naomi helped Doyle run the dry cleaning business. Bob had used the cleaners and he would visit with Naomi when he stopped in. Naomi had kept up with everybody. If it hadn't been for Naomi, Bob would never have known that Lockie Lynn Dees had moved to Greenville, or that Vivian Bunch had married a Jewish fellow and owned New Orleans now, or that Harold Cauker had smothered to death when he happened to be tying his shoe behind the wrong dump truck at Fort Worth Sand & Gravel. Bob said he might still be using Laymance Cleaners if Doyle and Naomi hadn't lost two of his suits and four pairs of slacks.

Anna Sue stood up, seething.

"Whur goan, baugh?" Bob's question.

"To the Casino, where I can listen to music instead of this crap!"

Three miles on out the Jacksboro Highway, the Casino was a grand ballroom on the edge of Lake Worth. The Casino was next to a kiddie park at which a mountainous roller coaster killed on the average of two kiddies a year. Normally, the Casino booked a big-name orchestra on weekends, a Jan Garber, Richard Himber, Abe Lyman, or Benny Goodman, or a personality like Lee Wiley, Ina Ray Hutton, or Little Jack Little, "radio's cheerful little earful"; but on this Friday night the Casino had settled for local celebrities: Jack Amlung and his band with Glenda Petty on vocals. Their reputations were being enhanced by their radio show, which originated from the Crazy Water Hotel in Mineral Wells, Texas.

As Ted paid the cover charge for everyone—eighty cents a

couple—Betsy commented on the fact that Mineral Wells, which was fifty miles west, a little town cradled in hills and white chalk cliffs, had once been a spring training site for major league baseball teams. The New York Giants once trained there.

"My New York Giants?" Ted said.

"Yours . . . John McGraw's . . . Christy Mathewson's."

The bandstand was on their left as they entered the ballroom, a long stand-up bar on the right. Couples were bustling around the dance floor beneath revolving crystal balls as Glenda Petty, a miniature blonde in a red satin dress, was bobbing up and down at the microphone in front of an orchestra in white dinner jackets.

It's only a shanty
In old shantytown . . .

At their table, from which they could catch a breeze from off the lake, they ordered bottles of Scotch and bourbon and mixers and a bucket of ice from an aging black waiter in a tuxedo.

Bob Walker made a joke about a stomach pump as Anna Sue took turns mixing her bourbon with ginger ale and Coke.

Anna Sue made Bob dance to "How Deep Is the Ocean?" and "I Cover the Waterfront." Betsy and Ted joined them on the dance floor, but they all four returned to their table when Glenda Petty rendered a bouncy version of "The Object of My Affection."

They ate potato chips for dinner.

After a trip to the men's room, Bob and Ted stopped at the bar for a moment. Ted's idea.

"I thought we should have a little talk," Ted said.

"What about?" said Bob, knowing very well that Ted wanted to talk about Betsy.

Ted said, "I know you and my wife are very close . . . that you go back a long way . . . that, well . . . there was a time when you two thought you were in love. I just want to say I understand the bond between you. You have an enviable friendship."

Ted stuck out his hand. Bob looked down at it. "Didn't we do that earlier?"

"I'm hoping you and I can be friends, too."

Bob shook Ted's hand. "Any friend of Betsy's. I'm happy she married a Yale man, Ted. If you'd gone to Baylor, I'd probably have to kill myself."

Ted smiled at him. "I have a suspicion you're a more serious fellow than you pretend to be."

Bob said, "Now, see there, darn it. You went to Yale, so you can detect those things. I went to the University of Texas. All I know how to do is work for a living."

Ted might have made something of that remark, but didn't. He said, "Betsy hasn't told me everything about you. Did you play any football at Texas?"

"I went out as a freshman, but the coach told me he already had one quarterback with a skinny neck. He didn't see how they could afford all the medical bills."

"So you went to the typewriter after that?"

"Well, it was sitting there. Nobody was using it."

Ted studied Bob for a moment. "Look, I really do want us to be friends," he said. "What can I do?"

"Get a divorce."

Ted assumed he was supposed to be laughing at that as they walked back to the table to join the girls.

Later in the evening, Bob got around to asking Betsy to dance. The number was "Don't Blame Me."

Bob held her close but tenderly. They didn't speak through most of the song, but a thousand nights raced through their heads. Light flickered on them from the revolving crystal balls overhead.

> *I'm under your spell,*
> *So how can I help it?*
> *Don't blame me.*

"You're happy for me, aren't you?" Betsy got around to saying.

"Of course."

"He's a good guy."

"Seems like it."

"He really is," she said softly, kissing Bob on the cheek, nuzzling him in a friendly fashion. "I've known the two best guys there ever were."

"I've known the greatest girl there ever was."

Betsy gazed up at him. "You say that to all of them, right?"

"No," Bob said with a look. "I'd never say it to anybody who couldn't type."

Nine

ALL ALONG, Betsy had been studying the *Times-Standard*. In the early mornings, after the paperboy caromed down Wildflower Drive on his bicycle and slung the paper up on the terrace or up on the roof, Betsy would sit in her upstairs study with a pot of coffee, a pack of Luckies, and a box of red crayolas, marking up the pages.

In words and phrases that would only have made sense to a newsperson, she would write:

"Strip ... sink ... indent ... should be lead ... bigger pic ... why not box? ... prefer square Gothic ... coin rule here ... boldface indent ... no need to jump ... can't find jump! ... no pix on this ... typos! ... where's agate? ... is this true? ... death to italix!" and other such notes for Ray Fletcher, the managing editor.

Betsy had announced to the staff that she would take over as editor on Saturday, September 21, the day of TCU's opening football game, but Ray Fletcher might have thought she was already in charge, judging by the phone calls he was getting.

It was now September 19, a Thursday, and Betsy was calling him again. "Ray, I'm looking at the front page."

The only art was a mug shot. Somebody who had been appointed to a WPA office in Washington.

"I'm looking at it, Betsy."

"The man in the picture ... ?"

"That's Frank Lanham. He used to be chairman of the Texas Highway Commission."

"I'm thrilled for him, but turn to page three."

"Okay."

"What do you see?"

"Mussolini, ain't it? Mussolini and the King of Italy."

"It's a hell of a picture, Ray. There they are in the Alps, all dressed up in their uniforms and medals, surrounded by generals. They're in the middle of the greatest peacetime army maneuvers in the history of Europe. Italy's recalling its consuls from Ethiopia, Ray. There's going to be a war!"

"Wouldn't be surprised."

"What's our lead story?"

"Let me look."

"I'll tell you what it is. It's the revelation that Galveston is going to get a new causeway."

"That's right," Ray said. "I moved it up to a banner over them boys who got lost in a boat down in Florida."

Betsy told Ray he was going to have to start thinking differently. She would work with him on it.

She said, "What Mussolini and Haile Selassie are up to is slightly more important than a causeway."

"I don't know about that, Betsy. An awful lot of people go to Galveston in the summer."

"I'm talking about a *war,* Ray."

The managing editor said, "Maybe so, but it's like old Shady Webster said out at the club, 'Niggers and wops, how can you root?' "

Nothing about the paper was pleasing Betsy that morning but the comics.

No editor could change Little Orphan Annie's dress. No editor could insulate Flash Gordon from the Witch Queen of Mongo. No editor could rip off Dick Tracy's yellow raincoat or keep him from protecting Tess Trueheart from evil incarnate by yelling, "Open up in there! I've got a tommy gun in my hands and it's in a barking mood!"

The editorials were usually written by Ray Fletcher or an aging rim-man named Joe Stogner. Today's lead editorial was happy about FDR's good health, now that the President was back from a deep-sea fishing trip. The second editorial said Claybelle should be thankful its polygamy laws were clearer than they were in other places, and that God would deal personally with the man in Kingman, Arizona, who had fathered nineteen children. The third editorial said the *Times-Standard* was behind the Claybelle Yellow Jackets win, lose, or draw in tomorrow night's opening football game against the Paschal Panthers from Fort Worth. The paper urged all

52,000 residents to go out to Clay Field and support the Jackets. *That* would be a story, Betsy thought, if the entire population tried to fit into the little wooden grandstands which seated only 8,000.

The paper's columnists were as hard to get through as the editorials.

Arthur Brisbane's syndicated column, which ran on page one and was always presented under an italicized paragraph explaining that the distinguished writer's views should not be interpreted as reflecting, necessarily, the editorial opinions or policies of the *Times-Standard,* commented this day on the revelation that certain stars in the universe gave off more heat than the sun.

Betsy was going to drop Arthur Brisbane.

Carolyn Moseley's society column, "Carolyn's Chit Chat," pointed out that Cecil Gill, "the yodelin' country boy," would make an appearance with Claude Utley and His Melody Scamps at the Shadowlawn Country Club tea dance Sunday afternoon.

"Sportanic Eruptions" was the standing head on Big 'Un Darly's sports column.

Today, Big 'Un had tried to lighten the burden on the shoulders of Claybelle's 137-pound quarterback, Eugene Herster, as the little pine knot got ready to start his first game tomorrow night.

Big 'Un's lead read:

> Eugene Herster has all it takes to do good tomorrow night against the heavier, faster, meaner, tougher Paschal Panthers, who will be after him like wolves and lions, but Eugene, who they call him Pine Knot, has been outstanding in practice workout sessions running Coach Dub Cooper's new Y-formation, as have the terminal posts and the boys down in the trenches, not to

overlook our secret weapon, Griff Waggoman, who has speed to burn if he can keep a handle on the football. Eugene is the little brother of Slop Herster, who caught the pass against Corsicana in '25, so he have some football heritage to call on, and I wouldn't be surprised if he didn't surprise the Paschals, but let me not make any rash predictions.

That was as far as Betsy could go, although "Sportanic Eruptions" ran for another two thousand words.

The only writer on the paper who may have been worse than Big 'Un in Betsy's estimation was Cloyd Bennett, who put out the oil page five days a week and wrote an oil column on Sundays.

Nobody could understand an oil story. She read part of one aloud to herself.

"Magnolia No. 2 Edwards, in section 2, block B-23, public school land, drilled main pay from 3,345 feet and flowed 320 barrels direct east offset to No. 2 Henderson, which showed production of 133 barrels in two hours from total depth of 3,515 feet."

She drew a circle around the story with her red crayola as, simultaneously, a one-column head caught her eye. The headline said: OIL RISING IN WEBSTER TEST.

The story said:

A mile and a half northern extension to the Strawn pool assured Wednesday with Shady Webster No. 1 Eva Jane showing for a producer at 3,498 feet. No. 1 Eva Jane in the southeast corner of section 13, block 77, was idle Tuesday after operators found oil had risen in casing overnight. Further testing at

present level is scheduled before operators determine whether the hole will be
deepened or shot at present level.

Betsy walked down to Ted's study, where he was making notes as he listened to KVAT.

"As near as I can tell from trying to read Cloyd Bennett," she said, "it looks like Shady Webster's hit another oil well, but that's not the most interesting thing. He's had the audacity to name it after Eva Jane McKnight."

"Name what?"

"The oil well. You know, like the Daisy Bradford."

"I've heard of Daisy Bradford. Actress or something?"

"It was the first oil well in the East Texas field—five years ago. Dad Joiner drilled it. We had stories about it in the magazine. East Texas is only the biggest oil strike in the history of the *world,* Ted. It's getting bigger every day. They're drilling wells inside people's living rooms over there. That's why the Daisy Bradford is famous."

"I know the name of the first radio station. It's KDKA in Pittsburgh, 1920. Ben told me."

"I've got to get on the job," Betsy said. "This paper's driving me crazy. Want to start to work Monday?"

"Fine with me. What's the name of Shady's oil well?"

"The Number One Eva Jane."

"That's kind of cute. I wonder how Mrs. Shady Webster will like it?"

Betsy said, "He'll probably tell Florine it's a typographical error. In *this* paper, that's believable."

She unfolded the paper to Big 'Un Darly's column and handed it to Ted. "I've noticed how tense you are about the Claybelle-Paschal game. Read this."

Ted smiled to himself as he looked over "Sportanic Eruptions."

"You know the most disturbing thing about it?" said Betsy. "He has a following!"

She went back down the hall to her own study.

Ted turned to the radio log in the paper. He had been wondering if any changes could be made in the daytime programming. None, if Ben Throckmorton had anything to say about

134—Fast Copy

it. From sign-on at 7 A.M. until *Amos 'n' Andy* at 7 P.M., every
Monday through Friday, KVAT offered a reliable dream factory. Why mess with it?

On this day of September 19, 1935, KVAT's daytime log in
the *Times-Standard* was free of typos. It read:

Time	Program	Sponsor
7:00a	Top O' the Morning	
7:15	News & Markets	
7:30	Press-Radio News	
7:45	Hymns of All Churches	Mohawk Rugs
8:00a	Happy Jack Turner, songs	Cheerios
8:15	Dot and Don, xylophone	
8:30	Ivy Strange, readings	
8:45	Vaughn de Leath, songs	
9:00a	Emily Post, etiquette	Knox Gelatin
9:15	Betty Crocker, cooking	General Mills
9:30	Myrt and Marge	Wrigley's Gum
9:45	Backstage Wife	Taystee Bread
10:00a	Just Plain Bill	Super Suds
10:15	Josephine Gibson's food talk	Heinz Foods
10:30	Ely Culbertson's bridge lessons	
10:45	Today's Children	Pillsbury
11:00a	Big 'Un Darly's sports talk	B's Cafe
11:15	Rev. H. W. Drews, homespun inspiration	
11:30	News & Markets	
11:45	Press-Radio News	
12:00n	Booty and Them Others, songs, swing	Fidelity Bank
12:15	Young Widder Brown	Bayer Aspirin
12:30	Mary Marlin	Kleenex
12:45	Our Gal Sunday	Anacin
1:00p	Romance of Helen Trent	Dreft
1:15	Coach Dub Cooper, Claybelle sports chatter	B's Cafe

2:00p	Pepper Young's Family	Camay
2:15	Road of Life	P&G
2:30	Big Sister	Rinso Blue
2:45	Honeyboy & Sassasfras, Negro comedy	
3:00p	Stella Dallas	Milk of Magnesia
3:15	Ma Perkins	Oxydol
3:30	Vic and Sade	Crisco
3:45	Betty and Bob	Bisquick
4:00p	The O'Neills	Ivory Soap
4:15	Lorenzo Jones	Bayer Aspirin
4:30	Buck Rogers	Cream of Wheat
4:45	Dick Tracy	Quaker Oats
5:00p	Jack Armstrong	Wheaties
5:15	Tom Mix	Ralston
5:30	Little Orphan Annie	Ovaltine
5:45	The Lone Ranger	Silvercup Bread
6:00p	News & Markets	
6:15	Gabriel Heater, news	Scott Tissue
6:30	Lum and Abner	Horlick Malt
6:45	Easy Aces	Anacin
7:00p	Amos 'n' Andy	Pepsodent

Ben Throckmorton's radio station, with offices and studios on the top floor of the Times-Standard Building, was a much smaller operation than the newspaper. All it took to run KVAT were a couple of sound engineers, an electrician—as Bob Walker said—a salesman, a bookkeeper, a secretary, and Estill Parch. Estill Parch read the news, delivered commercial messages, hosted local programs, like Booty Pettigrew's or Big 'Un Darly's or Dub Cooper's, and cued Aubrey Diggs on the phone when it was time for Aubrey to give his nasal market reports—"Hogs, up three-eighths."

And yet it had become a fact of life that radio was the most awesome advertising packager in the history of mankind. As small as the operation was, KVAT reached more people and exerted a greater influence on the community than the paper ever had, or could. Such was the dynamic of radio.

It was the cheapest ticket there was to music, adventure, drama, comedy, romance, even news. A newspaper cost five cents on weekdays, ten cents on Sundays. News was free on the radio. But news was far from the main reason people listened to the radio.

For literally millions, the characters on daytime serials were friends, neighbors, companions, more familiar and trustworthy than relatives.

The Leatha Wardlaws, Bertha Thompsons, and Joylene Blanchards of the world truly believed that Bill Davidson, the kindly barber of Hartville, could solve any problem with his homespun philosophy. Emotionally, the Leathas and Berthas were there on the porch with Ma Perkins in Rushville Center, where Ma might be chatting with her partner in the lumberyard, Shuffle Shober, or worrying about her troublesome daughter, Evey. They understood how Stella Dallas could have seen her daughter, Laurel, marry into wealth and society and why Stella, having realized the differences in their tastes and worlds, had gone out of Laurel's life. They had all known couples like lovable, impractical Lorenzo Jones and his devoted wife, Belle, and knew how Lorenzo's inventions had made him a character in the town, but not to Belle, who loved him. And they worried about an orphan girl named Sunday, who came from the little town of Silver Creek, Colorado, and in young womanhood had married England's richest, most handsome lord, Lord Henry Brinthrope. This was the story that asked the question of whether a young girl from a small mining town in the West could find happiness as the wife of a wealthy and titled Englishman. She seldom seemed to, which was why she spent most of her time pouring out her heart to her handsome and brilliant friend, Kevin Bromfield.

The true power of radio was reflected in a survey Ted had seen. Between seven and seven-fifteen every weekday evening, telephone use in America dropped off by 50 percent. The reason was *Amos 'n' Andy*.

Even the Tivoli and Liberty theaters in Claybelle switched off their projectors between seven and seven-fifteen to pipe in

Amos 'n' Andy, to let people hear Freeman Gosden and Charles Correll perform their comedy in black-voice, to hear Andy walk into the Harlem lodge known as the Mystic Knights of the Sea, and say, "Kingfish, I's regusted."

Betsy had never thought *Amos 'n' Andy* was *that* funny. For comedy, she much preferred *Vic and Sade* in the afternoons. At *Time,* she had been known to race back from lunch in time to catch the program.

Betsy judged her friends and acquaintances by how familiar they were with Vic and Sade Gook, who lived on Virginia Avenue in Crooper, Illinois, in the little house halfway up the next block. Paul Rhymer, the man who had created the show, and wrote it daily, was "an American treasure," Betsy would argue.

The show consisted of only four voices, those of actors Art Van Harvey (Vic), Bernadine Flynn (Sade), Billy Idelson (Rush, their son), and Clarence Hartzell (Uncle Fletcher), but through Paul Rhymer's dialogue, a much larger world had come to exist.

To be a close friend of Betsy's, it was a good thing to know that Ruthie Stembottom was Sade's gossiping friend; that Vic worked as a bookkeeper for the Consolidated Kitchenware Company; that his lodge was the Drowsy Venus Chapter of the Sacred Stars of the Milky Way; that Mr. Gumpox was the garbage man; that other friends included Ike Kneesupper, Cora Bucksaddle, Mr. Buller, Mervyn S. Spraul, the twins Robert and Slobbert Hink; that Rush read books about the adventures of Third Lieutenant Stanley; that Rush had good friends in Smelly Clark, Bluetooth Johnson, and Rooster Davis; that the Gooks knew someone named Rishigan Fishigan from Sishigan, Michigan, who married Jane Bane of Pane, Maine; and that Uncle Fletcher liked to sit around the Bright Kentucky Hotel and watch a half-wit fly crawl around on the ceiling, and tell a story about a man he once knew in Dismal Seepage, Ohio, who got a job as an armed guard at the State Home for the Criminally Tall. "Later moved to Belvedere," he would say. "Later died. Yes, sir. Stuff happens."

"Stuff happens" was one of the phrases Betsy and Bob Walker both liked to lean on as an explanation for most events that took place, worldwide or otherwise, seeing as how most events were out of their control.

Ted, meanwhile, thought *Vic and Sade* was mildly amusing, though he rarely built his day around listening to it.

If any one thing thoroughly baffled Betsy these days, it was the fact that she had married a man who only thought *Vic and Sade* was "mildly amusing."

But—stuff happens.

There in his study that morning, Ted was beginning to think that Bob Walker may have been right. Perhaps the best thing he could do for KVAT was keep the locomotive on the track. But then he got this idea. In a funny kind of way, it was Big 'Un Darly's column that gave it to him.

He went to Betsy's study to try it out on her. "What's Claybelle's fight song?" he asked her.

She was at her desk typing a note to Ray Fletcher. " 'Washington and Lee Swing,' " she said.

"Sing it."

"I hardly ever sing high school fight songs in the mornings," she said, pouring herself more coffee from the fresh pot Florence had brought her.

"Don't you know it?"

"Of course I know it."

"Then sing it for me."

"I don't want to sing it for you."

"I'm working on an idea."

"Who for—Morton Downey?"

"Betsy, will you sing the song, please?"

She sang two lines of it, softly.

> We are the gang from dear old
>   Claybelle High.
> Our boys have got that good old
>   do or die.

"Perfect," Ted said.

"For what?"

Hear him out, he said. Hold the laughter. It was corny, yes, but it just might go over. KVAT's signal for a station break was three bongs, like a door chime, after which Estill Parch would say, "KVAT, the voice of Claybelle, Texas." Ordinary. Commonplace. Boring. Most radio stations did it that way. What if the Claybelle High School band recorded the fight song and the station played eight bars of it on every station break? Estill Parch could come in after the music and say, "KVAT, the voice of Claybelle, Texas—home of the fighting Yellow Jackets!"

"You're right, it's corny," Betsy said, "but you know what? Daddy will love it. He'll love it so much, he'll want to do it with the TCU fight song."

Ted considered that for a second, then said, "Can't. Correct me if I'm wrong, but I don't imagine everybody in Claybelle is a TCU fan. Wouldn't there be some Texas Aggies living here? SMU Mustangs? Baylor Bears?"

"Noggin," Betsy said, pointing at her head.

"But," said Ted, "the high school fight song wouldn't be showing any partiality. It's patriotic!"

"Go, Jackets." Betsy smiled.

The phone rang and Betsy answered it.

"Well, we've got a news story *now,*" Ray Fletcher said excitedly.

"What?"

"The Texas Rangers just shot and killed a bank robber here on the square!"

"Is Smitty on it?"

"He will be. He had to go buy film."

Smitty McWhorter was one of the paper's two photographers, a runt of a man in his late thirties.

"Get Junior down there!" Betsy said.

Junior Dingle was the other staff photographer, a pudgy slow-moving kid of twenty-one. Junior was less known for his skill as a photographer than he was for the sandwiches he brought to work. He liked to slice up bananas and Baby Ruth candy bars and put it all between two pieces of light bread.

Ray Fletcher said, "I will as soon as he gets off the toilet."

Betsy slammed down the phone and could only laugh as she hurried to the bedroom to slip out of her robe and into a dress. A shooting had occurred on the doorstep of her newspaper, but one of her photographers was out of film and the other one was taking his morning shit.

Ten

IN THE street in front of the Fidelity Bank, Captain Lank Allred and Lieutenant J. T. Hines stood near a body crumpled under a blanket. The two Texas Rangers in their white shirts, khaki britches, and gray Stetsons were calmly filling out reports.

The street was blocked at both ends by vehicles. Black Ford sedans, blue police cars, a white ambulance, a purple ambulance, and a red fire truck were slanted this way and that.

Dozens of people in the square and on the sidewalks surrounded the Rangers, but were keeping a polite distance away, all of them looking on with fascination.

It was a fine golden morning. Birds were chirping in the trees on the square.

Betsy and Ted circulated through the crowd.

Leatha Wardlaw said she would have seen it all if she hadn't been talking to Olive Cooper on the phone. She said Ben Throckmorton had missed the excitement because he had gone out to Shadowlawn to play golf with Shady Webster.

Buck Blanchard, Joylene, and Wynelle Stubbs had come out of B's Cafe.

"Two of 'em got away, but the Rangers are chasin' 'em," Buck said. "I'd have seen it if I'd been lookin' out the window, but naw, I had to be takin' shit from Joylene."

Joylene said, "You steal another twenty out of my register and that'll be *you* in the street."

"We both could have seen it if you'd knowed how to shut up."

"I'll shut up when I'm not married to a thief."

"A thief? Listen to that. Like it ain't my restaurant."

Wynelle said she hadn't seen it either, but she couldn't be too unhappy about one less vagrant in the world who wasn't gonna leave her no tip.

140

O. L. Beaton puffed on a cigar, one thumb hooked around his suspenders.

O. L. said, "I was in my office. Inez stuck her head in and said all hell's broke loose. I guess they came in to rob us, but that Ranger over there—not Lank, the other one—was waitin' inside. Crooks ran out the door and wound up in a shootin' gallery. Rangers had a trap set for 'em."

He said Anna Sue would be sick she missed all the excitement, but she had taken the day off to go to Dallas and try on a dress.

Booty Pettigrew and his band were mingling in the crowd. They were due on the air in an hour. They had been upstairs rehearsing in a studio at KVAT. The whole Times-Standard Building had emptied out—people from the newsroom, the station, and from the ground floor, from advertising, circulation, classified, the money cage, reception, the back shop.

Staring at the body lying in the street, Booty was moved to sing two lines from a Jimmie Rodgers song.

Oh, why did I stray from the righteous path?
Nobody knows but me.

Smitty McWhorter and Junior Dingle were now shooting pictures of everything in sight. They were even shooting pictures of each other with their Speed Graphics. First one and then the other would slip over near the blanket-covered body and strike a funny pose.

Claybelle Police Chief Olin Musgrove and Sergeant R. G. Teague were leaning against a car when Betsy and Ted approached them.

Chief Musgrove, a dumpy man with a pencil mustache and a billed cap on the back of his head, was drinking a mug of coffee he'd brought out of B's. He looked glum. R. G. Teague, a husky young man in shirtsleeves and a billed cap on the back of *his* head, was nursing along a bottle of Dr Pepper.

Nodding at Lank Allred and J. T. Hines, Chief Musgrove said, "Looks like General Pershing and Marshal Foch got everything under control."

Nobody interfered with a Texas Ranger's business. A Texas

Ranger could exercise his jurisdiction over any other law enforcement officer in the State of Texas whenever he felt like it. A Texas Ranger had access to any evidence he might deem important to any investigation of any crime. Within the boundaries of Texas, even an FBI agent wouldn't get in the way of a Texas Ranger if he knew what was good for him. A Texas Ranger answered only to a Texas Ranger of superior rank, and the Colonel of the Texas Rangers answered only to the Governor. This was how it had been ever since the Texas Rangers were formed back in 1835 to guard the frontier during the Texas Revolution, back in the days when the only kind of man recruited for the Rangers was one who could "ride like Mexicans, shoot like Tennesseeans, and fight like the very devil."

All other law enforcement officers in the state treated the Texas Rangers with sober respect, cooperated with them completely, and for the most part were well versed in the legends of such famous Rangers as Matt Caldwell, Ben McCullough, Jack Hays, Big Foot Wallace, Lone Wolf Gonzales, B. M. Gault, and Frank Hamer.

"One riot, one Ranger," R. G. Teague said with sarcasm as he watched Lank Allred strutting up and down the street.

It had become a slogan of the Rangers. When the inmates of the state penitentiary at Huntsville had rioted one time, Captain Frank Hamer, the man who got Bonnie and Clyde, had walked into the prison yard all by himself and shouted through a megaphone, "I'm Frank Hamer—this riot's over."

And it was.

It was only when a law enforcement officer from another branch was talking about a Texas Ranger behind his back that he might be likely to tell you how much he despised the Goddamn phony-ass lightweight high-handed snobs.

Chief Musgrove didn't seem to be too worked up over the incident.

To Betsy, he said, "Aw, me and R. G. was havin' lunch at B's. Somebody came in and said the Texas Rangers shot somebody. I said, 'Hell, that ain't nothin' new.' I was in the middle of my chicken and dumplin's. They was a little light on the chicken today, but it was good. Then they said, Naw, it was right over here in front of the bank, is where it was. Me and R. G. come over, but there ain't much for us to do, as you can see."

R. G. said, "Chief, I been tryin' to remember. When was the last time somebody got kilt around here? I think it was that time Al Bates shot that old boy in the gas station."

"If you want to count a nigger deal."

"Yeah, that's right. I guess the last white man was Blanche Hubbard's husband. Damn, old Blanche did him up good."

"Had it done, you mean. She hired Gwendolyn Neal to do the dirty work." The chief laughed to himself. "Offered her a hundred dollars."

R. G. said, "I couldn't ever understand why they cut off his arm. What'd they do? They gave him ether till he passed out and then beat him to death with them monkey wrenches. Why'd they go and cut off his arm?"

"Spite, I reckon."

"Damn," said R. G., looking pained. "Cut a man's arm off."

Betsy tried to break in. "Chief, I was wondering if—"

But the chief and R. G. hadn't finished.

"Them bitches didn't come nowhere close to not gettin' caught," the chief said. "We picked up Gwendolyn a week later at the Claybelle-Cleburne game. She started singin' her song. The judge did *his* job. Blanche got 165 years, same as Gwendolyn."

"Judge didn't do his job by my taste," R. G. said. "I'd have made 'em ride Old Toasty."

Ted nudged Betsy. "Who's Old Toasty?"

"Electric chair."

The chief finally said to Betsy, "How's your daddy and them?"

She said, "What happened here, Chief Musgrove?"

"Dogass me." He sipped his coffee. "All I know's what Sloppy Herster and Tommy Jack Lucas told me. They seen the whole thing, apparently."

"Excuse us," Betsy said, her eyes widening.

She and Ted walked briskly over to Slop and Tommy Jack, who were sprawled on a bench in the square.

"Slop, you guys saw what happened?"

"Sure did. Eyewitness deal."

Slop and Tommy Jack looked more presentable than usual. It's possible they were all spruced up for a pleasant day of shoplifting in downtown Fort Worth. Tommy Jack was wearing a green checkered flannel shirt and khaki work pants. Slop was wearing a pair of blue rayon trousers, a white dress shirt, and a blue-and-yellow cableknit sleeveless sweater with the crest of a yo-yo champion on the front.

Slop had won the sweater two years ago in a contest sponsored by Thompson's Pharmacy. He had been twenty-five years old at the time, ineligible to enter a competition for ten-to-fourteen-year-olds, but Hansel Thompson, Bertha's husband, hadn't cared to risk his life to keep Slop out of the contest.

Slop had pulled his ice pick on poor Hansel and had said, "Now, I carry this thing to use on spicks in pool halls, but I'll use it on your ass. I been practicin' for a month. This is my day and there ain't no old fart like you gonna stand between me and that sweater."

Slop had performed all of the compulsory tricks—walk the dog, around the world, rock the baby, shoot the moon—and he had looped the loop sixty-seven times without missing, one more than a twelve-year old named Buddy Truett, and Sloppy Herster had won the coveted Claybelle yo-yo championship of 1933.

The kids had all gone away in tears, and their mothers had cursed and spat on poor Hansel Thompson, but Tommy Jack, who had been counting the loop-the-loops out loud, had pumped Slop's hand and yelled, "You did it, you did it—you the winner!"

"Yeah, and I didn't cheat neither," Slop had said proudly. "Some of them little fuckers put wax on their strings."

Slop and Tommy Jack described to Betsy and Ted what they had seen happen in front of the Fidelity Bank.

They had been sitting on the same bench, facing the bank, drinking a Country Red—half beer, half tomato juice—when they saw the Texas Rangers arrive. Three carloads of Rangers.

One car had stopped a block down the street, another had

kept circling the square slowly. The car with Lank Allred and J. T. Hines had head-in parked in front of the bank.

J. T. had gone inside the bank. Lank had walked around the corner and stood in front of Herschel Melton's barbershop.

Slop said that about ten minutes later this bank robber came walking down the street, and he stood around in front of the bank. Young guy. In his twenties, maybe.

"He was the lookout," Tommy Jack said.

Then a car drove up. Looked like a LaSalle, yellow, with Oklahoma plates. The driver left the motor running and a fellow got out and went inside the bank. Older man. Wore a hat and a suit.

"That's when the shit flew," Slop said.

The man had come running out of the bank. They had heard him yell to the lookout, "Get outta here, we been set up!"

The man in the hat had jumped into the LaSalle and the LaSalle had burned rubber, with J. T. Hines blasting away at it as he came out of the bank.

At the same time, Lank Allred had come around the corner and gone after the lookout.

The lookout hadn't known which way to run. He had almost been run over by one of the two cars that took off after the LaSalle.

"Old Lank, he's somethin'," Tommy Jack said. "He stood still and drew a bead and dropped that old boy right where he lays. It looked like he was shootin' a Indian in a picture show. Pow! Dropped him. Pow! Hit him again on the ground. Pow! Hit him again."

Slop said, "Them last two shots made him bounce, I swear I seen him bounce."

Betsy and Ted went to speak to Lank Allred, who was on a car radio, his boot on a running board, now in the company of O. L. Beaton.

Betsy introduced herself to the Ranger after he clicked off his radio. She reminded him that they'd met at the train station in Fort Worth, but she mainly wanted to know how the chase was progressing and could he identify the dead robber?

"They've cut through farm property south of town. I think we'll get 'em," Lank said.

And the dead one?

"My guess is he's a punk who busted out of a joint in Oklahoma. Fits the description."

"I gather you had an informant," Ted said.

Lank said, "A lawman can't do much to prevent a crime without sources. It's a lucky thing for society that most scum ain't acquainted with many people that are trustworthy."

"I'd like to see the body," Betsy said.

The Ranger glanced at Ted, as if this required Ted's approval.

"It's all right," Betsy said. "I'm a newshen."

Lank Allred led them over to the body and pulled back the blanket.

Betsy and Ted were shocked to discover that the dead man was Charley Atkins, the young hobo they'd spoken to at the Star of Hope Mission.

"My God, we know him!" Betsy said. "I mean, we talked to him one day at the mission. His name's, uh . . . Atkins. Charley Atkins."

J. T. Hines wrote down the name.

Staring down at the wasted young life, Betsy felt sad, bewildered, angry at the world.

"He was just a hobo," she said. "A young kid. He didn't look like someone who would rob a bank."

"No, ma'am," Lank Allred said. "He tried, is all."

The Ranger covered up the body with the blanket.

O. L. Beaton said to Lank, "My bank owes you and your squad a real debt. I'll be writing a letter to the Colonel and the Governor. I want 'em to know Claybelle, Texas, is proud of the Texas Rangers. You've got a reward comin', too."

"I can't accept another reward," Lank said.

"I'm talkin' about five thousand dollars, Captain!"

"I know. I took money for them others. I reckon my wife would have divorced me if I hadn't, but I can't accept any more rewards for doin' my job. Tell the bankers to donate the money to a church or something."

"May I quote you on that?" Betsy asked the Ranger.

"Aw, I wouldn't want to make no big thing out of it."

"It's news, Captain."

"If you say so."

They walked swiftly through the square toward the Times-Standard Building.

"I've got myself a scoop," Betsy said. "Ranger turns down reward."

Eleven

___

THE NEWSROOM at the *Times-Standard* was smaller by half than those of most big-city dailies, but it was every inch as squalid and cluttered, and it clacked and hummed and backfired with the same charming noises.

Occasionally, you could hear a frayed-collar literary genius holler, "God damn it!" as he wrestled with the ribbon reverse on his typewriter. Occasionally, you could hear another literary genius holler, "Pig's ass shit!" as he watched the cream curdle in his cup of coffee. You could hear somebody shriek at the discovery of a month-old cupcake in a desk drawer. Or some artistic person shout, "Goddamn motherfucking son of a Goddamn bitch!" as a bottle of root beer was accidentally knocked over on his prize-winning lead.

Cries of "Copy!" could be heard from writers or editors, and a copyboy would come shuffling away from the water cooler, or out of the bathroom, or out from behind filing cabinets where he'd been taking a nap or reading comic books.

People came and went. Messengers bringing zinc plates back from the engraver, or messengers sullenly going off to fetch more sandwiches and coffee. Visitors coming in to bring news of garden clubs or church activities. Visitors coming in to complain about stories that were too accurate about their personal lives and finances.

Some writers brooded endlessly over their typewriters, yanking out the paper and carbon, wadding it up, tossing it at wastebaskets twenty feet away, then rolling in more paper and staring at it with frozen eyes. Other writers typed a couple of paragraphs, lit up cigarettes, and sat back to admire the work.

Rewrite people hammered on their machines as they barked or cursed or laughed into phones. A columnist might be trying to type while joke-tellers annoyed him.

The occasional person would grab a hat and a notebook and dash out of the room, and the occasional person would come limping wearily in, fall into a chair, and reach for a flask in the drawer of a desk.

Unruffled editors sat in slots at large half-moon desks that were covered in dark green linoleum. They would be penciling in words and sentences, or drawing lines through words and sentences, and then cramming the copy into tubes and stuffing the tubes into suction shafts that shot the copy to the linotype operators in the back shop.

Phones rang constantly.

The wire machines pecked and dinged. Five bells on a wire machine meant something big hád happened—Huey Long had been assassinated, Will Rogers and Wiley Post had been killed in a plane crash, the Chicago Cubs had clinched the pennant.

Ashtrays were always on fire, cigars always burning the edges of desktops, pipes always stinking up the place—layers of smoke hanging heavily over the room.

This was how a newspaper went to bed, and Betsy loved every shabby, disgusting, derelict thing about it.

Most of the busywork took place in the center of the room, around the two half-moon desks, one with a slot for the city editor, the other with a slot for the state editor. Around the desks sat rewrite men, copy readers, and headline writers, who were one and the same, and they took their directions from the editors in the slots—when they weren't dozing, munching, bullshitting, taking leaks, putting jokes up on one of the bare plaster walls, getting in on ten-cent chain letters, working a crossword puzzle, or playing Monopoly.

Desks and typewriters for the "beat" writers and feature writers, where Betsy had taught herself to type and play twelve-year-old newshen, were scattered here and there on the perimeter of the half-moon desks. When these desks were unoccupied, it was hoped that the reporters were out working as hard on assignments as they were at getting drunk or laid, and when the desks were occupied, it was hoped the reporters weren't going to turn in something that rhymed.

At one end of the room, on the way to the morgue, were the special sections. These sections consisted of two or three desks with small bookshelves and filing cabinets inside a little pen. Each pen was separated from the other by the bars of a wood railing three feet high. One pen was known as "The Candy Store." This was Big 'Un Darly's sports department. One was known as "Pies and Cookies." This was Carolyn Moseley's society department. One was known as "Spindletop." This was Cloyd Bennett's oil and business department. Someone in the back shop had named the sections long ago.

Down at the opposite end of the room, across one wall, were two glass-enclosed offices. One now belonged to Betsy—it was her daddy's office—and the other belonged to Ray Fletcher, the managing editor. Ben had moved up to the third floor, up there with Ted and KVAT, to a broom closet where he could pick up his mail when he wasn't playing golf.

Betsy's office and Ray's office were divided by a ground-glass partition, but from their respective desks they could look out on the whole newsroom, or swivel around and look out at the square.

Betsy was now in her office, waiting for a city side reporter named W. M. Keller to finish his story on the attempted robbery, but she was talking to Ray Fletcher about something else at the moment.

Ray stood in front of her desk holding up the day's front page. "You want it down here in this corner, double column?"

"Every day, Ray."

"What besides the freight schedules?"

"Travel routes—the best places to board trains without getting into trouble. I don't just want the Claybelle freight schedules, I want Fort Worth's, Waco's, Cleburne's, everything around. I want it boldfaced, indented. See how it looks with a coin rule. I want to be able to *see* it."

"Betsy, if you don't mind me sayin' so, it seems like a waste of good space for . . . panhandlers."

"Some people call them *transients*. Some people talk about the red menace, like that idiot Father Coughlin. The thing is, Ray, these people have to ride the rails to go anywhere. They're broke, poor, hungry, helpless. I want to start it on Monday and I want it to run every day."

"People are gonna think—"

"People don't *think*," Betsy stopped him. "This is a public service. I don't care if some of them are worthless and lazy. The majority of them are unlucky. People with no food, no shelter, no sanitation, no medical attention, no hope! Just *do* it, Ray."

"How they gonna afford a newspaper?"

"They'll *steal* one."

Betsy rolled around in her chair and turned on the radio that was on a table to the left of her desk. Assuming the discussion was over, Ray left.

Betsy twisted the dial to KVAT and heard Booty and Them Others. The band was backing him up with a hint of Dixieland, and Booty was singing:

> *In a little cottage cozy*
> *The world seems rosy*
> *At sundown.*
> *Where a lovin' smile will greet me,*
> *Always meet me*
> *At sundown.*

The song ended and Booty spoke in his deep whiskey voice. "Friends, I reckon most of you heard all them sirens in Claybelle this mornin'. The Texas Rangers were at it again. A bunch of bandits tried to rob the Fidelity Bank. The Rangers dough-popped one of 'em. He's deader than the engine on your car. Two of 'em got away, and I've just been handed a note— it looks like they've given everbody the slip, but you can bet they ain't no closer to Claybelle than I am to bein' rich. Everbody can rest easy. Right now, me and the boys are gonna slick your hair down with a little number called 'Here Comes Cookie.' "

Betsy picked up the phone and called Ted upstairs.

She said, "It occurs to me that you might be tempted to use my exclusive on the radio before my paper comes out."

"I was thinking about it."

"I knew you were, that's why I called. You're not serious, I trust."

"I heard him say it, too."

"Ted, that was *my* interview. It's *my* quote!"

"What if I put it on at six o'clock? That's only four hours before your first edition comes out."

"You *are* teasing?"

"I'd give you credit. Captain Allred told the *Times-Standard* he was going to turn down the reward money—something like that."

"Not funny, Ted."

"I'm not being funny. I don't, actually, see anything wrong with it."

"Let me tell you what's wrong with it. If you use it, you're going to be married to the unhappiest bitch God ever put on this earth—for the rest of your life!"

And she hung up.

She'd hardly had time to light a Lucky when the phone rang. She grabbed it. "Yes?"

Ted said, "I'm curious. Why did you think I would do that to you?"

"Because you didn't go to my high school!"

"No, I'm not Bob Walker."

"What does that mean?"

"Nothing."

"Yes, it does."

"What did *you* mean, I didn't go to your high school?"

"It means you can't trust anybody from the East—not deep down."

"Oh, now the Texas comes out. Great."

"This is not the Texas coming out. It's the newshen coming out."

"The newshen, I forgot. Betsy Throckmorton, grown from the *soil* of journalism."

"He said, wittily."

The door to Betsy's office opened and W. M. Keller came in, a man in his thirties, his sleeves rolled up, a cigarette stuck in his lips. He was holding three pages of copy.

On the phone, Ted was saying, "Look, what are we fighting about? I'm not going to use it. It's your scoop. I love you."

"I love you, too, but I'm hanging up now. I'm busy."

W. M. Keller handed her his copy. "Dave said you wanted to see this first."

Dave Hawkins was the city editor of the *Times-Standard,* one of the somber men who sat in a slot.

Betsy read over the piece quickly. A workmanlike job, full of words like allegedly and supposedly.

Betsy asked, "How many bank robbers has Lank Allred shot?"

"Four now," W. M. Keller said. "I've got it in there someplace."

Betsy was looking at the story as she talked. "We can't identify the kid, huh?"

"You told somebody his name was Charley Atkins, but we can't confirm it. We can't find anybody in the hobo camp who claims to be his mama and daddy. I called Hollis, Oklahoma. No school records or birth records. No record of him in reform schools or prisons. Charley Atkins must be an alias."

"Okay, so what we've got is a screwed-up bank job, an unidentified dead guy, and two escaped."

Betsy grabbed the phone again and called the city editor, only fifty feet away. "Dave, I want a box to go with the lead— Lank Allred's trail of dead bank robbers. Their names, arrest records, dates, places of the heists."

Now she called Ray Fletcher. "Ray, have you see any art?" She tapped her fingers on her desk impatiently. "It's me. Betsy. Yes, the person next door. Have you seen any art?" He hadn't.

She said, "I want to go with something big on Lank Allred. Four-column and deep. Near the body. Maybe his holster showing. We've got a folk hero on our hands."

Now she spun around in her chair, this time to face a fast-action Remington on a table to the right of her desk. She put paper and carbon in the typewriter.

"Read over my shoulder," she said to W. M. Keller.

First she typed on the byline, centering it on the page, and then her fingers flew.

BY W. M. KELLER
Times-Standard Staff Writer
A Texas Ranger put another notch in his gun yesterday, and if Capt. Lank Allred is going to keep this up, he may have to strap a Winchester to his leg—

there won't be any room left on his trusty .45.

In the mid-morning sunlight on the town square, while people at home were listening to radio dramas, the Ranger stood in the street and pumped three bullets into a fleeing bank robber, stopping him cold.

It was the Ranger captain's fourth bandit victim in the past two months, but in an exclusive interview with the *Times-Standard,* Capt. Allred said he would refuse to accept the $5,000 reward from the Texas Bankers Assn.

"I can't accept any more rewards for doing my job," he told the *Times-Standard.*

Acting on a tip from underworld sources, Capt. Allred, 37, a tall, fearless Ranger, had set a trap for the bandits.

As the real-life drama then unfolded, with the robbers foiled and trying to escape, Capt. Allred dashed into the street in front of the Fidelity Bank and became the focal point of a scene that recalled the lusty days of the Old West, or the more recent days of Clyde Barrow and Bonnie Parker.

Betsy snatched the copy out of her typewriter and handed it to W. M. Keller. "Here, you finish it."

"I don't write like that," W. M. said limply.

"You do now. You're a good reporter, W. M., but you've got to learn how to make the words throb. You want people to read what you write, don't you?"

"Sure. I mean—"

"Jesus wept."

"What?"

"Jesus wept. Paragraph. That's the all-time lead."

"It is?"

"Go on. Go to work. Get the fuck out of here."

The reporter looked a little dazed by Betsy's haste and language.

She tried to put him at ease with a smile. "Just let it flow, W. M. Big stories tend to write themselves."

The party started at ten o'clock that evening, after Betsy had laid out the front page, seen all the stories through the composing room, made up the page in the form, corrected proofs, and watched the presses roll. She and Ted had left the building for a while, to have cube steak sandwiches at B's, where they kissed and apologized to each other for anything they may have said, and they had gone over to Felix's package store and bought bottles of whiskey for the staff.

It was a crude party, everyone drinking out of coffee cups or fruit jars, but Betsy wanted to have the get-together to help make amends for the yelling and cussing she had done throughout the afternoon.

Betsy, in a matter of a few hours, had given the paper a new look: larger, blacker headlines and a splashier use of pictures. Not every editor and writer on the staff would like it, but newspaper people shared a strange quirk: for free whiskey, they would pretend to like a grocery circular.

Ben had called twice during the afternoon from Shadowlawn to ask if he could be any help. He was spending more time at the country club now, trying to get his game in shape for the club's Fall Championship. He reported to Betsy that his new Spalding irons could hook *and* slice. He said he would drop by later.

A bar was set up on the desk of the city editor, Dave Hawkins. He was an unflappable little man with a slick bald head and cold eyes. He had once been a star reporter at the *Star-Telegram* in Fort Worth, but had resigned after he had been passed over twice for the managing editor's job.

Dave was best remembered for his coverage of Vernon Castle's death. The world famous dancer, the Fred Astaire of his day, half of the celebrated team of Vernon and Irene Castle, had been killed in 1918 in the crash of a Jenny when as a captain in the Royal Flying Corps he had been stationed at Benbrook Field in Fort Worth.

Castle had been coming in for a routine landing at the airfield when he'd had to pull his plane up sharply to avoid a collision with a young pilot training in another Curtiss JN. His plane had stalled, hung in the air, and plummeted to earth. He had been crushed in the pile of boards, canvas, and wire.

No news story before or since had sent the Fort Worth dateline rocketing around the globe like the death of Vernon Castle.

A hundred thousand people, including ten-year-old Betsy Throckmorton, had turned out to watch the funeral procession that moved through the streets of downtown Fort Worth to the muffled drums of the 36th Division band.

Dave Hawkins' lead on the funeral had read:

"To the sound of muffled drums and strong men weeping, a whole city said farewell to Vernon Castle yesterday, as an artillery caisson, drawn by six horses, carried the famed dancer and aviator through the streets of Fort Worth, and on to immortality."

Joe Stogner, the old rim-man, quoted the lead perfectly to Betsy.

"I'd have written it differently," she said.

"How?"

"He danced a million times with Irene, but his last waltz was with a Jenny."

Joe Stogner waited for her to go on and then realized he was supposed to laugh.

The front page lay flat on a desktop, and Red Hensch and Bert Swick were looking at it. Betsy joined them.

"Never thought I'd wind up working for a tabloid," said Red Hensch, the state editor, tall and stoop-shouldered, scarlet-faced, and almost never without a green eyeshade on his head, even on days off.

"Did you ever think you'd wind up working for a newspaper?" Betsy said.

Bert Swick, the feature editor, flabby and sweaty, a reformed alcoholic, was dipping into a can of cold green peas with a spoon.

"Glad to see we kept the masthead," Bert said.

"I thought of jumping it," Betsy retorted.

Ted was cordially playing bartender in the slot of the city desk.

Ben Throckmorton and Leatha Wardlaw walked into the party, and Ben received warm hellos all around. It was Red Hensch who called out, "Hey, Ben, you missed it—we been playin' newspaper."

Ben and Leatha studied the front page of the paper, Ben digesting the new look without expression, but Leatha said, "Is this what the paper's going to look like every day, Betsy?"

Betsy wasn't enthralled with Leatha's tone.

With a glance for her daddy, Betsy said, "We probably wouldn't have played it this big if it had happened in North Platte, Nebraska."

Ben smiled and Leatha kept looking at the front page with puzzlement.

An eight-column banner raced across the top of the page in fat black Gothic type an inch and a half tall.

TEXAS RANGERS FOIL CLAYBELLE BANK ROBBERY

Beneath the banner was a double-column deck.

Capt. Lank Allred Guns Down Fourth Bandit; Rejects $5000 Reward from Texas Bankers

Under this came W. M. Keller's double-column ten-point lead with the most prominent byline he might ever receive.

W. M. was almost as pleased with the layout as was Junior Dingle.

It had been Junior, not Smitty McWhorter, who had shot the picture of Lank Allred that filled up one-third of the front page—the Ranger looking sternly at the camera, his boot on a running board, his hand on his .45, the blanket-covered body of his victim in the lower right-hand corner of the frame.

The two smaller pictures on the page were Smitty's. One was an aerial of the cars and Rangers and onlookers in the street, taken from the roof of the bank. The other was a two-shot, O. L. Beaton shaking hands with Ranger J. T. Hines.

There had only been space on the front page for two other stories. Betsy had selected both of them off the wire. Mussolini's dive bombers had attacked some Ethiopians who had tried to fight back with rocks and spears. In the other story, Father Charles Coughlin, the radical Catholic priest, had accused President Roosevelt of being a "great betrayer, a Communist held captive by the Jewish bankers of New York."

The Father Coughlin story troubled Ben. "People are going to think we're criticizing the President," he said.

"The lunatic said it, not us," Betsy said.

"People don't read things that close. I know why you ran it, honey. You want everybody to know the man's a loony, but you'll have readers who'll take it the wrong way."

Ted said, "I know what you're saying. I know this writer who did a humor piece about FDR in *Vanity Fair*. It was slugged 'Humor.' It was slugged 'Fiction.' But he got fifty angry letters saying he had maligned the President."

"Are you suggesting I shouldn't run a piece because people are stupid?" Betsy asked Ben.

"No, I'm just tellin' you to get ready for the phone calls. You'll get a call from somebody wanting to know why we said those terrible things about the President. What'd we do, call him a Jew? A Communist? Who did he betray? You'll get a call saying what's got into your newspaper, anyhow? The very idea, calling FDR all those names. Oh, you'll try to explain that *we* didn't say these things, it was Father Coughlin. But they won't have heard him on the radio—they won't know what a damn fool he is. By the way, Ted, I won't carry the crazy son of a bitch on KVAT. Amon Carter don't carry him on WBAP, either. So, anyhow, honey, you'll take the time to explain who Father Coughlin is, but they'll say, well, if that's the case, what the dickens are you doing putting a story about him in your newspaper? You can't win. But—they'll get it all off their chests and say they're gonna cancel their subscription, but they won't. We'll run a nice story about the Yellow Jackets and they'll forget it."

Betsy said, "That's America, huh?"

"Near as I've been able to tell."

Junior Dingle sidled up to Betsy and said, "How 'bout my picture?"

"It worked out fine."

"I had him pose," Junior said.

"No shit."

Betsy was sipping her Scotch from a coffee cup.

Junior said, "He wouldn't pose for Smitty. He thought Smitty was a smart aleck."

"You did a good job, Junior."

"Smitty asked him what he'd heard from Tonto lately. He didn't give me no trouble at all. I shot it from three different angles. I think the one you used is the best one."

"Junior, you're going to have to do me a favor."

"What?"

"Don't eat that thing around me."

Junior smiled apologetically and backed away with his banana–and–Baby Ruth sandwich.

Twelve

———

DUB COOPER said he'd seen more people at a pissin' contest. The coach said he was pretty near close to being heartbroke that Claybelle's opening football game didn't draw a bigger crowd. Only two thousand turned out, which didn't fill up a third of Clay Field on Friday night. Looking around at the empty stands, the coach said, "There ain't enough folks here to make a pimple on a fat man's ass."

The explanation for the light turnout was the same as ever. Most people in town had adopted their usual wait-and-see attitude about the Yellow Jackets.

Each football season, the *Times-Standard* and KVAT and all of the local merchants would do what they could to get everybody excited about Dub Cooper's lads, but each year the Yellow Jackets would suffer some deplorable misfortune—an injury to a key player, a lousy call by an official, a crazy bounce of the ball—that would cost them the District and keep them out of the State playoffs.

All except that memorable year of 1925. It was in '25 that Claybelle had traveled on the fugitive heels and strong arm of Bobby Walker at quarterback; on the battering-ram plunges of Clarence (Big 'Un) Darly at fullback; on the line play of Tommy Jack Lucas, the watchfob center, Doyle Laymance, the caveman guard, and Sloppy Herster, the glue-fingered end, to win District 5-AA, upset Corsicana in Bi-District, and barely lose in the State quarterfinals to the Waco Tigers. The final score of the Waco game had been 26 to 6, but Dub Cooper maintained that if you took away the three blocked punts in the fourth quarter, something different would have happened.

The three blocked punts had largely been caused by Tommy Jack's poor snaps from center. For three quarters, Tommy Jack had taken a beating from Waco's bigger, angrier linemen, and by the time the fourth quarter rolled around, Tommy Jack had wanted to be anywhere but on the field. He had shut his eyes, gritted his teeth, centered the ball along the ground, off in a dumb direction, and then tried to dig a hole for himself. Bob Walker had retrieved the ball each time but had been unable to punt the ball over the huge wall of Waco beef storming down on him. All three punts had been blocked for Waco touchdowns.

"Tommy Jack, you yellow as butter," Dub Cooper had said to his center as he slapped him around on the sideline.

Most Claybelle fans hadn't blamed the crushing loss on Tommy Jack entirely. They had been aware that most of Waco's players were older and stronger, many of them more than twenty-five years of age. It had been a well-known fact that Waco's two biggest stars, Fatback Lillard and Gunnysack Weaver, had already played four years of ball for Cisco High under their real names of Melvin Waits and Burl Dunagan.

Gracious in defeat, Dub Cooper had said to reporters, "I want to congratulate the Waco Tigers on a great victory, but somethin' ought to be done about the Goddamn criminal element in high school football."

Aside from the usual skepticism regarding the destiny of the 1935 Yellow Jackets, there may have been other reasons for the disappointing crowd at the opening game.

On his radio show at 11 A.M. that morning, Big 'Un Darly had lost control of himself. Sitting at a table in the box-shaped studio and speaking into a microphone only slightly smaller than a helmsman's wheel, Big 'Un had said:

"I don't want nobody to get too excited about the Claybelle-Paschal game tonight, but we got us a omen goin' for us. A omen is a thing that tells you about the future, and our omen is Eugene Herster, who we call Pine Knot.

"Ten years ago this year—and I can't believe how time flies —Claybelle had another Herster on the team, and that team won District. It was my honor to be a cog on that team. I will never forget the pass old Slop Herster caught against Corsicana, which won us the Bi-District and sent us to the State quarterfinals where we would have beat Waco if they hadn't cheated.

"And I want to say something personal right here. I say it

don't matter that Eugene's older brother has turned out to be about half-sorry in his adult life. Slop Herster won us the Corsicana game when he doved and come up with Bob Walker's low-flung pass, which gave us a thirteen-to-seven victory.

"That was the most emotional minute of my life. We weren't supposed to win over there at Corsicana, as most of you may remember. We was hurt and underdogs and some of our helmets had been stolen, but by golly, we proved that if boys believe in themselves and they've got a leader like Coach Cooper—which they can talk about Howard Jones or Wallace Wade if they want to—it just shows what the never-say-die spirit can do.

"We wanted it real bad, and I can still hear our proud band playin' the fight song that day, and all the kids singin', 'We are the gang from dear old Claybelle High. Our boys have got that good old do or die. . . .' I'm sorry to get so choked up, but that was the greatest day of my life as I've knowed it, and . . . and . . . well, by God, all I can say about our game tonight against the cocky Paschal Panthers is, *Go get 'em, Yellow Jackets!*"

This was where Big 'Un had broken down and cried.

After a two-minute dead spot, Estill Parch had rushed into the studio and filled out the broadcast with some comments about the beef hash at B's Cafe.

Estill Parch was living proof that there was life after career failure. A fastidious gentleman in his forties, one who sported a bushy black mustache and combed his hair into a tall black mound, he fancied himself the town's leading celebrity and was quick to let it be known that if he had only been in the right place at the right time, he would have been the voice on the *March of Time*.

Along with his other duties at KVAT, Estill co-hosted Dub Cooper's radio show. This entailed asking the coach questions, most of them sent in by listeners. Dub upped his income by fifteen dollars a week doing the show.

It wasn't out of the ordinary for Dub to appear gloomy or evasive on the show, particularly on a game day. He didn't want to give the enemy anything they could use against him.

On that Friday, the show began with Estill Parch saying, "Well, here we go, Coacher, the 1935 season is getting *under way!* It's a little warm and muggy out, but I can sniff old autumn in the air. The boys are *raring* to go, I hear. Ready to put their stingers in the old Central High Panthers who are coming up here from Cowtown. The kickoff is at eight o'clock and tickets are still available at the high school gym or out at Clay Field, is that the case, Coach?"

"Paschal," said Dub in a voice that could barely be heard by Estill Parch, let alone the radio audience. "It's the Paschal Panthers."

"Right you are, Coach—it is the Paschal Panthers now, but they still play in that tough District Seven-AA with the Masonic Home Masons and North Side Steers. Have you ever faced a tougher opening game?"

Dub quietly said, "Some games is first, some games is last, some games is in the middle."

Estill Parch enunciated his words clearly. "What would you say is the key to tonight's game, Coach?"

"I don't know."

"Passing, running, kicking—anything along those lines?"

"Maybe."

"Defense?"

"Maybe."

"Can you speak up a little, Coach? We want our Yellow Jacket fans to hear the word from the man himself!"

Dub coughed into the mike.

"What about tonight's strategy, Coach? You were saying . . . ?"

"I wasn't sayin' nothin'."

Dub took out a handkerchief and honked his nose into the mike.

"Let's get to the questions," Estill Parch said. "Our good friend Homer Moody over at Bewley Mill wants to know how the new Y-formation is coming along."

"I wish I had me some orphans to run it."

"Orphans?"

"Them orphans who'll hitchee."

Estill chuckled nervously. "Our next question is from Mrs. Dale Trimble, 3219 West Lula. She wants to know if Coach Dutch Meyer at TCU stole his shovel pass from your playbook, true or false?"

Dub spoke up a little. "It ain't proper for a coach to comment on another coach's system. We all tryin' to do a job."

"But looking back in retrospect, Coach, didn't *you,* Dub Cooper, have a play like the shovel pass in your repertoire as far back as 1925?"

"Estill, I don't want to cast no dispersions on another coach, particularly a fine man like Dutch Meyer, but the answer is yes, I've had the shovel pass in my repertoire for ten years, although we ain't never employed it in a game."

"Now then, Coach, *I* have a question for you. If you were a Paschal Panther, what would you be most concerned about tonight?"

"Arithmetic."

"Beg pardon?"

"I 'magine they'll be pretty busy tryin' to count how many of us limp off."

Betsy and Ted went to the game with Ben and Leatha.

Their seats were in a reserved section near the fifty-yard line, about twelve rows up behind the Claybelle bench. These seats were ideal for another reason. Clay Field's lights were woefully dim inside the twenty-yard lines at both ends of the stadium. Usually before any Claybelle game ended, the owners of cars parked outside the wire fences behind both end zones would be requested by the PA announcer to turn on their headlights, please, in order for the players and officials to see better.

Ted took a moment before the game started to talk to the Claybelle band director, Colonel M. D. Cherryhomes, about bringing the thirty-four-piece band to KVAT to make a recording of the fight song for station breaks. The band director said, "Tata da-*dot,* ta-*dah!*" which meant he liked the idea.

In the reserved section were many familiar faces, and Sloppy Herster and Tommy Jack Lucas were down on the field with the Claybelle team, both of them wearing their old letter jackets. Dub Cooper had permitted Sloppy and Tommy Jack to be on the sideline, thinking it would help bolster Eugene's confidence.

Warren and Florence Richards supported the Yellow Jackets, but they were sitting near the ten-yard line in the "colored section."

Anna Sue Beaton was still boycotting Claybelle games, having never forgiven the school for not electing her cheerleader. She'd had better things to do that night, anyhow. Her alma mater, SMU, the college she had attended for two years, was opening its football season the next day, as was TCU in Fort Worth, and Anna Sue had gone to Dallas for three gala pep rallies. One pep rally had been scheduled in front of Neiman-Marcus downtown, another in the Highland Park Shopping Village, and the biggest rally would be in Ownby Stadium, a redbrick structure that blended in with the other buildings on a leafy Southern Methodist University campus that was known to its impassioned alumni as, alternately, "The Hilltop" and "The Sweet Old Lady on Mockingbird Lane."

Bob Walker had wanted to come to the Claybelle game, if only for laughs, but he'd had to stay in Dallas and go on a radio show at WFAA with Matty Bell, SMU's new head coach, and two of SMU's most versatile players, Bobby Wilson and J. R. (Jackrabbit) Smith. Bob would be covering SMU's opener on Saturday.

Betsy had spoken to him on the phone earlier in the day.

"You had some excitement, huh?" Bob had said.

"Just your basic murder."

"Murder?"

"The kid wasn't armed. He was only a young hobo."

"The Rangers didn't know he wasn't armed."

"It was such a waste. Dumb kid."

"You did a good job, babe. I saw the paper."

"The newshen took over. I just got out of her way. Are you seeing the lovely Anna Sue tonight?"

"I think so."

"I'm going to find you a woman. I may have to call Millie Saunders to move down here."

"From what I hear, she's a little too speedy for me."

"You'd love her."

"Well, mail me a contract."

"There's one problem."

"What?"

"You're not rich enough."

"That seems to be a problem with a lot of them."

Ben Throckmorton was a man with a renewed interest in life. Football season was upon him. Football Silly not only had tonight's game to look forward to, he would be going to the TCU–Howard Payne game in Fort Worth tomorrow, but all this didn't keep him from being irritated at Dub Cooper.

Before the Claybelle-Paschal kickoff, Ben worked his way over to Olive Cooper in the stands. Olive was resplendent in her lucky yellow awning and brown tam.

As Ben kneeled down near her, Olive was pouring a glass of strawberry polypop out of a thermos jug.

"Has your husband misplaced his brain cells?"

Olive said, "He's never had an abundant supply. What's he done?"

"Did you hear him on the radio today?"

Olive hadn't. She had been helping out at the Star of Hope Mission. She handed the glass of polypop behind her to Reverend Jimmy Don Tankersley, who had come to the game to pray that nobody got seriously injured.

The reverend said, "Lord bless this heavenly potion, though it be the scarlet color of Ezekiel's women."

Ben smiled at the reverend and looked back at Olive. "I can't believe your husband, on KVAT, said he invented the shovel pass and insinuated that Dutch Meyer stole it from him! The shovel pass was invented at TCU last year when Sam Baugh threw it to Jimmy Lawrence in the Baylor game! Nobody had ever seen a shovel pass before that, not even Knute Rockne—not even Knute Rockne *dead*. You tell Dub I want him to clear this up next week or he'll be a football coach with one less radio show!"

Olive said, "Why, Ben, that is the worst thing I have ever heard. I can't imagine what must have been goin' through the idiot's mind. You can rest assured the pea-brained son of a bitch will hear about it from *me*. Pardon my language, Reverend, but when Ben Throckmorton is upset, *I* am upset."

What Olive didn't add was that Ben had loaned the Coopers the money to buy their duplex. Ben's generosity was spread all over Claybelle.

Reverend Tankersley said, "The Lord forgives people's words if they hearts is pure."

Big 'Un Darly came trudging up the aisle looking grim. As was his custom, he had been in the locker room to hear Coach Cooper's last-minute pep talk and was on his way to the press box, a tiny wood shack atop the west stands which held ten to twelve people and swayed in a strong wind.

Betsy and Ted, among the Claybelle faithful, stood and clapped as the Yellow Jackets took the field for the opening kickoff. The Jackets hopped up and down in their uniforms of old gold with dark brown numerals and dark brown shoulders and dark brown stripes up their legs.

The Paschal Panthers took the field in their solid gray uniforms with purple numerals and black helmets. Olive Cooper let out a jarring boo and screamed, "Go to hell, you Fort Worth jackasses!"

The Claybelle band struck up the "Washington and Lee Swing." The Paschal band struck up "Across the Field," a fight song that belonged to Ohio State on those Saturdays when the Buckeyes played football.

Directly in front of Betsy's section, on the gravel behind the Claybelle bench, the Yellow Jacket cheerleaders turned cartwheels and did forward rolls and went into a yell.

"Hamburger, hotdog!
Come on, bunch!
Go, you Jackets,
Eat their lunch!"

The fans picked up the chant in the stands, but it wouldn't have been possible for Betsy to join in, even if she had been so moved, for in the next moment she was diverted by a sight she might have described on a typewriter as about two feet short of Byzantine.

Two couples had arrived at the game together and were moving into their seats a few rows below.

"My, there's a cozy little foursome," Betsy said, giving Ted a gentle elbow.

Shady Webster was with Eva Jane McKnight—they had gone public—and Captain Lank Allred of the Texas Rangers was with Shirley, the cowgirl waitress from Lola's Oasis.

Thirteen

IT TOOK about forty-five minutes for Leatha Wardlaw to decide that Shady Webster should be circumcised—she meant castrated—and also shot, blinded, crippled, starved, and left to rot in an Arab desert.

Leatha had expected to see Florine come along behind Shady and Eva Jane. She had even commented on how thoughtful it had been for Shady and Florine to bring Eva Jane to the game with them. A divorced young woman, trying to raise those two troublesome boys, Eva Jane probably didn't get a chance to go out much, Leatha said.

Shady and Eva Jane and Lank and Shirley had waved at everyone as they took their seats across an aisle and six rows down from Betsy and the others.

After ten minutes of the first quarter went by and there was still no sight of Florine, Leatha began to show concern.

"Florine must not be feeling well," she said to Ben.

"Guess not," Ben said absently—he was concentrating on the game.

Watching Leatha grow more restless, Betsy was wondering how long it was going to take her to realize that Shady was cheating on his wife in public.

As the first quarter ended with the score 0 to 0, Leatha said to Ben, "Maybe I should go ask him where Florine is."

"She must have had something else to do tonight," Ben said, more absorbed with Dub Cooper starting to act up on the sideline.

Dub was cussing his players, kicking them in the shins, shaking them by their shoulder pads, and trying to twist their noses when they were near him.

Smitty McWhorter tried to slip up behind Dub and snap a picture of the coach snarling and kicking at his players.

Dub wheeled on Smitty, swung at him, kicked dirt at him, and chased the photographer away from the Claybelle bench.

The crowd booed and hissed Smitty. "Get the press outta there!" "Kill that damn photographer!"

Olive Cooper moved down to the row where Betsy and the others were sitting. Olive made room for herself next to Leatha. "Where is Florine tonight?"

"I have been wondering the same thing," Leatha said.

"You should go ask him. You're her closest friend. You might also want to ask him why he has his hand on Eva Jane's thigh!"

Leatha stood up to get a better look at Shady and Eva Jane. She gasped.

Ben said, "Leatha, I'm tryin' to watch a football game."

Leatha sat back down. "Shady Webster is making a fool of himself in public. He's making a fool of Florine in public!"

"Florine's not here," Ben said.

"It's a disgrace!"

"What is?"

"Shady Webster is with Eva Jane McKnight! They're together! He's out on a *date!*"

"Wouldn't that be his business?" Ben said.

Olive said, "Betsy? Eva Jane is your age. What is going through that child's *mind?*"

"I'm not sure," Betsy said, "but you've got to give her high marks for spunk."

Leatha squeezed through the crowd and walked down the steps and out of sight in a tunnel. She had gone beneath the stands to gather up her courage, then she intended to confront Shady and ask him what was going on.

Out on the football field, Eugene Herster, who had been running in every direction except forward for almost two quarters, suddenly shook loose on a broken-field scamper. He went zigzagging through the gray-jerseyed Panthers on his way to a fifty-five-yard touchdown run.

Olive let out a blood-curdling yell. "Run, you little shitass, run!"

Sloppy Herster and Tommy Jack Lucas ran down the sideline, parallel with Pine Knot, and when the little quarterback crossed the goal line, Slop and Tommy Jack piled on him jubilantly in the end zone.

It was 6 to 0, Claybelle.

In all the excitement, the Yellow Jackets missed the try for extra point. A squat little player named Lester Cogwell tried to dropkick the ball through the uprights, but the kick was blocked.

Ben Throckmorton took it out on Olive. "That'll cost us," he said. "Nobody tries a *dropkick,* for Christ's sake! Nobody's dropkicked a football since Jim Thorpe! Goddamn it, Olive, sometimes that husband of yours makes my ass hurt!"

"I couldn't agree more," Olive said. "He's the stupidest idiot I know."

The half ended with Claybelle holding a six-point lead.

The Claybelle band moved onto the field, led by a high-stepping drum major in a tall fur hat. Colonel M. D. Cherryhomes climbed up on a stepladder and raised his baton. In their yellow coats and pants and their yellow policemen's caps, the band members formed a wrinkled S.

A voice on the PA system said the Claybelle band was dedicating its halftime show to John Philip Sousa, whose death had wrenched the hearts of all Americans.

The band played "Nobles of the Mystic Shrine."

Ted looked at Betsy and said, "John Philip Sousa died three years ago."

"It took a while for the news to get here."

Leatha Wardlaw was now in the aisle, stopping to have her exchange with Shady Webster and Eva Jane.

"Good evening," said Leatha. They both smiled at her.

"Not a bad game," Shady said.

"Is Florine feeling well?" Leatha said. "I haven't spoken to her today."

"Far as I know," Shady said.

"Where might she be tonight?"

"Well, let's see." Shady grinned. "I'd say she's either in Fort Worth or Dallas, havin' dinner with a divorce lawyer."

Eva Jane said, "Leatha, I know Florine's a good friend of yours, and I feel badly about what's happened, but sometimes people can't control their emotions. Shady and I are in love."

"That's about the size of it," Shady said. "We decided to

bring it out in the open. Slippin' around was makin' us feel like criminals."

Eva Jane was looking gorgeous in a bright red dress, although she was wearing more jewelry than would normally be seen at Claybelle football games.

"How long has this been going on?" Leatha asked.

Shady glanced at Eva Jane. "What's it been, puddin'—a year? Year and a half?"

"A *year?*" Leatha said, almost losing her serenity. "You have been humiliating Florine for a year?"

"Now, Leatha, what somebody don't know, don't hurt 'em," Shady said. "Nobody knew about us. We were pretty slick, if I say so myself."

"What do you call this—being out here? Being out here in front of Florine's friends? You call this being discreet? *Slick,* as you put it?"

Shady said, "Naw, this is called not givin' a shit no more."

Leatha looked at Eva Jane icily. "You don't have any shame at all, do you?"

"I'm not ashamed to be in love."

Shady said, "Leatha, nobody needs to worry none about Florine. She'll get a hell of a settlement. She'll be the richest woman in Claybelle."

"She better not be!" Eva Jane winced.

"Second richest," said Shady. He stood corrected.

Leatha returned to her seat in a huff.

Shady turned to Lank Allred and Shirley, whose full name was Shirley Watters. "Don't nobody understand love."

"Norma Shearer does," Shirley Watters said. "Norma Shearer finds love every time I go to the picture show—except for that time those Frenchmen cut off her head."

"They came right out and admitted it," Leatha was saying. "They've been cheating on Florine for more than a year!"

"You don't mean it?" Olive said, pouring another glass of polypop for Reverend Tankersley, who was now sitting next to her.

"I am sorry, but I am livid," Leatha said, refusing to stand and applaud the Yellow Jackets as they came back on the field for the second half.

She nudged Ben. "Are you not going to say anything about it?"

Ben said, "Leatha, I'm too old to be surprised by anything anymore, and besides that, I'm at a football game."

She said, "Shady Webster is a lying, cheating, deceitful so-and-so!"

"I can vouch for all that," Ben said. "I've seen him kick his ball out of the rough enough times on the golf course. Let's go, Jackets! Get *serious!*"

The two teams were ready to start the second half, but the Claybelle band was still on the field and was now playing "El Capitan." Dub Cooper shook his fist at Colonel M. D. Cherry-homes.

Slop Herster and Tommy Jack Lucas took it upon themselves to chase the band off the field. They pitched buckets of water on a trombonist and a tuba player.

The drum major in the tall fur hat threatened Slop with his baton, but Slop backhanded the drum major in the mouth, took his baton away from him, placed it between his legs, and pretended to jack off.

Tommy Jack fell down on the grass and clutched his sides.

Slop gave the baton back to the drum major and bowed to the crowd. Reverend Tankersley said a prayer for him.

Leatha and Olive couldn't enjoy the rest of the game.

They kept staring at Shady and Eva Jane and fuming, and discussing the various deformities that God should smite them with.

Reverend Tankersley said that perhaps prayer was called for in this case, too. He said he would go to the concession stand so that on his way back he could get a better look at the woman; it would help him to know how to talk to Jaysus about it.

The reverend came back with two hot dogs, both for himself. Gnawing into one of them, he said:

"Oh, Jaysus, you're in trouble—you ain't never been in the ring with nothin' like this, let me tell you! A dear friend of ours, oh Lord, he is in the clutches of evil. I have seen this racehorse, Jaysus. The devil has give her them long legs what could wrap around a buffalo and squeeze the life out of that scogie, and he has give her them eyes of a cat. Oh, Lord, this woman don't look like she can wait till the paint gets dry! Jaysus, I know you been around, but when you go up against this one, you better have your cleats screwed on, old buddy!"

Olive wiped mustard off the reverend's neck, and he continued:

"Jaysus, I know you believe in fair play, you've refereed all them games of life. I know you want to punish this man for the sin he's wallowed hisself in, but I ask thee not to be cruel —let him keep his oil, Jaysus, for he may giveth to my church, but I ask thee to help Mrs. Webster in her hour of need. Make it a fair fight, Jaysus. Help her to find herself a good Jew lawyer in Dallas."

Claybelle was still leading 6 to 0 late in the fourth quarter, but that's when the Paschal Panthers mounted their most serious drive of the night. They drove eighty yards, all the way down to Claybelle's five-yard line, where they had time for two, maybe three plays.

"Ain't this wonderful?" said Ben Throckmorton, throwing up his hands. "They score, kick the point. We lose, seven-six. We could have had a tie if it hadn't been for Marconi down there tryin' to invent the dropkick!"

Dub Cooper called a time-out. The coach gathered his battle-weary lads around him. Some of them had to push Big 'Un Darly out of the way. Big 'Un had left the press box to go down on the sideline and cheer on the Jackets.

In desperate moments like this, Dub Cooper was noted for his inspirational ways, for his knack of coming up with defensive adjustments.

Now, with his stalwarts gathered around him, Dub said, "Awright, here's the deal. If you let them fuckers score, I'll tell you what—ever one of you little farts is gonna get fifty licks on the bare ass Monday mornin'. You ain't run no laps compared to how many you'll be runnin' next week! I'll run you till your lungs look like a used rubber! Ain't none of you can tackle a turd in a toilet bowl. I'd just as soon be covered with lice as tryin' to coach you gutless, no-good, give-up, snivelin' little mama's-boy queers! Go on out there! Get your butts beat! See if I give a rat's ass fuck!"

The Panthers ran an off-tackle play to Claybelle's one-yard

line. Time for one more play. The Clay Field crowd was on its feet.

Olive Cooper asked Reverend Tankersley if he knew a prayer that would keep those Fort Worth shitasses from scoring.

No one could say for sure what may have happened on the last play. This was when the Claybelle fans in the cars behind the end zone turned off their headlights.

It may well be that a Paschal ballcarrier made it across the goal line, but no official signaled a touchdown, and the gun sounded at the timekeeper's table, and the scoreboard said the final score was Claybelle 6, Paschal 0.

When last seen, the Paschal team and a hundred of their fans were chasing the game officials into a tunnel beneath the stands.

Horns were honking festively in the parking lots as Betsy and Ted and everyone filed out of the stadium.

"All of the games were played in the daytime when I was in high school," Betsy said. "I wonder how we ever beat anybody? Character, I guess."

Big 'Un Darly must have written five thousand words for the Saturday morning paper, counting the game story, two sidebars, and "Sportanic Eruptions."

That he had managed to get all this done between the time the game ended, at 10:30 P.M., and the paper's final deadline around midnight was a tribute to his dedication but possible because of the quality of his prose.

Big 'Un's game story hadn't taken any time at all; he had only put a lead on top of the running.

By BIG 'UN DARLY
Times-Standard Sports
Editor
Purple sage and bronco-bustin' football rode into Claybelle last night, and yippie-ti-yi-yee if the hell-for-leather Yellow Jackets didn't upset the vaunted Paschal Panthers 6 to 0 in an

earthquake of a upset, you bet!

Paschal won the toss and elected to receive. The wind was out of the southeast. Claybelle kick to Paschal who receive. Schilder up middle for 2. Kring off-tackle for 5. Schilder around end for 6. Schilder no gain. Off-sides Jackets. (Bad call).

The game story ran on for two thousand words. It was easy enough for Betsy to see where Big 'Un had deserted the press box for the sideline.

Schilder through guard for 3. Kring hits middle for 7. Ball on Claybelle 19. Schilder fakes pass and

In an effort to save himself time, Big 'Un had written one of his sidebars before the game, a scene-setter.

By CLARENCE DARLY
Times-Standard Staff
Writer

The furor and holy crusade of football is in town again and was in evidence last night at Clay Field, which have a lusteral history to it, like all stadiums buried in a colorful past, which Clay Field harkens to its depths. This have been the place where terminal posts have roamed and scatbacks have dipsy-doodled and mayhem have seen its heroic days of melees.

Big 'Un's other sidebar covered the aftermath of the victory. The byline was that of a fictitious person. The sports editor liked to pretend he was in charge of a larger staff than himself, an elderly desk man named Hack Ables, whose major claim to fame was that he had defeated Hodgkin's disease three times and had appeared in Ripley's "Believe It or Not," and a retired railroad worker named Buster Dybwad, who answered the phone and typed up the bowling, softball, and local golf agate.

In part, the other sidebar read:

By CREW SLAMMER
Times-Standard Staff
Writer

"I ask 'em to dig down deep and they dug," Coach Dub Cooper said in reverence to Claybelle's emotion-packed verdict over the Paschal Panthers last night, who fought like wild dogs but came up short when the chips were on the sled.

"We knowed we could do it and we done it," said Eugene Herster, which scored the game-winner on a 55-yard journey to paydirt.

Coach Cooper asked the Jackets not to get any big heads because it was only the first game and this week they have the Masonic Home Masons coming up. "Them orphans is gonna be a lot tougher than Paschal," he said.

But of course Big 'Un saved his best effort for his column which always ran down the left side of the first page of the sports section. A column was where a writer could stretch out, go for literature.

SPORTANIC
ERUPTIONS
By Big 'Un Darly

You know how it was at the Somme when the little

> corporals limped out of the
> trenches with their purple
> guts in their hands and
> asked the Kaiser if that was
> the best he could do, but if
> you wanted to see a real war,
> you should have been at
> Clay Field last night when
> our brave . . .

Betsy called Big 'Un at home Saturday morning.

She congratulated him on his hard work, but told him his copy might improve if, from now on, it passed across her desk or Ray Fletcher's before it got into the paper.

"I know I need to work on my sims," Big 'Un said.

"Your what?"

"My similes. Man can do a lot with good similes."

Big 'Un thanked Betsy for her interest. He said he'd like to talk to her at greater length sometime, but right now, he had to get the flat fixed on his car so he could drive to Fort Worth to cover the TCU–Howard Payne game.

Betsy and Ted declined Ben's invitation to go to the TCU game. Betsy wanted to preside over her first Sunday edition, and Ted was curious to see how things would go at the station with KVAT picking up the feed of the TCU game from WBAP as Estill Parch acted as host in the studio and inserted the local commercials.

Ben's station carried as much football as possible on Saturdays. There would be a national game coming on from the East at noon. Betsy could do a fair imitation of Graham McNamee: "If Michigan scores, you'll hear a roar." The national game would be followed by the TCU game, or the Southwest Conference Game of the Week, which would sometimes involve TCU. Betsy could do a fair imitation of Kern Tips, who announced the Southwest Conference Game of the Week for the Humble Oil & Refining Company—"He's a rollin' bundle of butcher knives, down at Rice they call him Buckin' Bill Wallace!"

Sunday's *Times-Standard* was the biggest-selling edition of the week. People bought the paper on Sundays when they didn't buy it any other day. People wanted bulk, to get their money's worth.

Betsy planned to add bulk. The paper now had four Sunday sections: front, sports, oil and want ads, comics. With her daddy's money, she was going to add society, food, amusements, and rotogravure. The *Star-Telegram* in Fort Worth had a rotogravure press she could borrow, and she saw it as no problem to fill up these new sections. And the new sections would open up avenues for more advertising. Betsy loathed advertisers, but she understood the economics of the newspaper business. She loathed advertisers because she had never met one who didn't have trouble understanding that he was buying space, not your words.

Wedding announcements, tea dances, and chitchat would take care of the society section. Brine would handle food. Gossip columns and features off the wires would fill up amusements. As for rotogravure, a lot of Anna Sues and Eva Janes would simply have to go to a lot of horse shows.

Bulk for the people.

Betsy worked all Saturday afternoon and into the evening in her office, editing copy, *deciphering* copy. She kept her radio on and casually listened to parts of the TCU game, parts of the SMU game on WFAA, and parts of the Rice-LSU game, a clash of Top Ten teams, on KFJZ.

She listened to most of the scoreboard shows and wondered which scores were correct. Had Columbia beaten Cornell 20 to 13, or had Cornell beaten Columbia 20 to 13?

On Saturday night there was only one show worth tuning in, the one that began with the rapid patter of a tobacco auctioneer, Mr. F. E. Boone of Lexington, Kentucky, or L. A. (Speedy) Riggs of Goldsboro, North Carolina, saying, "Hey, twenty-nine, twenty-nine nine nine nine, thirty, thirty-one, thirty-two, *three,* thirty-three, thirty-three, *four,* thirty-four dollar-bill, dollar-bill, *five,* thirty-five, thirty-five five five, sold American!" Lennie Hayton's Lucky Strike Orchestra then struck up the song that was No. 7 that week among "the songs most requested of the Nation's bandleaders, the best sellers in sheet music and phonograph records, the songs most heard on the air and most played on the automatic coin machines . . . an accurate, authentic tabulation of America's taste in popular music!" On *Your Hit Parade* in that third week of September in 1935, Betsy was disappointed to hear that "East of the Sun" had been knocked out of No. 1 by "I'm in the Mood for Love," but was happy that "Cheek to Cheek" was moving up fast.

The show was signing off in its usual way, and Betsy was half-singing along with Barry Wood and Bea Wain—"So long for a while, that's all the songs for a while"—when the phone rang.

It was Millie Saunders calling from New York.

Betsy and Millie had been speaking over long distance at least once a week since Betsy had moved to Texas.

Millie had big news. "Guess who I'm going out with?" she said.

"Bruno Hauptmann."

"We broke up. I wouldn't slip him a saw. It's a guy who knows you and Ted. We met at Charley, Al and Sally's. The joint's still the same, Betsy. Grimy as ever—full of bums. They all say hello and want to know if you rope steers and things."

"Who's the guy?"

"Chet Weatherford."

"*Our* Chet Weatherford? The FBI's Chet Weatherford?"

"He's a doll. He's been transferred to New York. He called me at the store. He said he didn't know anybody in town and wanted to have a drink. He said you guys had talked about me. Who cares what you said—he called. I've been seeing him every night."

"I thought Chet was married."

"He is, it's great."

"Tell him hello."

"When I'm on top, I will. Betsy, it's a perfect situation. His wife is like nonexistent, get it? He works in the city, she's stashed up in Connecticut with the kids—one of those towns where people go antiquing and do over farms. I'm in love."

"How long have you known him, a *week?*"

"With you and Ted it was love at first sight—and Ted didn't even pack a rod."

As Betsy talked on the phone, Ray Fletcher brought her the layout of Sunday's front page. TCU had defeated Howard

Payne 41 to 0. SMU had defeated North Texas 39 to 0. It was a big opening Saturday for the two universities in the communal surroundings. Betsy was going to cater to the primeval instincts of her readers and put college football on page one, banner on the Horned Frogs. Art from the TCU game. Ray to rewrite Big 'Un's game story, or scrub it up.

Ray left the office after Betsy approved the layout with a nod, and she and Millie went on talking.

"Mill, what would you say if I told you I think I've made a mistake?"

"I'd say you're drunk—you've never admitted a mistake in your life."

"I shouldn't have married Ted."

"You *are* drunk."

It could be said that Betsy wasn't big on introspection. Why waste the time—and for what? You had a life, you lived it. You had a job, you did it. You had something to say, you said it. Betsy didn't care about what might have been, she acted on what *was*. Introspection was for the non-doers, and Ted was introspective. How could she not have known this? And why would he give up writing, give up New York, to move to Texas? You don't leave New York to come to this place if you have any real ambition, she said.

"*You* did," Millie reminded her.

"I came to edit my own newspaper. He came to run a radio station. Radio! Jesus. He says he's going to freelance magazine articles, but his typewriter looks like it's for rent!"

"Betsy, Ted moved to Texas because he loves you. It's what *you* wanted to do. To the ends of the earth—all that business."

"I wouldn't have done it for him."

"Of course not. You're a bitch."

"He wanted to marry an heiress."

A pause, and Millie said, "Oh, my God, I've got Mimi Baker on the phone."

"No, but I was the best he could find."

"Betsy, I have never seen two people more in love than you and Ted. To be honest, it was sickening. What's going on down there? Is the perfect couple having a marital spat? Are you two . . . ? *Uh*-oh."

"What?"

"Bob Walker."

"No," Betsy said, turning the word into three syllables, drawing it out through derisive laughter. "Bob *is* smarter than Ted. He's more aware. I'd forgotten it till I came back here, but Bob's family, Millie. I love him the way I love you. I love Ted the way I'm supposed to love a husband, I *think,* but it's starting to worry me about what he wants to do—what he wants to *be.*"

"Betsy, you ought to be on my end of the line. You'd be screaming with laughter and taking notes. How's the sex at home?"

"It's good. This has nothing to do with sex."

"So what is your *problem,* Bets? You have a career. You have your own newspaper. You have money. You have a handsome husband who loves you—and you can screw Bob Walker any time you want a change of pace."

"I don't want to screw Bob Walker. I spent my *girlhood* screwing Bob Walker. I just wish Ted were smarter . . . quicker . . . something."

"Well, it's your own fault he isn't smarter."

"*My* fault?"

"You shouldn't have fucked his brains out."

Fourteen

IN LATE October, Lank Allred was honored by the Governor of Texas for killing his fifth bank robber. The Governor, Jumpin' Jimmy Allred, was no relation to Lank, but in a speech on the steps of the capitol in Austin he said he would be proud to claim this servant of law and order as his "kissin' cousin." The Governor presented Lank with a scroll and a medal and, in effect, told the Texas Ranger to keep his .45 blazing away at all the trash that was disrupting society.

Lank's fifth victim had come as a result of another setup after another underworld tip. At the Farmers' Loan Bank in Hillsboro, which was halfway between Fort Worth and Waco, Lank had knelt down behind a pay window and waited for the bandits. Three men had entered the bank. One of the men had asked the teller a question. The other two men had pulled out pistols and demanded the money. That's when Lank had raised up with his .45 and, according to a witness, had said, "You came up short today, bubba."

The bandits had been so stunned to see Lank, they had panicked and run for the door. Lank had mowed down one, and the other two had been captured by the Rangers waiting outside.

The two men who had been caught by the Rangers were Joe Ed and Donald Watson, known "police characters" around Dallas. But the dead one had been a young man like "Charley Atkins" in Claybelle, an unarmed victim who had looked to the teller like nothing more than "one of them hobos you see around nowadays."

This had been one too many unarmed victims to suit Betsy, and it gave her a subject with which to launch the front-page column she had decided to write, that subject being the Texas Bankers Association and the $5,000 rewards they were offering for dead bank robbers.

Her daily column was called "Good Morning." It ran from below the masthead down the left-hand side of the page, no picture. The byline was that of Betsy Throckmorton. Not for a second did she consider using her proper name, Elizabeth Hood Throckmorton, on the byline. Elizabeth Hood Throckmorton might look appropriate on a book jacket someday, but for now she was shy, unassuming Betsy Throckmorton.

Her first column started off:

> A word of caution about going in a bank to cash a check these days. Don't leave your hand in your pocket too long —a law enforcement officer may blow your head off, thanks to the Texas Bankers Assn., which might be better named "The Texas Murder Machine."
>
> Far be it from me to criticize a hero like Lank Allred, who is only doing his job, but aren't these rewards being offered by the Texas Bankers making our brave lawmen a little trigger-happy?

It didn't take O. L. Beaton long to come striding into Betsy's office on the day the column ran.

"You ain't the little girl I've watched grow up!" he boomed. "You're the press! You're a menace! The very idea, a 'Texas Murder Machine'! Name me somebody a banker's killed? You make it sound like the banks are runnin' around killin' folks!"

"Your rewards are killing people," Betsy said. "Have you looked at what's going on in this state? Twenty bank robbers have been killed and almost none of them were John Dillinger. Cops are shooting at anybody who looks cross-eyed. Four of Lank Allred's five victims were unarmed."

"Who gives a shit?" the banker shouted. "He didn't know it! A Texas Ranger don't go up to a bank robber and say, 'Excuse me, sir, but are you *armed?* I need to know before I shoot your ass.' The man's doin' his job!"

Betsy calmly said, "I think your rewards are inviting trouble. Suppose this—and don't swell up and pop your suspenders, O. L. Suppose I'm a crooked cop and I want to pick up an easy five thousand dollars. What do I do? I go out and find a poor dumb kid to be a 'lookout' on a bank job. I pay him twenty, thirty, fifty dollars, but there's not going to be a bank job. It's a trick. I'm there to shoot the kid, the 'lookout,' and collect the reward."

O. L. looked amazed. "Lord God, you've got a worse criminal mind than a criminal!"

"It's not so far-fetched."

"You're not sayin' Lank Allred's doin' this, are you? I hope to God you're not sayin' that."

"No, I'm not. I think Captain Allred is only trying to make a reputation for himself. He'd like to be as famous as Frank Hamer. And because you bankers have made it open season on anybody who looks suspicious, he's become even more of a headline grabber. He'll be a *Time* cover any day now."

"Mr. Law and Order is who he is, young lady, and I'll tell you somethin' else. It's my personal opinion that if an old boy lets himself get talked into bein' a lookout on a bank job, even if there *ain't* no bank job, he deserves to get himself killed!"

"Somehow, I knew you would feel that way," Betsy said. "What have we got to lose, anyway—just another hobo, right?"

"Right! Clean up the streets!"

As Betsy got into the rhythm of writing a column five days a week, she found material all around her.

One afternoon she got so worked up over a regional story that moved on the wire, she played it above the 160,000 Ethiopians who were now throwing unripened fruit at Mussolini's dive bombers.

The story was about three Baylor University coeds who had been expelled from the Waco college for smoking cigarettes. The president of Baylor had read out the names of the girls at chapel, but the AP hadn't carried the names.

Betsy called W. M. Keller into her office and ordered him to find out the names of the girls, get their reactions, get other reactions, and, for her own information, find out the name of the AP reporter who hadn't used their names in his story so she would never make the mistake of hiring him.

W. M. had come back to Betsy in an hour with the girls'

names and with a quote from one of them, who revealed that she and her friends hadn't actually been smoking *on* campus but across the street in a drugstore. Another student had reported them.

"What a world," Betsy sighed.

W. M. went on to relate to Betsy that a year ago, the same president of the university had expelled a male student for reading a newspaper in chapel, and two other male students for climbing over benches on the campus lawn.

"Why, that silly Baptist fool!" Betsy said, whirling around to stick paper in her typewriter.

> In the next life, I want to come back as the President of Baylor University so I can expel every student who goes to see a movie in which Bette Davis smokes a cigarette.
> Where is Mussolini when we need him? He could be bombing Baptists!

After this, it was the State Legislature that made Betsy's pace quicken.

The legislators, long known for their rolled-down white socks, prison haircuts, and lack of courage, had buckled under to religious groups and voted out liquor by the drink in Texas. It had been close but the Drys had beat the Wets, 72 to 67, and soon whiskey could only be purchased in package stores.

Swell. Prohibition had finally come to an end in the United States, but the State of Texas had found a way to institute its own form of Prohibition.

Betsy was steaming as she wrote:

> Score another victory for stupidity. The Drys couldn't quite get it through their pious, Bible-bubbled brains that Texans are now going to consume more whiskey than ever since they will be forced to buy it by the bottle instead of by the glass.
> Here come the private clubs again. We

used to call them speakeasies, remember?

And so much for economic growth.

What company or industry will want to move here, or hold a convention here, in this archaic land of the brown paper bag?

Do the backward Fundamentalists seriously outnumber the intelligent people of this state?

I know what's coming next. The rumbles are already out there. Horse racing is doomed—so there goes Arlington Downs, our beautiful thoroughbred track on the Dallas Pike.

And next will come a ban on smoking. Then movies. Then books. Then radio. Then newspapers. Then suntans.

There may not be a revolution until the narrow-minded, tyrannical pedagogues try to pass a law against cornbread.

The day this column ran, Betsy was paid a visit in her office by Reverend H. W. Drews of Claybelle's First Baptist Church. He had finished his radio show on KVAT and dropped by to express his displeasure with her column. Reverend Drews was an unsmiling, dull-looking man in his sixties, starched and stuffy. Had he been a college professor, his course would have been the first one you dropped.

The reverend said to Betsy that given her education and upbringing, she of all people should know and understand the evils of consuming "spiritous beverages."

Betsy was exhaling a Lucky as she said, "What happened to freedom of choice, Dr. Drews?"

"The people have spoken," he said.

"The people didn't have a chance to think about it! The law was railroaded through. A handful of zealots made noise and a cringing bunch of legislators caved in."

Betsy remembered Claybelle's First Baptist Church from her childhood. A fire-and-brimstone preacher named Dr. B. Oras Candlin had assured her she was going to hell at the age of eight. She remembered wondering what she had done that was so bad in so short a life.

Dr. B. Oras Candlin had ruined congregational religion for her. As a child, the only place of worship she had been able to tolerate was the St. James Church, the Negro church, where Warren and Florence had taken her occasionally to hear gospel singing. She hadn't liked even that church after the music stopped.

"I would rather you didn't smoke in my presence," Reverend Drews said. "As the editor of this paper, Betsy, you should be conscious of your image in the community."

Betsy blew smoke away from the minister, and said, "Dr. Drews, I've taken Jesus into my heart. I spoke to him last night."

"You did? That's wonderful."

"Yes. He said Lucky Strike means fine tobacco."

Less than amused, the reverend marched out of the building.

Betsy reached for a black grease pencil and wrote a note to herself on a memo pad: TELL TED—CANCEL THE JERK'S RADIO SHOW!

The college football season was almost turning Ben Throckmorton into a hyena.

The TCU Horned Frogs were undefeated through seven games and were climbing steadily in the National rankings of the Williamson System, a weekly syndicated service that ran in most newspapers in the country, including the *Times-Standard*.

Betsy's daddy was beginning to dream about two things— TCU winning the National Championship in the poll and being invited to play in the Rose Bowl, both of which would be firsts for a school which had suffered the misfortune of being located in Texas. Football Silly was wearing a big button on his lapel, a purple and white button with a photo of a football player on it. The button proclaimed: I AM FOR SLINGIN' SAM BAUGH AND THE FIGHTIN' FROGS.

Ben had seen every TCU game, home and away, as the Frogs had whipped Howard Payne, North Texas, Arkansas,

Tulsa, Texas A&M, Centenary, and Loyola of the South. TCU was now ranked No. 5 in the nation by the poll, the highest the Frogs had ever been ranked.

At the time, there were two other authorities in the country that selected National Champions. Both waited until the end of a season to choose the No. 1 team. *Illustrated Football,* a magazine, chose one, and the other was selected by a professor at the University of Illinois, a man named Frank Dickinson, who had developed a mathematical formula for rating teams in 1926. The Touchdown Club of Chicago annually presented the Knute Rockne Trophy, symbolic of a National Championship, to the team which had best licked the professor's mathematical formula. But neither of these authorities furnished regular week-by-week ratings.

Williamson's weekly ranking had begun to cause hollering, bickering, and cursing among the millions of Football Sillies in America, for in these Thirties the only team sports that mattered were major league baseball, minor league baseball, and college football.

College basketball was still looked upon as a game played by skinny white boys and second-string football players, and pro football was a shabby undertaking, a game played by overweight factory workers and tramp athletes in the baseball parks of Northern industrial cities. Pro football was lucky to get three paragraphs on the sports pages.

Athletes who stood out in individual sports—prizefighters, golfers, tennis champions, jockeys, Indy drivers, hundred-yard sprinters—occupied a special place in the minds and hearts of fans, but where team sports were concerned, there was only college football in the fall of the year, "King Fooball," as Dub Cooper sometimes called it, and now a Fort Worth school was up there in the National rankings. No wonder Ben Throckmorton cavorted around the wire machines on those days he had watched TCU climb from thirty-third to twenty-fifth to nineteenth to eleventh to ninth to seventh to fifth.

Recognition at last—for the area, the state, the conference.

Colleges were supposed to be for academics, but Ben said academics could never do as much for a university as a winning football team. Build a library for you, is all. Who would ever have heard of Notre Dame, he would say, if it hadn't been for football? Or Stanford? Or Southern Cal? Or Michigan? Or Alabama? Or even Yale, by God.

The day the Frogs reached No. 5, Ben said, "They can't stop us now. We've got the greatest football team that ever took the field. Talk about your Four Horsemen, Red Grange, Pug Lund, all that Eastern crap—nobody ever had a passing team like we do. Sam Baugh can knock your dick off at fifty yards! Don't matter who we play in the Rose Bowl—Cal, Stanford, USC, who cares? They can't bring nothin' to the dance."

Standing at the wire machines with Ben that day, Ray Fletcher said, "What are you doing to do about SMU, Ben?"

Not an unreasonable question. The SMU Mustangs were looking even better than TCU. They, too, were undefeated through seven games, but more importantly, they had conquered the Rice Owls on October 19 in the biggest game of the season so far. Rice had rolled into Dallas as the Nation's top-ranked team, and a record crowd of 27,000 had spilled over onto the sidelines at SMU's Ownby Stadium. The teams had played a scoreless tie through three fierce quarters, but the Mustangs had prevailed in the final fifteen minutes and had won, 10 to 0, largely on the efforts of Bobby Wilson, a darting little halfback who had a habit of making big plays for SMU.

Bob Walker had covered the game and his lead had said:

"The best contest in college football would be to match SMU's Bobby Wilson against the wind."

The Mustangs were now ranked No. 3 in the Nation, close behind Ohio State and Notre Dame, and two notches above the Frogs, but Ben's answer to Ray Fletcher was "We've got SMU at home, right out there at TCU Stadium on November 30. How they gonna beat us at home?"

The Saturday of November 30, 1935, was definitely shaping up as the day of a holy war. In a column, Bob Walker had already looked to the future:

> Does anybody have any spare lumber and cement?
> TCU's stadium holds 30,000 people, but if the Horned Frogs and Mustangs

continue unbeaten until November 30, which seems likely, they are going to play a football game on that day with nothing less at stake than the National Championship and a bid to the Rose Bowl.

Since no team in the State of Texas has ever come close to claiming either of these tawdry prizes, one hates to think of how many wild-eyed fans, armed and dangerous, will try to jam into the Fort Worth stadium.

The Governor would do well to start mobilizing the militia now.

The excitement being stirred up in the Southwest Conference was a good thing for Dub Cooper, for it was diverting attention away from his hard-luck Yellow Jackets.

Things had not gone well since Claybelle's opening victory. The following Friday night they had lost to Masonic Home, 59 to 0, but Dub had said, "'At least we didn't quit. I ain't never had a team quit on me. We just couldn't handle them orphans—they have too much to prove, bein' orphans and all."

The Yellow Jackets had traveled to Breckenridge and had lost to the Buckaroos, 47 to 0, and they had traveled to Dallas and lost to the Sunset Bisons, 33 to 0, but Dub had said on his radio show, "I don't see nothin' but progress. That yellow streak on our back is gettin' thinner ever week."

The coach had reminded Claybelle's fans that all three of these losses had been to non-District foes; they didn't mean a thing where District 5-AA was concerned. "We gonna be in the family squabble," he had said to everyone in B's Cafe one day. "You can shit that in your toilet right now."

The Jackets were fortunate not to have sustained any serious injuries in those non-District games, other than to Lester Cogwell. The dropkicker had broken his foot in the Sunset game, but Big 'Un Darly pointed out in the paper that if Lester had made contact with the ball instead of the hard ground, it may not have happened, but what could you say about the cards you were sometimes dealt in life?

Dub had issued a warning on the radio. He had said that if he was Ranger, Eastland, Weatherford, Grandbury, Cleburne, and Palo Pinto, he would be a little bit worried about the Yellow Jackets. Grandbury had then tied the Jackets 6 to 6, but Claybelle had found a way to beat Ranger, 12 to 7, in a game that the coach described as an example of "good old-fashioned guts-up, knucks-down football."

Claybelle's record after six games moved Big 'Un Darly to put the season in perspective in "Sportanic Eruptions."

> We're on the ropes but our boat's not sunk yet. Our season record is 2-1-3, but we're 1-1-0 in District, so looking ahead it's possible we could wind up 6-1-3 or 5-1-4 or 4-2-4, which could get us to the State playoffs, depending on what other teams do as all of us in District 5-AA try to miss the icebergs that lay in our jungle path like puppies on a hardwood floor.

By now, the Claybelle fight song was being played on station breaks at KVAT.

One morning, to the horror and shock of everyone in the Times-Standard Building, Colonel M. D. Cherryhomes and the thirty-four members of the band, all in uniform, had marched into the building and up the stairs to heavy drum beats and the bashing of cymbals.

A problem arose when all of the band members hadn't been able to crowd into the studio where a sound man was going to seek levels and another technician was going to operate the weight-driven lathe that would press the needle into the wax for the recording.

Ted and the band director had refereed a rowdy argument among the kids over which eight or ten of them would form a Dixieland group to play for the recording. Ted had sent all of those not chosen over to B's for as much as they could eat and drink—his treat.

This group had included the drum major in the tall fur hat, to whom Wynelle Stubbs had said, "I'll kick your butt if any birdshit falls out of that thing on my clean floor."

The Dixieland group had played the fight song twice, once for the master and once for the playback, and the kids had made the recording in a studio next door to the studio where Estill Parch had been trying to read the news.

"You wouldn't believe what's going on around here, folks," Estill Parch had said over the air. "My goodness, it's louder in here than it must be over there in Addissty Adababa, or— heh, heh—whichever way you're supposed to pronounce it. I'm sure Mr. Haile Selassie could tell us. Meanwhile, the Jews are in more hot water in Germany. Adolf Hitler announced today that . . ."

October was a good month for the local scandal.

Shady Webster moved out of the house with Florine and into the house with Eva Jane McKnight and her two boys. Shady was spending most of his time calling private schools and military schools around the country to see if he could find an institution that would take the little shits—and soon.

It was beginning to look as if he would have to make a very large endowment to a school in order to get rid of Billy V. and Robbie D.

Shady and Eva Jane had been quite visible around town, and all around Fort Worth, ignoring the angry glances of people who felt sorry for Florine. Florine had been secluded for a while but had finally adopted the attitude that she was well rid of the asshole.

The three of them had been destined to meet in public eventually, and it happened at Shadowlawn Country Club at the Sunday afternoon tea dance.

Leatha had talked Florine into going to the club with her and Ben, and Betsy and Ted.

Shady and Eva Jane were on the dance floor when they arrived, and Florine saw them immediately. They were dancing a two-step to the music of Booty and Them Others. Booty was singing:

There's a feeling I can't lose.
Muddy water in my shoes.
When I get those Mississippi Delta blues.

"Oh, you poor thing," Leatha said. "I had no idea they would be here."

"Excuse me for a minute," Florine said. She marched straight toward them.

Shady saw his wife coming and said, "Uh-oh. Paging Mr. Fault. Mr. At Fault."

Florine addressed him in the middle of the dance floor, as several of the members watched.

"I thought you might want to know I'm filing suit tomorrow, big shot. You can speak to me through my attorney from now on. I'm only sorry I didn't do it sooner. We wasted some good years."

Eva Jane, unmoved and unshaken, said, "Don't go to court, Florine. I've been through it. You and Shady can settle things among yourselves. You'll come out better off. Shady will be very generous."

Florine threw her head back and laughed. "Why, you little cunt! You're going to stand here and tell me what *I* should do?"

"Call me names if you want to. I'm only trying to help."

Shady said, "Let me explain something, Florine. All them oil wells are divided up in different corporations, different partnerships. If you think a Jew lawyer's gonna get you half of them oil wells, you're wrong. Shady Webster don't own nothin' in his own name."

"See?" said Eva Jane calmly. "Texas is a community property state, Florine. When I split up with Bubba Dean, I was lucky I got to keep my grandmother's silver."

"I'm gonna do right," Shady said. "I'm gonna take care of you. You're gonna be a rich woman, Florine—richer'n a Goddamn Baptist preacher with a circus tent. All we got to do is keep them Jews out of it. You can trust Mr. Fault."

"Mister who?" Florine said.

"Mr. At Fault. That fellow you been livin' with all these years."

"Very funny," Florine said. She went to the buffet table and came back with a large bowl of fruit cocktail.

"Naw, you ain't gonna do that, are you?" said Shady. "Not here at the club."

"It will make me feel better."

"This is my best coat."

Florine started to dump the bowl of fruit cocktail on Shady's head, but stopped.

"What am I doing?" She laughed. "I'm acting like I give a shit."

Florine took the bowl of fruit cocktail back to the buffet and joined Betsy and the others at a table.

Shady and Eva Jane left the club. Shady grinned and waved at everybody as they were walking out. "This is my lucky day," he said to Eva Jane. "It could have been acid."

November brought a few cold days but no blue northers. It would be topcoat weather one day, sweater weather the next, shirtsleeves the next, then back to topcoats. This added to Ted Winton's confusion as to what the well-dressed hobo should wear.

Ted was going to spend the night in Claybelle's hobo camp.

He had spoken to an editor at *Collier's* about doing an article on transients. The editor had liked the idea.

Betsy was delighted that Ted wanted to get back to his typewriter. The radio station was running smoothly.

The night he was going to the hobo camp for the first time, he asked Warren Richards to help him select an outfit.

If he could look like a hobo himself, it would put his subjects at ease.

"What you gonna do about the way you talk?" Warren asked.

"People in the East are out of work, too."

Warren supplied Ted with a pair of his frazzled coveralls, two faded sweatshirts, and an old pair of brown shoes on which the toes had been cut out to make room for Warren's corns.

"Beats anything I ever saw," Warren said. "Man wants to go in the jungle. Most folks wants to get *out* the jungle."

Ted got dressed in his hobo costume and went in the kitchen

to ask Florence what he could take with him in the way of food.

"Have mercy on *me!*" said Florence, gaping at Ted.

She poked around in the cupboard and gave him three cans of salmon and a box of crackers. This was what she had seen a hobo buy at the A&P one day.

Warren gave him a black wool cap to wear and a blanket to take along.

As he was leaving the house, Ted looked at himself in a full-length mirror. "Portrait of a Yale man," he said.

He drove around the square on his way to the hobo camp. The Tivoli was showing a new double feature: Sylvia Sidney and Herbert Marshall in *Accent on Youth,* and *Every Night at Eight* with George Raft and Patsy Kelly. The Liberty was showing an old double feature: *Murder in the Fleet* with Robert Taylor and Jean Parker, and *Mark of the Vampire* with Bela Lugosi and Lionel Barrymore.

He parked at the Santa Fe depot, about a hundred yards from the camp. He walked over to the camp and began to wander around among the tin sheds and dugouts and crate-box shelters in which two hundred people were trying to subsist.

Tiny fires burned in the camp. Rags and clothing flapped on clotheslines that were strung from one shed to another.

He stood near a campfire for a moment. A man was strumming a ukulele and singing in a halfhearted voice as four boys and an older woman looked at the fire. Ted listened to the man sing the mournful, lilting anthem that Jimmie Rodgers had written for hobos.

> *Though my pocketbook is empty,*
> *And my heart is full of pain,*
> *I'm a thousand miles*
> *Away from home,*
> *Waitin' for a train.*

He walked on to another campfire and invited himself to sit down with three older men who were making cigarettes out of tree bark.

For all of his trouble, Ted's costume hadn't come close to

making him look like a hobo. He immediately confessed that he was a journalist working on an article.

Ted got the men talking, about the jobs they couldn't find nowadays, the families they had lost, the land they had lost, their war wounds, about a society that had forgotten them.

A hobo named Milton said he had seen the worst dust storm God had ever bestowed on Oklahoma. Big old brown clouds two hundred feet high. Folks had to dig their way out of their houses.

Milton said, "God give us dust storms because He don't want nobody to forget what the Thirties looked like."

The hobo named Albert said he had seen the worst tornado God had ever sent to Brownwood.

"I seen that twister pick up a ice wagon and sling it four blocks," he said. "You can tell when them things are coming. Might be high noon but the sky turns black as midnight. Everything gets still. Then here it comes. A bad tornado sounds like a hundred freight trains comin' down on your head. Your twisters always come out of the southwest. That's why you don't ever see rich folks livin' on the southwest side of a town. It's a fact."

Rodney, another hobo, said, "How's a twister know where it's at?"

"It knows," Albert said with assurance.

Ted passed around the canned salmon and crackers.

The hobos ate it all, but Milton was disappointed that Ted hadn't thought to bring whiskey and cigarettes.

There were these two old boys named Mister Man and Brains who came to the camp occasionally, and they always brought whiskey and smokes, Milton remarked.

"Who?"asked Ted.

"Mister Man and Brains is all I know 'em by," Milton said.

Sounded like a comedy act, Ted said. Lum and Abner. Honeyboy and Sassafras. Mister Man and Brains.

"Do they work for the Salvation Army?"

"Could be," Milton said, "although I ain't knowed the Salvation Army to be fond of whiskey."

Ted asked what the fellows looked like.

Of all people, the descriptions curiously seemed to fit Sloppy Herster and Tommy Jack Lucas.

Ted mentioned this to Betsy after he returned home the next morning—how there was a possibility that her two old classmates were doing social work in the hobo camp but were going by the names of Mister Man and Brains for whatever arcane reasons they might have.

Betsy said, "Mister Man is an old colored term. It means the Boss. Brains sounds suitable for Tommy Jack."

Then she laughed as something occurred to her. If Slop and Tommy Jack *were* hanging around the hobo camp, she said, they were probably trying to recruit orphans for Dub Cooper's football program.

Made sense to Betsy.

PART THREE

Stuff Happens

Fifteen

———

THE CIGARETTE smoke was thick enough to dish up and serve as a soufflé. Betsy was smoking at her desk. Ben smoked as he paced back and forth.

"Daddy, who's the editor around here?"

"Who's the owner?"

"Who's the heiress?"

They were arguing about journalism, specifically about a story Betsy wanted to run and Ben wanted to kill.

It was the second week in November and Shadowlawn Country Club's Fall Championship, a partnership golf tournament, had been played over the weekend and had ended in what some people might have said was disarray but others would have said was a cheating scandal.

The winners of the tournament had appeared to be Shady Webster and O. L. Beaton. They had posted a best-ball score of eight under par for the forty-four holes of play.

It would have been a normal thirty-six-hole tournament, of course, if it hadn't been for the unhappy design of the Shadowlawn golf course. Because of the eleven-hole layout, a complete round of golf at Shadowlawn was considered to be twenty-two holes, unlike the eighteen holes a person would play on almost any other golf course in the world.

Shady and O. L. had beaten the field by six strokes, and they were drinking whiskey in the clubhouse and congratulating each other when they heard they had been disqualified.

A dozen members had come off the course to testify that they had seen Shady and O. L. kicking their golf balls out of the rough and into the fairways, tossing their golf balls back in bounds from the other side of fences, and lifting their golf balls out of sand traps and ditches.

The oilman and banker protested. They said they had only been taking the free drops to which they had been entitled under the "casual water" rule of golf.

The tournament committee, of which Ben Throckmorton was a member, had reminded Shady and O. L. that it hadn't rained in Claybelle in over a month, and it should have gone without saying that the club didn't have a watering system. What "casual water"?

Shady got mad and accused certain members of acting out of envy and jealousy. "Don't none of you like it because I've went out and found myself some young pussy," he said. "Tell the truth!"

It hadn't mattered to Ben who won. He and his partner, Ray Fletcher, had finished far back in the tournament. They had been in contention until they both triple-bogeyed the same hole, Shadowlawn's intimidating fifth, which required a carry of 165 yards over a dry creek, piles of rocks, and nests of assorted reptiles.

Owing to the disqualification, the winners' silver trophies had been awarded to the team of Buck Blanchard and Buster Dybwad of the *Times-Standard*'s sports department, but they had only been champions for a few moments.

It had been brought to the committee's attention that Buster Dybwad was only an honorary member of the club, as were others on the paper's sports staff. Buster played golf free, but he wasn't a social member; therefore, he was ineligible for club championships. "The freeloadin' dipshit don't even pay for his lunch," Shady Webster said to the committee.

The trophies had wound up in the hands of Hansel Thompson from the drugstore and his partner, Errett Babcock, the co-owner and butcher of Sterch & Babcock's Meat Market.

Shady had tried to argue that Hansel Thompson should also be disqualified for only carrying four golf clubs in his bag, a spoon, five-iron, nine-iron, and putter.

"Lightens his load," Shady said. "If the old fart carried a full set like the rest of us, he'd die of a stroke."

Betsy had rewritten Buster Dybwad's story, moving the disqualifications into the lead. She was planning to box the story prominently under a headline that said:

**BANKER AND OILMAN
CAUGHT CHEATING IN
LOCAL GOLF TOURNAMENT**

Ben had guessed his daughter would do something like this, which was why he was in her office now.

"You can't run the story and that's that," Ben was saying.

"It's true, isn't it?"

"Unfortunately, yes."

"Then give me one reason why I can't run it."

"I'll give you three." Ben was looking extremely serious. "Shady and O. L. are friends of mine. Anna Sue is a friend of yours."

"Everybody in town's going to be talking about it, anyhow."

Ben said, "Everybody in town talking about it and everybody in town seeing it in print are two different things."

Ben put the copy on her desk. He'd gone to the back shop and snatched it off Squirrely McCall's linotype machine.

"Shady and O. L. can deal with the gossip. They can't deal with the print. I want you to rewrite the story. Just say who won and that two teams were disqualified over a misinterpretation of the rules. Something like that."

Betsy fought back a laugh. "A misinterpretation of the rules? Climbing over a fence and throwing your ball back in the fairway?"

"Damn it, honey, most people cheat on a golf course. They don't even think of it as cheating. The game's hard enough to play without the rulebook. I'm not gonna ruin their lives over this."

Betsy took a long moment to think about her journalism ethics. "Do I get the society section?" she said.

"I guess so."

"Food?"

"I suppose."

"Amusements?"

"It's a blackmail deal!"

"Rotogravure?"

"My own daughter!"

"I want them all *now,* Daddy."

"I've told you what all that's gonna cost."

"We'll make money in the long run."

"All right, you win," Ben said, going to the door in a slump. "Sometimes I wish *I* had me for a friend."

"They're lucky people."

"Now I got to go argue with your husband."

"What about?"

"Aw, he's trying to jack around with my nighttimes."

The charts were on the wall in Ted's office at KVAT.

Ted stood and Ben sat while they talked. Dot, a secretary, brought them both coffee. She told Ben he smoked too much. Ben told Dot she ate too much.

"The only change I think we should make on Monday night is at eight-thirty," Ted said, using a pointer on the chart. "I'd like to replace *Those We Love,* which precedes the *Lux Radio Theater,* with Raymond Gram Swing. No need to have two dramas back-to-back. Doesn't this make sense to you?"

"*Those We Love* is one of my favorite shows," Ben said. "Have you talked to Betsy about this?"

"Not really."

"She likes it, too. I've heard her talk about how sophisticated it is. Too sophisticated for radio, she says. We better leave it alone. Betsy loves Aunt Emily. Everybody loves Aunt Emily."

"Aunt Emily?"

"Everybody's favorite character on *Those We Love.* Personally, I'd put Agnes Ridgway up there with Carlton Morse."

"Who is Agnes Ridgway?"

"She writes it."

Ted moved on to Tuesday night.

No worries with *Fibber McGee and Molly* or *Jimmie Fidler's Hollywood Gossip,* but there might be a possibility for improvement at eight o'clock, he said. He had in mind picking up *Information Please* from NBC-Blue and substituting it for *Big Town.*

Big Town starred Edward G. Robinson as Steve Wilson, the crusading editor of the *Illustrated Press,* and Claire Trevor as Lorelei Kilbourne, the paper's wisecracking society editor who somehow seemed to uncover corruption behind every door she opened. Sponsored by Ironized Yeast, the show began each week with an announcer saying, "Freedom of the press is a flaming sword—use it justly, hold it high, guard it well!"

Ben looked hurt. "We can't lose *Big Town,* Ted."

"It's pretty corny. I know Betsy likes Lorelei Kilbourne, but—"

"Ted!" Ben stopped him, his voice sounding a warning. "Betsy thinks she *is* Lorelei Kilbourne."

On to Wednesday, a blockbuster evening.

Even Ted, now a radio executive but only a casual radio listener, had enough sense not to mess with Wednesday night.

Wednesday night began with *One Man's Family*, written by Carlton E. Morse, brought to you by Tenderleaf Tea. It was dedicated to the mothers and fathers of the Younger Generation and to their Bewildering Offspring. Father Barbour was usually sitting by the fire muttering, "Yes, yes, Fanny." Paul —writer, aviator, war hero—was usually in the library wondering how to break up with Beth Holly without breaking Beth Holly's heart. Hazel, a widow, was usually in the kitchen. Jack was usually up at the Sky Ranch with Hank and Pinky. Claudia was usually going out to dinner with Nicholas Lacy, unsure of her feelings about him. And Clifford was usually down on the seawall daydreaming about Hong Kong. The show seemed destined to run for a quarter of a century, all the way to Chapter 3256, Book 134.

Time, then, for the *Raleigh and Kool Show* with Tommy Dorsey, that Sentimental Gentleman of Swing . . . his trombone, and his orchestra. Next came Fred Allen's *Town Hall Tonight*, with Portland Hoffa, Harry Von Zell, Peter Van Steedan's orchestra, Kenny Delmar, and a cast of Allen creations: Senator Claghorn, Titus Moody, Mrs. Nussbaum, Falstaff Openshaw, and One Long Pan, the Chinese detective.

This was followed by *Mr. District Attorney*, who on behalf of Vitalis, Ipana, and Sal Hepatica, promised not only to prosecute all persons accused of crimes perpetrated within his county but to defend with equal vigor the rights and privileges of all its citizens. As Vicki Vola stood ably by in the role of Miss Miller, Len Doyle, as Harrington, would say, "Let me at him, Chief!" But Jay Jostyn would restrain him. "No, Harrington. We're going . . . *downtown*."

A change of pace, then, as KVAT's listeners heard: "Evenin', folks, how y'all?" Time for *Kay Kyser's Kollege of Musical Knowledge* and an array of vocalists: Ginny Simms, Harry

Babbitt, Sully Mason, and Merwyn A. Bogue, better known as Ish Kabibble.

Wednesday night's prime shows concluded with the clatter of machine guns, the screeching of tires, and a voice for Palmolive soap that said, "Calling all cars, calling all cars! Be on the lookout for a man, thirty-five, scar over his left cheek, wanted for murder and robbery." And the calmer voice of Phillips H. Lord said, "Now picture our setting as a special office, turned over to *Gangbusters* by Lewis J. Valentine of the New York City police . . ."

"I can't remember the last time I went out on Wednesday night," Ben said, admiring the Wednesday lineup on Ted's chart.

Ted had a notion about Thursday night. Why, he wondered, should an evening of splendid music—*Show Boat, The Kate Smith Hour,* Bing Crosby's *Kraft Music Hall*—be climaxed with a horror show like *I Love a Mystery,* a show that required you to suspend so much belief? Might it not be better if—

Ben interrupted him again. "Now you're talkin' war, son."

Jack Packard, Doc Long, and Reggie Yorke had become Ben's buddies as they roamed the globe for the A-1 Detective Agency, prowling through one creepy mansion after another, solving murders that occurred every time a baby cried or an organ played the Brahms Lullaby. Ben's favorite adventure on *I Love a Mystery* had been "The Island of Skulls," but Betsy was partial to "The Decapitation of Jefferson Monk."

"You're firm on this?" said Ted.

"I'm savin' you a divorce," Ben said.

Friday night, Ted felt, was somewhat overloaded with sports commentary, what with Grantland Rice and Ford Bond on the *Cities Service Concert,* followed later by Bill Stern's *Colgate Newsreel,* but the evening was saved by *First Nighter* with Barbara Luddy and Les Tremayne.

No recommendations, and none for Saturday night, but he suggested they take a hard look at Sunday.

Ben said, "I don't want to take too hard a look at it. Sunday gets Hoopers like Wednesday."

"It could do better."

"Can't do any better than Jack Benny, Edgar Bergen and

Charlie McCarthy, Ozzie and Harriet, and Walter Winchell —no way."

"You've made my point," said Ted as Ben downed the rest of his coffee. "What we have here is a night of comedy and show business. But look what's blocking these shows in front. Look what's intruding in the middle. Look what's killing them at the end."

Ben didn't have to look. He wasn't about to cancel *The Shadow*. Cancel Lamont Cranston? A man of wealth, a student of science, a master of other people's minds? A man who devoted his life to righting wrongs, protecting the innocent, and punishing the guilty? A man who used advanced methods that might ultimately become available to all law enforcement agencies, a man never seen, only heard, as haunting to superstitious minds as a ghost, as inevitable as a guilty conscience? Cancel an amateur criminologist ably assisted in conquering evil by his friend and constant companion, the lovely Margo Lane? Ted must kidding.

And Ben wasn't going to get rid of *Manhattan Merry-Go-Round* either.

"Betsy likes that song."

Ted said, "Yes, I know, but the show itself—"

"She'll claw our eyes out."

"We'd better keep it," Ted said, upon reflection.

On more than one late evening in New York, Ted had heard Betsy and Millie Saunders harmonizing as they hopped from one saloon to another.

Jump on the Manhattan Merry-Go-Round.
We're touring alluring New York town.
Broadway to Harlem, a musical show.
The orchids that you rest at your radio.
We're serving music, songs, and laughter.
Your happy heart will follow after.
And we won't be home until morning
On the Manhattan Merry-Go-Round.

"Music does blend with comedy and show business," Ted said, "which brings up ten o'clock. It would seem to me that if we were to pick up Phil Spitalny's All-Girl Orchestra, the *Hour of Charm,* it would top off the evening more suitably than—"

Another gesture from Ben stopped Ted a third time. "Lose *Grand Central Station?*"

Ben had heard Betsy and Millie do their routine. So had Ted, for that matter.

Betsy: "As a bullet seeks its target, shining rails in every part of our great country are aimed at Grand Central Station, heart of the nation's greatest city."

Millie: "Drawn by the magnetic force of the fantastic metropolis, day and night great trains rush toward the Hudson River, sweep down its eastern bank for a hundred and forty miles, flash briefly by the long red row of tenement houses south of a Hundred and Twenty-fifth Street . . ."

Betsy: " . . . dive with a roar into the two-and-a-half-mile tunnel which burrows beneath the glitter and swank of Park Avenue, and then . . ."

Both: "Grand Central Station! Crossroads of a million private lives—a gigantic stage on which are played a thousand dramas daily."

Ben Throckmorton put out his cigarette as he stood up. "This has been very productive, Ted."

"It has?"

"I think we got quite a bit accomplished."

Ben left the building in a good mood that day. He'd kept his nighttimes intact.

On the morning of Tuesday, November 26, the bells dinged on the AP machine and the Williamson football rankings began to be displayed on the cylinder of yellow paper. "God damn, they finally came to their senses," Ben yelled out. He had been waiting for the story to move.

Ben ripped the story off the machine, a story which said TCU had unseated SMU that week as the No. 1 team in the Nation. He walked all around the newsroom saying, "How 'bout *this?* TCU number one, SMU number two, Rice number eight! Good God-a-mighty!"

The race for the National Championship in 1935 was more turbulent than usual. Rice had begun the season with the No.

1 ranking and held it for four weeks, until the Owls lost to SMU in mid-October. This put Ohio State on top. But on November 2, the Buckeyes lost a rollicking game to Notre Dame, 18 to 13, on a last-minute pass from Bill Shakespeare to Wayne Millner. Notre Dame went to No. 1, but on the following Saturday the Irish were upset by Northwestern. Now SMU went to No. 1. The Mustangs were still as undefeated as TCU, but over the past three weeks the Horned Frogs had been winning their games in a more impressive fashion, and the poll acknowledged it. Sam Baugh was throwing three touchdown passes a game, and it was the view of "Sportanic Eruptions" that Jimmy Lawrence was lugging the football "like a bee-zerk mental patient with mice in his pants." TCU looked invincible, as Ben saw it, and Betsy's daddy was doing a little dance as he entered her office with the wire copy in his hand.

"We're number one," Ben said. "If this ain't a page-one banner, I've never seen one."

"It'll be old by tomorrow." Betsy looked up from trying to make sense out of a Cloyd Bennett oil column. "The *Evening Star-Telegram* will have it this afternoon. It'll be all over the radio tonight. I'll put it out front, but it's not the lead."

"What's a better lead?"

"The Japanese have entered Peking, for one thing."

"Chinks over *football?*" Ben spun in a circle. "Let me tell you something, honey. They can strike oil on the square, right out here! They can kill Vernon Castle again! The Japs can *eat* Peking! You're not gonna get a bigger story than this—not around here, not *this* week!"

This was, in fact, the week of the long-awaited TCU-SMU game.

Ben raised his voice. "What I've got in my hand right here says the Texas Christian University Horned Frogs from Fort Worth, Texas, are the number one football team in the whole Goddamn United States!"

To keep Ben from having heart failure, Betsy led the paper with that news.

All 30,000 seats in TCU's stadium for the SMU game had been sold weeks before, and when the school found a way to add 4,500 more seats by erecting temporary bleachers in both end zones, these tickets were gone an hour after it was announced on the radio that they were available.

Rumors persisted that scalpers in Fort Worth and Dallas were asking—and getting—a hundred dollars for a ticket to Saturday's game.

The game was a page-one banner the rest of the week, not only in the *Times-Standard* but in the *Star-Telegram* and *Press* in Fort Worth and in the *Journal, Morning News,* and *Times Herald* in Dallas.

On Wednesday night, the Rose Bowl announced it would officially invite the TCU-SMU winner to Pasadena to play Stanford, which had again won the Pacific Coast Conference. Betsy wrote a banner that said: ROSE BOWL AT STAKE AS NATION'S FOOTBALL SPOTLIGHT WHIRLS TO FORT WORTH.

As the tension and suspense continued to build, there was news that swarms of Hollywood and Broadway celebrities were coming to the game, that famous coaches from around the country were coming, among them Minnesota's Bernie Bierman, Northwestern's Pappy Waldorf, and Princeton's Fritz Crisler; that the game would be broadcast coast-to-coast by Bill Stern for Mutual and by Kern Tips for NBC; and that the Nation's sportswriting elite would be in the press box: their worships Grantland Rice of the *New York Sun,* Paul Gallico of the *New York Journal-American,* Joe Williams of the *New York World-Telegram,* Arch Ward of the *Chicago Tribune,* and Bill Cunningham of the *Boston Globe,* among others.

Big 'Un was as excited about the big-time sportswriters coming to the game as he was about the game itself. He was already wondering how he was going to write his own story while he was trying to watch Grantland Rice type.

Every feature angle of the game was exhausted by every paper.

In the *Times-Standard,* even Carolyn Moseley's society pages were filled with stories about the fans who were pouring into Fort Worth for the big event. Carolyn's idea of news was to report that Mr. and Mrs. Alpheus Hammond of Rising Star would be the guests of Mr. and Mrs. H. G. Tucker, 3702

Pembroke, and were looking forward to Brenda Tucker's tamale pie.

On Friday morning, Betsy plastered the game over the entire front page under a banner which said: HIGHEST HONORS IN SOUTHWEST HISTORY ON LINE TOMORROW.

The season records of the teams were set in large boldface type.

TCU (10–0)			SMU (10–0)	
41	Howard Payne	0	39 North Texas	0
28	North Texas	11	60 Austin College	0
13	Arkansas	7	14 Tulsa	0
13	Tulsa	0	35 Washington (Mo.)·	6
19	Texas A&M	14	10 Rice	0
27	Centenary	7	18 Hardin-Simmons	6
14	Loyola (La.)	0	20 Texas	0
28	Baylor	0	21 UCLA	0
28	Texas	0	17 Arkansas	6
27	Rice	6	10 Baylor	0

Pictures of every starting player adorned Betsy's front page, and the lineups were also presented in large black type.

SATURDAY'S PROBABLE STARTERS

	TCU				SMU	
No.	Player	Wt.	Position	Wt.	Player	No.
30	Willie Walls	180	L.E.R	185	Maco Stewart	21
15	Drew Ellis	200	L.T.R.	210	Maurice Orr	49
38	Cotton Harrison	190	L.G.R.	185	Billy Stamps	43
22	Darrell Lester	215	C.	190	Art Johnson	26
9	Tracy Kellow	172	R.G.L.	195	Iron Man Wetsel	40
11	Wilson Groseclose	210	R.T.L.	210	Truman Spain	47
25	Walter Roach	185	R.E.L.	185	Bill Tipton	23
45	Sam Baugh	182	Q.	195	Johnny Sprague	36
5	Dutch Kline	178	L.H.	150	Bobby Wilson	11
8	Jimmy Lawrence	185	R.H.	165	Jackrabbit Smith	19
33	Tillie Manton	190	F.	180	Bob Finley	27

Possible Substitutions: TCU—L. D. Meyer (39), end; Solon Holt (43), tackle; Glenn Rogers (35), guard; Rex Clark (50), Scott McCall (36), Harold McClure (6), halfbacks. SMU—Charlie Baker (42), Paschal Scottino (48), guards; Buster Raborn (13), center; Harry Shuford (37), fullback; Shelley Burt (20), Bob Turner (24), halfbacks.

Coaches: TCU—Leo R. (Dutch) Meyer, head coach; Bear Wolf, Howard Grubbs, assistants. SMU—Madison (Matty) Bell, head coach; Vic Hurt, Charlie Trigg, assistants.

Referee: Abb Curtis (Texas University). Kickoff: 2 p.m.

"May their names live in the eternity of gridiron treasure," Big 'Un Darly said admiringly.

Despite all of the attention the papers were giving the game, Bob Walker managed to score a mild scoop in his column Friday morning in the *Dallas Journal,* a column which no longer appeared under its old head of "Fan's Fare," but had been given a more unique name: "Bob Walker."

His idea.

Bob's column that morning began:

> You know the winner of tomorrow's big game is going to the Rose Bowl on New Year's Day to meet Stanford, but what you don't know is that the loser is going to be invited to play the LSU Tigers in the Sugar Bowl in New Orleans. Not a bad consolation prize, and more than fitting in so far as this is the first time in all of college football history that two great teams, ranked No. 1 and No. 2 in the Nation, have collided so late in a season with so much at stake.

Betsy phoned Bob Friday afternoon. "How did you know about the Sugar Bowl?"

"The more I thought about it, the more it made sense," he said. "I called a guy I know in New Orleans. He's on the Sugar Bowl committee. He cleared his throat once too often. 'Well, Bob, as you know . . .' I had him. They're going to announce it after the game."

"You might have shared it with me."

"I didn't think about it, to be honest."

"That's nice."

"Actually, I think about you a lot—I just didn't think about your newspaper."

"How's Anna Sue?"

"Anna Sue Beaton?"

"Never mind."

"What do you think of the column head?"

"I was going to ask. Why did you pick that name?"

"I thought about 'Ring Lardner,' but somebody told me it had been taken."

"Will we see you tonight?"

"Wouldn't miss it."

The place to be on Friday before the big game was the Fort Worth Club. Ben Throckmorton had reserved a large table in the ballroom, the party to consist of himself and Leatha, Betsy and Ted, the Beatons, Bob and Anna Sue, and Florine Webster.

Leatha had urged Ben to include Florine, and Ben had, although he didn't want to have to worry about Florine causing a scene if Shady and Eva Jane were there. He had a football game to concentrate on.

"Florine would never embarrass herself, or us, at a place like the Fort Worth Club."

"I'm trusting you to ride shotgun," Ben said.

Betsy and Ted drove to Fort Worth alone and got to the dinner party late. Betsy had been detained at the paper, trying to convince Ray Fletcher that the China Clipper landing safely on its maiden flight to Manila was worth more than two paragraphs on page fourteen.

They parked three blocks from the Fort Worth Club building and walked up Seventh Street, beneath a flapping banner that said BEAT SMU, which was strung over the street from Ellison's Furniture Store to Wally Williams' fashion shop.

Every window within sight had a statement to make about the big game, if only a comment on the dubious ancestry of a Dallas person.

The mannequins in the windows at The Fair were dressed in the purple and white of TCU and the red and blue of SMU, and they were joined by large cut-out photos of TCU and SMU players that had been pasted on plywood and were stiff-arming and growling at window-shoppers.

Betsy imagined she would have enough drinks tonight to press her conspiracy theory on O. L. Beaton again.

She wasn't sure she believed it herself—and Ted thought it was preposterous—but it would make interesting conversation.

Her theory *now* was that somebody was going into the hobo camps and recruiting reckless, uneducated young men to be "lookouts" on phony bank jobs so *Lank Allred* could kill them and collect the $5,000 rewards from the Texas Bankers Association.

"Nobody could have such little regard for human life," Ted said as they were waiting for an elevator in the lobby of the Fort Worth Club. "Least of all a law enforcement officer."

"Boy, you still don't know Texas very well, do you?" Betsy said. "Hobos aren't human beings to Lank Allred or most people down here."

"What are they?"

"Germs."

The most compelling argument against Betsy's conspiracy theory was the one she made to herself.

Lank Allred was a Texas Ranger.

The club was jammed. Purple and white crepe paper crawled around the ceilings and streamed down door facings. Only the enormous Remingtons and Russells covering most of the walls had been spared a TCU motif.

Ben's reserved table was in a corner, far removed from the bandstand. They wouldn't be annoyed by the Travis Glenn Quintet with Genevieve Reed on vocals. At the moment, the vocalist was having a swell time with "She's a Latin from Manhattan."

Betsy hated the Latin beat and wouldn't have minded seeing Carmen Miranda sent to the Big House.

Bob Walker received a kiss on the mouth from Betsy before she sat down.

"Do you always have to kiss her?" Anna Sue asked Bob.

"She kissed *me*. I don't mind."

"*I* mind!"

"You can kiss somebody if you want to," Bob said. "Grantland Rice is over there."

"Is he really?" Betsy said alertly.

Bob Walker pointed out Grantland Rice, who was dining at

a table with Paul Gallico and Joe Williams. The illustrious writers were being entertained by two rich-looking Texas couples, friends of Amon Carter's.

Amon Carter himself, graying and distinguished, was at the head of another table in a large group of people that included the parents of Sam Baugh, who had driven in from Sweetwater and were staying at the club as guests of the publisher.

"Excuse me a second," Betsy said to all. "I have to go do some business."

Betsy circulated through the ballroom, stopping to say hello to Amon Carter and meet Sam Baugh's parents, and then she went to the Grantland Rice table and introduced herself.

Rice was dressed sportily in a hound's-tooth jacket, sweater, and bow tie. He rose to shake hands with Betsy, a smile on his pink, pudgy face.

She said, "Mr. Rice, I'm the editor of a newspaper you've never heard of, but I want to buy a copy of your game story tomorrow. Can you tell me who I should contact at the syndicate, or . . . maybe we can reach an agreement right now. Money is no object."

"You're a newspaper editor?" Rice said, surprised.

"It's my daddy's paper, the *Claybelle Times-Standard.* I used to work at *Time,* but I've moved back home. I'm the editor-in-chief, which means I get to holler at people."

"Where is Claybelle?"

"It's twenty-five miles from here—that way. Go to TCU Stadium . . . and keep going."

"The newspaper business is looking up." Rice grinned.

Betsy said, "I just got this idea a minute ago. This game is the biggest thing that's ever happened around here. I'd rather run your story than anybody else's. I think it would be a great stunt for our paper."

"I'm flattered," Rice said. "Nobody else has asked me. But you can't buy it, young lady. I'll give it to you. You have somebody look me up in the press box tomorrow when I'm finished. They can have my carbon."

"That is *great,*" Betsy said. "Thank you! And welcome to Texas!"

"I wouldn't have missed this game," he said.

Betsy went back to her daddy's table.

"What was that all about?" Ted asked as Betsy took a chair between Ted and Bob.

"Grantland Rice is covering the game for the *Times-Standard*! He said I could have his carbon."

"You screwed up again," Bob Walker said.

Betsy laughed. "I could have had yours, right?"

Ben Throckmorton was sitting between Leatha and Florine, two decorous ladies. Florine was looking younger than her forty-two years, and even a trifle racy in her off-the-shoulder party dress. Her divorce would be final in a few more weeks. She had reached an out-of-court settlement with Shady. He had given her the house, a Cadillac, and $2,000 a month until such time as she married again.

When the Travis Glenn Quintet played "Red Sails in the Sunset," Florine asked Ben to dance. Ben sighed heavily and rubbed on his knee, as if an old wound was acting up, but Leatha ridiculed him into dancing with Florine.

On the dance floor, Florine said, "What is it, Ben? Are you the most stubborn man in the world or the most selfish? Why haven't you and Leatha married?"

Ben didn't have a quick answer.

Florine said, "You like your life the way it is, don't you?"

"It took me a long time to get over Elizabeth," Ben said. "Now, I'm so comfortable . . . independent . . . I guess I don't want to change anything."

"If you didn't have Florence and Warren, you'd have another wife. If Leatha had everything you wanted in a woman, you'd be married to her—not that I'm saying anything bad about Leatha. I don't mean it that way . . . I don't think."

"Leatha's a fine lady," Ben said, smiling at an unfamiliar couple on the dance floor.

Florine pressed herself closely to Ben. "I can tell you I'm looking forward to being single."

Ben looked down at her. "You know, Florine, you ought to think about moving to Fort Worth or Dallas. Meet some new people. There's a whole other world out there—so they tell me."

"I'm thinking about it," she said. "I may very well do it. If it looks interesting, I'll let you know."

Ben didn't say anything. They weren't dancing so much as they were shuffling slowly.

"Do you know how much I admire you?" Florine said softly.

"For what?"

"Just for being who you are."

"Tell you what I am right now," Ben said. "A man who'd like to sit down. Do you mind?"

"I could use a drink myself," Florine said.

On their way to the table, Florine squeezed Ben's hand and said, "Don't ever come out of your cocoon, Ben Throckmorton. Something interesting might happen to you."

Tonight was one of those evenings when Bernice Beaton didn't look like she would be happier in a coffin. Bernice was gazing around the ballroom, taken with the crowd.

"Isn't that Dr. Webb Walker at Amon Carter's table?" Bernice said. "I'm sure it is. I see Dr. Terrell and Dr. Anderson over there with Dr. McLean."

"Dr. Duringer's here," Leatha said. "I saw him talking to Dr. Clayton and Dr. Beaver."

"I'll bet Dr. Jackson's here somewhere. He would be sitting with Dr. Kingsbury."

Ben said, "I hope nobody in Fort Worth gets sick tonight."

It was during dinner that Betsy asked O. L. Beaton about Lank Allred and the reward money. Had Lank changed his mind and accepted any of it, aside from the money he had taken in the beginning? After all, five dead people—that was $25,000 on almost anybody's multiplication table.

"I told the board to give it to charity, like Lank said. I can't tell you where the board sent the money. I haven't bothered to ask."

Betsy said, "I called the headquarters of the Texas Bankers in Houston. I asked them for records of the reward money. A secretary told me the information was confidential. She had instructions not to give the information out to anybody, especially the press."

"For a good reason, too," the banker said. "Most of the officers who've shot bandits haven't been identified in the newspapers. That's how they want it. Some of these gangs are known for their reprisals. By dern, that's somethin' else you can say for Lank Allred. He goes after the scum and he don't care who knows it!"

"He does relish publicity."

"He likes the limelight, no question about it," O. L. said. "But Lank's a great American, a great Texan. There'll be a statue of Lank Allred someday."

Ben Throckmorton sent the conversation drifting momentarily when he said, "They're having a good fight in Austin about statues right now."

Betsy had brightened up the front page with the story.

As the State of Texas moved closer to its hundredth birthday, the Centennial Historical Board was arguing among itself about how to spend a million dollars in federal funds on memorials.

Nothing was happening. The board members were locked in a deadly game of trying to one-up each other on obscure aspects of Texas history.

The board had agreed on the predictable—statues of Davy Crockett, Jim Bowie, Sam Houston, Ben Milam, that crowd— but on little else. Some board members were threatening to resign and boycott all literary teas forever if Fort Concho in San Angelo wasn't restored, or if the old stone fort at Nacogdoches wasn't rebuilt.

Every member seemed to know a lovable old schoolteacher or rancher who deserved a statue.

J. Frank Dobie, the author and leading lore collector in Texas, had filed a minority report saying, "We would be exactly where we are today if most of what the board wants to memorialize had never existed. Nobody seems to give a hoot about the important things, such as Tom Lubbock and the brave men who went on the Sante Fe Expedition."

Ben was the only person at the table who knew anything about the Santa Fe Expedition.

"A bunch of real estate developers is what they were," he said. "They got this idea back in 1841 that Texas wasn't big enough. They rode off to claim everything between the Alamo and the Pacific Ocean for Texas. Most of 'em got drunk and lost on the Plains. A lot of 'em were killed by Comanches. Some of 'em wound up in Mexican prisons. It's what ought to happen to most real estate developers."

"I can get a court order," Betsy said to O. L. Beaton, letting him know by her expression that she wasn't kidding.

The banker moved around uncomfortably in his chair and put his cigar down. "Can I talk to you off the record?"

"Nothing is off the record," she said. "You can give me some information if you like, and I may keep it confidential, but I'll be the judge of whether it's news or not."

"Folks talk off the record all the time!" O. L. said in a wounded tone. "But they can't to *you,* is that it?"

"Nothing is *ever* off the record, O. L. I don't care what you think you know about my profession. I can say, sure, mister, you're talking off the record if I want to get information out of somebody, and I *will* protect a source if it's necessary, but if it's news, it's going to find its way into print, somehow, some way, attributable to somebody—so what did you want to tell me?"

"It ain't news, it's, uh . . . I don't know what you call it."

"What?"

"Background?" Ben suggested. Everybody was listening.

"Lank's been collecting the reward money, but now, damn it, Betsy, don't get all fired up—there's not a thing wrong with it!"

Betsy said, "He's taken twenty-five thousand dollars? All of it?"

"His wife's in poor health," O. L. said. "His mama and daddy is poor as rats. He wanted to give some of it to charity, but the Bankers Association couldn't find a charity that didn't look like a thief was runnin' it. He earned that money, Betsy. He's a hero. He's prevented five banks from gettin' robbed. I hope he kills five more of the sons of bitches!"

Running a comb through her hair, Anna Sue said to Bob Walker, "Somebody killed five people—where?"

"Sam Baugh."

"He did?"

"Hit 'em right in the heart with the football. Doesn't know his own strength."

"Makes our story look good," Betsy said to O. L.

"Your story was just fine," the banker said. "When Lank made his statement to you, he absolutely meant it. He took the money later."

"That girl I've seen him with at Clay Field? That's no poor sick wife!"

Lank had taken Shirley Watters to more than one Claybelle football game.

O. L. laughed nervously as he said, "Little Shirley from the Oasis? Heh, heh. No, I'm afraid that's your basic Texas Ranger showin' us his human side. Well, I reckon if a man's wife is ill . . . can't get out much. You know what I'm sayin'."

"Uh-huh." Betsy nodded, pretending to understand, not that very many women had ever understood such behavior.

Driving back to Claybelle later that evening, Betsy sat in silence most of the way, thinking, smoking, as Ted handled the wheel of the Dodge and watched the road.

Lighting her forty-third Lucky of the night, Betsy said, "Cheating on his wife doesn't make Lank Allred a criminal, it only makes him average; and taking the reward money doesn't make him any different from a lot of other cops in this state, *but* . . . shooting five people, four of whom were unarmed young kids with no record or criminal history, *that* intrigues me, particularly when you put it together with his taking the reward money."

"Interesting but circumstantial," said Ted. "I'm sure it's only coincidence. I think you were right the first time. He's a trigger-happy headline grabber."

Betsy looked at Ted sharply. "You know, if there really *is* a 'Texas Murder Machine,' and if I could prove it—and write it —you know what I'd have?"

"A good story."

"Better."

"A book?"

"You're not trying."

"A movie?"

She looked at him impatiently.

"What?" he said.

"It's called a Pulitzer, Ted."

Sixteen

___

GOD INVENTED football so grown boys would have something to do between wars.

Bob Walker's line.

Bob wrote that the reason it had taken so many years for the game to develop in America was because God had wanted young men to learn how to use their brains as well as their bodies. This, like all refinements, needed time. The first college football game had been played between Princeton and Rutgers in 1869, but the contest had only resembled a form of the rugby scrum, which consisted of many male bodies falling into a pile and trying to see how many eyeballs they could detach from their sockets.

It wasn't until 1880 that the scrum had been abandoned in favor of the scrimmage line, and the number of players reduced to eleven on a side. In 1906, the rules makers had established the length of a game at sixty minutes, divided into two thirty-minute halves. That was also the year somebody had thrown the first forward pass. Fellow from Wesleyan. Probably in panic. It had been a quaint thing to do, but nobody had taken it seriously as an offensive maneuver.

Then came 1912 and the notion to allow the offense four downs to advance ten yards and retain possession, the idea that the playing field should be a hundred yards long and fifty yards wide, and the decision to count a touchdown as six points. By now, Bob went on, the game was not only Americanized to the fullest, it was spreading across the land, attracting rabid crowds, igniting and rallying alumni, encouraging monstrous stadiums to be built.

But who could have guessed that the next revolutionary advance in the modern game would occur on the Saturday of November 30, 1935, in the unsuspecting city of Fort Worth, Texas? Surely no one. And yet that's what happened when a

Texas Christian University student in his junior year, Samuel Adrian Baugh, had awakened the Nation to the fact that the forward pass could be used as a consistent, reliable, deadly weapon. Slingin' Sam Baugh had been on the losing side in the bigger-than-life football game that day—though just barely, and through no fault of his own—but he had thrown the ungodly, unheard-of, and unworldly number of forty-five passes during the sixty minutes of swirling action, most often with great artistry and accuracy, and football would never be the same again.

S.M.U. TAKES THRILLING GAME FROM T.C.U., 20–14

This was the big black banner which swept across the front page of the *Times-Standard* on Sunday morning.

The decks told more.

**44,000 JAM STADIUM
TO SEE WILD CLASSIC**

———

**Ponies Snatch Victory
With Long Pass While
Score Tied in Fourth**

———

**Daring Style of Play
Viewed by Largest Crowd
In Texas Football Annals**

Then a famous sportswriter's game story told the rest.

By GRANTLAND RICE
Copyright, 1935, by
NANA, Inc.
FORT WORTH, Texas, Nov. 30.—In the most desperate football this season has known from coast to coast, Southern Methodist beat Texas Christian 20 to 14 today, and thereby carved

out a clear highway to the Rose Bowl beyond any argument or doubt.

In a TCU Stadium that seated 30,000 spectators, over 44,000 wildly excited Texans and visitors from every corner of the map packed, jammed and fought their way into every square foot of standing and seating space to see one of the greatest football games ever played in the sixty-year history of the Nation's finest college sport.

This tense, keyed-up crowd even leaped the wire fences from the tops of automobiles to watch a 60-minute swirl of action that no other section of the country could even approach. Elusive running and forward passing that electrified the packed stands—especially by TCU's All-American, Sammy Baugh—turned this climax game of 1935 into a combination of all-around skill and drama no other football crowd has seen this year.

With the Rose Bowl bid at stake, SMU got the big jump by taking a lead of 14 to 0. In the first period, Fullback Bob Finley plowed over the line at the end of a 73-yard march that featured every known method of attack. In the second quarter, SMU scored again. A 33-yard pass from Finley to End Maco Stewart, who made a diving catch, set up a 9-yard dash around end by SMU's brilliant All-America halfback, Bobby Wilson, the greatest running back of 1935.

(TURN TO PAGE 12, COLUMN 1.)

A moment after the opening kickoff, the two hundred extra policemen who had been hired had given up trying to control the ranting thousands outside the stadium and had joined them in a thunderous dash to claim whatever space was available inside the stadium.

Betsy saw Chief Olin Musgrove and Sergeant R. G. Teague among those who flooded the portals, squeezed into rows in the stands, lined the aisles and steps, ringed the playing field, and knelt in clusters behind both end zones. The chief and R. G. were behind the north end zone. Lank Allred and J. T. Hines were standing behind the south end zone.

Ben Throckmorton's excellent box was thirty rows up on the west side, the press-box side, near the fifty-yard line. Ben's precious eight seats were for himself and Leatha, Betsy and Ted, Ray Fletcher and his wife, Jo Ellen, and Shady Webster and Eva Jane McKnight.

Leatha had asked Ben to try to scare up a ticket for Florine, who had lost her seat to the big game in the divorce, but Florine had let Ben off the hook. She had said she would be happy to listen to the game on the radio. She had been invited to a "listening party" at B's Cafe, where Wynelle Stubbs was going to serve potted-ham finger sandwiches and Vienna sausages on toothpicks.

Leatha had promised Ben she would "act nice" to Eva Jane. Ben had said she might as well start learning to get along with Eva Jane, because he and Shady weren't going to stop playing golf together or rooting for TCU together.

In the box before the game started, Shady said he was sorry he'd missed the dinner party at the Fort Worth Club, but he had been called away to Ranger to watch one of his oil wells turn into a wolf camp.

Ted asked what a wolf camp was.

Shady said it was a hole in the ground that looked like it was going to produce oil—for about three days. Then it ran dry. Turned into a wolf camp.

"Yep, I finally made the ocean," he said. "Offhand, I'd say it's doubly unfortunate, because I'm drillin' three more of them fuckers nearby."

"What do you do in the case of a wolf camp?"

"You break the news real gently to your partners."

Shady didn't mention it, but there was something else he would do, something typical of wildcatters. He would sell off part of his valuable production in order to drill more holes, keep on gambling. An oilman would bet on two bugs crawling up a wall. Too much was never enough for most oilmen. They either wanted to hit a major field or go busted trying. "Money ain't important," as one of them had said, "but it's how they keep score."

Amon Carter and his friends, most of whom looked like Postmaster Generals and Railroad Commissioners, had experienced some difficulty getting into Amon's reserved box next to Ben's.

That's because Slop Herster and Tommy Jack Lucas had been occupying it until three policemen threw them out.

"I believe you lads are in the wrong seats," Amon Carter had said to Slop and Tommy Jack.

"Habla español?" Slop had said, and he and Tommy Jack hadn't moved.

Amon Carter had motioned to a policeman to come do something about the intruders.

Knowing who Amon Carter was, the policeman had brought two other cops with him, and the police had been aching for Slop and Tommy Jack to make trouble.

Slop had accommodated them by saying, "What can I do for you six-dollar-a-week motherfuckers?"

The cops had pulled out their pistols and grabbed Slop and Tommy Jack and put them in handcuffs.

"Look at this shit," Slop had said as he and Tommy Jack were being led away. "What are we, black?"

Slop and Tommy Jack had been taken outside the stadium and given a lecture and then released. But they somehow managed to get back in and spent the rest of the afternoon down on the field circling the stadium and looking up in the stands in the hope that from their vantage point they would be rewarded with an occasional glimpse of some lap moss.

Everyone had dressed warmly for the cold gray afternoon.

Betsy wore a double-breasted tweed coat with a fox collar and a cloche hat. Leatha and Jo Ellen Fletcher were in beaver, and Eva Jane in leopard. Ben and Shady and Ray had donned their camel's-hair overcoats and their businessman's Stetsons. Ted was in a trenchcoat and a snap-brim.

When the SMU Mustangs had exploded for a two-touchdown lead in the second quarter, Ben and Shady had gone into shock, bordering on serious illness.

Shady had said, "It was too big for us—too much pressure. Too much publicity. Goddamn newspaper people!"

"What did the press do?" Betsy asked.

"Blowed the damn thing out of proportion," Shady said. "Publicity ain't ever helped nobody but a Dionne quintuplet. If it was a normal game, we'd be kicking their ass."

Betsy said, "You know, it's a funny thing, Shady, but I swear I don't see a single newspaperman out there in a TCU uniform."

Ted, the ex–football hero, made the astute observation that it was early. If the Frogs settled down, they could still make a game of it.

(GRANTLAND RICE—CONTINUED FROM PAGE 1.)

Facing this smothering margin, Texas Christian came back from the middle of the second quarter with a counter charge that almost swept the Mustangs off the field.

TCU's attack featured the incredible passing of Baugh and the driving runs of Jimmy Lawrence, a truly great back who might have made All-America himself this season had there not been so many others from his sector. The Horned Frogs, with savage drive, repeatedly knocked on the Mustang goal and finally scored as Lawrence fought his way in from the 4-yard line.

Trailing 14 to 7 at the start of the fourth quarter, Lawrence again climaxed a long march with a tying score as Baugh whipped the ball into his open arms from 6 yards out.

Tied at 14 to 14, the big crowd sensed a TCU victory against a fading SMU team, even though

Jimmy Lawrence injured his ankle on his second touchdown and was helped from the field, never to return. Lawrence's loss to TCU in the telling fourth quarter more than offset the fact that SMU played without the services of Harry Shuford, the Mustangs' regular fullback and captain, who was also nursing an injury.

"I'll settle for a tie," Ben was now yelling. "I'll take it. This is the greatest comeback in the history of football!"

"Who'll go to the Rose Bowl if they tie?" Leatha asked.

"We will!" Ben howled. "Anybody with sense can see we're the best team—we're outgaining 'em two to one! What's wrong with you, woman?"

Eva Jane made the mistake of saying, "Well, I don't know who's going to win, but SMU has cuter uniforms."

The Mustangs were wearing their red leather helmets, red jerseys with blue numerals and vertical blue stripes running up each ribcage from the waist to the armpit, and two-tone pants that were khaki in front and red stretch-knit in the back. This in contrast to TCU's solid white jerseys, skinny purple numerals, black leather helmets, and khaki-colored pants with a purple knit stripe going up the rear of each leg.

"Eva Jane, you don't know what you're talkin' about!" Ben said. "SMU dresses like bellhops. This is a football game. We're wearin' our work clothes!"

(MORE RICE—CONTINUED)

On the ropes though they were, outgained in every department, it was still the Mustangs who had the winning drive left. Taking the ball from the kickoff after TCU tied the game, Jackrabbit Smith ran three times to the Horned Frogs' 47. Bobby Wilson got 10 more. Three line plunges failed, which brought up fourth down at the TCU 37. Needing seven yards for a first down, Southern Methodist then pulled the most daring play of a daring game.

From punt formation, Bob Finley suddenly dropped back to pass. Bobby Wilson went racing down the northeast sideline toward the TCU goal. Wilson was open. He had slipped behind TCU's Harold McClure, who was substituting for the injured Jimmy Lawrence. Finley unleashed a forward pass that must have sailed 50 yards in the air. As the ball cleared the flying Wilson's shoulder, the 147-pound back made a leaping, twisting catch that swept him across the goal-line for the winning score. It was a great pass but an even greater catch.

"Son of a bitch, nobody could catch that thing!" Ben shouted. "Where'd he come from? How'd he get down there?"

"A great back made a great play," Ted said. "You have to hand it to him."

"Piss on the bastard!" Shady said. "How many times you want to fuck me, Lord?" He was looking at the sky. "Want me to bend over, make it easy for you?"

(MORE RICE—CONTINUED)

TCU fought back with desperation in the game's last 6 minutes. Baugh drove TCU to SMU's 30 and 25 without scoring, and Baugh was eating up ground at the SMU 22 when the final whistle blew, and SMU's supporters were in a panic from Baugh's deathly machinegun fire.

Baugh's passing was brilliant. He threw an unbelievable forty-five passes, completing 21 of the aerials, but many were dropped in the early stages, some due to nervousness and some because he had thrown too swiftly for his receivers to handle. On one occasion, Baugh knocked his receiver down with as much speed as Dizzy Dean ever saw.

TCU had a fine running attack as well, and the Frogs far outgained SMU in total yardage, but the Mustangs played a cooler, smarter game.

With its victory over Texas Christian, SMU's fine squad now picks up the Rose Bowl challenge. TCU will settle for the Sugar Bowl. Their opponents had better be ready, for SMU and TCU are the two strongest, most spectacular teams I have seen this year.

Betsy found herself yelling for TCU—for her daddy, really —in the game's last two minutes, as Sam Baugh drove the Frogs fifty-five yards to what could have been a touchdown and a winning extra point. In their glee over Bobby Wilson's catch, the Mustangs had missed the conversion attempt, leaving TCU a ray of hope to win the game, 21 to 20.

Baugh completed passes for fourteen yards, eight yards, and ten yards, and then flicked one to an end, L. D. Meyer, good for twenty more yards, but the receiver couldn't scramble out of bounds to stop the clock at the SMU twenty-two, to give Slingin' Sam one last chance to pull it out. The game was over.

Ben Throckmorton slumped in his seat, head hanging, elbows on his knees. The defeat was a stain on his soul, something he would have to live with forever.

Betsy tried to console him. "Daddy, it was one of the greatest games ever played, and we saw it. We were here."

"Nothing to be ashamed of, Ben," Ted said. "I saw two great teams out here today."

"Jimmy Lawrence," Ben moaned. "If Jimmy Lawrence hadn't got hurt, we'd have beat 'em easy. We had 'em. What a shame. What a dirty, rotten shame."

Ben and Shady had both brought flasks with them. They

all sat in the box for an hour and a half after the game, passing the flasks around, letting the traffic thin out.

"I ain't steppin' foot in Dallas again," Shady said. "I ain't shittin'."

"You don't mean that," Eva Jane said.

"I don't, huh? I don't mean it? Fuck you, bitch!"

"Shady Webster!" Leatha said, springing uniquely to Eva Jane's defense.

"He doesn't mean that either," Eva Jane said.

"You're right, honey," Shady said. "It's only a game. I'm sorry."

But then he leaped to his feet and called out to the world:

"FUCK DALLAS IN THE ASS! SMU IS LOWER THAN WHALESHIT AND WHALESHIT IS ON THE BOTTOM OF THE OCEAN!"

Bob Walker came down from the press box. He had finished his story and brought Betsy the carbon from Grantland Rice. Big 'Un Darly hadn't been able to work up enough nerve to approach Grantland Rice and ask him for it.

Bob said Big 'Un was apparently having difficulty getting started on the sidebar he was supposed to write. Big 'Un seemed to be paralyzed at his typewriter, overwhelmed by the magnitude of the event.

Bob had glanced at the paper in Big 'Un's typewriter. In an hour and a half, all Big 'Un had written was:

> **By BIG 'UN DARLY**
> **Times-Standard Sports**
> **Editor**
> Into the valley of football
> death rode the

Patting Ben on the shoulder, Bob said, "Sorry, old-timer, but some game, huh?"

"Jimmy Lawrence," Ben said, staring off vacantly.

"What did you write?" Betsy asked Bob. "Anything that rhymed?"

"We all choked," Bob said. "I wound up talking about the coaches. I was down on the field before the kickoff. Matty Bell had the Mustangs laughing, telling jokes. I don't know what Dutch Meyer did to the Frogs, but they had tears in their eyes and looked like they were going to the Crusades."

"I'm afraid that's the whole story," Ben said. "They were loose, we weren't."

"Fuckin' newspapers," Shady said.

Betsy got back to the *Times-Standard* around seven o'clock. She went with nothing but pictures and Grantland Rice's story on page one.

Smitty McWhorter and Junior Dingle had been no different from the hundred other photographers in the stadium. They, too, had missed the shot of Bobby Wilson catching the pass.

"It's just as well," Ben Throckmorton said. "I'll never stop seeing the damn thing in my mind."

Seventeen

THE TCU Horned Frogs were scheduled to play one more regular-season football game, against the Santa Clara Broncos in Kezar Stadium in San Francisco, a big intersectional game—the school's first trip to the West Coast—but after the bitter loss to SMU, Ben Throckmorton said he wouldn't go to California now if he could cut the balls off every sorry son of a bitch in Dallas and hang 'em from the roof of a mansion on Nob Hill.

He said this all through Saturday night, and all day Sunday, and most of Monday, but by Monday night Betsy had convinced him he should go; the trip would be fun. He could pretend it was the Rose Bowl. He should take Leatha along, as planned, on the special train that the *Star-Telegram* was sponsoring, a train that would be carrying the TCU team, the band, and two hundred fans.

At a cost of only $72.30 for a round-trip ticket, the trip was going to take seven days in all, there and back, with all of the exciting stopovers Betsy remembered from her trip to the Rose Bowl for the Columbia-Stanford game.

Betsy told her daddy he could file her a story or two, if he felt like it, but mostly she thought he ought to enjoy himself.

Ben weakened on Monday night and called Leatha to tell her to go ahead and pack, but he couldn't change Shady Webster's mind.

Ben drove over to Shady and Eva Jane's to have a drink with his pal and try to talk him into going to California. While Shady was mixing drinks, Billy V. poured a bottle of blue ink on the beige carpet in the living room, and Robbie D., a fair shot with a BB gun, shattered an antique vase. All this before Ben and Shady could lock themselves in the den.

"I'll be rid of them little pricks in January," Shady said.

"Their ass is off to a military school in Virginia. They don't get to do nothin' the first year but clean toilets. They can't write home, they can't get a letter, they can't make a phone call—and if they climb over the wall, the niggers'll kill 'em. That's what the commandant says. The commandant says when they get out of there, we won't hear nothin' but yes, sir; yes, ma'am; gee, Mom, can't I run another errand for you? Sounds like a great place."

"How can I talk you into going to California with us?"

Shady said, "I can't leave now. I'm sittin' out there in a fuckin' wolf camp. I've got two more dusters comin' in for sure. What I have to do is get my ass back in the Bryson Sand. I'm holdin' some good leases over near Possum Kingdom."

"Maybe you'd be better off in California when the dry holes turn up."

"Hell, it don't bother me none. It's part of the game. But my partners put up two-thirds of the money this time. Dry holes make money nervous. I'd better stick around."

Later that Monday night, Ben phoned Leatha to ask if she could hold her luggage down to two suitcases. That's when Leatha suggested taking Florine with them.

"Why?"

"It will be more fun for me," Leatha said.

"There's no room."

"There's loads of room, Ben. We have an upper berth and a lower berth. Florine can sleep with me."

"All right, ask her."

"I already have."

Florine called Ben to say thank you, she was thrilled; she was packing.

Hell of a thing, Ben thought to himself. Forget the football game. Forget the sightseeing. It was only a guess, but he was now going to spend a week on a train trying to keep Leatha from finding out that her best friend, a divorcée on the loose, might try to crank up Old Wilbur in the vestibule.

He would have to be nimble, he decided, but it was only a guess.

The Fort Worth and Denver Special shoved off from the T&P station at 10 A.M. Tuesday, December 3. Three days later, a story from Ben came into the *Times-Standard*. Betsy made room for it on the front page, though competition for space was stiff.

The Thelma Todd story was shocking. The platinum-haired movie star had been found dead in her garage in Santa Monica, the victim of monoxide poisoning.

Hollywood was stunned, but no more so than Estill Parch, who, over KVAT, had said the movie star had died of "carbon peroxide."

"It could happen," Betsy said to Ray Fletcher, "but not in this case, evidently."

In the other big story of the day, Haile Selassie was predicting an end to the Italo-Ethiopian war, now becalmed because of the rainy season and a lack of interest on the part of Mussolini's troops. "Mud is our strongest ally," the Emperor was quoted on the wire. "With mud and spears, we will rid our land of demons."

Ben's story wound up in the lower left-hand corner on the front, then jumped to sports.

By
BEN THROCKMORTON

ABOARD T.C.U. FOOTBALL SPECIAL EN ROUTE TO SAN FRANCISCO, Dec 5.—The final leg of this long journey has started for the Fort Worth team and fans. After rousing welcomes and stopovers in Amarillo and Denver, where the Frogs went through light drills, the train arrived in Salt Lake City for the highlight of the trip, an organ recital in the Mormon Tabernacle. The deluxe 11-car train now moves across the salt desert into Nevada and will enter California through the Feather River Canyon. From there, the route will lead through Sac-

ramento and Oakland. The
train will be ferried across
the Bay into San Francisco.

A little less rusty, Ben had done better on the game story
for Sunday's paper.

By
BEN THROCKMORTON
KEZAR STADIUM, SAN
FRANCISCO, Calif., Dec. 7.
—Sam Baugh's aim was true
and knocked all the cable
cars off their tracks this
afternoon as T.C.U. defeated
Santa Clara University 10 to
6 in a game that gave the
40,000 spectators a fair example of the kind of football
played in the Southwest.

Ben's file went on to say the trip—and the game—had
helped doctor the wounds of the loss to SMU. The Frogs had
ended their regular season with a record of 11-1, and though
they would have to settle for the No. 2 ranking in the Nation,
all of the fans who'd made the California journey were looking
forward to the special trains that would take them to New
Orleans over New Year's for the Sugar Bowl game against
Louisiana State. Meanwhile, an even greater number of Texans would be going out to Pasadena with the SMU Mustangs.
Thus, Ben wrote, the most exciting football season in Texas
history wasn't over yet.

Ben called Betsy at the office Saturday night to see if his
story had arrived, to make sure the Western Union telegrapher hadn't garbled it so much it looked like a page out of the
Moscow phone book.

"It reads fine, Daddy," Betsy said. "Tell me about the trip.
Nobody's had a cocktail, I guess."

Ben said, "The trip has been wonderful. Florine's been a
great addition. There's more to that woman than I knew. Of

course, the tree was a setback for Leatha. She took to her bed."

"The tree?"

"Leatha's magnolia. You haven't heard?"

"Heard what?"

"It ain't there any more."

"Leatha's magnolia?"

"Nothin' left but a stump. Somebody cut it down last night. Rhoba Nims called Leatha at the hotel to tell her."

"Who in the world would cut down that tree?"

"Rhoba Nims thinks it was Sloppy Herster and Tommy Jack Lucas. She saw 'em drunk on the street earlier in the evening. They were mad about the Claybelle-Cleburne game and looking for trouble."

The Yellow Jackets had been having their problems in District 5-AA. They had been mauled by Weatherford, Eastland, and Palo Pinto, but Dub Cooper had said on the radio that they could end the season with dignity if they could beat Cleburne.

"If we beat Cleburne we'll be three-one-six on the year, which is batting three hundred. They's more than one Ducky Medwick who'd like to have it. I'm proud of this bunch. They a little light on ability, but their hearts is big as feed sacks."

Out at Clay Field on Friday night, the Jackets had played their best game of the season for three quarters, taking a fourteen-point lead into the final quarter. But they had given up three touchdowns in the last fifteen minutes, all on intercepted passes thrown by Pine Knot Herster. Pine Knot's last interception had given Cleburne its 28 to 21 victory.

After that pass, the little quarterback had ditched his helmet and run for his life with Slop and Tommy Jack chasing him. Pine Knot had hopped over a fence and vanished into the night.

In Big 'Un Darly's report of the game, Coach Cooper's quote contradicted his previous statement about the character of his team. Dub said, "There ain't much a coach can do when he's at the mercy of a bunch of gutless wonders. Them yellow bellies make me want to puke."

"Tell Leatha I'm crushed about the tree," Betsy said to her daddy on the phone.

"She won't eat, won't drink, won't talk to anybody. I told her I'd get her another tree. She said it wouldn't be the same."

"Tell her we all mourn the tree."

"I better go, honey. Florine and I are going to dinner at some Chinese joint she read about. I'm not much on boiled shoestrings, but I reckon they'll have whiskey. The train leaves for Los Angeles tomorrow. We'll be home Wednesday."

"Florine, huh?"

"She read about this restaurant where they put umbrellas in your drinks. We thought we'd give it a try. No reason for us to hang around the hotel because Leatha don't want to go anywhere. It's worked out real good having Florine on the trip."

"I'll bet it has."

"She's quite a woman."

"I'll bet she is."

"She knows about all kinds of things I'd never given her credit for."

"I'll bet she does."

"What say, honey?"

"Nothing. Tell Florine hello. Thanks for typing, Daddy."

The copy spread out on the desk before Betsy demanded her attention, but as she hung up she found her mind wandering. There had been something in her daddy's voice when he spoke of Florine Webster that made her happy for him. He had never sounded like that when he talked about Leatha.

Now a silly thing happened. Tears welled up in Betsy's eyes, for she began to think about her mother and what an incredible loss it must have been for her daddy when Elizabeth had passed away.

What a special lady he had once found. Born in a covered wagon, yes. Daughter of a mule trader who became a barber, yes. But a college graduate! After Poppa Clinton had settled in Georgetown, what had driven that pioneer woman to want to go to Southwestern University? Had she studied religion at this oldest college in Texas? What could you have studied back then? Had it only been a way to get out of the house, away from Poppa Clinton's barbershop? Was it the genes?

In Florine, Betsy could see a slight resemblance to her

mother, but Florine was attractive in a more vibrant, athletic kind of way.

Betsy wondered if Elizabeth had possessed a sense of humor, if that delicate, exquisite lady, always so conscious of her charm and bearing, had ever in her whole life uttered a cussword.

She would have liked to know her better. It would have been fun to have a mother.

Betsy dabbed at her eyes with a tissue and went back to work.

On Sunday morning, Shady Webster bought a *Times-Standard* at Thompson's Pharmacy and walked over to B's Cafe to meet his oil partners for breakfast. He sat at a booth in the back of the room and turned to Cloyd Bennett's oil column in the paper.

> Well, you never know, do you? No. 1 Mary Ruth, Erath County wildcat in section 12, block A-33, public school land, is drilling below 2,344 feet with top of anhydrite picked at 1,925 feet and top of salt at 2,010 feet. Operators think Yates sand has creeped into rotary and can be reached below 3,000, and then it's up to the lime top.

"This dumbass don't even make sense to a oilman," Shady remarked to Wynelle Stubbs as she brought him a cup of something she called coffee and he called molten bridle path.

"Hear about Leatha's magnolia?"

"What was I supposed to hear?" Shady said.

"Somebody cut it down."

"Cut down that old magnolia?"

"Sawed it off. I seen the stump comin' to work this morning. I know who did it. Slop Herster and Tommy Jack Lucas was drunk all over town Friday night after the football game. They're the only ones sorry enough to do something like that."

"Damn, I feel like I've lost an old friend."

"Leatha might as well stay in California. Her house don't look no better than mine without that tree in her yard."

"That tree must have been a hundred years old."

"Pine Knot come in here yesterday. His face was a mess. Slop and Tommy Jack kicked his ass for throwing those interceptions. He says he's gonna transfer to Masonic Home. He's got two years eligibility left."

"Can he get into Masonic Home?"

"He hasn't got no mama, I don't see why not. If you haven't got a mama or daddy and you can play football, you can get into Masonic Home. I said he ought to do it. He can play on a championship team for Rusty Russell. Dub Cooper's been impersonating a football coach for as long as I can remember. Pine Knot says Dub sent in those stupid pass plays. That's why we lost. You couldn't find Dub Cooper's brain with a search warrant and two subpoenas."

Lank Allred and O. L. Beaton joined Shady in the back booth. Neither man looked happy.

"Y'all gonna eat?" Wynelle said to the two men.

"Two poached," O. L. said. "Put 'em on buttered toast. I don't want no golf balls—and crispy-chewy on the bacon."

Lank Allred said, "Two over-easy. Yellow runnin', white hard. Sausage, biscuits, cream gravy on the side."

Wynelle said, "I don't know if Leonardo da Vinci is in the kitchen today but I'll see what I can do."

She left.

The Texas Ranger fixed a cold stare on Shady. "Let me see if I understand this correctly. After telling me how good our core samples are, how we're sittin' on top of the 'pay horizon,' you're saying we're in a wolf camp, is that right?"

"You knew it was risky, Lank."

"Let me ask you this, then. What were we doin' throwin' our dice as far from all them gushers as we could get?"

Shady rolled his eyes in exasperation. "Because I had ever damn lease tied up that was anywhere close to us. If we'd hit, you'd be suckin' my dick right now."

"You callin' me a queer?"

"No, I ain't callin' you a queer," Shady said. "It's a figure of speech."

"I ain't never sucked no dick."

"I know *that*."

"I'll take your dick and tie a knot in it and hand it back to you."

"I was makin' a joke, Lank. Shit. Look, I'll tell you what. I know I've let you down—both of you. I want to make it up to you."

Lank said, "You've sucked my dick for twenty thousand dollars, is all I know."

"I'm gonna help you get it back, hoss. I've been rat-holin' some leases over in Young County. I was saving 'em for myself because I know they're gold. They're in the Bryson Sand. That sand ain't too tight. We can reach the pay with cable tools, and what's down there is heaven. It's a fallin'-down cinch."

O. L. said, "Thirty thousand. That's what you've fucked me out of, Shady."

Shady said, "God damn it, O. L., you of all people know there ain't no guarantees in this business. And I haven't made you any money, have I? I've made you three times that much, asshole!"

"What about this Bryson Sand?" said Lank.

"I'll tell you how good it looks," Shady said. "I'm gonna sell off some of my production to drill three wells. Could be another Yates."

Lank looked intrigued. "It's a lock? This ain't some more of your bullshit?"

"I'm sure enough of it to break a cardinal rule: Don't ever take points off the scoreboard. How many coaches you heard say *that*?"

"So you want more money?" O. L. said. "We've broke our pick but you want more money. That's some gall, boy. That's what that is."

Shady lowered his voice. "Let me tell y'all something. Where them leases are? If it was a fishin' hole, you'd have to hide behind a tree to bait your hook."

"How much?" Lank asked.

"I'll put you each in for a third," Shady said. "I'll need twenty grand apiece."

"Jee-zus Christ!" said O. L.

"You got to spend money to make money," Shady said, leaning back in his seat. "Listen, I don't care whether y'all are in or out, but when I hit me a Yates, I don't want to hear no crap from you."

O.L. said he didn't have that kind of money right now.

Shady laughed cynically. "Bankers," he said. "You yank a man's dick when he comes in the front door, fuck him in the ass when he goes out the back. Give a banker an enema, you can put him in a shoe box."

"I guess I'm in," the banker said gravely. "I'll figure out something."

Shady looked at Lank for his answer.

"It's a can't-miss deal?" The Ranger squinted. "You swear that on the grave of your lightweight chokin'-dog give-up TCU Horned Frogs?"

Shady said, "All I know is, there ain't nothin' around them leases but three hundred barrels a day."

"I'll go," Lank said. "I hate to dip into my inheritance again, but I'm with you."

The men all shook hands.

"The things I do for friends," Shady said, sighing heavily.

Eighteen

TED WAS going back to the hobo camp on the cold, gloomy night of December 12—it must have been his fourth visit—but first he met Betsy for a bite to eat at B's Cafe.

She dashed over from the paper, where she was working on a column about Nazis.

Chancellor Adolf Hitler seemed to be passing a new law every day in Germany, and the latest one decreed that if someone's husband or wife didn't believe in Nazism, it was grounds for divorce.

Column stuff.

> An evening at home with Heidi and Ernst in Bavaria:
>
> "Darling, you're not going to wear that silly old armband to bed, are you?"
>
> "You don't like our swastika?"
>
> "Of course I like it. I like it on our drapes. I like it on our living room carpet. I love it on our tank. I simply think it's a bit much on the pajamas. But don't be upset, darling. Give Heidi a kiss."
>
> "Don't come near me, you Marxist witch! You'll be hearing from my attorney in the morning!"

Betsy had been working so hard at the paper and on her column, she had almost forgotten she was married. Ted was trying to do his own work on her schedule, but her schedule kept changing. Blame the news, she said.

At the radio station, Ted had begun to direct his energy toward sales, now that he was unable to make any changes in the programming, but he was mostly keeping busy with his research for the magazine piece about hobos.

Which annoyed Betsy, the more she thought about it. It seemed to her that she could have written three magazine pieces in the time it was taking Ted to write one. She knew he was a bleeder at the typewriter, but this was ridiculous.

A day earlier she had walked into his study at home and found him doing something that would have made her whoop and holler and call Bob Walker on the phone if it hadn't been Ted, and hadn't been, in a way, so sad.

He had written the first page of the story for about the sixteenth time, and had thumbtacked it to the wall and was standing across the room looking at it through binoculars in an effort to get a detached attitude about his prose.

Now they were in a booth at B's having smothered steaks with mashed potatoes and green beans and salad.

"When are you going to finish the hobo piece?" Betsy said. "Is it a novel? Have I been misled?"

"It *could* be a book," Ted said. "There's so darn much material. *Collier's* wants five thousand words. I've been thinking I'll deal with three different themes. Lost hope. The economy. Life in the jungle. It's taking some organizing."

"Why don't you just say what the camps look like and let the people talk? When they get through talking, you're finished."

"That will be part of it."

"So write."

"It's not a column, Betsy."

"No, it's five columns."

Ted put his fork down. "Betsy, a magazine piece requires more depth than a column—you know that."

"I've always been known for my lack of depth," Betsy said, looking at her plate.

"I didn't say that."

"It's okay, I understand. All a columnist has to be is rude ... self-righteous ... arrogant ... meddlesome ... harassing ... accusatory. A *magazine writer,* on the other hand ..."

They ate silently for a moment.

Then Betsy said, "Thank God that's what we are! We happen to be the link between the people and their institutions. The link between the people and the political phonies! Take me, take my excesses, but remember, you're getting a free press in the bargain!"

"The newshen has spoken."

"Yes!"

"You're angry."

"I'm not angry."

"You're disappointed—in me."

"Why would I be disappointed? You've just given me a column topic."

"We'll talk about it later," Ted said, sliding out of the booth. He kissed her goodbye on the cheek and, in a pair of old corduroys, a heavy sweater, and a wool cap, left for the hobo camp.

Joylene Blanchard was at the register as Betsy paid the dinner check, Betsy in her dungarees, boots, a baggy sweatshirt under a fur coat, no makeup, and her hair looking like a Yorkshire terrier had been running through it.

Seeing her reflection in the window glass, Betsy said, "God, *I* belong in a hobo camp."

"The paper's looking better, Betsy," Joylene said. "I like those big pictures. Your column's good, too. I don't understand it half the time, but it's good."

"Thanks, Joylene. It's kind of shallow, but I try."

A day before, Ben had returned from California with his two ladies, one grieving about her magnolia tree, the other looking radiant for reasons she was keeping to herself.

Warren met the train in Fort Worth in the burgundy Packard, and Ben drove straight to Leatha's house.

From a block away, they could see the stump where the magnolia tree had been, and Leatha burst into tears—again.

They all stood around the stump.

Leatha said, "Sloppy Herster and Tommy Jack Lucas ought to go to the penitentiary for this!"

"I'll plant you two nice mimosas, Miz Leatha," Warren said. "I'll put one here and one over there. They'll grow up big before you know it."

Florine put her arm around Leatha. "Want me to stay with you tonight?"

"No, that's sweet, but I'm going to have to start getting used to it. Oh, my."

Leatha got hold of herself.

"It was a wonderful tree," Ben said. "We'll all miss it."

To Leatha, Florine said, "You call me later if you want company."

Ben had driven to his house next, to drop off Warren and the luggage, and then he had taken Florine home alone.

Ted picked up a fifth of Schenley's and filled his pockets with packs of Camels before he want to the hobo camp, and now he was sitting around a campfire with Milton and Albert and two other hobos.

The hobos were enjoying the whiskey and smokes.

It was close to midnight, and Milton was talking about the chalk marks. "You make a X on the sidewalk," he said. "That's so the next old boy will know them folks will give you food."

Albert said, "Some don't leave a mark. They keep it to themselves. Greed's all that is."

"It's unlucky not to put a mark," one of the other hobos said. "But you'll see women out in the yard with a hose washing off them marks. It's a fact."

"You can carve something on a tree, if they've got a tree," Milton said.

"Rich folks is the worst," Albert said. "I ain't never got nothin' to eat at a rich man's house. Call the police is all they do."

Mister Man and Brains were in the camp tonight, somebody said. Ted perked up.

"I seen 'em earlier," Milton said. "They might have left by now. They were handin' out fried pies."

"I think I saw 'em with Willis," Albert said.

"Who's Willis?" Ted asked.

"He's a new kid come in," Milton said.

Ted excused himself from his friends. He thought he might wander through the camp, see if he could find Mister Man and Brains. It would be fun to find out for sure if Mister Man and Brains were, in fact, Sloppy Herster and Tommy Jack Lucas —or another comedy act.

As he approached one of the tin sheds, he heard voices and laughter coming from inside.

Three men were discussing the universal subject.

From in back of the shed, Ted stopped to listen.

"Any moss around this shithole?" a voice was saying.

"Any what?"

"Moss. Lick. Chewy."

"Pussy," another voice explained.

A giggle.

"You like pussy, Willis?"

"Who don't?"

"My friend here, he don't think about nothin' else. Moss ruint his brain. That's why we call him Brains."

"Money'll get you all the pussy you want."

"I reckon so."

"Pussy don't like but two things. A hard dick and money. You know that, don't you, boy?"

Another giggle. Then: "There's this whore-lady in Fort Worth. Down there at the Stewart Hotel. Man, she'll take you for a ride. Big old blonde. Got them titties out to here. She can't get enough dick."

"Tell him what she said to you last time."

"Aw, hell."

"Tell him!"

The voice said, "Aw, we was jackin' around there in the hotel room. I'd done screwed her once, but she wanted more. She went kind of wild—like they do, you know? She grabbed her moss and started playin' with it. Next thing I know, she's down on her knees on the floor. I'm sittin' on the side of the bed. She's got one hand on her moss and the other hand on Leroy here. She squealed and said, 'Oh, baby, fuck my mouth, fuck my mouth!' "

"Damn," said the younger voice.

The laughter stopped, and one of the voices grew serious. "Willis, I've got a job for you if you're interested."

"Sure."

"Pays fifty dollars. How's that sound?"

"Are you jokin'?"

"Ain't much to it. See, there's these people I know who plan to pay a visit to a bank over here in Arlington. They don't like that bank. That bank took their daddy's farm. They plan to relieve that bank of some money."

"Rob a bank?"

"Well . . . they call it gettin' even."

"I ain't never broke the law."

"I don't know as though you could call it breakin' the law. All they need is a lookout. Somebody to keep an eye on the bank, make sure there ain't no police around, give 'em a signal when the bank looks empty."

"Why don't one of y'all do it?"

"We've got other assignments. You don't need to know too many details. It's for your own good. John Dillinger and them? Bonnie and Clyde? They was real good at banks, but they went and got dead because they told too many people too many details."

"Fifty dollars buys lots of pussy, Willis."

"I ain't sure I'd spend it on pussy, but it would get me to California."

"It's just a piss-ant bank. It's over here in Arlington, between Fort Worth and Dallas. We'd drive you over there. You'd get your money before anything happened. It'll be a few days from now, I'll let you know when. Hell, Willis, it's easy as strokin' old Leroy. All you do is mosey around on the sidewalk, have a cigarette, let 'em know when the coast is clear. Then you're gone. You're on your way to California."

"Sounds pretty good."

"*Good?* Heh, heh, Your dick's hard, ain't it?"

Shifting his weight, Ted accidentally mashed down on some twigs. An empty Coca-Cola bottle rolled into a rock and made a noise, a ping.

"What's that?" said a voice inside the shed.

Ted walked away briskly.

Mister Man and Brains and Willis came out of the shed.

"Hey!" Mister Man hollered at Ted, a figure in the moonlight.

Ted broke into a jog.

"Stay here," Mister Man said to Willis. Mister Man and Brains took off after Ted, who was cutting across a deserted lot, angling away from the hobo camp.

Ted saw them coming and stopped. What the hell. Why not confront them?

Catching his breath, Mister Man said, "What were you doin' back there, ace? If you wasn't listenin', why are you runnin'?"

"I was listening," Ted said. "I heard enough. That kid's as good as dead, isn't he?"

"What are you talkin' about?" said Brains.

"There's no bank job," Ted said. "*He* may think there is, but we know better, don't we? Set the kid up, kill him, collect the reward. Nice little scam you fellows have going. Who are you working with? It wouldn't be a Texas Ranger, would it?"

"You crazy?" Brains faked a laugh.

Mister Man said to Ted, "Let me ask you this. What do you care if a chickenshit bank gets robbed?"

"Oh, come on," Ted said. "You have no intention of robbing a bank. I know it and you know it. You fellows can make it easier on yourselves if you cooperate with the police."

"You goin' to the police?" Brains asked.

"It *has* crossed my mind."

Mister Man grinned as he casually reached behind him. "Well, I'll tell you," he said. "Since you're so smart—"

And with that, in a sudden move, Mister Man plunged an ice pick into Ted's stomach. Grabbing Ted's shoulder with his left hand and with the ice pick in his right hand, he buried the point deeper into Ted's midsection as Ted let out a gasp.

"Motherfucker!" Mister Man sneered. "You should have minded your own Goddamn business!"

Mister Man jerked out the ice pick and quickly stabbed Ted again, grinding the point around in Ted's stomach.

Ted sank to his knees, into the weeds. The stab wounds sent a sharp, burning sensation through his whole body. His brain was in shock.

As Mister Man and Brains stared at him, Ted clutched his stomach. His head dropped. Could he be dying? He had never thought of dying before. If he was dying, how could it happen like this? Here. Now. In the weeds and gravel of a little town in Texas. He engaged a fleeting coherent thought of Betsy, another of his mother and father, and still another of how stupid it was if his life was ending this way—and he toppled over.

Ted Winton was dead.

Brains said, "Shit, we ain't never killed nobody."

Mister Man looked around. The lights of the hobo camp were a hundred yards away. They were alone.

"Fuck it. Nobody saw nothin'."

"What about Willis?"

Mister Man said, "I'll handle his ass with money. He can lose his memory and hit the road."

The phone call awakened Ben Throckmorton at seventhirty in the morning. Police Chief Olin Musgrove broke the news to Ben in a low, sad drawl.

"Oh, no," Ben said weakly. He groped for a Chesterfield on a bedside table.

"I don't know what happened," the chief said. "One of them hobos, I guess. A fight. A robbery. Who knows? I'm sure he's hightailed it by now, whatever punk did it."

The chief said a hobo had discovered Ted's body as he walked through the field on his way to the Santa Fe station for his morning coffee. Ben's son-in-law had been dead for six or seven hours, apparently. The body had been taken to Baptist Hospital, which was on the edge of town, near the grain elevator.

"We're questioning everybody in the camp, Ben, but I don't expect much. What in the world was Ted doin' over there, anyhow?"

"He was working on a magazine story."

"Well, it's a damn shame."

"Olin, thank you for calling me first."

Ben hung up. Not knowing what else to do at the moment, he sat on the arm of his leather chair and smoked. His eyes began to shine with tears as he thought of Betsy. He wasn't sure he would be able to tell her about this alone.

He threw on a pair of pants, a shirt, a long-sleeve cardigan sweater, and went out to the garage apartment to tell Florence and Warren.

They were up and dressed. Florence collapsed in tears. "Oh, my poor child," she said, thinking only of Betsy.

Warren said, "I knowed there wasn't nothin' good could come out of goin' to that jungle. I knowed it for sure."

Ben patted Florence and said, "Florence, I want you to get hold of yourself. I'm going to need you now."

From the telephone in the garage apartment, Ben called Bob Walker in Dallas.

Hurt, frustrated, and angry, Bob Walker cussed everything in the universe, on up past God and into the cosmos.

"Betsy's still alseep," Ben said to him. "I hope she'll sleep for another hour or so. Bob, I'd sure like to have you with me when I tell her."

"I'll be there as quick as I can," Bob said.

Ben phoned Leatha. She was still mourning her tree—and now this. Leatha said she would try to pull herself together and come by later.

Ben called Florine Webster.

"Oh, Ben, I'm so sorry," said Florine. "What can I do? Shall I come over now?"

Thinking quickly, Ben said, "Maybe you better wait till Leatha tells you about it."

Ben placed a long-distance call to Millie Saunders who cussed the news as vigorously as Bob Walker had.

Ben said, "Millie, I can't think of anything but my daughter right now. I was wondering if—"

"I'm coming down there!"

"Would you? That would be wonderful."

"I'll get a plane. Maybe I can be there by tonight. Tell her I'm on the way."

"Thank you, Millie. I won't forget it."

"Mr. Throckmorton . . . ?"

"Yes."

"I know that girl. She'll be all right."

Nineteen

BETSY ONLY had to look at her daddy and Bob Walker to know something terrible had happened. Bob Walker's very presence at this hour told her it was serious.

She was wearing a robe over her nightgown and brushing her hair at the dressing table when they rapped gently on the bedroom door and entered.

"What is it?" she said, reaching for her Lucky in the ashtray. Names raced through her mind: Warren, Florence, Leatha, what?

"Honey," said Ben, but no more words would come out.

Betsy looked at Bob Walker. "Ted . . . ?" she said.

Ben and Bob moved toward her.

Bob said, "It's a tough one, babe."

Betsy stood up. "That tough?"

"Yeah."

She pitched the brush onto the table and squashed out her cigarette. She folded her arms and stared at Bob and her daddy, her eyes starting to glisten. "He's dead, isn't he?"

Bob looked down and nodded.

Ben's eyes glistened.

"How, Daddy?"

Betsy ached all over. Her throat was in a knot.

"Nobody knows," Ben said. "He was . . . stabbed. Over near the hobo camp."

Betsy walked to a window and put her forehead against the pane. She was looking out on the front lawn but seeing nothing.

Ben and Bob stood close.

"God damn it," Betsy said. "God *damn* this crummy world."

Ben Throckmorton pulled his daughter around in his arms.

"Oh, God, Daddy," she said—and the tears gushed as she held tightly to Ben.

Bob fought back a tear as he lit a cigarette.

"God damn this place," Betsy said, sobbing. "God damn this miserable town . . . this miserable state."

Ben kept holding her.

Florence and Warren came into the room. Warren carried a tray of coffee and orange juice.

"Come here to me, child," Florence said, taking Betsy from Ben and leading her to the bed. They sat on the bed and Florence cradled her. "My poor baby girl," Florence said more than once. "You go ahead and cry."

Quietly to Ben, Bob said, "I'd have a drink if it wasn't so early."

Betsy heard this. "God, get me one . . . please."

Warren left the room and was back in three minutes with a bottle of Scotch, ice, glasses.

"It ain't fair," Warren said. "Lord took her mama. Lord taken her husband. It ain't fair."

Bob poured Betsy a double and handed it to her.

She gulped half of it down. Caught her breath and drank the rest. "Where is he?" she wanted to know from somebody.

"Baptist Hospital," Ben said. "We'll go over there after a while—if you want to."

"I want to see him."

"We'll take you," Bob said.

Betsy said, "We don't know who . . . what . . . how? All those journalism things?"

"They think it happened around midnight," Ben said. "He was stabbed twice . . . near the camp. We don't know any more than that right now."

Betsy held her glass out to Bob for another drink. Bob poured Scotch into the glass.

Choking with emotion, she said, "He cared about those people."

Florence was still holding her as Ben said, "Honey, God knows who was in the camp. Olin says it looks like a simple robbery. Nowadays, I reckon, a man'll kill for a dollar."

Bob knelt on the carpet in front of Betsy and took her hands in his. "Millie's on her way. Ben called her."

Moved by this, Betsy gushed another torrent of tears.

"Somebody has to call Ted's folks," Bob said. "I guess that's a job for me, huh?"

Her eyes closed, Betsy squeezed Bob's hands.

"You all right?" he said. "We can get some pills . . . knock you out."

She shook her head no. "I want to see Ted," she mumbled.

But she stretched out across the bed. Florence covered her with a quilt.

Florence told Bob and Ben to go downstairs for a while, she would stay with Betsy.

Down in the kitchen, Bob and Ben sat at the butcher-block table. They drank coffee and smoked.

Ben phoned KVAT and left word for Estill Parch to put the story on the noon news, but keep it brief. He phoned Ray Fletcher at his home and suggested that Ray assign W. M. Keller to the story. There ought to be a sidebar obit on Ted, he said. There were pictures of Ted at the house. Somebody could come over and pick out something.

"I'll write the obit for you," Bob said.

"You will?"

"I think I know enough about him. I'd rather be typing than sitting here."

First, Bob made the thankless phone call to Ted's father in Bridgehampton, Long Island, reaching him at his grocery store in the heart of the village, on the main road that led to Easthampton and on out to Montauk.

There was no manual for this kind of phone call.

Bob identified himself as a close friend of the Throckmorton family, and said, "Mr. Winton, I've got some bad news for you. I hope you're strong enough to take it. It's about Ted. There's been an accident"—Bob knew this was the wrong word—"and I'm afraid Ted's been killed."

The awkward pause.

"We don't know much right now, sir. It happened around midnight. He was stabbed. There must have been a fight or something. He'd gone to a hobo camp here in Claybelle. He was working on a magazine story. We've just told Betsy about it. I know she'll want to talk to you and Mrs. Winton later. Sir, I can't tell you how sorry we are, all of us. Ted was a great guy. The name of the police chief is Musgrove. That number is 4-1561."

Bob hung up the phone in the kitchen. "I think I'm ready for a Scotch, Warren."

Bob took the drink to Ben's bedroom-office-den. He looked out of the big picture window. Ben was down on the boat dock.

The day was cold and overcast. The back lawn had turned the color of a Manila envelope. The trees were a tangle of wire. In a topcoat and bareheaded, Ben was a lonely figure on the dock.

Bob plunked down at the typewriter on Ben's desk and wrote the obit.

Ted Winton, the radio executive who died of stab wounds Thursday night, was a former football star at Yale and one of America's brightest journalists.

Mr. Winton, 30, a native of Bridge-hampton, New York, was working on a magazine story for *Collier's* at the time of his death.

Mr. Winton had moved to Claybelle from New York City. Since September, he had been the station manager of KVAT. He was married to Betsy Throck-morton, editor-in-chief of the *Times-Standard*.

Funeral arrangements have not been made but it is expected that Mr. Winton will be buried in Bridgehampton. A memorial service will be held in Claybelle.

Mr. Winton had been a staff writer for *Time* magazine before moving to Texas. He had covered the stock market crash, the Lindbergh kidnapping, and the demise of such crime figures as John Dillinger and "Ma" Barker.

Henry Luce, the editor and publisher of *Time,* said, "We are all greatly saddened. Ted was one of our most versatile writers. He and Betsy were two of the most likable young people I have ever known."

Having made up the quote from Henry Luce, Bob went on to say that Ted would be remembered among the true greats of Yale football; that his name would be mentioned along with those of Stagg, Heffelfinger, Frank Hinkey, Ted Coy, Albie Booth. Bob gave Ted credit for almost single-handedly leading Yale to the National Championship of 1927.

Bob slipped on his jacket, pulled up the collar, lit a cigarette, and carried his drink down to the dock.

"This was never much of a lake," Ben said, "but you kids used to spend a lot of time out here."

"Those were good days."

"I guess she'll come through this, one way or another."

"She will."

"Life's been good to me, except for some things." Ben was looking off.

Bob said, "I haven't had any whiskey this early since college."

"I'd give anything if I could bring Ted back for her, Bob. She's about the only thing I ever did right."

"That's not true, Ben. You've done most things right in your life, but she's the best thing you ever did."

Florence helped Betsy slip into a skirt, blouse, sweater, and poured Scotch into a flask and put the flask in Betsy's purse.

"You go to that hospital, then you come home to me," Florence said.

Wearing a pair of dark glasses and with a fur coat over her shoulders, Betsy was led to the Packard by her daddy and Bob Walker.

She didn't utter a word on the drive to the hospital, though she twice took a swig from the flask.

The hospital was an old redbrick building with a modern wing built on. As Ben parked the car, Betsy finally spoke. "I don't think I've been in here since Mama died."

If that one had been easier somehow, it was only because everybody had been resigned to it. Betsy had watched Elizabeth, a gorgeous woman, gradually become a yellowing, misshapen invalid. She had watched her mother's sweetness disappear as the pain had grown worse. The kidney infection was causing other complications, somebody had said. Ben would ignore her mother's irritability and sit for hours by the bed, holding Elizabeth's hand, speaking to her gently, reliving the good days. Ben wasn't seeing that bloated dying person in the hospital bed. He was seeing the Gibson Girl. After school, Betsy would go to the hospital room and sit in a corner doing homework or reading Mark Twain. Betsy would wander around on the hospital floors and return to the room to find more tubes and contraptions hooked up to her mother. One night Florence and Warren came in, and two more doctors, and more nurses, and they had all looked peculiar. She remembered the faint sound of the death rattle. And she remembered how her daddy had been holding Elizabeth's hand as a nurse said, "She's gone, Mr. Throckmorton."

Florence was the only one who had smiled through her tears. Florence had said, "Thank the Lord, she won't suffer no more."

Death might have been a good break for her mother but it was a lousy break for Ted.

Now in that hospital again, being led down a corridor, Betsy's mind was a junkyard—and she was angry.

What ignorant person had done this? It was ignorance that killed most things on the stupid planet. Here lies another human being who was worthwhile. Cause of death: life.

Ben and Bob gripped Betsy firmly as she looked at Ted.

There was still color in his face as he lay on a pad atop a table, still in his hobo costume: handsome, youthful, sleeping peacefully.

Betsy's eyes flooded. "What a waste," she said in a low voice. She touched Ted's cheek and ran her hand through his hair. "I'm sorry, sweetie," she said. "God, you were special."

She almost bent over and kissed him, but didn't. She looked at him for another agonizing moment. Suddenly she turned away and shuddered. "I can't do this," she said unsteadily, grabbing Bob Walker's arm. "Get me out of here, Bob. Get me the *fuck* out of here."

Twenty

MOST PEOPLE called them wakes, but Betsy called them death parties. Fortunately, for her sanity's sake, she was aware that in Texas a death party couldn't be prevented any more than it could be brought to an end in mid-cry, mid-drink, or mid–meat loaf. A death party simply invented itself and kept growing, as food and whiskey and people came from every direction. A death party was one of nature's miracles. Cakes and pies and casseroles made it okay that somebody had died.

The death party at the house on Wildflower Drive started around five o'clock, two hours after Betsy came back from the hospital. This was when Leatha arrived with the potato salad. A few minutes later, Olive Cooper arrived with the macaroni and cheese. And a few minutes after that, Bernice Beaton arrived with the black-eyed peas and cornbread.

Within the next hour, virtually everyone Betsy had ever known in Claybelle was in the house. If the residents of the hobo camp could have seen all the food in the kitchen, there would have been a riot in Ben Throckmorton's front yard.

It was Anna Sue Beaton who brought the angel-food cake, and Eva Jane McKnight who had been thoughtful enough to make fudge.

Betsy had gone back to bed after she returned from the hospital, but Leatha came over, handed her bowl of potato salad to Florence in the kitchen, and marched straight up the stairs and into Betsy's bedroom and flung herself into Betsy's arms. The usually serene Leatha wanted to show Betsy that she knew what near-hysterics were all about.

Betsy could only look at Leatha through a blur, an alcoholic haze.

"Oh, my dearest darling, what are we going to do?" Leatha kept saying. "Oh, you poor thing, you poor darling thing."

Betsy couldn't think of anything to say, except that she was sorry about Leatha's magnolia. But Leatha's presence urged her to get out of bed and hit the Scotch again.

Now Olive Cooper entered the room, having stopped in the kitchen to put Florence and Warren in charge of her macaroni and cheese.

"It's God's will," Olive said, without tears. "Betsy, this hit me like a physical blow, I can't tell you, but you must take Jesus into your heart."

"I don't have a heart," Betsy said, a little wobbly.

"God the Father, God the Son, God the Holy Spirit," Olive said.

"That'll make the front seat pretty crowded."

"I brought some macaroni and cheese. I'm not saying mine's better than Florence can make, but I use sharper cheese."

Betsy went to her dressing table and thought about trying to repair the damage to her face.

"If you'll give me a minute, I'll come downstairs," Betsy said, looking into the mirror, wondering where to begin.

"You stay right here," Leatha said. "No one is going to bother you."

"They won't?"

"Ben looks terrible," Olive said. "He's heartbroken."

"Betsy, what can I do?"

"Nothing, Leatha."

"Are you all right? You are so brave."

"I'm not brave. I'm mad."

Olive said, "Betsy, I want you to take Jesus into your heart."

"Would one of you ask Warren to bring me some ice?"

Leatha said, "Ben keeps an ice pack around here somewhere. I'll go look."

"I don't want an ice pack." Betsy sighed. "I want a glass of ice."

"I'll go," Olive said, starting for the door. "I'll send you up a nice big pitcher of ice water."

"Thanks."

"Dub will be over in a while. He is so angry at what happened. I wouldn't want to repeat what he said he'd like to do to everyone in that hobo camp." Olive left.

Leatha said, "Betsy, I know it's painful to talk about, but arrangements will have to be made. I want to do anything I can to help."

"Christ," Betsy said, dreading the fact that she was going to have to speak to Ted's folks. Surely they were hating her this moment for dragging their son to Texas and getting him killed. "I'll take him to Bridgehampton," she said to Leatha. "That's what his mother and father will want."

"You tell me how I can help."

"I don't know, Leatha. I can't think right now."

Leatha asked if Betsy had known Ted's parents at all.

"Not well," Betsy said. "They came to the city a few times. We went out to the island once or twice. He has an older brother I never met, but Ted was . . . he was their . . ."

"I know. He was their pride and joy."

"They'll hate me," Betsy said, getting weepy again, though she was fighting it.

"They will do no such thing," Leatha said. "They know how much he loved you."

How much was that? Betsy wondered. And how much had she loved him? And what did it matter now?

Leatha left the room, and five minutes later Florine Webster came in. Florine brought the pitcher of ice water, which she put on the table by the bottle of Scotch. She walked over and squeezed Betsy on the shoulders.

"It's a cafeteria downstairs," Florine said. "I didn't bring any food. Can I stay?"

"Hi, Florine." Betsy managed a weak smile.

Florine fixed two Scotch and waters. Stiff. Serious amber. She handed one to Betsy, then took a seat on the chaise lounge near the dressing table.

"I think you're a little ahead of me," Florine said.

"I am *way* ahead of you."

"I'll catch up."

"Not likely."

They sipped their drinks and both lit cigarettes.

"Ted and I had dinner together last night at B's," Betsy said. "We argued about something stupid. Journalism. Perfect, huh? You have an argument with somebody and you never see them again. Funny. Last week we talked about death. Those schoolteachers? That story bothered us. Ted's mother is a teacher. There they were, three ladies from Stripling High in Fort Worth, driving to Austin for a convention, but a minute later—gone. A car comes out of a side road and they're dead. They no longer exist. I kissed Ted goodbye last night . . . now *he's* gone. Just like that. It's all so pointless."

"You don't have enough Scotch for me to try to explain the meaning of life," Florine said.

"All day long I've been telling myself it's only a merry-go-round. Some people fall off quicker than others. No big mystery."

Florine put a top on her drink and sat back down.

"I can't help being angry, Florine. I'm furious. The world is turning into a great big comic strip, but Ted's not going to know how it all comes out."

"The news has always been funny."

"Look at it now," Betsy said. "The Italians are killing the Ethiopians. The Russians are killing anybody who smiles. They can't wait to start killing each other in Spain. The Nazis are committing wholesale murder in Germany. Presumably intelligent people say, 'Gee, I wonder what Hitler's up to?' *I* know what he's up to. He wants to start a war. Look at their swastika. Is that an evil-looking thing or not? I ask you, would a nice person wear that? I honestly can't figure out the German people. They're highly cultured, sober, hardworking, creative . . . but here they are, letting this ranting psychotic drag them into spiritual ruin. England and France will have to fight them again. That means us, too. Anybody who reads a newspaper knows this, but of course nobody reads a newspaper. So . . . you and Daddy, huh?"

"Stuff happens." Florine shrugged, smiling.

"Where does this leave Madam Serenity?"

"Your father and Leatha haven't been to bed together in five years. You know Leatha. She's an old friend of mine, but she's always cared more about the way things *seem* than the way things *are*."

"You and Daddy probably haven't been to bed together in three or four days."

"Three," Florine said. "I don't know what's going to happen, Betsy. I'm just going to take things as they come. My divorce was final last week. Here I was, looking forward to throwing myself on the open market, but now I only want to be with Ben."

"Sly old Pop," Betsy said.

Downstairs, the death party had spread through the house. Two hundred people wandering in and out of rooms, sitting, standing, mixing drinks, holding drinks, holding plates of food, going back for second helpings, discussing football, business, children, auto repair, vegetable gardens.

Betsy, having made herself presentable, came down the stairs with Florine; and they were met in the foyer by Ben and Chief Olin Musgrove.

Millie Saunders was on the way, Ben told Betsy. Millie had phoned from Memphis, where she was changing planes. Bob Walker had driven to Meacham Field in Fort Worth to meet her flight. She ought to be at the house by nine or ten o'clock.

The police chief, eating a plate of cornbread with cream gravy poured over it, took Betsy, Ben, and Florine into a corner to bring them up to date on what his investigation had uncovered.

The chief said, "Betsy, we've interrogated everybody in the hobo camp. Me and R. G. been working pretty hard all day, but I'm afraid we haven't come up with much. Some of them hobos knew Ted by description. A couple of 'em said they'd seen him last night, but they hadn't seen him after he'd gone wandering off in the camp somewhere, around eleven o'clock."

"So what you've found out is nothing, is that it?"

"That's what I was leadin' up to."

"Thank you, Chief."

"Betsy, let me say somethin'. There ain't but a hundred vagrants in that camp who could have done this. It was just a damned old robbery. Whoever did it ain't waitin' around to get caught. They gone Dixie. That's what I'd bet on. We'll continue our investigation, but I don't want you to get your hopes up about justice bein' done."

"The only justice would be for Ted not to be dead."

"There you go."

"The irony is, he cared about those people."

"Who did?"

"My husband."

"Cared about them hobos?"

The chief looked at Ben. "What for?"

Betsy walked away, leaving her daddy with the problem of trying to explain it.

Shady Webster and O. L. Beaton were in Ben's bedroom-office-den eating the black-eyed peas and cornbread that Bernice had brought. Shady was saying he had hired the driller he wanted and they were about ready to stick their straw in the ground.

"I see where they've hit a duster over by our lease," O. L. said with a worried look.

"Cloyd Bennett don't know shit. That duster is two miles from us. We'll be stem testing in sand at two thousand feet. We'll be in heavy flush at thirty-five hundred."

"I don't need me any more dry holes, Shady. My butt's gonna be in a crack if we don't hit this time."

"I don't exactly *collect* the sons of bitches myself."

"My main problem is with Lank."

"How's that?"

"He says he ain't gonna pay back the bank if we don't hit." O. L. glanced around to make sure no one was listening. "I've loaned him the money to get in on these last two deals. He said it wasn't right for a celebrity like him to piss off twenty thousand dollars with you. He said he didn't get in the oil business to lose money. He got in the oil business to get rich. Well, I wanted to help him out. He's a hero. And your track record was good. But now he's into Fidelity for thirty thousand. Between you and me, it ain't even a legitimate loan. I didn't ask him for any collateral. If a bank examiner came in tomorrow, I'd be swimmin' in a tub of shit. The other day, I said, 'Lank, what if I get a bank examination?' He said I could juggle the books and handle it. I asked him if he was some kind of a lunatic, and when I said that, he started to *look* at me like a lunatic. He said, 'Don't ever call me no lunatic again.' Scared the hell out of me, is what he did. You know what I'm startin' to think? I'm thinkin' we're mixed up with a lunatic."

"Hey, whoa," said Shady. "What's this *we* shit? You fuckers are investors. You came to me, remember? He's *your* partner, not mine."

"All I know is, I've got thirty thousand dollars with wings on it and nothin' but your word it's gonna fly back into my coop."

"Relax, old buddy. No need for you to worry unless you see me pullin' pipe and standin' ass-deep in salt water."

Shady's little joke.

"I hope to God I don't see that," the banker said prayerfully.

"What you need is some young pussy, O. L. Take the pressure off."

"How *is* Eva Jane?"

"Now you're talkin' about a gusher," Shady said. "Don't I look thinner? You couldn't plug that fuckin' hole with eight hundred pounds of cement."

Big 'Un Darly came by to pay his respects to Betsy. He found her sitting in the kitchen at the butcher-block table having another drink with Florine.

Big 'Un said that Ted was a fine fellow and he would never forget that Ted had put the Claybelle fight song on the radio.

"I brought you something," the sports editor said, handing Betsy a large brown envelope. "It was in our files. I thought you might like to have it."

In the envelope Betsy found an old AP wirephoto of Ted carrying the football in the Yale-Army game of 1927. Betsy was touched by Big 'Un's thoughtfulness. She gave him a hug.

As long as he was there, Big 'Un said, he wondered if he could ask Betsy a business question.

"Am I gonna get to cover the Sugar Bowl?"

"I don't see why not. We should have our own man there."

"It won't cost much," Big 'Un said. "I've worked it out in arithmetic. I'll drive to New Orleans. It's around a thousand miles, round trip. We're allowed three cents a mile. That's thirty dollars. A hotel can't be more than twenty dollars for four days. I figure a dollar a day for meals. The whole trip can't cost no more than sixty-five or seventy-five dollars."

"I think we can manage."

Florine looked away to hide her smile.

Big 'Un said, "I've never been to a bowl game."

"It should be a good one."

"I've never been to New Orleans."

"It's an interesting city."

"You'll get your money's worth, Betsy. I'll write a column every day, a lead every day, and a sidebar every day."

"I'm sure you will."

"I been workin' on my sims, too. I think I got some pretty good ones."

"Your what?" Florine asked.

"His similes," Betsy answered, and Florine turned away again.

Big 'Un went to the buffet in the dining room to see if anybody had brought any cream gravy he might pour over the snacks and casseroles.

A moment later, Anna Sue and Eva Jane were in the kitchen.

They had come to the death party together with their angel-food cake and fudge, each in a new frock that had made its way from the Rue de la Paix to Dallas.

Betsy was given a hug by both women. Eva Jane and Florine exchanged a cool smile.

"I wish I knew what to say, Betsy," Eva Jane said. "It is a human tragedy, is all. To think something like this could happen in Claybelle."

"Isn't it the truth?" said Anna Sue. "You would expect it to happen to niggers or Mexicans, but my God—real people?"

"Anna Sue, do you mind?" Florine said, indicating with a look that Warren and Florence were in the kitchen now, tending to the dishes and the food.

"Oh, I'm sorry," Anna Sue said, covering her mouth with her hand, looking embarrassed. "Betsy, they say it was one of those hobos. I hope they catch him. I hope he fries till there's nothin' left but his shoes! Are you all right?"

"I'm fine," Betsy said.

"You don't look good."

Eva Jane said, "Well, naturally she doesn't look good, Anna Sue! She's lost her husband!"

"I know, but—"

"I'm drunk," Betsy said.

Anna Sue said, "Betsy, you know I've never been very religious. I mean, I've never gone to church regularly, but this whole thing started me to thinking about God today—which I believe in, of course. I think a person can believe in God even if they don't go to church, I really do, don't you, Eva Jane? Anyhow, Betsy, the thing we have to keep in mind is how God acts in strange ways. You know, if you look at Africa and places? That kind of thing? It is *very* strange. But I don't think there's any question that God acts different when He's dealing with America. He is definitely partial to America— and thank the stars! We almost never have the terrible things happen to us that foreigners do. Catastrophes and things. Earthquakes and tidal waves. My Lord, they have those things all the time. You would think those people would get tired of it and *move*. One reason foreigners have all this, *I* think, is because they dress so funny. I mean, how is God supposed to know what they *stand for* if they are going to walk around looking like they do? Veils. Robes. Sandals. Feathers—"

"What is your point, Anna Sue?" Florine asked, afraid to look at Betsy, even for a second.

"My point is that God must have been in one of His moods where He wanted to balance things out. Betsy, God just happened to look down here, accidentally—I think it was purely accidental—and see that there was this person—you—who has had everything she ever wanted. You've always had looks, money, everything. You were a cheerleader for two years. You were class favorite for three years. You have a talent. You've lived in New York. And then you got Ted. I wish God hadn't looked down here and noticed, but He did. So He took Ted away from you. I don't know what other explanation there could be. God thought you had too much for one person. The unlucky thing is, He just happened not to be busy with tornadoes and things while He was passing over Claybelle."

Betsy was too amazed to make a comment, but Florine said, "Now I know why Will Rogers got killed. He had too many polo ponies."

"Will Rogers?" said Anna Sue, her nose wrinkled. "Will Rogers was a totally different thing. Will Rogers was a tragic accident. God had His back turned. God would never kill anybody like Will Rogers if He hadn't been busy with something else. Where was Will Rogers when his plane crashed? I've forgotten."

"Alaska," said Florine.

"Well, see there? What in the world would God be doing in Alaska?"

Anna Sue changed the subject to clothes. She was going out to the Rose Bowl on one of SMU's special trains, and she wondered if Betsy could give her any tips on what to take.

"I am *so* excited," she said. "I want to see it all—a movie studio, Catalina, Hollywood, Santa Monica. Bob's covering the game. Everybody in Dallas is going. There must be ten or fifteen special trains."

"We're going to New Orleans with TCU," Eva Jane announced.

"That'll be cozy," Florine said. "So am I."

"Oh?" said Eva Jane. "Are you on the train with the team? We are."

"Actually, I'm not sure I'm going now. It was supposed to be Ben and Leatha, a bunch of us."

"Of course you're going," Betsy said. "That's two weeks from now. I'll be in New York, anyhow."

"How long will you stay?"

"I'm not sure when I'm coming back, Florine."

Florine took her hand. "Don't hate Texas, Betsy."

"I don't hate Texas. I'm just going to let Texas entertain somebody else for a while."

Twenty-one

———

MILLIE SAUNDERS flew into Fort Worth on an "aluminum broom," as she called it, a Stinson Trimotor. The plane carried ten passengers and belonged to Mid-Continent Airlines when it was on the ground, Millie said, but to fate alone when it was in the air.

It was eight o'clock at night and the wind was whipping an icy mist across the pavement as Millie stepped down from the Trimotor. Through a plate-glass window in the dining room at Meacham Field, Bob Walker picked her out among the passengers. She was the young woman in the full-length leopard coat and a hat that looked like an upside-down flowerpot.

"You must be Millie Saunders," Bob said, halting her in the terminal lobby where carved eagles were crawling up the corners and convening on the ceiling of the building.

"The former Millie Saunders," she said. "Right now, I'm a walking bedpan. Did you see that landing?"

"No."

"Neither did the pilot!"

"I'm Bob Walker."

"Of course you are."

They went to the luggage area to claim Millie's suitcase, if it hadn't fallen out of the plane somewhere over Little Rock.

"How is Bets?"

"Drunk."

"Good!"

"The house was swarming with people when I left. How do you stop a wake?"

"Hand grenades help. How long a drive is it?"

On these roads tonight, Bob said, it would take them an hour and a half.

"Do we pass any cowboys?"

"I might be able to find one."

The airport was north of downtown Fort Worth. The stockyards area lay in a direct path to downtown, which lay in a
direct path to Claybelle.

Bob drove Millie through the stockyards area, in and
around cowboy hotels, saloons, saddle shops, a hacienda-type
structure that housed the Livestock Exchange, the Swift and
Armour meat-packing plants, and the stock pens where
hundreds of head of cattle were groaning in the night. Millie
saw a building she thought was an armory. It was the rodeo
coliseum, home of "the world's championship indoor rodeo."

"An *indoor* rodeo?" Millie smiled.

"This was the first one," Bob said. "I never thought it was
unusual until right now."

Bob parked on Exchange Avenue and took Millie in the
Buck Horn Bar for a drink. She broke into laughter at the bar
stools. They were actual leather saddles.

She removed her leopard coat and hat and climbed onto a
saddle. "Hidy, partner," she said to the bartender, a lean little
man with a limp, scars on his forehead and chin, and bloodshot eyes—an old bronc rider.

"This is great," Millie said, swiveling around on the saddle.
"If I have time, I want to rent a car and go see Dodge City.
How far is it?"

"About six hundred miles."

"What?"

"Roughly."

"How far is Tombstone?"

"Eight hundred miles."

"Be serious!"

"You asked me."

"What about Reno?"

"Fifteen hundred miles."

"Jesus Christ, I thought I was out West!"

On the drive to Claybelle, they traded sips from a carton of
black coffee Bob had stopped to buy at a Pig Stand.

"You and Betsy are like sisters," Bob mentioned.

"Closer," Millie said. "We chose each other."

Millie confessed that she had always envied Betsy for having a skill, for knowing she wanted to be a journalist. Millie

had wanted a career, too, though she hadn't known what kind. Her goal had been to become a female executive somewhere. Any old corporation would do.

She had taken the first job offered to her after she had graduated from Barnard, the job at Lord & Taylor. In five years, she had moved up from assistant buyer in Better Dresses to the head of the couture department.

"I may become the first woman vice-president at the store, which is hilarious because I hate fashion; *but*—they send me to Paris twice a year to get drunk, so how can I knock it? I'm in charge of the rich bitches. That's my job. The rich bitches don't ask for anybody but me. I must get paged thirty times a day."

"You sound like a powerful person. Has it gone to your head?"

"Listen, power is the only thing men understand, the only thing they *respect*. I don't know why I can deal with the rich bitches so well, exactly. Well, I *do* know. They're mentally deficient. I tease them . . . gossip with them. Then I sell them a suit Joan Crawford wouldn't wear. They buy the crap because they don't have anything else to do. Fashion is white-collar fraud."

"Women dress for other women, don't they?"

"Of course we do—but at least we get variety this way. All a man wants to see a woman wear are high heels and lingerie. You and Bets go back to the crib or something, right?"

First grade, Bob said, but they didn't fall in love until the second grade. The best times in elementary school were when their desks had been close together, through the luck of alphabetical seating. They had been able to pass notes of sinful hilarity.

In junior high, Bob admitted, he had gone through a period when girls weren't as important to him as sports or vandalism. It had been more fun to hang around with the guys. Ringing doorbells. Stealing peaches. Throwing rocks and breaking out school windows in the night. Watching Tommy Jack Lucas shit in a paper bag, put it on Mr. Kinkel's front porch, set fire to it, ring the doorbell, and hide behind a hedge across the street. Mr. Kinkel would stomp out the fire and get shit all over his shoes. "Doyle Laymance!" Sloppy Herster would yell, and everybody would romp off down the street and collapse in gut-wrenching laughter.

Bob and Betsy had fallen back in love in Claybelle High, this time for keeps. Betsy was the high school queen, arbiter of all taste, decider of all fads. She may have invented the Slam Book. Other girls were considered prettier, like Anna Sue Beaton and Eva Jane McKnight, but no girl combined the wit, the intelligence, and the looks of Betsy Throckmorton.

Nothing was more painful or at the same time more blissful than high school love, Bob said. Sneaking kisses and feels in the hallways. Vowing never to be parted the rest of your lives. Tearing yourselves apart to go to class. Necking on picnics until your faces were raw.

"I'm surprised we had tongues left after our last summer together before we went off to college."

"It broke my heart to leave Pete Michero," Millie said. "He promised to write me in New York every day. By Thanksgiving, he was married to a hunky named Paula who worked at the Heinz plant."

Bob figured that if Betsy had stayed in Texas and gone to college, they would have made the drastic mistake of getting married. They would have *had* to get married, most likely. Their careers would have been fouled up, and now where would they be? Settling for less. Weary and unhappy. Barely able to find the energy to change the dial on a radio.

It was better for things to have worked out as they had, he said. Their passions had been calmed by distance and absence. Their interests had expanded. They had both changed for the better. They would always have each other, as close friends, sharing memories that were burned into their minds.

"Betsy will always belong to me in a certain way," he said. "I'll always belong to her in a certain way. She really cared for Ted. He was a great guy. I liked him a lot. It's a funny thing, but I was happy just seeing her happy."

Bob noticed Millie gazing at him.

"What . . . ?" he said inquisitively.

"Nothing," Millie said. "I was just looking at a man who's in love."

The death party was over by the time Bob and Millie reached the house. Leatha and Florine were still there, sitting in the living room with Betsy and her daddy, when Bob's car came into the circular drive. Betsy saw the headlights and rushed out on the front porch.

Millie raced up the steps. They hugged and cried and hugged some more.

"You're supposed to be drunk and passed out," Millie said.

"I drank myself sober."

After introductions to Leatha and Florine, and Florence and Warren, Millie was given a Scotch and offered some of the food that was left over—enough to feed all the teams in the Southwest Conference, but for no longer than a month.

Plans were discussed.

Waggoman's funeral home in Claybelle was going to ship Ted's body to a funeral home in Bridgehampton. Betsy would fly back with Millie and stay in New York City for an indefinite period, with Millie in her apartment.

While Bob had been going to the airport to meet Millie, Betsy had spoken to Ted's parents on the phone. Not an enjoyable phone call. The Wintons had cursed Texas and everything it stood for. Ben had gotten on the phone and said he wanted to pay for the funeral. The Wintons had said they didn't need his charity.

Ted's older brother would be handling the funeral arrangements. Ted would be buried in a cemetery in Bridgehampton. Ted's brother would try to round up some of Ted's old Yale teammates, and perhaps some of his friends at *Time,* for pallbearers.

Though it was getting late, past ten o'clock, W. M. Keller stopped by the house to offer Betsy his condolences. He had wanted to come by earlier but he had been working on a story about Thornton's Dairy selling tainted milk to the Claybelle High lunchroom.

Betsy took W. M. up to her study to speak to him privately.

"W. M., I'm going to New York. I don't know how long. Daddy's going to be running the paper again, but I want you to do something for me. Can I swear you to secrecy?"

The reporter said yes, of course, and looked intrigued.

"I want you to keep an eye on Lank Allred . . . do some checking up on him."

"Why?"

Betsy tried out her theory on W. M. about a possible "Texas Murder Machine."

"Damn," said W. M. "A Texas Ranger?"

"Maybe I've been reading too many detective stories, maybe not."

"Hell of an idea. Kill a hobo for profit. Hell of a *story*."

"Doesn't it seem to you like too much of a coincidence that four of the five people he's killed were unarmed?"

"I hadn't thought about it."

"How many attempted bank robberies were there in this state before the bankers started paying those rewards?"

"Not as many as we've got goin' on now."

"He's collected *all* of the reward money, W. M. I found that out from O. L. Beaton. I'd like to know what he's done with it. He may have gambling debts, who knows? He has a girlfriend in Fort Worth. Shirley Watters. She works at Lola's Oasis. Find out what you can about her. I haven't mentioned this to anyone, not even Daddy. Ted and I talked about it, but—"

Betsy turned away for a second. It hurt to say Ted's name.

W. M. said, "Betsy, you don't think what happened to Ted was connected in some way, do you?"

"No," she said. "It wouldn't make any sense. W. M., I don't know if I'm right about any of this. I know it's hard to believe about a Texas Ranger. I've tried to tell myself he's nothing but a trigger-happy headline grabber."

"That sounds more like it."

"I know it does, but these rewards bother the hell out of me. People are getting knocked off all over the state, and it's awfully strange to me that most of them are 'attempted' bank robbers."

"If I find out anything interesting, what do I do?"

"Call me in New York."

Before the evening was over, Betsy, Millie, and Bob Walker retreated to Betsy's bedroom upstairs. Betsy and Millie slipped on robes. Bob kicked off his shoes and pulled out his shirttail.

Florence brought up a pot of coffee, a pitcher of milk, a plate of lean ham sandwiches, and a plate of oatmeal cookies, no raisins.

Warren built a fire for them.

In the warmth and coziness of that room, then, with her two closest friends around her, Betsy was reassured of love and loyalty in this sordid world.

The three of them talked far into the night, of old times and better times. They occasionally mentioned Ted but were always careful to deflect their pain, their sorrow, with a cynicism they might never again find so useful.

So ended the worst day of Betsy Throckmorton's life. So ended a phase of her life. She swore that night that a mindless act of violence had stripped her of all vulnerability—there was nothing left now but the newshen.

Millie and Bob knew better, but they let her have the moment.

Twenty-two

DRUNK WAS the only way a person of sound mind could get through the squalid ritual of a funeral at which the casket was going to be left open.

"I have spoke," Betsy said in pure Texan.

"I'll be drunk, too," Millie predicted. "Maybe we should hire a couple of big fat nurses to go along. You know, keep us propped up, slap us around?"

They were in the back of a Cadillac limousine. They were being driven out to Long Island. It was the day before Ted's funeral.

The limo was dense with cigarette smoke, and the floor was trashed with newspapers. Betsy had been criticizing editorials. Millie had been criticizing ads.

"Why do people want an open casket?" Betsy said. "I guess they don't think they're going to get their money's worth if the casket's closed."

"That's part of it, but there's something else. If the casket's closed, how do you know who's inside? It could be anybody. It could be empty."

Millie had reserved a suite for the two of them in a little hotel in Sag Harbor, only seven miles from Bridgehampton. The hotel was named the Seaview. Millie had shacked up there once. If the hotel had ever offered a view of the sea, it no longer did. A hardware store and a Woolworth's were more like it. But the rooms were clean, Millie promised, and it had a dark bar that catered to fishermen, potato farmers, and worldly authors who might even see their work published someday.

The plan, as Millie saw it, was for them to drink themselves into a stupor tonight, wake up with a hangover, get drunk again to cure the hangover, claw their way through the services, and be driven back to the city.

That was how to handle this funeral.

Betsy wouldn't have minded being drunk now. Ted's parents had made it clear to her that she wasn't welcome to drop by their house in Bridgehampton. They weren't even happy about the fact that she would be sitting with them at the funeral—and it had been their wish that the casket be open.

"They want me to have one last look at the man I killed," Betsy said.

"No, they don't, Betsy. They know better than that. They want to grieve. You can grieve better when the casket's open."

"I want to be cremated."

"God, I don't." Millie flinched.

"Why not?"

"Doesn't it hurt?"

And there was another thing about cremation. "How do you know whose ashes are in the urn?" Millie said. "You only have the funeral director's word for it. I mean, is it Uncle Chester or is it Oxydol?"

It was early evening when they checked into the Seaview. They sent their bags up to the suite and went directly to the bar, where, aside from a brooding book author slumped in a corner, they were the only customers.

"You ladies have escorts?" asked a gray-haired bartender.

Millie said, "The prince is docking the yacht. Give us two Scotches and paste this to your forehead, old-timer."

She slid him a ten.

They drank for two hours, chatting with the bartender mostly. They heard how much he hated the summers out there. Rich guys didn't tip. Millie got around to asking if they could get something to eat at the bar; they didn't want to fool with the dining room.

"Can't eat at the bar, it's against the rules," he said.

Millie slid him another ten.

"What would you like?"

"Anything I can eat with a fork," Betsy said. "I need one hand free to smoke."

The bartender brought them each a plate of spaghetti and meatballs. One-hand food.

They drank through dinner, and beyond, and now Betsy said, "Funerals do have a certain amount of suspense. Will the minister get everyone's name right? 'Our hearts go out to his lovely wife, Patsy.' "

Millie's drink went down the wrong way.

Moments later, Betsy sang from a hymn.

> *He comes to the garden alone*
> *While the dew is still on the roses.*
> *And the voice I hear—*

"That's it," Millie said, taking Betsy by the arm. "What's the damage, old-timer?"

Betsy and Millie had breakfast in the room and started spiking their coffee with brandy at ten-thirty.

At noon, when the limousine arrived at the funeral home, a white two-story house that looked like a summer inn, Betsy said, "Just get me past the casket. There'll be a nice tip in it for you."

The largest wreath had come from Henry Luce. This had been Betsy's guess, and Stillwell Padgam-Norris confirmed it later. Still Norris had led a group of *Time* people to the funeral: Hazel Hanrahan, the head of research; Mabe Forrest, the doughnut queen; Andrew Cheshire, an editor; and Nina, the sly kitten.

In a summer month, there would have been more of them. They could have tied the funeral in with a croquet tournament.

When Betsy entered the chapel and saw the open casket from a distance, her knees buckled, but Millie held her firmly.

They were ushered to the second row of seats, behind Ted's folks and older brother, a banker or something. He offered Betsy a look of sympathy, but Ted's mother and father, who could not have been mistaken for anything but a grocer and a schoolteacher, refused eye contact.

Boris Karloff, the minister, talked for ten minutes about eternity and its place in everyday life. Then it was time for the crowd-pleasing trek past the casket.

Boris Karloff invited Betsy to go first.

Her knees buckled again, this time more fiercely, but Millie supported her as she looked down at Ted's powder-white face, his hair parted on the wrong side, the body dressed in a brown suit, light blue shirt, and dark blue tie, none of which she had seen him wear in the whole time she had known him.

At the cemetery, Ted's casket was lugged by six sturdy young men to a burial plot under a tent.

Again, Betsy and Millie sat in the second row of chairs, behind Ted's parents and brother.

Boris Karloff said some more words about death, trying to make it sound like such a neat deal everybody ought to commit suicide.

When the service ended, a lawn party began.

The pallbearers introduced themselves to Betsy. None of their names were familiar. If any of them had been Yale All-Americans, Bruce Caldwells or Bill Websters, she would have recognized the names.

Ted's parents left the cemetery without a word to Betsy.

The *Time* contingent had stood off to one side during the burial service. Betsy and Millie gravitated into their conversation group.

Betsy told them she would be staying around New York for a while. She promised to drop by the office.

"We'll be in our new building by the end of the summer," Still Norris mentioned. "Forty-eighth Street. Everybody wants an office overlooking the skating rink. You know about Harry's new magazine, I gather?"

"It was in the works before I left."

"He hasn't named an M.E. yet. It's only a rumor on Promenade Deck, but I'm told I'm in the running. I rather think he liked what I said in a meeting the other day. We should see *Life* . . . see the world, I said. Mammoth budget. Harry's very excited."

Still Norris reflected on how Ted had been one of the "fastest learners" he had ever edited. Mastered the *Time* art of writing a "round" story rather quickly, Ted did.

This theory had always fascinated Betsy. A *Time* piece needed to be round, Still Norris had once said, making a big circle with his arms. Vertical and horizontal stories were for newspapers.

"To be sure," he had lectured, "our pieces must have a beginning, a middle, and an end, *but*—if we do our job well, we fatten them on the sides, you see? Which is what makes them round."

The editor asked if there was any new evidence surrounding Ted's death. Clues, suspects?

"Nothing," Betsy said. "I'm inclined to go along with the police. Some poor hobo did it for eight dollars."

"Hmmm," Still Norris said. "Tragic. Senseless. Education's the answer. That's Harry's view—*and* mine, by the way."

Hazel Hanrahan hugged Betsy and said she would always remember Ted's neatness and courtesy.

Mabe Forrest, the doughnut queen, hugged Betsy and said she would always remember Ted's friendliness.

Nina, the sly kitten, hugged Betsy and said she would always remember Ted's thoughtfulness.

In what way? Betsy wondered.

Andrew Cheshire apologized to Betsy for Lafester Cleed's absence. "Laffy," as he liked to be called, the managing editor, had wanted to be there, but he and Harry Luce were leaving tonight for Peking. They were going over to talk to Yin Jukeng and Sung Cheh-yuan and try to straighten out this darn mess in northern China.

Betsy curled up in the limousine and slept most of the way back to Manhattan, to Millie's apartment amid the glitter and swank of Park Avenue.

Twenty-three

—

BEN THROCKMORTON was reasonably sure he had fallen into the same thing as love with Florine Webster, but what was he going to do about it?

Florine was the recent wife of one of his best friends, and the best friend of the woman he was *supposed* to be in love with.

You could put this shit on the radio, Ben was thinking to himself as he carried a mug of coffee into Ray Fletcher's office at the paper and sat down to confide in his old friend and managing editor.

He and Florine had been sneaking around to be with each other, and it had been making both of them miserable. Neither of them wanted to hurt Leatha, though Florine was slightly less emphatic about it.

Leatha ought to be told for her own good, Florine was suggesting.

Not necessarily, Ben was saying. It had been his experience that when people were told something for their own good, they resented you for it for the next sixty or seventy years and never looked at you the same again.

Ben knew it would make things easier on himself and Florine if he could find a way to tell Leatha that they had no future together, but this would involve having to explain the basic reason he had reached such a conclusion was because he had discovered this marvelous, intelligent, witty, beautiful woman who had introduced him to his first sustained hard-on in ten years.

Chances are, he said to Ray Fletcher, this would send Leatha flying through the air like one of Sam Baugh's spirals, and when she came back to the ground she would scream at him till he went deaf in both ears.

"Chance are," Ray said with a grin.

279

"So what do I do?"

"Bunt."

"Bunt?"

"Stay in the game," Ray advised. "Leatha is bound to see the signs sooner or later. Women pick up on those things. She'll figure out something's going on. But when she confronts you with it, lie. Launch a counterattack. Bad-mouth all the people who could have started an ugly rumor like this. Leatha will go to Florine with it. Florine will break down and tell her the truth. Then you can confess and say you lied because you didn't want to hurt her."

"Do you think I'm that big a chickenshit?"

"You can call it chickenshit if you want to. I call it smart."

"I was thinking Florine and I should go to Leatha together, like adults. Straightforward, honest, decent people. Take the high road."

"Throw yourself on the mercy of the court."

"Something like that."

"Fine. Do it Christmas morning. Dress up like Santa Claus. 'Here's your present, Leatha—I'm fuckin' your best friend.'"

"That's real funny, Ray."

"Can I bum a smoke?"

Handing him his pack of Chesterfields, Ben said, "I thought you quit."

"Only when the Colonel's around."

The Colonel was Ray's endearing name for Jo Ellen, his wife.

"Leatha's going to get hurt, Ben. You can't get around the fact. Are you sure you're in love with Florine? Seems kind of sudden, if you don't mind me saying so."

"I didn't think I'd ever feel like this about anybody again. She's a wonderful woman."

"Why'd she marry that runt?"

"She was young. Shady's okay. You don't know him as well as I do. You have to take half of what Shady says and divide it by two."

"Well, she's a damn good-looking woman, I'll say that. She'll probably be worth it."

"Worth what?"

"That opera you're gonna have to sit through."

"Thanks, Ray. You're a lot of help—like you are on the golf course."

Ben saved his Christmas shopping for Christmas Eve day, as was usually the case.

He and Florine drove to Fort Worth that morning. They checked into a room at the Westbrook Hotel and stayed in bed until three in the afternoon, *then* went shopping.

Ben always felt foolish when he arranged these matinees— a man his age doing this shit—but Florine would take him on yet another physical adventure, something that would make him think his brain was being attacked by humming-birds, and he would find himself plotting the next matinee.

They went to The Fair on Seventh Street to shop. Florine picked out a brooch for Ben to give Leatha, a gold basket with rubies and sapphires in it. She picked out a wool coat for Ben to give Florence and a hunting jacket for Ben to give Warren. As part of their Christmas, Florence and Warren would receive money, too. It was always a ridiculous amount, up in the hundreds of dollars. Florence would cry and they would refuse the money, but Ben would force it on them. For the past several years, they had taken to putting the money in the bank and not touching it, in case Ben ever needed it for an emergency.

Ben had already mailed a diamond watch to Betsy to open on Christmas morning. Florine had picked it out on the day of another matinee.

In the department store, Ben asked Florine to entertain herself for a half-hour while he went to shop for her present.

"I don't want anything," she said. "I already have what I want.

"You've got me something, don't you?"

"It's nothing."

It was an oil painting. Florine had found it at an auction, a painting of a Confederate cavalry charge. It was called "Lee's Texans." It wasn't easy to buy something for Ben that he didn't already have.

"I won't be long," he said. "Meet you at the soda fountain."

Ben's idea was to leave nothing to chance when it came to Florine's present. He walked three blocks down the street to

Haltom's, the finest jewelry store in town, and bought a ring that almost made the saleslady faint.

In was a ten-carat diamond set in platinum. The stone was the size of a swollen nickel.

They drove back to Claybelle with Ben complaining about the fact that he was going to have to endure his traditional Christmas Eve dinner with Leatha tonight, nor was he looking forward to Christmas Day either, to his traditional all-day Christmas brunch for friends and employees.

"The brunch will be gala," Florine said. "Shady and Eva Jane will be there. She'll be the one who's uncomfortable, not me."

Ben said, "Listen, this present I've got for you . . . if you like it and decide to keep it . . . you'll have to tell Leatha you bought it for yourself."

"Does it float?"

"Maybe you can say you inherited it."

"What have you done, Ben?"

"Bought you a present, is all."

"Have you spent a lot of money?"

"I have a lot of money."

"Still?"

Ben laughed. "Damn, I hate all this slippin' around," he said. "What in the world are we gonna do in New Orleans?"

"I don't know about you, but I plan to root for the Frogs."

"I'll be with Leatha and you'll be with *us*. Every time she turns her back, I'll want to touch you."

"Do I get to pick the spot?"

Ben and Leatha dined at a table by the window at the front of her house. They had a view of her magnolia stump.

Leatha had cooked one of Ben's favorite meals, a beef brisket, new potatoes, navy beans, green salad. They drank red wine and made small talk and talked about Betsy.

Ben gave Leatha the brooch at an appropriate moment. It may have been the third or fourth brooch he had given her for Christmas. She gave him a new leather briefcase. Every other Christmas, Leatha gave Ben a new leather briefcase. On the odd years, she gave him a pen and pencil set.

Leatha said Ben shouldn't have given her the brooch. It was much too expensive.

"Nonsense," Ben said, knowing the brooch could have come out of a gumball machine compared to the cost of Florine's ring.

Presently, Ben yawned and stretched.

"I have to get up early and go to the office so I can get back for the brunch," he said.

"The wine's making me feel a little romantic," she said, taking his hand. "Must you leave?"

Ben faked another yawn. "We still put out a newspaper on Christmas Day, Leatha. Most of the staff wanted the day off. I said fine."

Ben didn't need to go to the office at all, of course. Ray Fletcher, Dave Hawkins, Red Hensch, and Bert Swick had all volunteered to work on Christmas Day, to get out of the house.

Early the next morning, Florine phoned Leatha to wish her a Merry Christmas but actually to make sure Leatha was still at home and not over at Ben's, helping Florence and Warren prepare for the brunch. Leatha said she would be home for another hour.

All clear. Florine had time to take Ben her present for him.

Ben was delighted with "Lee's Texans." He hung it in a prominent place on the wall of his bedroom-office-den. He stood back and admired it.

"That's old John Bell Hood right there," he said, pointing to the gray-clad Confederate general leading the cavalry charge.

He opened a drawer of his desk and handed Florine a tiny white box with a pink ribbon. "You can take it back if you don't like it."

Florine opened the package and gasped. "Oh, Ben," she said.

She put the ring on. She went to a mirror and looked at her hand in the mirror. Ben stood behind her, looking in the mirror.

"Well, it's absolutely obscene"—she laughed—"but I love it." She turned to him. "And I love you."

They kissed and held each other.

"This is just the flashlight," Ben said. "You'll get the tool kit on your birthday."

Florine scurried back home to dress for the brunch, but the first thing she did was call Betsy in New York.

"Merry Christmas, sweetheart. How you doin'?"

"Hi, Florine. Merry Christmas."

Betsy claimed to be doing fine, given the fact that she had been hit in the head with a hammer. She and Millie had been to Charley, Al and Sally's last night. A lot of her old newspaper pals had shown up. There had been this journalism seminar which had required several gallons of whiskey. Today, they were going to treat themselves to a long lunch at The Plaza and maybe go see *Top Hat* at the movies.

"I love my watch," Betsy said. "I know you picked it out. Daddy would have sent me a football."

"Have you talked to him?"

"A few minutes ago."

"Did he tell you what he gave *me?*"

"Yeah, jewelry."

"*Jewelry?* He called it *jewelry?* Betsy, it's the most gorgeous diamond ring you've ever seen! It's a Barbara Hutton deal. It'll be yours someday—I'm just the custodian."

"Marry him, Florine."

"I do love him, Betsy. I'd like nothing better, but we have one small problem."

"Leatha?"

"We can't keep sneaking around. We're going to have to tell her."

"She may surprise you."

"How?"

"You never know about Madam Serenity. She won't take it well, but she might get over it quicker than you think. She may value your friendship so much—for social reasons— she'll wind up wanting to be in your wedding."

"In a way, I hope there's more to her than that. If there isn't, why have I been her friend for so long?"

"Good question."

Florine wore the ring to brunch.

Many of the other guests were already at Ben's house when Florine waltzed in looking casually chic, neighborhoodish, in a sporty sweater and skirt.

The sight of the diamond made Ben nervous. He wasn't big on tension. But Florine quickly announced that she had bought the ring for herself, as a divorce trophy.

"Have you lost your mind?" Leatha said to Florine as she looked at the diamond. "I don't have to guess what this must have cost!"

Everybody had a comment about the ring.

Olive Cooper said it was a sinful extravagance, what with so many people starving in China.

Dub Cooper said, "I ain't much on rings if they don't say 'State Championship' on there somewhere."

Bob Walker and Anna Sue Beaton were there as a couple. Anna Sue asked Florine if she could try on the ring. She slipped it on her finger and held it out for Bob to see.

"I better go check the hood of my car," Bob said. "I think something might be missing."

"I know where you bought this," Anna Sue said to Florine. "Henri's? Highland Park Village?"

"No."

"Neiman's?"

"It came from Haltom's."

Anna Sue's regard for the diamond was suddenly diminished by the news that the ring had been purchased in Fort Worth, not Dallas.

Eva Jane McKnight wasn't altogether thrilled that the ring far outclassed the small diamond earrings Shady had given her for Christmas. She took off the earrings, saying one of them was pinching her.

Eva Jane and Shady had brought the incorrigibles with them, Billy V. and Robbie D., but Warren Richards had done everyone a favor by taking them outside to play the moment they arrived.

Florence Richards, who had been cooking for three days, now put out the turkey and dressing and all the other food on the dining-room table, buffet-style.

Florence had a whole other turkey in reserve.

Everybody ate in the living room, on sofas, in chairs, kneeling at tables, standing at mantels and bookshelves.

The indomitable Billy V. came roaring through the house, all dressed up in the replica of a TCU football uniform Shady had given him for Christmas. Billy V. wore No. 45, Sam Baugh's number.

Billy V. threw a body block on O. L. Beaton, who wasn't looking so hot in the first place. The oil business was troubling him greatly.

"Get off me, you little shit," O. L. said, trying to shake Billy V. loose from his leg.

"Big job!" Billy V. yelled.

Bob Walker lifted up Billy V. and dangled him playfully by his heels.

Billy V. let out a screech that rocked the ceiling.

"Want to go outside, buddy?"

"Big job on you!" Billy V. shouted.

Anna Sue said, "Eva Jane, can't you do something with that child?"

Eva Jane went over to her eight-year-old as Bob put him down. "Billy V., don't make me spank you on Christmas."

"Go to hell!" said Billy V.

"Don't you talk to your mother that way, you hear me?"

"Piss-fart, big job!" Billy V. scampered to the doorway.

Eva Jane started after him. "Come here to me!"

"No!"

"I said come here to me!"

"Shit-bitch!" Billy V. gave his mother the finger.

"Oh, boy, are you in for it!"

Billy V. gave his mother two fingers. Both hands.

"Billy V.!"

"Bag of snot!" Billy V. bolted outside, slamming the door behind him.

Eva Jane smiled apologetically at everyone. "I am *counting* the days," she said.

Shady Webster, with a grin of satisfaction, told the group that the boys would be leaving town soon. At this school in Virginia, as he understood it, Billy V. and Robbie D. would be kept in what amounted to a prison for the first six months, and would be tortured and abused beyond recognition.

"There's only one thing wrong with the place as far as I can tell," he said.

"What's that?" somebody asked.

"The little fuckers can't leave this afternoon."

Anna Sue monopolized the conversation for twenty minutes, describing the complete wardrobe she was taking to California on the Rose Bowl trip. She and Bob Walker were leaving the next day on one of the SMU Specials.

"SMU's gonna roll over Stanford like a big wheel," Shady said.

His opinion was based on the fact that Stanford had lost to UCLA, 7 to 6, during the regular season, whereas SMU had gone out to Los Angeles for a game on Armistice Day and had whipped UCLA, 21 to 0.

"The SMU players aren't thinking about the game, from what I've seen," Bob Walker said. "All they're doing is buying up Rose Bowl tickets. The game's a sellout. They think they're going to scalp the tickets out there and get rich. They better plan on playing a football game, too."

"We've got a football game on *our* hands," Ben Throckmorton conceded. "LSU is as good as anybody in the country."

The TCU Specials to the Sugar Bowl in New Orleans weren't leaving until December 28. Ben had a suite reserved in the Pontchartrain Hotel that would accommodate himself, Leatha, and Florine. Shady had reserved his own suite in the hotel. Ben preferred to stay near the Garden District rather than in the French Quarter. If he was an alcoholic or a dope fiend, he said, he would stay in the French Quarter.

A little later in the day, after the guests had recovered from the food and were beginning to mix cocktails for themselves, Ben and Florine met by accident in Ben's bedroom-office-den.

Florine came out of the bathroom as Ben was waiting to go in.

Ben closed the door to the bedroom, took Florine in his arms, and they kissed.

Though listening for footsteps and fearful of an intrusion, they kissed again, more passionately this time, as their hands roved about.

What they didn't notice was Billy V. watching them through the window from the backyard.

Florine returned to the living room.

Ben relieved himself, washed his hands, straightened his tie, and when he walked back into the living room, Billy V. was jumping up and down, pointing at Florine, and yelling, "He kissed her, he kissed her!"

To her son, Eva Jane said, "Stop jumping around, you'll break something."

"I saw it, I saw it!" Billy V. hollered.

"You saw what?"

"Them!" Billy V. pointed at Ben and Florine again. "They was kissin' and she grabbed his pee-pee!"

Ben's face turned the color of an apple.

Florine was striving to keep her poise.

"I saw you, I saw you!" Billy V. chirped. "Yah-yah-yah!"

Billy V. leaped about the room. He slapped at Ben. He poked at Florine. He skittered through the house and out the back door, and on down to the boat dock, where Robbie D. was throwing Warren's lawn tools into the lake.

Everyone but Bob Walker, who couldn't contain a grin, was looking at Ben and Florine with expressions that ranged from disbelief to contempt.

Leatha rose from an armchair. "I want to know what that child is talking about," she said to Ben and Florine.

"I don't have any idea," Ben said innocently.

"You are a liar!" Leatha said.

"Yeah, I am," Ben said, drawing a look of surprise from Florine. "I never was any good at it."

"You were kissin' my *wife?*" Shady said.

Eva Jane jabbed Shady in the ribs. "She's not your wife, she's your ex-wife!"

Leatha rudely smeared her thumb across Ben's cheek. "You might have the decency to wipe off her lipstick!"

Ben looked at himself in a wall mirror. He thought he had.

"I knew something was going on," Leatha said. "You two have been acting strange ever since we were in San Francisco, but I said to myself, no, it's not possible. Florine is my best friend. Ben Throckmorton is the most honorable man in this town. Well, it just goes to show you, doesn't it?"

Florine said, "Leatha, nobody wants to see you hurt. It happened. We couldn't do anything about it."

Anna Sue spoke up loudly. "I wish someone would tell me what's happened, if you please."

Shady said, "Ben and Florine, that's what's happened."

"Ben and Florine *what?*"

Shady made a speech: "My good friend, Ben Throckmorton, standing right there, and my wife, Florine, standing beside him, they are havin' an *affair*—that's what's happened! Behind my back!"

"She is your *ex-wife,* damn it," said Eva Jane.

"Don't matter," Shady said. "It was behind my back."

Her eyes closed, Olive Cooper said, "God, forgive these sinners."

"I don't see no sinners," said Dub. "Florine's a divorced woman. Ben's a single man. If he wants to dip old Wilbur in Susy Q, who they sinnin' against?"

Ben was looking at Leatha sympathetically. "I can't feel any lower than I do," he said to her. "We both hated to be deceiving you. We were trying to get up the courage to tell you. Leatha, you're a fine woman, a good friend, an old friend. We've had some good times together. We go back a long way. But deep down, you and me both know we've never been in the kind of love where folks get married."

"I thought we would," Leatha said.

"When? After we were in wheelchairs bein' fed through straws? You deserve better than that. I hope you'll find it someday."

"Find what?" Anna Sue asked Bob Walker, who was relaxed on a sofa, his hands clasped behind his head, enjoying the entertainment.

"Ask Dub," Bob said.

Leatha raised her voice as she said, "Ben Throckmorton, you bought her that diamond ring, didn't you?"

Ben's expression gave him away.

Leatha tore the $500 brooch off her tailored suit. "You gave me *this,* but you gave her *that!*" She slung the brooch across the room.

"Whoa, wait a minute," Shady Webster intruded, peering at Ben. "A man don't spring for a rock like that unless this shit's been goin' on for a *long time,* no sir!"

"Tell us about it, big shot," Florine said.

"What's that supposed to mean?"

"Do you think I'm stupid? Do you think for a minute I haven't known about all the ladies you've had before Eva Jane?"

Shady looked indignant. "Name one!" he said.

"Mildred West."

"That's one."

"Emily Stoker."

"Okay, that's two."

"Virginia Blackman at the Boat Club. Doris Weekly. You took her to Honolulu, in case you don't remember. Frances Horn. Cherry Jean Deakins. Fay Cameron, Molly Burkett, the one who liked to go horseback riding. That waitress at the Dixie Hotel—what was her name? Jennie Beth Clifford."

Even Eva Jane was staring at Shady in astonishment.

"A waitress don't count," Shady said.

"Why not? You gave her a car!"

"Count her, then. Fuck it. What's the score?"

Leatha was on the brink of tears as she said to Florine, "Does Betsy know about this?"

"I told her," Florine said.

"What did she say?"

"She feels badly about you—like we all do."

Leatha drew herself up, holding herself rigid, and ran out of the house.

Olive Cooper, who was wearing her red and green Christmas awning, moved to the door. "I'll go home with her. I'll see if I can get Brother Tankersley to stop by."

"That'll fix her up," Dub said, tagging along with his wife.

Bob Walker, still on the sofa, still looking amused, said, "Ben, can I ask a question?"

"I'm not sure I like the look on your face," Ben said.

"It's a serious question. Do you lovebirds have any plans to get married?"

"I resent that question!" Shady said. "The woman was married to *me* eight weeks ago!"

"Happily, that's only a vague memory," Florine said.

Ben took Florine's hand and pulled her closer to him. He slid his arm around her waist. "I believe I could handle being married again—if the lady will have me."

"Is that a proposal?" Florine asked.

"It's a question I never thought I'd ask again."

"Wait till I get my hat, I'll go with you."

"Shady!" Eva Jane said, excitedly. "If she marries again, you save two thousand dollars a month!"

"God damn, that's right," said Shady, breaking into a grin. He raised the glass of bourbon in his hand, a toast to the room. "Merry fuckin' Christmas!"

Twenty-four

ELIZABETH HOOD Throckmorton, who was known by that name only on her birth certificate and on her college degree, was of an age where she could still remember most New Year's Eves distinctly, as if each was a great lead by Herbert Bayard Swope or W. O. McGeehan or Damon Runyon.

The New Year's Eves from her high school days were all the same: rowdy, squealing parties in a tourist court where the football boys would eventually break furniture, where everybody would vomit from the poisonous rum, and where she and Bob Walker would have to slip off to another cabin if they wanted to do their dry-fucking in private.

Who could forget the New Year's Eves from her college days? Rowdy, squealing parties in Manhattan hotel suites where the girls outnumbered the boys and the only fellow you were likely to meet was either a car thief from Queens or the son of a Wall Street embezzler from Harvard, Yale, or Princeton.

In her days at *Time,* she had usually been working on New Year's Eve, checking the facts in stories that would tell readers more than they cared to know about railway pensions or Post Office deficits. Then the New Year would be rung in with a "pouring," as it was called, and she would watch the bigtime editors, Still Norris and the others, get their hair mussed and be dragged off to supply closets by Nina, the sly kitten, and Janice, the slinky temptress.

And then there was the New Year's Eve Millie Saunders had once arranged by getting them dates with two advertising executives she had befriended the night before in a speakeasy. One of the men, Forgie Baldwin, professed to be a widower. The other, Ross Clayton, was recovering from a recent divorce, he said.

The two couples went to the Astor Roof and had a fine time,

drinking champagne and dancing, until the men got drunk and began to talk about their adventures in the "ad game." They claimed credit for two slogans that had changed the buying habits of America. Forgie Baldwin boasted that he had thought up the phrase "Quick, Henry, the Flit!" Ross Clayton said that "Palmolive soap for that schoolgirl complexion" had been his.

Drunkenly, the men had then let it drop that they weren't single at all—they were married and lived in Greenwich, Connecticut.

Millie had reacted to this information by suddenly developing a persistent itch on her thigh and saying she couldn't remember the last time she had been to bed with a "white man."

Forgie Baldwin and Ross Clayton had fled the Astor Roof, leaving Betsy and Millie with the check.

Now, Betsy was going to spend another New Year's Eve with Millie. Well, with Millie and any or all newshounds who might wander into Charley, Al and Sally's.

Betsy's plan was to drink Scotch until her jaw turned to stone, and she was already looking forward to New Year's Day. Millie would sleep but Betsy would have a wonderful time not getting dressed, slouching about, stuffing herself with deli sandwiches, and listening to every moment of the Sugar Bowl and Rose Bowl football games on the radio.

They got to Charley, Al and Sally's early, around seven in the evening, and staked out stools at the bar that were near the baskets of hard-boiled eggs, the baskets of pretzels, and the pot of coffee. That would be dinner as they drank their way into the promising year of 1936.

The owner of Charley, Al and Sally's made a rare appearance. He joined the ladies for a drink.

Lennie Zurzolo, a carelessly dressed, unshaven man in his early fifties, seldom came around. He was always at a racetrack somewhere around New York or down in Florida. The management of the joint was left up to Chuck, a longtime bartender, or Fritz, a longtime waiter.

Charley, Al and Sally's always seemed to have a new cook in the kitchen, another parolee, who would only be seen when he came out front to use the phone to bet against a jockey with forearms that could pull an elephant or on a left-handed pitcher who could wet it down.

Betsy had been assuming all these years that Charley, Al and Sally's was named for the original owners, possibly an old song-and-dance team in vaudeville.

At the bar, Betsy asked Lennie Zurzolo if he had known Charley, Al and Sally personally.

"No," he said.

"What year did you take over the place?"

"I opened it in '31 as a speak."

"It wasn't already here?"

"Why?"

"Who are Charley, Al and Sally?"

Lennie Zurzolo said he had named the place after his three favorite personalities. Charley Farrell, handsomest guy in Hollywood, Al Capone, toughest guy around, and Sally Rand, hell of a fan dancer.

Never assume, Betsy was reminded.

The ink-stained wretches began to filter in around nine.

Hitch of the *Daily Mirror*. Rauch of the *Graphic*. Bates of the *Herald Tribune*. Steen of the *Sun*. Ruth Leary came in with her husband, Bart. Ruth was a sob sister for the *Daily News,* a plump, gaudily dressed woman with frosty eyes and dyed-blond hair. Her husband was an assistant picture editor on the same paper. Ruth Leary's ambition was to get off of tear-stained sidebars about the mothers of dead cops and become a three-dot gossip columnist so she could eat free in good restaurants.

Before long, everybody was clustered at the bar, drinking heavily and enjoying one of their pastimes: quoting from many of journalisms's most revered leads—"literature in a hurry," Matthew Arnold called it—and challenging each other to guess the bylines.

Hitch started it off. " 'Out of the grave came the voice of the dead today in the form of musty letters that smoked with the reverend's love for the little choir singer.' "

Betsy got it first. "Runyon. Hall-Mills case."

"My favorite of Runyon's was the Capone trial," Rauch said, and Betsy quickly quoted the lead:

" 'Al Capone was quietly dressed this morning, except for a hat of pearly white, emblematic, no doubt, of purity.' "

Betsy was a tough customer at this game.

Hitch said, "What was that great lead of Swope's? Herman Rosenthal something."

Betsy took a sip of her drink and recited Herbert Bayard Swope's most celebrated lead from the *New York Herald:*

" 'The whisper ran through the pallid underworld. It was heard in the East Side dens. It rang in the opium houses in Chinatown. It crept up to the stuss and crap games on Fourteenth Street. It reached into the select circles of uptown gambling where business is always good and graft is always high. Herman Rosenthal had squealed once too often.' "

Steen of the *Sun:* "What did the grizzled Marine sergeant say as he went over the top?"

Rauch said, " 'Come on, you sons of bitches, do you want to live forever?' "

"Floyd Gibbons," said Betsy, and she lapsed into Gibbons again:

" 'I stood on the slanting deck of the big liner and watched the lowering of lifeboats and heard the hiss of escaping steam and the roar of rockets as they tore lurid rents in the black sky and cast their red glare over the roaring sea.' "

Betsy motioned to Chuck the bartender to give everybody a round on her.

"Here's one," she said. " 'Beyond anything but inarticulate sobs, a mother held her girl close to her again; her girl, given up for dead.' "

Ruth Leary, who was chatting with Millie about society divorces, overheard this one. "Majorie Driscoll, L.A. *Examiner,*" said Ruth. The sob sisters read each other.

"What story?" somebody asked.

"Aimee Semple McPherson," Betsy said.

"The story was a phony." Hitch laughed.

"Not when she wrote it on deadline," Betsy contended. "The whole country thought Aimee Semple McPherson was dead."

"All evangelists should be dead," Rauch said.

Bates said he had seen Aimee Semple McPherson in person. She was quite an act. "Here's this ritzy dame, a real looker, and she's got this Bible in her hand. A lot of guys in this country wanted to make it with Aimee Semple McPherson, even if they had to go to church."

They all laughed at how Aimee Semple McPherson had "mysteriously" disappeared for thirty-seven days. Her disappearance had been a national sensation in 1926. America feared she was dead. But one day the fetching evangelist had staggered out of the Arizona desert saying she had been kidnapped and tortured but with God's help she had escaped from her abductors. Majorie Driscoll had made the wires with her story of Aimee's reunion with her mother. In the days that followed, however, it became evident that Aimee Semple McPherson hadn't been kidnapped at all—she had only been hiding out with her boyfriend for over a month, a boyfriend America didn't know she had.

The game went on a while longer.

" 'John McGraw is dead—so what?' " somebody said.

"Pegler!" a voice said.

" 'Only in the Coca-Cola belt can an Episcopalian be regarded as an atheist.' "

"Mencken!"

" 'The Wild Bull of the Pampas, brutally gored by the Manassa matador in the second round, rolled over near the ropes, inert, unconscious—knocked out.' "

"McGeehan!"

Betsy tried one. " 'The Olympic Marathon was run on Tuesday. It is now Thursday and I'm still waiting for the Americans to finish.' "

No guesses.

"Henry McLemore, dummies."

And she tried another. " 'The Rebel line was five miles long and a Nation's very existence trembled before its clangor—the great, desperate, final charge was about to come.' "

"What the hell is that?" asked Hitch.

"Whitelaw Reid at Gettysburg," Betsy said.

"Who cares about that crap?"

"Southerners!" Betsy retorted. "And I'll tell you something else, *buddy*. If Jeb Stuart had got there with his cavalry, you'd need a passport to go to Washington, D.C., now!"

Rauch pleaded for quiet. He wanted to share his all-time lead with everyone.

Slowly, he said, " 'The fat, arrogant general was surrounded by his stolen art objects and armed guards, but I propped my feet up on his gilt-edged desk and told him exactly what I thought of his grimy little banana republic.' "

"Who's that?" Betsy was stumped for once.

"Me," Rauch said, pridefully.

"*You?* When?"

"I haven't used it yet, but if I ever get a foreign assignment . . ."

Betsy changed the game to something she called "second graf."

"Okay," she said. "The lead is 'Jesus wept.' "

"Who wrote that?" Bates asked.

Betsy said, "I don't know. St. John, St. somebody—some Bible guy. Gimme the second graf."

They all thought it over.

Betsy looked at Bates. "Jesus wept. Paragraph."

"His car wouldn't start."

To Rauch, she said, "Jesus wept—paragraph."

"Lou Gehrig was at the plate."

Hitch said he could play this game. "Try me," he said to Betsy.

"Jesus wept," said Betsy. "Paragraph."

"They'd rewritten his lead."

A half-hour before midnight, Betsy was paged to the phone. Ben and Florine were calling to wish her a Happy New Year. It was only ten-thirty in New Orleans. They were finishing dinner at the Pontchartrain and were getting ready to go to the French Quarter to watch the demented and neurotic celebrate.

"I'll be listening to the game tomorrow," Betsy said.

"TCU may be in trouble," Ben said. "It's supposed to rain. A slick ball don't help our passing game."

Fifteen minutes later, Betsy got another Happy New Year phone call, this time from Bob Walker at the Roosevelt Hotel in Hollywood, where it was only eight forty-five in the evening.

The first thing Bob had to report was that Anna Sue was into her second hour of trying to decide what to wear to a round of Rose Bowl dinner dances, one of which would be at the Cocoanut Grove in the Ambassador Hotel.

"Are you kids having fun?"

"Great time," said Bob. "I drive to Pasadena to workouts. Anna Sue hires a car and goes shopping. You probably didn't know they have some of the most exquisite shopping centers in the country out here."

"Seen any movie stars?"

"Who's that guy that slicks down his hair and dresses like a sheik?"

"Rudolph Valentino?"

"That's the one."

"Rudolph Valentino is dead."

"That's what I told Anna Sue. I said what do you want that guy's autograph for? He's dead. I wrote a good column today."

"Not again?"

Bob had been stockpiling quotes over the past twelve months, the actual words of various personalities.

Subscribers to the *Dallas Journal* would read:

PASADENA, Calif., Dec. 31.—I don't know about you, but 1935 was a 365-reel talkie that kept me on the edge of my seat. It had everything—war, politics, death, treachery, romance, disaster, drama, heroism, thrills.

Almost everybody you can think of was in it, and they all had speaking parts. The action was so fast, I missed *Vic and Sade* twice trying to keep up. Here are a few of the best lines:

PRESIDENT ROOSEVELT (ignoring the Dust Bowl): "American life is improving everywhere."

ADOLF HITLER (admiring his troops and tanks): "We have a fanatical belief in the future."

HUEY LONG (dying on the steps): "I wonder why he shot me?"

GEN. FRANCO: "Those who are spoiling for a fight shall have one."

HAILE SELASSIE: "We will not retreat from the Roman tyrants."

BABE RUTH (after hitting three homers out of Forbes Field): "Boys, I'm through."

KING LEVINSKY (to the ref in his fight with Joe Louis): "Don't let him hit me no more."

J. EDGAR HOOVER: "Debauchers are un-American."

SHIRLEY TEMPLE: "I'm not really a princess."

SEN. BILBO (in response to one of his many critics): "He is a contemptible, dirty, vicious, pusillanimous, with malice aforethought, damnable, self-made liar."

BARBARA HUTTON: "It's just a simple string of jade beads."

HENRY McLEMORE: "Omaha is not a bad horse, considering he can only win Triple Crowns."

FATHER COUGHLIN (on FDR): "The man is anti-God."

SEC. HAROLD ICKES: "Anybody who criticizes this President suffers from mental saddle sores."

WILL ROGERS (excluding Wiley Post): "I never met a man I didn't like."

LLOYD GEORGE: "The world is heading for a great catastrophe."

The New Year arrived.

Betsy and Millie hugged at the bar, vowing not to let anyone they knew or cared about do something silly, like die, in the coming year.

They each kissed all of the ink-stained wretches. Chuck the bartender led the crowd in a rendition of "Auld Lang Syne," serving drinks on the house. Moments later, Betsy committed her first official act of 1936. She ate a hard-boiled egg. Dinner at last.

To no one's surprise, Leatha Wardlaw did not make the trip to New Orleans. Ben and Florine had both tried to contact her after that fateful Christmas Day, but she wasn't answering her phone or the doorbell, and a CLOSED sign hung in the window of her dress shop.

Ben and Florine found out that Leatha was only communicating with Olive Cooper, so they each wrote her a note in which they tried to explain themselves. These were pleas for Leatha's understanding and forgiveness. They each expressed the hope that everybody could be friends again someday.

Olive delivered the notes and brought back Leatha's reply. It was something to the effect that she hoped Ben and Florine came down with rectal cancer.

Ben and Florine and Shady and Eva Jane were the two most adorable couples on board the Sugar Bowl Special that carried the TCU football squad, the band, and 150 of the university's most generous contributors to New Orleans.

Since they were acquainted with many of the people on the train, they found themselves being stared at, and the object of whispers.

Before the train was three hours out of Fort Worth, Amon Carter, the publisher of the *Star-Telegram,* cornered Ben for a private talk in a passageway.

Amon Carter said, "Ben, I'm not one to pry into somebody's personal affairs, but what in the world's going on?"

As delicately as possible, Ben tried to explain the situation. Yes, he was with Shady Webster's wife—er, ex-wife—and Shady was with Eva Jane, and they were all probably going to get married, but not at the Sugar Bowl.

"And everybody's friends?" Amon Carter said.

"Leatha Wardlaw hasn't taken it too well, I'm afraid."

Amon Carter shook Ben's hand and wished him luck and said, "I guess Claybelle's a more interesting town than I thought."

Their first night in New Orleans, the two couples settled on dinner at Arnaud's after the mandatory debate of whether they should dine at Arnaud's, Gallatoire's, Brennan's, or Antoine's.

Florine had wondered what possible difference it could make—the entrée was going to be Moby Dick Meets Orange Ketchup, with claws and whiskers coming up on the blind side.

Shady Webster made an effort to clear the air, remove the strain, so the women could become friends and everybody could live happily ever after.

At Arnaud's, Shady said, "This is nice, ain't it? The four of us friends? That's the way it ought to be. Hell, we're all just victims of life."

Ben felt bad about Leatha. He couldn't help it.

"Why?" said Eva Jane.

"She's been hurt . . . embarrassed."

"Serves her right," Eva Jane said. "She was using you. All she ever talked about was Ben Throckmorton this, Ben Throckmorton that, and Ben Throckmorton said somethin' else!"

"She *was* known for that," Florine said.

"Anybody who went in her shop had to hear about Ben Throckmorton before they could buy anything, not that she ever stocked anything *I* wanted. If you didn't know Ben Throckmorton, you hated him after ten minutes in Leatha's shop."

"That makes me feel better," Ben said.

The Sugar Bowl football game was played under conditions that were, in the studied opinion of Ben Throckmorton, horseshit. Dark and cold from the start, Tulane Stadium was battered by rain throughout the whole second half.

But in light of the awful weather, Ben was all the more proud of the TCU Horned Frogs for defeating the LSU Tigers in this severe test of character, even if it had only been by the baroque score of 3 to 2, a field goal over a safety.

Despite the lack of scoring and the weather, it was a great game, Ben thought, one of the finest TCU had ever played. There was a lot of *near* scoring—long runs, goal-line stands —and Sam Baugh had put on an exhibition of punting that might never be duplicated. With a water-logged ball, Baugh had punted an amazing fourteen times, averaging over forty yards a kick, often spiraling the football out of bounds inside LSU's five-yard line, the old "coffin corner." TCU's fullback, Tillie Manton, placekicked the winning field goal from twenty-six yards out in the second quarter, but Baugh had been the player of the day, not only with his punting but by completing the occasional pass to keep the Frogs on the move, and by slithering away on a forty-five-yard run, longest of the afternoon, which had put the game out of danger and would have produced another score if time hadn't expired.

"The best team won," Ben said, "and they can stick *that* in their gumbo."

It had taken Big 'Un Darly two and a half days to drive to New Orleans, because of a combination of car trouble, Louisiana road signs, and a problem with the Cajun language in asking directions.

He had made it to Shreveport without incident, but then he had wound up in De Ridder when he'd been trying to find Alexandria. He had made it to Opelousas but had missed Baton Rouge and found himself in Thibodaux. At Thibodaux, he was close to New Orleans but hadn't realized it and got talked into going backwards, to Abbeville. From there, he had driven to Baton Rouge and on over to Gulfport, Mississippi. Finally, it had only been a straight shot to New Orleans, once he came back from Bogalusa.

But Big 'Un reached New Orleans in time to celebrate New Year's Eve on Bourbon Street, where he paid sixty-four dollars for two drinks and a cover charge to hear a Dixieland band. He had slept in his car.

Up in the Tulane Stadium press box, before pounding out his story, Big 'Un had consulted Betsy's notes. He had been carrying them with him since a day back in the fall when Betsy had gone to the trouble of writing the sports editor a memo on how to improve his craft.

Dear Big 'Un:

I certainly don't know everything about it, but here are some things you may find helpful in writing game stories:

1. Most readers already know who won. Try to see how many grafs you can write without putting in the score. This is a sly trick that may force you to think of other elements in the story.

2. In any sports event, there is always a key moment, a big play, which turns the tide. Seize on this moment. Hammer it. Kick it to death. It is worth sacrificing some play-by-play to do this, and it will add "depth" to your story.

3. When you have a strong angle, try to weave it all through the piece, reinforcing it with quotes and your own observations.

4. You *must* write shorter. Nobody reads a garden hose, I don't care how good it is. Writing short is very hard, of course. Like the man said, "If I'd had more time, I could have really screwed it up."

5. Sights, sounds, and smells. Take the reader to the event with you.

6. Don't strain. If descriptions come naturally, fine, but otherwise, just say it's "cold as ice" and get on with it.

7. Don't try to force things in when they don't fit the theme, no matter how fascinating or hilarious you may think these anecdotes are. You can use this information later in a story when it *does* fit.

8. Never begin a story with a quote. This is no law of journalism, but it's a phobia of my own, so don't do it!

9. Avoid jargon. A game is a game, not necessarily a clash or a melee.

10. Write with confidence. I know this isn't easy. We all know what it's like to stare at blank paper, especially on deadline. But it will help to remind yourself of three things: *you* were there and saw the event, most readers didn't; *you* interviewed the principals involved, the readers didn't; and *you* are the professional whose job it is to tell the readers what happened and why. In my own case, I tend to take the position that if the readers don't like what I write, that's *their* problem. I can't account for their stupidity.

Above all, relax at the typewriter and try to have fun, Big 'Un. You love what you do for a living, and that is a big, big edge.

Betsy.

Big 'Un did his darnedest to follow Betsy's guidelines in his Sugar Bowl game story.

By BIG 'UN DARLY
Times-Standard
Sports Editor
NEW ORLEANS, Jan 1.—
Playing hog-waller football in a stadium that was cold as ice, the purple-clad T.C.U. Horned Frogs whupped the

Terrible Tigers of Louisiana State University, champions of the Southeastern Conference, here this afternoon in the Sugar Bowl melee that some called a game. It's a good thing T.C.U. didn't wear their usual white jerseys in all that slime.

The game was played before 40,000 fans, the largest crowd ever gathered to see a sports event in the state of Louisiana. These fans, who were mostly from the Bayou and talk funny, survived a freezing wind, puddles of mud, and torments of rain, but they couldn't survive Sammy Baugh. Slingin' Sam punted, passed, ran, tackled, intercepted, and played one of the greatest games of his life. He did everything but kick the winning field goal. That was somebody else.

There's no way to describe the miserable conditions. After one quarter, the players all looked like minstrels, which was okay in L.S.U.'s case, seeing as how the Tigers speak a language called coon-ass.

Of Betsy's ten helpful hints, Big 'Un made best use of the first one, though perhaps inadvertently. In his entire game story, he never mentioned the score.

A limousine and driver were waiting outside the Sugar Bowl for Ben and Florine and their now-close friends, Shady and Eva Jane, to speed them back to the hotel so they could listen to the Rose Bowl on the radio.

Drinks and food were ordered up to Ben's suite from room service. Football Silly tipped more generously than usual— TCU had won a big game.

The Rose Bowl game turned Ben into a split personality. One moment, he would take sinister pleasure from the fact that the SMU Mustangs were playing poorly—they clearly weren't themselves, not the team which had defeated TCU—and the next moment he would be embarrassed for the Southwest Conference, for the State of Texas.

The Stanford Indians scored in the first quarter on a dull, ordinary drive and took a 7 to 0 lead; and it was beginning to look as if the vaunted, ballyhooed Mustangs, National Champions in the Dickinson Rankings, were going to sputter around, fumbling and doing nothing, for the rest of the afternoon.

"Serves 'em right," Ben said. "Cocky bastards. They shouldn't have been out there in the first place. *We* should have been out there. But, damn, this is horrible—they're lookin' like clowns in front of eighty-seven thousand people and the whole country on the radio!"

Only once did the Mustangs resemble themselves. In the third quarter, Bobby Wilson threw a pass to Maco Stewart, the end, who flipped a lateral to Harry Shuford, who in turn tossed a lateral to Bob Finley. The play covered thirty-five yards. "Football, Texas-style!" Ben hollered. The play swept the Mustangs to a first down at Stanford's five-yard line.

"*Now* things are starting to pop," Ben said.

Unfortunately, the thing that popped next was the football —out of somebody's arms on the next play. Stanford recovered the fumble. Dejected and confused after this, the Mustangs simply wilted away. Stanford never scored again, but SMU had trouble even making a first down.

Grantland Rice would later describe the game as "dull and disappointing in every detail." Stanford won, 7 to 0.

The result made Ben Throckmorton "about half-bilious." SMU was a great team. Bobby Wilson was a great player, "a little old rubber-legged doohickey from Corsicana." Ben hated to see him wind up his career like this.

Betsy called the suite from New York to discuss the two games with her daddy.

"They made us proud," she said of the Mustangs.

Betsy said she had missed LSU's safety when she had gone to Millie's kitchen to get another corned beef sandwich, and the radio announcers hadn't explained it very well.

Ben said, "Sam was in punt formation in his end zone. It

was a fake punt. He tried to throw a quick pass but the wet ball slipped off his hand and fell incomplete in the end zone. That's an automatic safety."

The safety had put LSU ahead, 2 to 0, at the time.

"That would have been a great way to lose a football game."

"Oh, we weren't gonna lose the game, honey. We had too much character."

Betsy had tried to call Leatha, she said. Olive Cooper had answered the phone. Leatha had refused to speak to Betsy, but Olive had mentioned that Leatha had decided to put her house and business up for sale.

"Olive says she's moving to Waco. She has a sister there."

"She doesn't have to do a fool thing like that."

"Olive says she's very bitter. She says she can't stay in the same town with all of us, even me. What did *I* do?"

"I never made that woman a single promise."

"I know you didn't, Daddy."

"Dang, I can't believe we're runnin' her out of town."

"I think it's the smartest thing she could do. We all have to get on with our lives."

After hanging up, Ben shared the news about Leatha with Florine, Shady, and Eva Jane.

"*Waco?*" Florine said. "There's nothing in Waco but tornadoes and Baylor. If the Baptists don't get you, the funnels will."

Ben checked in with Ray Fletcher at the paper to see how he was going to play the two bowl games.

Page one. Banner. Four-column action shot from each game. The wirephotos were already being transmitted. Stories straddling the art, Big 'Un's yarn running down the right-hand side of the page, Bob Walker's running down the left-hand side. Bob had offered to file his carbon from Pasadena. Better to have Bob's piece than a workmanlike AP report.

Ray had written the banner and decks.

FROGS BEAT L.S.U. AS S.M.U. TEAM LOSES!

87,000 in Rose	Field Goal by
Bowl See Ponies	Manton Provides
Fall by 7 to 0	3-to-2 Victory

Stanford Scores
Early; Mustang
Attack Sputters

Record Crowd
Survives Rain
Driven in Sheets

Bob Walker's story didn't please SMU's fans, but of course it was written under unhelpful circumstances. Anna Sue was pouting before they even arrived at the stadium, asking him not to take too long. She didn't come to California to sit in a car all day!

More inspired by a close deadline, Bob wrote as fast as he could.

By BOB WALKER
Copyright, 1936, Dallas Journal

PASADENA, Calif., Jan. 1.—For a whole crazy week, there's been nothing in southern California, it seemed, but thousands of wild, rowdy Texans, terrorizing the innocent people of Los Angeles, Hollywood and Pasadena as they paraded everywhere in their ten-gallon hats and whooped it up for their world-beating S.M.U. football team. They had even marched into the editorial offices of Los Angeles newspapers and serenaded the ink-stained wretches with drunken baritones. Tonight, however, it is not easy to find a Texan anywhere—there are empty saddles in the old corral, for the score of the Rose Bowl was Stanford 7, S.M.U. 0.

Never had a football team come to California with such a frenzied buildup. Never had a team received so much gushing notoriety. Never had a region fallen in love so deeply with a football hero and his sweetheart as this place had with All-American Bobby Wilson and his cute pepperpot cheerleader, Betty Bailey. If they had known how to tap-dance, the careers of Fred Astaire and Ginger Rogers would have been over.

But then came the football game, and
never has there been such a let-down.

Bob Walker's speculation was that SMU's listless performance could be blamed more on economics than anything
else. The Mustang athletes who had stocked up on Rose Bowl
tickets in the hope of becoming wealthy had been unable to
unload them at any price. Even before the opening kickoff,
several key players on the SMU team had been resigned to a
crushing financial loss.

In the story, Bob concluded:

> There can be no other explanation for
> why this normally alert, highly skilled
> SMU team would spend an entire after-
> noon in a coma, lackadaisically allowing
> two Stanford ends, Keith Topping and
> Monk Moscrip, to become honorary
> members of its backfield.
>
> The Texans were 21 points better than
> Stanford on paper—but not at The Last
> Roundup.

Two weeks later, in the middle of January, Ben Throckmor-
ton was no longer humiliated by SMU's defeat in the Rose
Bowl, for that numbing upset coupled with TCU's victory in
New Orleans had resulted in the Horned Frogs being declared
the National Champions of 1935 in the Final Williamson
Rankings, the other reputable poll of the day.

The race for National honors had been so close throughout
the regular football season that the Williamson System had
announced it would let the post-season games count in its
final evaluations, particularly since three of the top contend-
ers, SMU, TCU, and LSU, would be involved.

After the bowl games, it had crossed Ben's mind that the
Williamson Rankings might—just might—elevate the Frogs
to No. 1, and on the morning of January 15, he had again
loitered in front of the wire machines awaiting the word. Big
'Un Darly was with him.

Suddenly the AP machine clattered and there it was.

"Shithouse Rosy, we got it!" Ben yelled out.

"Dern," said Big 'Un, almost too emotional to speak. "I wrote behind a National Champion."

Ben and Big 'Un shook hands.

Aside from Florine and Betsy, Ben guessed he would never gaze upon anything prettier than this chart he now tore off the machine.

Which read:

FINAL 1935 WILLIAMSON RANKINGS

The Williamson System primarily rates the strength of football teams by weighting their won-lost records against the quality of their opposition. Here are the Final Rankings of the Top Twenty teams for 1935:

Team	Record
1. T.C.U.	12-1
2. S.M.U.	12-1
3. L.S.U.	9-2
4. Minnesota	8-0
5. Stanford	8-1
6. California	9-1
7. Notre Dame	7-1-1
8. Auburn	8-2
9. Ohio State	7-1
10. Princeton	9-0
11. U.C.L.A.	8-2
12. Pittsburgh	7-1-2
13. North Carolina	8-1
14. Fordham	6-1-2
15. Rice	8-3
16. St. Mary's	5-2-2
17. Vanderbilt	7-3
18. Alabama	6-2-1
19. Duke	8-2
20. Nebraska	6-2-1

Ben did a merry little dance as he glided into Ray Fletcher's office with the chart.

Ray was reading over Dorothy Thompson's syndicated column for tomorrow's paper. Dorothy Thompson's column was one of Betsy's favorite things in the world.

In this column, Dorothy Thompson was saying she had no real interest in running for President of the United States despite the encouragement she was receiving from a number of her good friends, among them Adolf Hitler, the Dalai Lama in Tibet, Rudy Vallee, Leni Riefenstahl, Ted Fiorita, Bronko Nagurski, Emily Post, the Maharaja of Jaipur, who always sent playful birthday cards, and Vice-Admiral Isoroku Yamamoto of the Imperial Japanese Fleet, who had invited her aboard his aircraft carrier to go on some tricky naval maneuvers near the Hawaiian Islands.

"Guess who's Number One *now?*" Ben said.

"Stanford?" said Ray, looking up from his desk.

"They wish," Ben said, grabbing a pencil and scribbling a headline on copy paper.

"Minnesota?"

"Who'd they play? Wisconsin eight times?"

"Princeton?"

"Uh-huh, Princeton—in 1922."

Ben shoved the copy paper in front of Ray. "I want to see this *big* in the morning."

Ben had written: T.C.U. FROGS NAMED FOOTBALL CHAMPS OF U.S.!

"Congratulations," Ray said.

"You don't know what this means, do you, Ray? It means about two million dollars in endowment for the school! It means we're livin' in the football capital of the world! Look what football's done for Stanford, Yale, USC, Notre Dame. You think anybody would ever have *heard* of South Bend, Indiana, if it hadn't been for football?"

Ben held out the chart and looked at it with adoring eyes. "That's something, isn't it? National Champions!"

Football Silly kissed the wire copy and held it out again.

"Ben, can I have that?" Ray Fletcher said. "I'd like to put it in the paper before you get too much lipstick on it."

Twenty-five

IT WAS a long-running joke among Betsy and her friends that she was the voice of the people, always fair and open-minded, objective and tolerant, so it was no surprise to any of them that she had resisted, avoided, and condemned the game of contract bridge ever since it had become a national craze during her college days. She was on record as having said in numerous conversations that bridge was a pseudo-intellectual pastime invented by a rich guy to give socialites something in common with their hairdressers and decorators.

Millie Saunders had been taught to play bridge by her mother, who was a member of four different bridge clubs in Pittsburgh and wrote fan letters to Ely Culbertson; but Betsy had refused to take the time to learn, from Millie or anyone else. Poker, fine. Dominoes, sure. Rummy, pitch, fan-tan, crazy-8. Betsy had learned all those games from her daddy, or Florence, or Warren. But bridge? Bridge was why Jesus wept.

Bridge *talk* was worse. In a speak one night, back around '31 or '32, Betsy had listened to this man, one of Millie's co-workers, describe in gory detail the king-queen-jack finesse in diamonds he had managed to pull off the night before, only because he had been shrewd enough to mention a no-trump in the bidding, purely as an irritant.

"Incredible," Betsy had said. "All that hair in one finesse?"

"All that what?"

"Hair. Didn't you say the king, queen, jack?"

"Oh, yes, I see," the gentleman said. "Hair. Heh, heh. That's rather quaint."

Betsy had turned to Millie. "If you ever see me play a hand of bridge, ring for the nurse. Tell her it's time for my shot."

Things were different now. At Millie's insistence, Betsy had tried an evening of bridge and liked it. The game had confused, frustrated, and intrigued her because she hadn't been able to master it immediately. Everything about the game went against her nature. Counting trumps and other suits seemed trivial. There wasn't enough room to bluff. She couldn't get used to relying on her partner to be holding good cards, too, or bad ones. She would thoughtlessly renege at times, causing gasps among others at first, but then laughter. It was like trying to learn math or a foreign language, neither of which she had ever come close to comprehending. The game became a challenge, and though she was still learning, she had made the discovery that bridge wasn't all that boring if you gambled at it. Thus it came about that in the winter and early spring of 1936, with the most infectious, tantalizing, engrossing city in the world outside Millie's Park Avenue apartment, Betsy and Millie were staying home four, five, six nights a week to play vicious, bitter, snappish, nickel-a-point bridge with Dennis and Claude.

Betsy's days were much the same. Millie would breeze off to work. Betsy would go to a luncheonette in the neighborhood for breakfast, occupying a booth for up to two hours while she read six newspapers. She would return to the apartment and fiddle around, cleaning, reading, writing letters, while she listened to the radio. After *Vic and Sade,* she might take in a movie or go browsing in bookstores, museums, or galleries; but then she would go back to Millie's and get ready for bridge. Slowly, with each passing day, Ted's death grew more distant.

Through phone calls and letters to and from Bob Walker, Florine, her daddy, Florence, and others, she kept up with what was going on in Claybelle.

It was during these months that Leatha Wardlaw followed through on her threat to sell her home and business and move to Waco.

One day in February, without a farewell to anyone but Olive Cooper, Leatha vanished. She sold her house and magnolia stump to Olive and Dub Cooper. The coach and his wife had been wanting to move to a better neighborhood—a trailer camp had begun to encircle their duplex. Dub arranged for a loan at the Fidelity Bank to buy Leatha's house. As collateral, O. L. Beaton had made Dub put up his car, icebox, Victrola, lawn mower, and a promise that he would entice four good football players from outlying high schools to change their names and enroll in Claybelle High.

Shady Webster bought Leatha's Creations. Not out of sympathy for Leatha, but because Eva Jane and Anna Sue wanted it. They saw it as an opportunity to go into business together. Their idea was to turn the dress shop into a high-fashion specialty store, something Claybelle badly needed. There was a hole in the market, Eva Jane said. They were taking great pains with the remodeling and restocking and making plans for a grand opening.

There was still a problem with the name. Eva Jane wanted to call it Eva Jane & Anna Sue's. Anna Sue wanted to call it Anna Sue & Eva Jane's. Suggestions for a name were coming from everyone. At B's Cafe, Wynelle Stubbs came up with "Slim and None." Carolyn Moseley's society column was recommending "Clothes Doors." Booty Pettigrew suggested "Them Two Girls." Olive Cooper preferred "Fat Chance." Estill Parch thought of "Chic to Chic." Shady liked Florine's "Hanging by a Thread," but the girls didn't.

Eva Jane's boys, Billy V. and Robbie D., were sent off to the Virginia military academy in late January. Shady Webster paid the school's commandant $1,000 extra to come to Claybelle and personally escort them out of town.

Shady and Eva Jane had seen the boys off on the train at the Santa Fe depot. One of Robbie D.'s parting gestures was to snatch a doughnut out of a hobo's hands and mash it in his mother's nose. On the train, before the commandant had handcuffed the boys to their seats, Billy V. had thrown a lighted book of matches at Shady and had given his mother the finger.

As the train pulled away, Shady and Eva Jane had smiled and waved at the boys in the window.

"Goodbye!" Eva Jane had sung out melodically. "Have fun! See you in thirty years!"

"Gosh, I'm sure gonna miss those carefree little tykes," Shady had said as they drove away from the depot.

Shady and Eva Jane had celebrated the departure of Billy V. and Robbie D. by getting married a week later.

The ceremony was held at Eva Jane's house, the old Pem-

berton home, where the couple already lived. Only their closest friends were present. A larger crowd had been invited to
the reception at Shadowlawn Country Club. O. L. Beaton was
best man, though not looking well at all. Anna Sue was maid
of honor. Shady and Eva Jane had shown no preference in
ministers. The Reverend H. W. Drews had performed most
marriage ceremonies in Claybelle, but Olive Cooper had per-
suaded Shady and Eva Jane to use Reverend Jimmy Don
Tankersley. He needed the exposure, she said. Olive was
trying to help Reverend Tankersley raise enough money to
buy Harlan's Automatic Blinds & Awning Fixtures so the
reverend could turn the old Victorian house into his Church
of the Heavenly Furrows.

Shady had promised Reverend Tankersley a sizable dona-
tion if the reverend would keep the ceremony brief.

This didn't happen. Reverend Tankersley strayed off into a
long story about Jedediah and how Jedediah would have
owned a top-down four-seater Cadillac Phaeton if there'd been
a dealership in Biblical times, and then another long story
about Matthew, Mark, Luke, and—a camel?

"Excuse me!" Shady said, interrupting the reverend.

"Huh?"

Reverend Tankersley was shocked to be interrupted during
a wedding ceremony.

Shady said, "Can we skip all this Jedediah crap and get on
with the I-do's?"

Eva Jane pinched Shady. "This is supposed to be a solemn
occasion, butthole!"

Reverend Tankersley said, "Yes, sir, we sure can. Uh, do
you, Eva Jane McKnight, take this man to—"

"She does and I do," Shady said, interrupting again. "Now
what?"

The reverend looked up to the ceiling to ask his good friend
Jaysus to forgive Shady's impetuosity and to try to understand that a Texas oilman had a perfect right to speak up any
time he felt like it. The ceremony ended on a sprightly note a
minute later.

Lank Allred and Shirley Watters came to the wedding reception.

They were hard to miss in the crowd. Lank was decked out

in a dark suit and tie, but he kept his hat on, his badge on the breast pocket of his coat, and his coat unbuttoned and flung back so that the .45 on his hip was visible. Shirley was dressed in the tight-fitting bell-bottoms, red satin shirt, boots, and Stetson of a rodeo trick rider.

In a purposeful stride, Lank bypassed the food, the bar, and the bowl of black-bottom punch, and pulled the bridgegroom and the best man off to a corner of the club for a private discussion. He wanted to know the latest on the wildcat Shady was drilling for them out near Possum Kingdom.

"It's coming along fine," Shady said. "We're at twenty-seven hundred feet. We've run into some hard lime, but it's no problem. Slows us down a little, is all."

" 'Hard lime'?" Lank said sarcastically.

Shady said, "It don't mean nothin'. Forget it. We ain't gonna make more than ten feet a day for a while, that's all."

"And it costs us more money," O. L. brooded.

"It will, you're right," Shady said. "But think what's waiting for us. Three miles from where we've stuck our straw in the ground, Gulf's reaching pay at thirty-five hundred. They hit one the other day. Spewed forty barrels in two hours."

"How much more money you need?" Lank asked.

"I'm guessin' this sucker will come in at around forty-one hundred feet. Another ten thousand dollars ought to do it."

"Suck on this," said the Ranger.

Shady casually looked at O. L. and said, "Hey, it don't make a damn to me. I'm gonna keep drillin'. But if I go the rest of the way on my own, I'm keepin' half for myself. We got a new divvy. It's up to y'all."

Now Lank had a look for the banker.

"Come by next week," O. L. said to Shady with heavy fatigue. "I'll think of something."

"That hard lime?" Lank said, his cold eyes on Shady. "Yeah?"

"I don't want to hear no more about that shit." The Ranger went to the buffet table.

Under his breath, Shady said to O. L., "I think you're right. The man is somewhat less than mentally stable."

Since no one else would bother, least of all Eva Jane, Florine engaged Shirley Watters in conversation.

"Hello," Florine said cheerily. "I'm the groom's ex-wife—which means I'm the happiest person here."

They drank a cup of black-bottom punch together.

"This is real nice," Shirley said, looking around. "I hope me and Lank can have a wedding like this."

"Oh? Are you and Captain Allred talking about marriage?"

"You can call him Lank."

"Okay."

"Just don't ever call him Burford."

"Burford?"

"That's his real name. I got it out of him one night after he took drunk. He's been Lank ever since high school, he says—when he played ball for Amarillo. He was a Sandie."

"Was he really?"

"I don't know if they were as good then as they are now. Ever time I pay attention, Amarillo High School is winnin' the State Championship."

"I attribute it to their nickname."

"I like it, too. You can find Lions and Tigers anywhere, but there's only one Golden Sandstorm. Lank says they've always been good at football. He says it's because West Texas breeds a person of higher caliber. I'd never thought about it before, but he may have somethin'. You know, when you get over in East Texas, you're up to your ass in niggers. Same thing down around Houston. And you can't go south to San Antonio or nowhere—it's nothin' but spicks."

Florine uttered a sound of the noncommittal variety.

"North Central Texas is all right," Shirley said. "That's where we are."

"As we speak."

"Lank says it's the next best thing. He says if he didn't have Company C, in charge of North Central Texas, or if he didn't have charge of a company somewhere in West Texas, he'd have to quit the Rangers. He says he's not gonna live around no niggers or pepperbellies."

Florine said, "So you might get married, huh?"

Shirley said it was more of a possibility these days, now that Lank had made his intentions known to his wife and to Shirley's present husband, B. R., who worked in the garage of a Phillips station on the Jacksboro Highway. Shirley said it was high time their spouses had been told the facts of life, that they were on the verge of being dumped. True love couldn't let nothin' stand in its way. Shirley felt bad about Lank's wife down in Mott, near Waco, her with a withered arm and that birthmark on her neck and all, but Lank would see that she was taken care of financially. Lank had told his wife, Emma, that she could have the trailer and everything in it, all except the ort on his walls. Lank had some good ort he was proud of, all framed and everything—big blowed-up pictures of Bonnie and Clyde after they was dead.

Lank had explained to B. R. about true love, too. Only the other night. That was when Lank had dough-popped B. R. after B. R. had come into Lola's Oasis and seen Shirley and Lank kissing one another.

"I told B. R. he better not start nothin' and keep his mouth shut, but the fool don't know how. Lank had to shut it for him. B. R. said, 'Well, lookie here if it ain't old Big Hat, No Cattle.' Lank went into a blind rage. He grabbed the hair of B. R.'s head and drug him out to the parking lot and gave him a goin'-over he won't forget. Lank hit him upside the head with his fist and his gun barrel both. Told him if he ever came around my house again, he'd shoot his pecker off. Between you and me, it'd take more than one shot—that's one thing I can say for B. R. I was real flattered. It's the first time two men ever had a fight over me. Not that it was much of a fight. Lank turned B. R.'s face into catfood, is all."

"God," said Florine. "That's sickening."

"I know, I couldn't hardly look at it myself," Shirley said. "Lank's a different story, though."

"What do you mean?"

"Girl, he's a Texas Ranger. Don't nothin' turn his stomach but two warm tits on his back."

Betsy was getting a letter a week from Bob Walker. Most of his letters were examples of a columnist avoiding the task of writing a column, as Betsy informed him in a note of her own, but she was happy to receive his letters.

In February, one of Bob's letters said:

Dear Cheryl:

I saw your dad at the TCU football banquet last night. He was the man waving a checkbook in the air and shouting at the coaches to go out and buy some more Sam Baughs.

He was also holding hands with a woman who looked like Irene Dunne.

Those two lovebirds are talking about a wedding, as you undoubtedly know, but I'm sure they won't do it until you come home. When are you coming home? Are you ever coming home? The question is on everybody's lips; or it was until they wiped it off.

I have discovered Anna Sue's secret hobby. She collects clothes.

We should be back from Alaska any day now, unless . . .

Holy shit, Wiley, pull up!

> Your friend,
> Will.

A letter in March said:

Sybil, darling:

So you will know how to plan your social calendar, circle this date: July 18. That's the day the Fort Worth Frontier Centennial opens. Billy Rose announced his lineup of stars this week, and it is no small thing that I recognized well over half the names.

At Casa Mañana, Everett Marshall and Ann Pennington will sing to each other, not to forget the audience, while Paul Whiteman conducts his orchestra underwater. Eddie Foy Jr. and Poodles Hanneford will liven things up at Jumbo, the singing circus. A lady named Hinda Wassau will take off her clothing twice nightly at Pioneer Palace. With no clothing to take off, Sally Rand and friends will caress large bubbles at the Nude Ranch —no children under 18.

But the big thrill every night will come at the Casa Mañana Revue when Faye Cotton of Borger, Texas, "Texas's No. 1 Sweetheart," parades around the stage in her $5,000 gold mesh gown.

That's all of the show-business news. I guess I better see if I can fix the valves on this truck.

> Safe driving,
> Royce.

The afternoon that Florine called Betsy to ask, officially, for her father's hand in marriage, they must have talked for an hour over long distance.

In the course of the conversation, Florine said, "Did you know I used to be a newspaper person?"

"You're kidding?"

"Nope," Florine said. "I was a reporter at the *Star-Telegram* for ten years. I went to work there as a secretary when I got out of TCU. I'd never thought about writing or reporting, but the woman who covered hydrangeas and Johnson grass quit the paper one day and they gave me the job. I wrote a garden column once a week. I eventually got around to writing features, too. I wouldn't put my own name on the garden column. I was 'Trixie Lilac' when I wrote about the pesky hydrangeas, but I was Florine Maples when I wrote features."

"Trixie Lilac?" Betsy said. "Did you know Daddy then?"

"Heavens, no. I didn't know anybody but aviators, doughboys, and con men. I hate to say it, but I never had more fun in my life than I did during the war. Don't you remember how big Camp Bowie was? There were thirty thousand men out there—and three airfields in town! They hit oil in Breckenridge in 1917—smack in the middle of the war—and Fort Worth was where all the promoters gathered, mainly in the lobby of the Westbrook Hotel. They turned the Westbrook Grill into an officers' club. It was *the* place. I danced on a few tables down there."

"Trixie Lilac liked to dance, did she?"

"Sugar, Trixie Lilac could *do* the rag."

"Is that where you met Shady?"

"No, that's where I met Vernon Castle. Shady didn't come along for five or six years. I met Mr. Big at the Buck Horn Bar. It was during the rodeo. He bought me a drink and introduced me to his good friend Chester Byers. Chester Byers was the world's champion trick roper. I was impressed. I didn't know Shady had only known Chester Byers for five minutes, long enough to buy *him* a drink. Shady and I got married because we both liked to go out every night. He was working for a roofing company when we met, but he wanted to build his own houses. No Fort Worth bank would loan him the money, but O. L. Beaton did. That's why we moved to Claybelle. I started having miscarriages and he built his dream neighborhood. All those houses over by Clay Field? The ones that lean?"

"How did he get in the oil business?"

"The usual way. Lie, cheat, and steal. He would knock on doors and try to talk a farmer into leasing him his land. He would promise the farmer anything—a one-half override—figuring he would screw the farmer out of it in the fine print. Most of the farmers were too smart. But one day he found this little retarded lady out near Strawn. Mrs. Waddell. She owned a lot of acreage. There were rigs all around her. Nobody had been able to deal with her, but she liked Shady. He imitated animals and she thought he was funny. Well, he got the lease land, but now he needed money to drill. That's when he rented a bulldozer and went out east of Claybelle and cut a path through some trees on property he didn't own. He took O. L. out to the property, told him he'd acquired the land and was going to build a golf course with beautiful homesites around it. He showed O. L. the path he'd bulldozed through the trees. 'There's the first hole,' he said. 'It's a par-four.' O. L. believed him. O. L. didn't invent the steamboat, as we know. O. L. loaned him thirty thousand dollars, and Shady drilled a well with the money."

"And hit."

"Yep. I don't know what he would have done if he'd made the ocean, but he hit—and then he hit eight more. Now he's an insufferable asshole, but it's Eva Jane's problem. How tall is Adolf Hitler?"

"I don't know—five-six?"

"That's what Shady is. Never marry short."

Betsy was also being kept up to date on Lank Allred through the occasional note or phone call from W. M. Keller.

Lank's .45 had been silent through the winter, but the Texas Ranger's legend was growing in other ways.

In February, a "Lank Allred Day" was arranged by the citizens of Waco, and Lank was given a downtown parade. In a ceremony in front of Waco's city hall, W. M. reported, Lank had made a moving speech in which he said, "I am an American by birth and a Texan by the grace of God."

A magazine writer from New York, a man with two hyphens and an umlaut in his name, had come down to Texas to do a piece on Lank for *The Saturday Evening Post*. The writer had wandered around Claybelle for a couple of days interviewing everybody who would give him any time. Wynelle Stubbs had called him a queer because he asked her to hold the gravy on his chicken-fried steak. The *Post* story would be out sometime this summer, W. M. said. A man with two hyphens and an umlaut in his name was undoubtedly a slow writer.

The biggest thing Lank had done to enhance his reputation was solve a kidnapping crime. It had taken Lank only two days to track down and catch Cynthia Ilene Woods, a twenty-two-year-old platinum blonde who had kidnapped the wife of Hubert Curry, a Fort Worth oilman. Cynthia Ilene Woods turned out to be Hubert Curry's secretary and mistress. She had kidnapped Anita Curry and was keeping her bound and gagged in a closet of her apartment until Anita agreed to give Hubert a divorce.

Cynthia Ilene Woods's red Chevrolet coupe had been the clue that led to her arrest. Neighbors of the Currys told Lank they had often seen the car speeding back and forth in front of the Curry home, the horn honking loudly, a girl of Cynthia's description behind the wheel, a message painted in white on both sides of the car. The message had said: I DATE YOUR HUSBAND.

Lank had found the car parked on the street in front of Cynthia's apartment and had crashed through the front door to rescue Mrs. Curry and apprehend the kidnapper.

Some people said it hadn't been all that hard for Lank to crack the case.

Partners were rotated in the bridge game so that Millie, Dennis, and Claude would each have to withstand a rubber with Betsy, the weakest player.

Dennis and Claude would bring dinner to Millie's apartment at Park Avenue and 87th Street, often prepare it, and Millie and Betsy would provide the beverages. The bridge game would begin after dinner. Depending on how the cards were running, the game might last until one or two in the morning.

Dennis and Claude were partners in a decorating business. They were tall, dark-haired, expensively dressed young men —difficult to tell apart unless you knew them. Claude was more outspoken, most often on the subject of the theater and movies. Claude had never seen a play or a movie he liked. As a consequence, Dennis had never been permitted to sit all the way through any Broadway show or motion picture. Occasionally, Dennis would ask Betsy or Millie to tell him what happened after Carole Lombard got off the boat.

Millie had met the two men at Lord & Taylor one day when she had helped them select birthday presents for their mothers. Dennis and Claude were smoothly attractive young men, and Millie had flirted with them. A friendship had developed before Millie realized that Dennis and Claude were "that way."

Dennis's and Claude's sexual preferences didn't matter to Betsy or Millie. The girls found them entertaining in a gossipy, bitchy kind of way, and the decorators played serious bridge.

As Millie saw it, Dennis and Claude were coming in quite handy during this period of what she referred to as Betsy's "convalescence."

Millie was still seeing Chet Weatherford, the happily married FBI agent, one or two nights a month, whenever Chet could work it out.

Their romance was strictly physical now. Fine with Millie. She cared for Chet, though not enough to encourage him to get a divorce and marry her.

The thing was, Chet had these three small children. A

mother Millie wasn't. A stepmother she wasn't. She was a career woman, one who still had party-girl urges and enjoyed her freedom.

She would see Chet just often enough for their encounters to transform them into panting, sweating, slurping animals. It was great. There was a lot to be said for "selective promiscuity," Millie said. She recommended it.

Maybe in five years she would be ready to settle down, she told Betsy, but right now she wasn't ready for what she liked to refer to as "skillet duty."

Millie had a one-bedroom apartment. Betsy would take the living-room couch on those evenings when Chet Weatherford stayed over, when it would be time once again for Millie to prove she could outfuck a Connecticut wife.

By early April, Betsy had become an adequate bridge player.

She couldn't wring as many tricks out of an ordinary hand as Millie or Dennis or Claude, but she could make game, and sometimes slam, if the cards were there, and she could now be relied upon to bid sensibly. Well, okay, she had a tendency to overbid, but didn't this add spice and suspense to the game?

Ironically, the bridge game came to an end just as Betsy was getting good at it.

The last hand was played on the night of April 4. Easy to remember the date because it was the day Bruno Richard Hauptmann had finally ridden Old Toasty, paying his debt to society for the kidnapping and murder of the Lindbergh baby.

Betsy had drawn bad cards all evening. No hair at all. She had made a couple of one-bids, but only because Claude insisted on playing one-bids.

"Of course we play one-bids," Claude said. "I would cut off an arm before I would throw in a one-bid. A one-bid can be *extremely* hard to make."

Betsy voiced the opinion that all one-bids should be fed to monkeys at the zoo, but she played them.

Then, with Claude as her partner, she got a hand. Not just a good hand. A full head of hair and two butcher knives. She was holding a six-card spade suit to the ace, king, queen. Five hearts to the ace, king, queen. A singleton ace of diamonds. A singleton club. It was a lay-down six spades, a small slam, possibly a grand slam.

Millie dealt and passed. Claude opened with a club. Her partner had opened! Dennis passed.

Betsy said two spades, giving her partner a jump-shift—a "demand" bid. The least he could say was two no trump, to keep the bidding open for her. It was only a question of whether she would go to six or seven spades.

The bidding went around again.

Millie: "Pass."

Claude: "Pass."

Dennis: "Pass!"

Dennis, with great relief, passed so quickly, it sounded like Claude's echo.

Betsy was stung with anger. This was a serious money game. Her bid of two measly spades would stand. A sure slam had gone down the toilet because of her partner's unforgivable response.

"You passed two spades?" she said to Claude as she calmly took a sip of coffee from the cup at her right elbow.

"I didn't actually have an opening hand," Claude said nonchalantly, putting out a cigarette in an ashtray on the card table. "I not only should have passed, darling, I should have slithered into the *woodwork* as I passed."

Betsy stood up. "You *passed* two spades?"

"Darling, I know it was a demand bid, but—"

"You PASSED . . . two spades?"

Betsy sailed the cards across Millie's living room. In the next instant, she lifted up the table with both hands and turned it over on Claude, knocking him backwards onto the floor, the coffee cups and saucers and ashtrays crashing down on him.

Betsy stormed into the bedroom and slammed the door behind her.

In her rage, she missed seeing Dennis, moved to tears, trying to help Claude, also in tears, dig himself out of the ashes, cigarette butts, cups, and saucers.

Betsy also missed seeing Millie stagger over to the couch and collapse in laughter.

The girls hadn't gone to sleep easily that night. Every time one of them started to doze off, the other would say, "You *passed* two spades?"

And they would start laughing again.

Near the end of April, Betsy received an invitation to a "pouring" in Stillwell Padgam-Norris's office at *Time,* to celebrate the fact that "Harry" Luce had named him assistant managing editor of *Life.*

The top job, that of M.E., had gone to Lafester Cleed, who would leave *Time* in the capable hands of Andrew Cheshire, and take on the greater responsibility of launching Luce's new magazine, which had a chance to make a bundle of money and at the same time bring a much-needed "maturity" to photojournalism.

Still Norris would have liked to have the No. 1 job, but this was the next best thing, for being the assistant managing editor also meant stock options, bonuses, unquestioned expense account lunches, and it might even involve journalism.

It was a noon "pouring," and Betsy could handle only one drink at that time of day.

She congratulated Still Norris and left, but not until the old wordmaster had told her there would always be a position for her at *Life* if she ever decided to come back to the "big top."

Betsy got back to the apartment in time to catch *Vic and Sade.* She sat on the couch and started a note to Bob Walker as she listened to the show.

UNCLE FLETCHER: Got something in your tooth, Vic?

VIC: It's five-thirty in the morning.

UNCLE FLETCHER: Fine.

SADE: It's awfully early, Uncle Fletcher. We're barely awake.

UNCLE FLETCHER: Vic's got something in his tooth.

SADE: Good morning, Rush.

RUSH: I'm sleepy.

UNCLE FLETCHER: Rush, you scalawag. Glad to see you up. Goin' over to Dixon today. Wondered who you want me to say hello to.

VIC: I'll just lay down here for a minute.

UNCLE FLETCHER: Henry Fedrock had friends in Dixon. He left Belvidere in nineteen-aught-nine, went to Dixon. Married a woman twenty-eight years old, went bail for his brother-in-law that skipped the country, invented a fingernail file that run by electricity. Later died.

SADE: I don't guess I know anybody in Dixon anymore.

RUSH: Dad, can you move over a little?

UNCLE FLETCHER: Jim Fashrope don't live there anymore. Some give it out he moved to Tallahassee, Georgia, married a woman thirty-nine years old and later died, and others give it out he moved to Fargo, Minnesota, married a woman forty-nine years old, later died. You can search me which story is true. Vic? Sade? Rush, honey?

The phone call from W. M. Keller came later that night. Lank Allred had done it again, but he had killed *two* bank robbers this time. Two young Mexican boys. They had been attempting to break into a bank on the south side of Fort Worth. W. M. had sped to the scene after getting a call from a friend on the *Star-Telegram*.

Everything about the incident strained his imagination, W. M. said, although it didn't seem to bother any of the other reporters or police officers on the scene. As Chick Murphy, a Fort Worth homicide detective, said, "Aw, it ain't nothin' but a spick deal."

But W. M. had noticed something unusual about the evidence. Might be important, might not. It struck him as curious, however.

It was W. M.'s observation about this shred of evidence that prompted Betsy, there on the phone at that late hour, to reach a decision.

"I'm coming back," she said.

PART FOUR

Which Asks the Question: Can a Girl from a Small Town in the West Find Happiness in a Small Town in the West?

Twenty-six

IN THE ten months that had gone by since the Texas Bankers Association had begun paying out $5,000 rewards for dead bank robbers—"and not one cent for live ones"—law enforcement officers in the State of Texas had shot and killed a total of forty-six people. Some of them may have even been bank robbers. Betsy's line.

A detective in Dallas had killed three. Down in Gonzales, where the first shots were fired in the Texas Revolution, a deputy sheriff had killed four. A policeman in Houston had killed three. A U.S. marshal in El Paso had killed two. But Lank Allred was the leader in the clubhouse with, as of now, seven.

Betsy summed all this up in her first "Good Morning" column upon her return from New York.

She wrote that it was a joy, a comfort, to live in a place where you knew you were so secure, where the only thing you had to worry about was getting hit by a stray bullet. We are all sleeping peacefully at night, she wrote, knowing that Captain Lank Allred is always out there, ever alert, his six-shooter cocked, ready to gun down any man who might not have shaved cleanly or might be wearing his hat at a jaunty angle.

Betsy's column was so rich in sarcasm, it outraged most of her readers and caused a problem with one of the paper's biggest advertisers.

The readers let her know through their phone calls and letters that they were incensed she would ridicule a Texas Ranger.

Betsy threw the letters in the wastebasket, only half read, and hung up on the phone callers about five seconds after they stated their business.

The perplexed advertiser was Russell Shelburne, the owner

and manager of the largest grocery market in town. The ads he placed in the *Times-Standard* for Shelburne's inundated the paper on Thursdays—the long-accepted day to advertise weekend bargains. He placed many other ads in the paper throughout the rest of the week and bought spots on KVAT.

Russell Shelburne was a big man in the community—big at the Rotary, at Shadowlawn Country Club, at the First Baptist Church. Betsy remembered him from her youth as a person who would call the police if a kid ran across his lawn. He looked a little like Ming the Merciless, only without the beard and helmet.

He came to see Betsy in her office, as the Reverend H. W. Drews once had.

"Your story was a disgrace!"

That was how Russell Shelburne opened up with Betsy, who was working at her desk.

"It wasn't a story, it was a column."

"It was there on the front page!"

"That's true."

"The press don't know where to stop sometimes, if you ask me!"

"That's true, too—and people are better off because of it."

"Everybody I know is upset about your story. The very idea, making fun of a policeman!"

"He's a Texas Ranger, not a policeman. Have you always been this observant?"

"He's keeping our streets safe, and this newspaper chooses to laugh at him for it! It beats anything I ever saw. I'm not sure Shelburne's Market wants to keep advertising in this newspaper!"

"You no longer do."

"I what?"

"I'm not running any more of your ads."

Russell Shelburne wasn't prepared for this. "You can't do that," he said, flustered.

"I just did it."

"You're sitting here telling me I can't buy an ad in this newspaper? Why, that's . . . that's against the Constitution— or something!"

"Sue me."

"Who do you think you are, young lady?"

"I'm the editor of this paper."

"Your father owns this paper!"

"Uh-huh," Betsy said. "Lucky break, huh?"

"You have lost your mind!"

"No, but I imagine you'll be losing some business."

"I've never heard of such a thing! I come in here to tell you something for your own good, and you tell me I can't put an ad in your newspaper! You happen to be in business, too, in case you don't know it!"

"I'm in the news business, not the grocery business." Betsy lit a cigarette. "You buy space. You don't buy my words. You came in here to throw your weight around, Mr. Shelburne. It doesn't work. I'm sentencing you to a month—no ads in this newspaper for one month—but if you keep pissing me off, you'll get *life*."

"We'll see about that!" The grocer steamed out of the office.

Betsy watched him through her glass window. Russell Shelburne stopped at Dave Hawkins's desk. He babbled and pointed at Betsy's office. Dave Hawkins laughed and slapped his thigh. Russell Shelburne walked over to Bert Swick's desk and babbled. Bert Swick broke into laughter and said something to Red Hensch, who started to laugh and, from a distance, gave Betsy a thumbs-up sign.

The advertiser sulked out of the newsroom, thoroughly mystified by all of this glee.

Ten minutes later, Betsy's phone rang. From downstairs, it was J. B. (Hap) Townsley, the head of advertising, who, like all others in the advertising and business departments, was forbidden to come on the editorial floor unless personally invited.

"Did I hear right?" Hap Townsley inquired.

"Yes, you did."

"Do you think you've acted in a responsible way, Betsy?"

"No, but it was fun."

Not for her daddy. Ben had to endure the wrath of Russell Shelburne at Shadowlawn Country Club, and the wrath of Shady Webster and Hansel Thompson and Buck Blanchard and almost every other businessman in town.

Up to his ass in wrath, Ben walked into Betsy's office, his

old office, intending to give his daughter a lecture on the economics of the newspaper business.

He said, "You want me to do some mathematics and tell you how much you're going to cost our paper over a month?"

Betsy stiffened. "I don't think that will be necessary."

"Retail is the backbone of a damn newspaper, Betsy, and you've cancelled a month of retail advertising to satisfy some kind of journalistic integrity, which is all right in its place as long as it don't tear a hole in my pocket!"

"You're saying Russell Shelburne is right and I'm wrong?"

"No, I'm not sayin' he's right! I'm sayin' he's rich!"

"So any rich guy can come in here and tell me what to do, is that it?"

"You could have your revenge without costing us money! You wrote your column. Let the man complain about it—you don't have to insult him!"

"I don't have to listen to his shit either! You of all people should back me up! And don't stand here and tell me how a newspaper operates. Retail breaks us even. The gravy is in classified, or is it *you* who doesn't understand the business?"

"Well, I've had my say."

"Fine." Betsy smiled. "Go play golf."

It was a beguiling week all around.

A drama unfolded in Fort Worth that captured the hearts of everyone in the communal surroundings. An eight-point blacktail deer somehow escaped from the Fort Worth Zoo and was missing for three days.

Animal lovers organized hunting parties. Schools organized scouting expeditions. Where could the deer have gone? The area around the zoo was well populated. Many of the city's finest homes were in that neighborhood.

Two Fort Worth policemen finally confessed that only hours after the deer had escaped, they had found it grazing in a river bottom, close to where the new Colonial Country Club golf course was under construction.

The policemen had shot the deer and had taken it home for dinner.

Betsy's headline on the story said:

COPS EAT KIDS' PET.

Alfred (Junior) Dingle, ace photographer, earned a new nickname that week: "Bloody" Dingle. W. M. Keller gave him the name after they had gone out on an assignment together.

A woman named Velma Latson, thirty-five, 1701 W. Moxley, had shot and killed her husband, Horace, in the midst of a marital quarrel. Horace, who was home on his day off from work at Cowden's Bicycle Shop, had turned on the radio and thought something was wrong with it, forgetting that it had to warm up before any sound could be heard. Horace had banged on the radio with his fist and had broken it beyond repair. Unluckily, this had occurred only one minute before *Backstage Wife* came on the air.

One word had led to another, and Velma Latson, who had a psychiatric history dating back to her previous marriage to a Church of Christ minister, had gone to a chest of drawers and got a .38 Horace kept in the house to protect the family from niggers and prowlers.

Velma had chased Horace into the street in front of their little wood-frame house. There in the street, Velma, at close range, had shot Horace six times—in the head, in the stomach, in Leroy.

She had gone back into the house to reload when her mother-in-law, Elberta, had knocked her cold with a rolling pin. The "alleged assailant" had been taken to Baptist Hospital with a concussion.

W. M. Keller and Junior Dingle arrived at 1701 W. Moxley while Horace was still lying in a river of blood. Junior started snapping pictures as W. M. went up on the front porch to interview Elberta.

Moments like these were never easy, but W. M. was a pro. He knew how to act sympathetic, considerate, kind, whatever it might take in order to obtain a picture of a deceased to run in the paper.

W. M. was leading up to asking Elberta for a snapshot of Horace when Junior came bounding up onto the porch.

Elberta let out a godawful scream—"Oh, dear God, no!" She covered her face with her hands and fled into the house.

W. M. and Junior didn't know what had happened for a moment, but then W. M. looked down.

Unknowingly, Junior had tromped Horace's blood all over the porch.

The month of May was tornado season in Betsy's part of Texas, and tornado warnings were being broadcast on KVAT the night she asked W. M. Keller to join her for supper in the dining room of the Dixie Hotel.

Because of the tornado warnings, Betsy had chosen the sturdy Dixie Hotel as a safe place to eat. A good tornado could turn B's Cafe into a pile of toothpicks in a matter of minutes.

Betsy was terrified of tornadoes. The Great Tornado of '25 had seared her soul.

In the late spring of that year, her junior year in high school, she and Bob Walker and a bunch of other kids had been having a picnic and swimming party in her backyard. The day had been hot and sticky, but in the late afternoon the sky had slowly grown dark and the temperature abnormally cool, not a leaf moving on the trees.

Warren and Florence had known what was coming. They had flung open the doors of the storm cellar behind their garage apartment and rounded up the kids. Before Betsy and everyone could get to the cellar, lightning had exploded and balls of hail larger than lemons had fallen—and then here it came, dropping out of the sky to the southwest, the blackest, thickest, most hideous-looking funnel she would ever see.

Down in the cellar, Betsy and the others could only cringe and listen to the booming, grinding roar of the twister.

They had all emerged an hour later to a bright blue sky, but six residential blocks near Wildflower Drive had been wiped out. Almost one-third of Claybelle had been blown to Alvarado, one-third of Alvarado had been blown to Waxahachie, and part of Waxahachie had wound up in Ennis. More than seventy people had been killed.

Betsy and W. M. dined in The French Room at the Dixie Hotel. The French Room was the most expensive restaurant in Claybelle, and supposedly the most elegant. Two busy chandeliers hung from the ceiling above a carpeted floor and linen tablecloths. A four-course meal in The French Room could cost up to a $1.80, though the food came out of the same kitchen as the food in the Dixie Hotel's coffee shop, which was considered by most connoisseurs to be grossly inferior to B's Cafe.

A gargantuan oil painting covered one wall of the dining room. The work of art was said to have been done by the wife of General Riley Jefferson Clay. It was a painting in which various armies, being led by various Robespierres and Bonapartes, appeared to be attacking each other while various maidens were being chased by various Charlemagnes and Louises. Here and there, the odd Gaul appeared to be feasting, weeping, sword-fighting, or committing rape. The painting had no name, so far as anyone knew, but Betsy had once given it a name: "France."

The service was not the best at dinner, because the two waitresses on duty in The French Room, Clemence and Modesta, kept going outside to look for a funnel and to see how Reverend Jimmy Don Tankersley was coming along.

Brother Tankersley was in the square, his Bible in his hands, his feet planted near the statue of General Clay, his eyes fixed on the brooding sky. He was asking the Lord to reroute the tornado to Cleburne.

Amid periodic reports from the waitresses on Brother Tankersley's progress, Betsy and W. M. talked about the bank job at which Lank Allred had shot the two young Mexican boys and increased his reward fund to $35,000.

W. M. related Lank's version of what had taken place at the Lone Star Bank in Fort Worth.

Lank had been in Fort Worth on an investigation of another nature, something he wasn't at liberty to talk about. Any time he was in Fort Worth at night he made it a habit to drive through Buttermilk Junction, the unsavory neighborhood where the bank was located. It was a "crime pocket," as most people knew.

The Ranger had been driving past the bank when something caught his eye—a flicker. Flashlight, he had thought. Might be a burglary in progress.

Lank had stopped his car, drawn his .45, and slipped up on

the two Mexicans. He had seen that they had broken out a window, and there had been no question in his mind that they intended to climb inside and crack open the safe.

Lank's story was that he had hollered at the Mexicans: "Hold it right there, greasies!"

They had cussed him in spick, he said, and had come at him with knives.

Lank had fired two bullets into each of the boys.

After the police and reporters arrived, Lank had said, "I kilt this one first, then I kilt that one."

"Not exactly hardened criminals," W. M. had said to Chick Murphy of Fort Worth Homicide, seeing that the boys were only eighteen or nineteen years old.

"Naw, don't look like it," Chick Murphy had said. "Two less problems for the world, though."

An acetylene torch had been found on the ground near the broken window. This seemed to be all the proof anybody needed that the Mexican boys were going to rob the bank. And yet when W. M. looked at the acetylene torch he had noticed that the tips were missing. The nozzles. An acetylene torch without the nozzles to keep the air from escaping wouldn't work. It would be of no more use than an automobile without spark plugs.

W. M. said he had learned this in metal shop in high school. It was about *all* he had learned in metal shop in high school, but it was a fact.

So that night, he had casually asked Lank Allred, "Where are the tips?"

"The who?"

"The nozzles?" W. M. had said, explaining in front of everybody that the acetylene torch wouldn't work without them.

"What's that got to do with anything?" Lank had said.

"I'm not sure," W. M. had said, "but don't you think two guys who are going to crack a safe would know how an acetylene torch worked?"

"I don't know about no 'tips,' " the Ranger had said with a chuckle. "Only kind of tips I care about are them that tell me where a punk's gonna pull a job. You sayin' this wasn't no bank robbery?"

"No, I didn't say that," W. M. had replied.

Lank had said, "Good! Because here's your acetylene torch, there's your bank, and here's your two dead spicks. You boys know what a cue ball and a Mexican have in common, don't you? The harder you hit 'em, the more English you get."

Everybody had laughed and that had been the end of it.

Now at the dinner table in The French Room, Betsy and W. M. could hear thunder and heavy rain outside, an indication that Claybelle was only getting a thunderstorm, that the danger of a tornado was over.

Modesta, one of the waitresses, said she was willing to give the credit to Reverend Tankersley, although she hoped that the funnel had only touched down on a vacant lot in Cleburne, where Reverend Tankersley had sent it. The waitress had good friends and relatives in Cleburne and she wouldn't wish a funnel on them.

"What did Lank look like when you mentioned the nozzles?" Betsy asked W. M.

"He was surprised. He was shook up—for a minute, anyhow."

"This is great!" Betsy said. "He's made a mistake. It's obvious somebody set up those kids for him—like they do all of his 'bank robbers.' Somebody got those kids there on one pretext or another. Somebody had already broken out the window. Somebody planted the 'evidence'—the acetylene torch. But somebody screwed up. They forgot the nozzles."

"He got away with it."

"Maybe not."

"You can't write it, Betsy. It's too thin."

"I'll have to think about it."

"It's also—" W. M. stopped short.

"What?"

"I was just thinking. If the man is crazy enough to kill six or seven innocent people, it might not bother him to shoot up a newspaper office. It might be dangerous to write it . . . wouldn't it?"

Twenty-seven

WYNELLE STUBBS autographed the plaster cast on Slop Herster's hand after she seated Slop and Tommy Jack Lucas as far away from the other customers as possible—they smelled like ten pounds of spoiled meat.

"Don't you ever bathe?" Wynelle asked Slop. "I know Tommy Jack don't. Somethin' crawled up his ass and died so long ago he's forgot about it."

Tommy Jack sniffed under his armpit. "I don't smell nothin'," he said.

Wynelle said, "You have *body odor,* is what you have. Both of you! Lord God, if y'all ain't rank!"

Slop said, "We can't smell no worse than what's between your legs."

"What's between my legs has been out of commission so long, you couldn't find it with a claw hammer."

"I could find it."

"I'd fuck a donkey first. What do y'all want to eat?"

They ordered meat loaf sandwiches on light bread and a beer.

Left to themselves, Slop said, "He's gonna pay. You can put that in the *Times-Standard* right now."

Tommy Jack said, "I wouldn't mess around with him if I was you."

"I ain't gonna mess with him. I'm gonna April Fool his ass, is all."

"How?"

"Get me a gun."

"You can't shoot no gun with your left hand."

"I'm gonna wait till my cast comes off."

"You better be careful. Sumbitch is mean."

"I don't know that, do I, *Brains?*" Slop held out the cast on his hand. "You aptly named."

338

Three days earlier, Lank Allred had gone into Scooter's Pool Hall looking for Slop. Scooter's was a block off the square, three doors from the Liberty Theater, which had been showing the same double feature for two months: *Ride, Tenderfoot!* starring Ken Maynard, and *Escapade* starring William Powell and Luise Rainer.

Scooter's consisted of three pool tables and one snooker table, a table and chairs where dominoes could be played, and all of the other niceties of a recreation parlor: a cold-drink box, a candy and cigarette case, a peanut machine, and an exceptional collection of "fuck books," which were kept in a drawer behind Scooter Pittman's counter and had to be asked for.

Scooter Pittman, the owner, was a bent-over man of thirty-six with purple sacks under his eyes. His war wound still bothered him. He had been shot in the back by his own commanding officer, the captain of Company H, 5th Infantry, only moments before he was supposed to go "over the top" at a place called St.-Etienne.

Scooter had always said that shooting him in the back had seemed like an extreme thing to do to a man who had realized in the nick of time that he was a conscientious objector.

Slop was practicing on the snooker table—running the six-ball—when Lank walked into Scooter's. Tommy Jack and Scooter were lounging on a wooden bench, laughing at one of the pocket-size "fuck books," the one titled *Greta Garbo Meets Mutt and Jeff.*

"Lookie here," Tommy Jack said, handing the book to Lank.

Lank studied a naked, frantic, voluptuous Greta Garbo holding Mutt's rod in one hand, Jeff's rod in the other, and pleading, "Fook me, fook me, I vant more fooking!"

"I seen better," Lank said, giving the book back to Tommy Jack.

Lank strolled over to the snooker table and picked up the cue ball as Slop was taking aim.

"Let's you and me take a ride," the Ranger said. "We got bidness to discuss."

Lank drove Slop out to the Valley View Inn, a crackerbox tourist court on the edge of town.

Lank had a key to one of the cabins. As he unlocked the

door, Slop said, "I hope you got some money for me today. I'm runnin' short."

This wasn't why Lank had brought him there.

No sooner had Lank closed the door, he doubled up his big fist and almost tore Slop's head off with a right cross that sent Slop flying against a wall. Slop sank to the linoleum floor.

Lank stood over him, and said, "You try to April Fool me, boy? What happened to them nozzles on the acetylene torch? You come close to makin' me look like a idiot."

Slop got to his hands and knees, groaning, coughing, spitting blood. "What you talkin' about?"

"The fuckin' tips that go on the fuckin' torch. The fucker don't work without the fuckers!"

"I told him what to do. We went over it real good."

"Who's *he?*"

"Tommy Jack. He went and got the torch, took it over there."

Lank said, "It was your responsibility, not his. You ought to know better than to trust Tommy Jack to do somethin' right. Tommy Jack's unlucky. He could stick his arm in a barrel of pussy and pull out a dick!"

Slop was still on his hands and knees.

"You're a right-handed pool shooter, ain't you, hotshot?"

With that, Lank Allred put the heel of his boot on Slop's right hand and crushed it. Slop wailed in agony. He cried out even louder when Lank stomped on the hand for good measure.

"You're left-handed now," Lank said.

Slop and Tommy Jack were still sitting in B's Cafe. Slop was reading *Tess Trueheart Meets Clark Gable.* Tommy Jack was reading *Jack Armstrong Meets Cleopatra.*

Dub Cooper came in and saw his two former players in the back booth and elected to join them, bringing along a friend.

Dub said, "Boys, I want you to meet the hoss who's gonna lead the Claybelle Yellow Jackets out of the wildnerness. This here is C. L. (Carload) Sealy."

Carload Sealy was a strapping youth of twenty-one, barefoot, wearing coveralls and no shirt, a sullen, greasy-haired hulk of six feet two, 210 pounds, the skin on his stone face offering proof enough that you couldn't outgrow acne.

"Somethin' stinks," Carload said as he slid into the booth.

"It's that damn liver and onions in the kitchen," Slop said.

Despite Carload's age, he was only a junior at Masonic Home in Fort Worth, except that Carload was going to transfer to Claybelle High and he would be eligible to play football next season.

"Them Masonic Home piss ants robbed me of Eugene," Dub said, "so I done robbed them of their best fullback. I'll tell you about Carload here. He ain't just big. He's fast and he's eat up with what I like to call want-to. He'll hitchee. You like to hit, Carload?"

"I'll hit. Can we eat?"

"Anything you want, hoss."

Dub glanced at Slop's cast. "What happened to *you?*"

"Construction accident."

Wynelle came to the booth to take the order.

"Say hello to the future," the coach said to her. "This right here is Mr. C. L. (Carload) Sealy of the Masonic Home variety. He's transferring to Claybelle. It's all over but the winnin' around this town!"

Carload ordered the chicken and dumplings, the roast beef lunch, two breaded veal cutlets, and four side bowls of pinto beans.

As she wrote down the order, Wynelle said, "Remind me to be on the other side of town when you fart."

Tommy Jack asked Carload where he was going to live in Claybelle.

"Coach's house."

It was true. Dub and Olive had more room now they had bought Leatha Wardlaw's place. There was a spare bedroom for Dub's out-of-work brother, Volney, and Olive's sister, Ida Brite; and the dining room could be converted into a bedroom for the terminally asthmatic Dorrance and his new cousin, C. L. (Carload) Sealy.

Dub and Olive had adopted Carload. It was the only way the Claybelle coach could get him released from Masonic Home.

Dub finally had him an orphan.

Twenty-eight

———

"GOOD GOD, there's niggers in the wedding!"

Anna Sue blurted it out as she stood in the back of the living room. Providentially, nobody heard it up near the altar, or over on the staircase, or out on the porch, where it may have been a little cooler on this Sunday afternoon in the latter part of June.

Anna Sue had just realized that Warren Richards, in his rented tuxedo, was going to be the best man and that Florence Richards was going to be the matron of honor. Florence had moved in next to Betsy in front of the altar.

The altar was a podium borrowed from the Rotary Club. Around it were flower arrangements from Opal Delle Scrafford's florist shop.

Dr. Wheeler Beckham of the TCU faculty and the University Christian Church in Fort Worth was at the podium. A spry little man despite his eighty-one years, Dr. Beckham's wavy gray hair blended in nicely with his purple blazer and white duck pants, his white shirt and purple tie, and the Bible he held, which was bound in purple leather.

Dr. Beckham had been associated with TCU since the institution was founded at Thorp Springs, Texas, not all that far from Claybelle, by the Clark brothers, Addison and Randolph. Dr. Beckham had been the university's president in the days when it was known as Add Ran College and was located in Waco. He was an ordained minister and to this day taught three courses in the New Testament at the university. But as most of the guests were aware, it was of slightly more importance to Ben Throckmorton that Dr. Beckham was a schizophrenic off-the-trolley fan of the TCU football team.

Florence Richards sang two songs in her gospel voice. First, "Oh, Promise Me," and then:

Oh, beautiful, beautiful Texas,
Where the beautiful bluebonnets grow.
I long to be in Texas,
Beside the Alamo.

Ben had requested the second song.

Florine Webster had wanted to have a wedding at which she could wear a gown, like a bride. She couldn't recall what she had worn when she and Shady, in a drunken stupor, were married by a judge in Weatherford, a town known as much for its quickie weddings and divorces as it was for its watermelon and cantaloupe.

Florine came down the aisle in a sleeveless cream-silk gown with a short train and sweetheart neckline with matching diamond clips. Her auburn hair was parted in the middle, plaited into a thick braid, and coiled into a coronet at the back of her head. She had never looked classier, and Ben Throckmorton had never looked or felt younger.

"Hi, Mom," Betsy said as the bride reached the altar.

Florine whispered, "I'm exactly fourteen years older than you. That's not a mom."

"You look great, Sis."

"Call me Trixie."

Between dearly beloved and repeat-after-me, Dr. Beckham detoured to an autumn Saturday in 1897, the day TCU had played its first big football game. The University of Texas had been the opponent. Dr. Beckham remembered the crowd of four hundred in the grandstands of Waco's Cow Palace Park, and he remembered how a "rich man" had come to him that day and offered to give the school a $2,000 endowment if he, as president, would discontinue the "brutal sport."

Dr. Beckham recalled how he had given the "rich man" a piece of his mind, stating that in his opinion work *and* play should be a part of the educational process.

"Oh, how right I was," Dr. Beckham said to the wedding guests. "Had I yielded to the temptation of commercialization, lo, those many years ago, we would not be standing here today as the National Champions of college football!"

"Go, Frogs!" The cry came from Shady Webster, who followed it up with a shrill whistle.

On the who-gives-this-woman part, Betsy took a step forward, placed Florine's hand in her daddy's, and said, "We do. Her mother and father in spirit, the daughter of the groom, and the Fighting Frogs of TCU."

"Ha!" Florine couldn't hold it in.

Inasmuch as Ben and Florine's wedding was Claybelle's biggest social event of the summer, Betsy had taken charge of the reception.

An enormous party tent was erected on the back lawn. Both the Dixie Hotel and B's Cafe were hired to cater the food and drink. Music for listening and dancing was provided by Booty and Them Others.

Shortly after Ben and Florine were joined together in holy matrimony, guests were roaming the house and lawn, crowding around the three outdoor bars, and Booty and Them Others were merging Western swing with Dixieland. Booty, with a drink in one hand and a microphone in the other, was singing:

> *I love you,*
> *Yes, I do,*
> *I love you.*
> *It's a sin to tell a lie.*

The bride and groom weren't going to dash off on a honeymoon any time soon. They didn't want to miss the opening of the Texas Frontier Centennial in Fort Worth.

Ben was flattered that Amon Carter came to the wedding and reception, and didn't mind at all that the publisher brought along a celebrity, Billy Rose.

Betsy requested a tune from Booty Pettigrew: "You've Got to See Mamma Every Night or You Can't See Mamma at All."

"There's the man who wrote it," Betsy said to the bandleader as she pointed out Billy Rose.

"That's a Broadway producer?" Booty said. "He don't look big enough to carry the plague."

Billy Rose was taken with the looks of Anna Sue Beaton and Eva Jane McKnight, now Eva Jane Webster. He sought them out at one of the outdoor bars and asked if they were interested in show business.

The Casa Mañana Revue, he said, was going to feature "the one hundred most beautiful girls in Texas." He and his stage manager, John Murray Anderson, were almost through casting, but they could still make room for two beauties like Anna Sue and Eva Jane.

Eva Jane thanked the producer for the compliment but said she couldn't dance a step and would have to settle for a good table in the audience on opening night.

"Dancing doesn't have a great deal to do with what I have in mind," Billy Rose said. "We've chosen all of our dancers. We're looking for gorgeous girls who carry themselves well and can wear glamorous costumes."

"I have loved show business my whole life!" Anna Sue said, to Eva Jane's amazement.

Billy Rose stepped back and took a harder look at Anna Sue. "Would it embarrass you if I asked you to lift your skirt? A little above the knee will be fine."

Anna Sue raised her skirt beyond mid-thigh.

"Very nice," the producer said. "How old are you?"

"Twenty-two," said the twenty-eight-year-old, twice-divorced Anna Sue.

Billy Rose handed Anna Sue a business card and said, "I don't mind saying this will be quite an opportunity for kids looking for a career on the stage. The theme of the revue is a Cavalcade of World's Fairs. Very splashy, very musical, very costumey. The show will run for four months. I personally know thirty talent scouts from Broadway and Hollywood who will be coming to Fort Worth."

Anna Sue said, "Do I call you . . . come to the theater . . . what should I do?"

"Come to the theater," Billy Rose said. "You're in the show, sweetheart."

As soon as Billy Rose walked away, Eva Jane said, "You can't be serious!"

"Why can't I?"

"Since when do you want to be a chorus girl?"

"Being in the Casa Mañana Revue at the Texas Frontier Centennial is *not* being a chorus girl, Eva Jane. It is being one of the one hundred most beautiful girls in Texas, which I am!"

"I thought we had a business to run?"

Their chic specialty store, which they had named "Ritzy Business," had opened on the first of the month. Esther Agee, a young woman who had helped run Leatha's Creations, was managing the shop by herself. So far, the co-owners had been the best if not the only customers.

There were few items in the shop for under fifty dollars. A lot of people had come in to look around the first week, but none of them had come back. Esther Agee's mother would stop in once a day, but she didn't count as a customer. She would only want to see how her daughter was getting along with the polio brace on her leg.

Anna Sue said, "You know very well the store can get along without me for four months. You don't want me to be a star!"

"Did I hear the word *star?*"

"You'd like to keep me in my place, wouldn't you? You were a cheerleader like Betsy, and you can't stand the thought of me doing something glamorous—something you haven't done!"

"I could do it," Eva Jane said stiffly. "He asked both of us, you know!"

"He obviously liked me better."

"Well, I guess he did! After you hiked your dress up to your rose bush!"

Betsy was dancing with Bob Walker as Booty Pettigrew sang:

> *I'm gonna smile and say*
> *I hope you're feelin' better,*
> *And close with love the way you do.*
> *I'm gonna sit right down and write*
> *   myself a letter,*
> *And make believe it came from*
> *   you.*

They kept holding hands after the song ended, as they stood on the wooden dance floor Warren had constructed for the party tent.

"Want to drive down to Austin with me one day next week?" Betsy asked.

"What for?"

"I can use some moral support. I have to go see somebody."

"Does it have anything to do with the story you're working on that your father doesn't want you to print but you probably will, anyhow, knowing you?"

"I have an appointment with Frank Hamer."

"Himself?"

"He doesn't know what it's about. All I told him when I called was that I might have some information he would be interested in. I said it was in connection with the reward money the bankers were paying out for dead robbers. He says he's opposed to the rewards, too. I thought I'd let him read a draft of the piece—see what his reaction is."

Betsy had been laboring over the story, writing different versions, some tougher on Lank Allred than others, some flirting with the serious possibility of a libel action if she were mistaken.

"What if he says you're wrong?"

"If he can convince me, fine."

Betsy had not seen much of Bob since her return. When she had flown back from New York—Newark, to be exact—on an American Airlines DC-2, he had met her plane at Meacham Field and had driven her to Claybelle. On the drive, he had listened to her rave about the wonders of air travel. "It's the only way to go," she had said. "We only made three stops. I was here in ten hours. Hostesses bring you cocktails . . . fried chicken . . . apple pie. You know the best thing? No phones."

Betsy had gone shopping with Florine in Dallas, and Bob had met them for dinner at the Adolphus Hotel, and he had taken Anna Sue to O. L. Beaton's dinner party for Ben and Florine at Shadowlawn Country Club, but otherwise they had been busy at their jobs, Bob writing his column and traveling now and then with the Dallas baseball team, and Betsy somehow finding the time to work on her exposé while putting out a newspaper every day and writing her own column.

One of Betsy's columns drew a response from Bob, in one of *his* columns.

Loons were bothering her. Too many loons had been released from the asylum prematurely and were overrunning the globe. Haile Selassie had fled Ethiopia, surrendering his country to Mussolini, who didn't know what to do with it now that he had it. The goose-stepping Nazis were doggedly fortifying the Rhineland, the old Siegfried Line, but the English and French were only concerned about the athletes they were going to send to the Berlin Olympics. Hitler had turned a place called Dachau into an internment camp for "undesirables," but the little shrimp was denying it and blaming the "vicious rumor" on his "political enemies." The Japanese were waging an undeclared war against the Chinese in Manchuria. And General Francisco Franco was massing troops in Morocco and training them for a full-scale civil war in Spain.

Bob had taken note of all this and suggested a way for the United States to deal with it. The New York Yankees presently had five men hitting over .350—Gehrig, Dickey, Lazzeri, Selkirk, and a rookie named DiMaggio—so why didn't we send them overseas with their baseball bats?

"We'll have to spend the night in Austin," Bob was saying. "I'll reserve us a room at the Driskill."

"You'll reserve us *two* rooms at the Driskill."

"Want to go to the ball game tomorrow night?"

"Do I *what?*"

Hardly a question she anticipated.

"The Cats and Dallas are starting a big series. LaGrave Field is the place to be tomorrow night. Sit in the press box with me."

"Women aren't allowed in the press box."

"You're not a woman, you're an editor."

"Thanks."

"Come with me. You have a legitimate right to be up there. First woman in a press box. Think of it. You'll make the wires."

"I'll get arrested."

"What more could you ask?"

Shady Webster and O. L. Beaton were down on the boat dock, away from the crowd.

Shady wondered if O. L. had seen a doctor lately. The

banker was looking far too gaunt and sickly. He had lost twenty pounds.

"A psychiatrist is what I need," O. L. said. "Maybe he could tell me how I ever got into this."

Shady Webster was drilling the slowest wildcat in the history of the oil industry. This had been partly due to bad weather, partly due to equipment failure, and partly due to the depth. Shady was down to 6,389 feet now, and going deeper. It was the deepest well an independent operator had ever drilled.

But things were still looking good, Shady said. Gulf and Texaco had hit pay in nearby sections. Shady's core tests were more than promising. He had been throwing around terms like drill stem, seven-inch casing, Caddo lime, Yates sand, but all O. L. knew was that he'd had to cough up another $30,000 for himself and Lank Allred, and he had stolen the money from his own bank.

He had phonied up a loan note for Hansel Thompson at the drugstore, another for Russell Shelburne at the grocery market, and another for Reverend H. W. Drews at the Baptist church, in case a bank examiner paid him a surprise visit.

If this oil well didn't hit soon, or if it didn't blow in at all— God forbid—O. L. guessed he would have to lie down and let Bernice put a lily on his chest.

Shady gave O. L. a goodhearted slap on the back. "Don't sweat it so much, podna. I was out there the other day. There's dinosaurs down there, all right. I can hear 'em grunt."

Warren and Florence Richards were drinking a toast with Ben and his bride when a hot gust of wind kicked up and specks of sand landed on Warren's tuxedo.

"Uh-oh, here come one," Warren said.

"I mean!"

Their word was good enough for Ben and Florine. All four of them rushed into the house and began soaking towels and rags in water.

Less than five minutes later, on the horizon to the north, here came a rolling wall of brown dust, three hundred feet high.

Bob Walker was lighting a cigarette for Betsy when he saw it.

"Am I wrong," he said, "or is that the whole State of Oklahoma?"

Betsy, Florine, Bob, and Ben pitched in to help Warren and Florence cram wet rags and towels around the windows and doors in the house.

Junior Dingle, who had been hired to take wedding pictures, refused to go indoors. Junior fetched a tall stepladder out of the garage and climbed onto Ben's roof to challenge the elements with his Speed Graphic.

Junior shot an exceptional photo of the dust storm. Betsy ran it six columns on the front page. Junior had caught a row of houses in the bottom of the frame only a second before the big dark billowing wall of dust had rumbled over the rooftops. For his effort, Junior earned another nickname around the *Times-Standard*. Some of his co-workers were now calling him "A-rab."

LaGrave Field was one of the largest and nicest ballparks in the minor leagues. It held 14,000 when full, as it was this night for the opening game of the series between the Fort Worth Cats and the Dallas Steers. A roof covered the stands all the way down the left-field line to the towering fence advertising Washer Brothers Clothiers, and all the way down the right-field line to a low fence advertising Vandervoort's Ice Cream.

The bleachers behind the right-field fence were reserved for "colored people" and the knothole gang. Warren and Florence went to as many Cat games as they could and had been following the team for years, since the days of old Panther Park, a mile closer to downtown on North Main, where Jake Atz and Big Boy Kraft had led the club to six straight Texas League championships. In those days, Warren and Florence would take Betsy on the Interurban from Claybelle to Fort Worth, then board a streetcar in downtown Fort Worth and make it to the ballpark in time for the four-thirty start. Betsy would sit in the "colored" section and root for the Cats. There were nothing but day games back then.

Sportswriters detested this relatively new thing called

night baseball. Night games forced strenuous deadlines on them and cut sharply into their social life.

When night baseball came in, Bob Walker said, "It's the end of literature as we know it."

Warren and Florence were like thousands of other fans of the Cats. If they didn't get out to the games at LaGrave Field in person, they listened faithfully to Zack Hurt's play-by-play broadcast on KFJZ. Zack Hurt was the "voice of the Cats," a man who liked to refer to the team as "Kittens" if they were behind on the scoreboard, who rang gongs to specify the number of bases a player reached after a hit, who always remarked that a ball club had "ducks on the pond" if runners were on base.

In their bright white flannels with blue caps and blue socks, the Cats were taking the field as Betsy and Bob entered the press box, Betsy having no problem getting past the guard on the door because the guard had limped off to take a piss.

The press box extended from home plate down the first-base line, high above the brilliant green grass of the playing field, which somehow looked richer and greener under the lights.

They entered the box behind Zack Hurt and stopped to listen as he ran through Fort Worth's lineup, calling the players by the nicknames he had given them and lavishing praise on each man as a credit to the community.

They heard about "Maestro" Homer Peel, the manager and right fielder; "Scoop 'Em Up" Hugh Shelley; "Flyin' " Freddie Frink; "Rabbit" McDowell; "Loopin' Lee" Stebbins; "Jolly Cholly" English; "Bouncin' " Buster Chatam; "Fireball" Frank Metha—and the big fellow himself would be on the mound tonight, Ed ("Bear Tracks") Greer.

"Where can we get a beer?" Betsy asked. She noticed that all of the sportswriters were drinking one.

Only half of the men in the press box were sportswriters. Every other person was a friend or a relative of a sportswriter. Two of the men were Western Union operators.

Zack Hurt heard the female voice behind him and spun around in his chair. The announcer gave Betsy the once-over, Betsy in her cool white summer dress and heels, smoking, taking everything in.

Back to his microphone, Zack Hurt said, "Well, folks, we

don't have any ducks on the pond yet, but we've got us a swan up here in the press box. That's a first!"

Bob got them each a bottle of beer out of the help-yourself cold-drink box that was up against a wall near the Western Union machines. They walked to the far end of the press box, Betsy getting looks from some of the men, Bob nodding hellos.

"Where's Big 'Un?" Betsy asked. "He's supposed to be covering the game."

"He sits in the dugout."

"Why? This is the best seat in the house."

"He likes to be close to the action so he can hear it and smell it."

"That's good, don't you think? For a writer?"

"Not particularly."

"It isn't?"

"Have you ever smelled a baseball player?"

Through the open windows of the press box, Betsy scanned the crowd below. She spotted Lank Allred in an aisle behind the home-plate screen. He had entered a portal and was signing autographs for a circle of law-and-order fans.

"It's celebrity night," Betsy said. "There's old Big Hat, No Cattle."

"I'm surprised you haven't called him that in print."

"I'm saving it for the right occasion."

As Betsy's eyes continued to roam, she was surprised to see two familiar faces looking up at her. She waved to them.

The men were Leland and Lawton, two of the rural intellectuals she had met on the Sunshine Special last summer.

"This feller can hit," Leland seemed to be saying to Betsy with a gesture toward the playing field.

The batter at the plate in gray flannels, dark red cap, and dark red socks was Les Mallon, Dallas's second baseman.

Bob said Les Mallon couldn't hit the deuce. Drop a deuce on Les Mallon and he would go south like a migrating bird.

At the plate, Les Mallon spit tobacco juice, tugged at his crotch, and glared at the pitcher.

Out on the mound, Ed ("Bear Tracks") Greer spit tobacco juice, tugged at *his* crotch, and glared at the hitter.

"I've never understood a baseball player's abiding love for his penis and balls," Betsy said.

"It's a slow game," Bob said. "A man's got to have something to do."

After a tedious windup, Ed ("Bear Tracks") Greer delivered a pitch that looked as if it had three different speeds and a jar of Vaseline on it. Les Mallon fell down swinging. Two more pitches and the hitter was out. The crowd cheered. The umpire examined the baseball. The crowd booed. The umpire threw the ball back to the mound. The crowd cheered. Les Mallon walked to the dugout and responded to the hooting of fans by showing them where they could come get their dinner.

Betsy now drew a look of displeasure from two sportswriters. Even such widely traveled authors as Pop Boone of the *Fort Worth Press,* Flem Hall of the *Star-Telegram,* George White of the *Dallas Morning News,* and Jinx Tucker of the *Waco News-Tribune* had never seen anything like a woman in the press box.

None of the writers spoke to Betsy, but they each had a private chat with Solon Dunlap, the business manager and publicity director of the Cats, a shy, creepy fellow known affectionately as "Sorry" to his friends. Sorry Dunlap kept ignoring Betsy, pretending she didn't exist.

No one seemed to know what to do about Betsy's invasion of their sanctum.

There might not have been an incident if it hadn't been for Anna Sue Beaton.

Anna Sue had gone to the game with Shady and Eva Jane because Bob Walker had said it was such a big event he wouldn't have time to worry about her, but Anna Sue now looked upstairs and saw Betsy standing with Bob.

In a fury, Anna Sue became the second woman in America to enter a press box. The guard on the door hadn't noticed her breezing past him, preoccupied as he was with a pocket-sized book titled *Jean Harlow Meets Daddy Warbucks.*

Anna Sue made a straight line for Betsy and Bob Walker. "Rats!" she said. "Two rats in a cage!"

"What?" said Bob.

"Lice! It's high school all over again, isn't it?"

"Are we talking about me?" Betsy asked.

"Yes, you! The attractive widow!"

To Bob: "She whistles and you come crawlin'!"

To Betsy: "I guess you've decided you want to go with a quarterback again!"

To Bob: "Go on! Fall in love with her again and see where it gets you!"

To Betsy: "It must be nice to go through life getting everything you want."

"Anna Sue, you're making a fool of yourself," Betsy said, trying to keep her voice low. "You aren't supposed to be up here. Women aren't allowed in the press box."

Bob laughed at that.

"Laugh!" said Anna Sue. "Make fun of the world like you always do! Both of you! Newspaper *degenerates!* Y'all would laugh at a cripple orphan!"

"Only if he played for Dub Cooper," Bob said.

Now Betsy laughed.

"I've only got one more thing to say to you, Bob Walker," said Anna Sue. "You have not broken my heart—not by a long shot! And you won't see me again unless it behooves you to come to Casa Mañana and look up on the stage!"

"Hey!" The shout came from somewhere down the press row.

"Do you women *mind?*" a Western Union telegrapher said. "We got us a ball game goin' on here!"

Anna Sue brushed past the man on her way out. "Mister, I don't know who you are," she said, "but if you've got anything to do with the newspaper business, you can climb on this and *rotate!*"

Sorry Dunlap, looking like a man suffering from a stomach disorder, approached Betsy timidly.

"Miss Throckmorton, I know who you are," he said. "That's why I asked the boys to mind their manners tonight. I didn't want to ask you to leave or have you ejected. It would have made the wires, and that wouldn't have done baseball no good, would it? Miss Throckmorton, I want to offer you my personal box—it's down there behind home plate—and I want you to use it any time you want to come out here to see the Cats play. We would be tickled to death to have you as our guest. But, uh . . . I'm gonna have to ask you a favor. For the sake of baseball, the game we all love, please don't come up here to my press box no more. It ain't right. With a woman up here, you see, the boys don't feel like they can cuss or spit or scratch where it itches—know what I mean? I hope you understand."

Twenty-nine

A BEGGAR squatting in the streets of Calcutta, with the sun at its zenith, would have been more comfortable than Betsy on this scalding July day in Austin, Texas.

To combat the heat and humidity, Betsy was wearing a backless yellow dress with the hemline climbing above the fashion dictates of Claybelle. Betsy's skirt was up to her knees, New York style, and her bare tan legs, to Bob Walker, looked more shapely than anything in the hosiery ads.

Bob teased Betsy about trying to look sexy for Captain Frank Hamer of the Texas Rangers.

"I'm trying not to melt, is what I'm doing."

He said, "I know smart women who try to look sexy to prove they're not one-dimensional. I know sexy women who try to look smart for the same reason. I'm not often fooled."

"The last thing I'm trying to do is look sexy for Frank Hamer."

"It must be for me then."

They had come out of the Driskill Hotel in downtown Austin. They were walking up Congress Avenue toward the state capitol.

The drive had taken six hours, counting the stop for lunch at a roadhouse that specialized in greaseburgers, and a stop in Waco, where they thought it would be nice to drop in on Leatha Wardlaw for a few moments.

Leatha had opened a new Leatha's Creations in Waco, and Betsy had obtained the address from Olive Cooper, but when they had driven up to that block, they had found nothing but a row of small buildings halfway under construction.

A worker said the entire block had been blown away by the tornado back in May. The funnel had picked up Leatha's Creations and put it down on top of Tindall's Poultry & Eggs.

They had driven on to Austin, checked into their hotel

rooms, bathed and changed clothes, and were on their way to
the five o'clock meeting with the Texas Ranger.

"Some women know how to sweat," Bob said, "You do.
You've always known how to sweat. You only get moist."

"Moist?"

"You glow."

"That's me. Miss Sweat Glow of 1936."

Bob put his hand on Betsy's back, which was bronzed from
the mornings she spent in the sun on the boat dock before
going to work.

"Yep, you're moist," he said. "Oh, shit."

"What?"

"I've got a hard-on."

Austin was the most charming city in Texas. Nobody argued about this except people from San Antonio, who liked to
pretend that their river wasn't stagnant. Austin was a city of
great old mansions, darkly shaded streets, florid buildings
that blended the influences of Europe with those of the Old
West, rippling creeks, hills rising beyond a tree-lined lake,
and rustic saloons and restaurants hidden in groves and
hanging from limestone ledges.

Bob had cherished memories of Austin. He always enjoyed
going back to the scene of his four-year crime, that of stealing
a degree from the University of Texas. He had stayed drunk
and disorderly, like most students he knew, for the whole
four years and had cheated his way through every course he
hated, which was everything but English, journalism, and
history.

"This is a great town," Bob said. "I'll drive you around
later."

"Swell."

Across the street from the capitol grounds, they entered a
white antebellum mansion that had been converted into a
state office building. A receptionist directed them up a stair-
way and down a hall to an office where the sign on the door
said:

CAPT. FRANK HAMER

COMPANY G

TEXAS RANGERS

In the outer office they found a secretary surrounded by walls of memorabilia: guns, knives, chains, handcuffs, swords, stirrups, photographs of lawmen, photographs of bullet-riddled automobiles. The secretary, a drab, efficient-looking woman, a dedicated bureaucrat, told them to have a seat, the captain would be with them shortly. Betsy was happy to find a window cooler in the outer office.

"Wow, is it hot outside," Betsy said, standing in front of the window cooler.

"Oh?" said the secretary. "I thought it was very pleasant when I had my lunch in the shade. Austin has more shade trees than any city in Texas. That's in an official report I've seen."

"You must be from Austin." Betsy smiled.

"Isn't it lovely? Why would anybody live anywhere else?"

They waited forty minutes for Frank Hamer. They smoked and looked at magazines.

In an issue of *Time*, Bob came across a picture of Adolf Hitler and Joseph Goebbels standing in a crowd of tall Nazi generals. They looked like Chihuahuas compared to the towering officers.

"I didn't know these guys were dwarfs," Bob said, holding up the magazine to show Betsy.

"That's why they're dangerous."

The secretary's radio was on, and the secretary hummed along to the themes that could be heard: "Wave the flag for Hudson High, boys, show them how we stand. . . . When it's Ralston time for breakfast, then it surely is a treat. . . . Who's that little chatterbox, the one with pretty auburn locks?"

A radio voice was saying something about "a fiery horse with the speed of light" when Frank Hamer's office door opened. Betsy was startled to see the man who came out. It was Mr. Johnson, of Johnson, Leland, and Lawton.

"Why, hello," Betsy said as Johnson touched his Stetson. "What are you doing here?"

"Frank's one of my fishin' buddies," Johnson said. "Sorry if I kept you folks waiting."

Frank Hamer stood up behind his desk as Betsy and Bob entered. He was a tall, stern-looking man with a narrow head and dark receding hair. The Ranger's coat was off, his tie loose. He wore no gun, but a pearl-handled .38 in a shoulder holster hung on a wooden coatrack behind him.

Betsy introduced Bob, who shook the Ranger's hand.

"I've read your column, Mr. Walker. You're pretty good with the needle."

"I'll take that as a compliment," Bob said. "Somebody has to keep the immortals honest. We wouldn't want a bunch of spoiled brats running loose in the streets."

Betsy opened the large black leather shoulder bag she had bought at "Ritzy Business" and handed Frank Hamer a copy of the story she had written. "Captain Hamer, this might save us some time. Read this, then we can talk."

She and Bob sat down in armchairs across from the Ranger's desk. Betsy watched Frank Hamer's face closely as he read her story. Bob's eyes shifted to an enlarged photograph on the wall—it must have been twenty by twenty-four inches —of Bonnie and Clyde's gunshot-battered automobile with Frank Hamer standing beside it, his foot on a running board, a sawed-off shotgun under his arm, a cigar in his mouth.

Frank Hamer's solemn expression never changed as he read:

By BETSY THROCKMORTON
Copyright, 1936, Claybelle Times-
Standard

This is a true horror story. It's about murder for money.

Innocent people in Texas are being murdered for profit, the Times-Standard has learned, and the blood of the witless victims flows straight to the doorstep of a cynical, cunning, unscrupulous law enforcement officer whose identity is known to this newspaper.

Under the guise of law and order, the lawman has been running a Texas Murder Machine for the past 10 months. Quite simply, he kills for money.

Ironically, the Texas Murder Machine was inadvertently created by the Texas Bankers Assn., which persists in offering $5,000 rewards for dead bank robbers "and not one cent for live ones," as its posters blatantly advertise.

Since the rewards were established, a survey shows that the number of attempted bank robberies has only increased in the State of Texas. The Times-Standard believes—and intends to prove—that these rewards have only aroused greed and evil desire in the minds of at least one psychotic lawman and his accomplices.

For months, the gang has been preying on the weakened character traits and Depression-induced hopelessness of young drifters and jobless hobos.

It works like this: these sad young men are recruited as "lookouts" on phony bank jobs but are then murdered as "bank robbers," for which $5,000 rewards are collected.

The story went on to say that six of the young men who had been killed in the North Central Texas area had no prior record of arrests and were not carrying weapons at the time they were slain.

The story never referred to Lank Allred by name, but only a mental defective might fail to figure out who "the cynical, cunning, unscrupulous law enforcement officer" was.

Captain Hamer finished the story, folded it in half, and handed it back to Betsy. "Print it."

"Really?" said Betsy, elated. "It's accurate?"

"Right down the line," Frank Hamer said.

She lit a Lucky and looked over at Bob Walker to accept his congratulatory smile.

Frank Hamer said, "Miss Throckmorton, it may interest you to know we've been working on this ourselves. Not long enough, I reckon. We didn't want to believe it about Lank at first—one of our own. We're watching him. We've *been* watching him. All we need is for him to make a wrong move— something we can nail him on."

Betsy told Frank Hamer about the missing nozzles on the acetylene torch.

"That's interesting for *us* to know, but a slick lawyer could make it look fairly unimportant in court."

Something occurred to Betsy. "You want me to print this story because you think it'll shake him up, don't you?"

"I'd be lying if I said no."

"Can I put in the story that the paper's findings have been confirmed and substantiated by investigators?"

"I don't want you to do that," Frank Hamer said. "I've got me a killer to catch. I don't want Lank to know we suspect him of *anything*. I'd rather have him think the story's a result of your own investigation. It'll make him nervous, put pressure on him—like I hope it does the bankers when they see it in print. Those sons of bitches—pardon my French—they represent all the wealth in Texas, and I've known horses smarter."

Bob Walker said, "Captain Hamer, isn't Betsy going to be in danger when she runs this story?"

"She's *been* in danger ever since she wrote her first smart-aleck column about him."

"*You?* A smart-aleck column?" Bob was looking at Betsy.

"It was the typewriter," she said. "I only went along for the ride."

Frank Hamer pushed a buzzer on his desk.

His secretary stuck her head in.

"Maureen, tell my undercover boys to come on in," the Ranger said.

Johnson, Leland, and Lawton shuffled into the office.

Frank Hamer introduced them properly: Captain A. T. Johnson, Lieutenant Tom Leland, Lieutenant Roy Lawton, all Texas Rangers.

Betsy felt stupid. "I told my husband they sold encyclopedias," she said.

Frank Hamer said, "When you met these fellows on the train they were on their way home from an FBI seminar in undercover work. They've been on a case down in the Valley. Some old boys were up to the same thing as Lank, only on a smaller scale. I've got my suspicions about a sheriff over on the Gulf Coast, too. We caught the boys in the Valley, but I don't think the story even made the wire. What's one less dead hobo? That's the attitude of most people I run into. The man who's chairman of the Texas Bankers Association, fellow down in Houston, said to me that as far as he was concerned, any hobo who could be talked into helping rob a bank, even if there wasn't a robbery, *ought* to get killed."

"I've heard the same thing from a banker in Claybelle," Betsy said.

The Ranger said, "Miss Throckmorton, your husband's death might be tied into all this."

"Did Lank Allred kill Ted?"

"No, ma'am, I can tell you for sure he didn't. But I think I know who did. I don't want to say any more about it right now, but if I'm right, it may help us throw a net over Lank."

"Captain Hamer, you can't sit here and tell me you know who killed my husband and not tell me who it is!"

"You have it in your story there. We think it was one of Lank's accomplices. We think your husband stumbled onto something in the hobo camp . . . overheard something . . . heard too much for his own good—had to be silenced."

Betsy said, "If there's a God, Lank Allred will rot in prison."

"We'll get him," Frank Hamer said. "Miss Throckmorton, we've only had one Lank Allred. The Texas Rangers are a proud organization. Brave men. Honest men. Men like B. M. Gault, Lone Wolf Gonzales—"

"Frank Hamer," said Betsy, rising.

The captain got to his feet. "When do you plan to run the story?"

"Soon, I suppose. I want to polish it a little."

"I'd run it before the Frontier Centennial opens. Nobody's apt to give a hoot about nothin' after that thing starts up."

A. T. Johnson said, "Cowtown's in for a four-month drunk, near as I can tell."

As she and Bob were leaving, Betsy thought she had better satisfy her curiosity about one other thing.

"After this story comes out, exactly how much should I be concerned about my health?"

Captain Hamer said, "I'd watch my step, if I were you, but my boys here will be stickin' to Lank like a grassburr on a wildcat. They'll be keeping an eye on you, too, young lady."

Bob drove them around Austin for an hour. He wanted to cruise past some of his old haunts—the tavern on Lake Austin where Wenonah Graves got hers, the nook out by Barton Springs where Prissy Harwood got hers, the lodge up on the cliff where Peggy Weir got hers, and the saloon in an alley off Guadalupe, the drag, where Maxine Chilner got his gold football.

Bob chose a shack on the edge of downtown for dinner, a place where gringos weren't altogether welcome unless they knew the owner, which Bob did. "Mexican Eats" was the name of the cafe, but Bob always called it "El Grub-o."

The food was served family style, and they stuffed themselves with cheese enchiladas, tamales, rice, refried beans, chili con queso, corn tortillas, and beer.

Betsy said, "Two things you can't find anywhere in New York—this or real barbecue. The closest you can come to barbecue is a Chinese rib."

"I ate a Chinese rib in California. It tasted like a Milky Way."

Bob had never been to New York, but there was a trip coming up next fall. The SMU Mustangs would be playing an intersectional football game against the Fordham Rams at the Polo Grounds.

A sportswriter's out-of-town travel was determined by the football and baseball teams he covered, if those teams paid his expenses. Traipsing after the Dallas Steers in the Texas League, his byline had flown in splendor over the datelines of Beaumont, Galveston, Tulsa, Oklahoma City, Houston, San Antonio, and Fort Worth.

His journeys with the SMU Mustangs had been more adventurous. Out to California for the Rose Bowl and twice before in '31 and '33, when the Ponies had gone out to play St. Mary's in Moraga, which had enabled him to take a peek at San Francisco. He had gone up to Annapolis in '31 to watch Speedy Mason and the boys whip Navy. In '30, he had made the trip to South Bend when SMU had barely lost to the Fighting Irish, 20 to 14, almost scoring a big upset over the team that would win the National Championship, the last Notre Dame team Knute Rockne had coached before his death in a plane crash. If Bob had been out of college and working for the paper at the time, he would have seen New York City in '28. That's when an SMU team had gone up to West Point and unveiled a ballcarrier named Redman Hume who had scared the long gray dignity out of Army before SMU had lost the game 14 to 13.

"I was there," Betsy said. "The SMU band stole the show. They came out at halftime in a two-step and played jazz. Nobody in the East had seen this before. They thought it was sacrilegious."

They drank for a while in the lobby of the Driskill after dinner. What passed for conversation was a high school memory test, savage games of What-Ever-Happened-To and Remember When. Betsy thought she won the night when she hit him with Yvonne Genelle Bozeman, but Bob had held back Qumy Kay Fuqua.

They went up to their rooms around ten o'clock. Betsy had wanted to get an early start back to Claybelle in the morning.

Bob gave her a hug and good-night kiss on the forehead in the hall outside their rooms.

"Thanks for coming with me," Betsy said as they were unlocking their doors.

"It was worth it for El Grub-o."

Betsy had brought along two feature stories to edit. She was sitting at a wobbly French desk in her room when Bob opened the connecting door and jammed it with the doorstop so it would stay open. He was bare-chested and barefooted but wearing his blue pajama bottoms that tied with a string at the waist. He held a copy of *Gone With the Wind,* a hefty new novel of the Old South which outweighed a forest of butternut trees and had sold over 50,000 copies its first day in America's bookstores.

"What do you think you're doing?"

"Safety first," Bob said. "I'm trying to read this book in bed, but if I fall asleep with it on my chest, I'll get crushed to death. If you hear any strange noises—gasping, something like that—will you come rescue me?"

"Good night." She laughed.

Bob read and smoked for an hour, then switched off his bed lamp. He was still awake when Betsy came into his room and stood by his bed. She was in a silk dressing gown.

He could see her in the faint glow from the moon coming in his windows. "Scarlett . . . ?"

"Just shut up."

She let the gown drop to the floor, and in her panties and brassiere she quickly crawled into his bed and under the sheet.

He slipped his arm around her.

"I don't want to do anything," she said. "Will you just hold me? Is that all right?"

"I could hold you forever."

They snuggled and got comfortable, Bob with one leg between hers, a hand on her hip, the other hand at her back. Betsy's arms were around him.

"Jesus, you feel good," Bob said. "You feel like . . . high school."

"Damn you," she said softly. Words of surrender.

Suddenly they were kissing madly on this quaintly blissful night of the Great Depression—Betsy Throckmorton and Bob Walker, old sweethearts, best friends, lovers again.

Bob's hand on Betsy's smooth back slowly began to struggle with the hooks on her brassiere, and one of her hands beneath the sheet began to struggle with the knot in his pajama string.

"I used to be able to do this with one hand," he said.

"Me, too," she giggled.

Thirty

THE STORY of the Texas Murder Machine rang bells on wire machines all across the state, all across the country.

But in an effort to reach a greater number of people in the communal surroundings—the dunce cap—Betsy went on KVAT twice on July 15, the day the story appeared in the *Times-Standard*. What better way to reach the multitudes of non-subscribers who tried so diligently to stay uninformed about almost everything?

She pre-empted *Just Plain Bill* at 10 A.M. and *Ma Perkins* at 3:15 P.M.

That morning at home, Betsy was nervous about going on the air. In the kitchen, Florence had watched her make a stab at opening a can of peaches for breakfast.

Either the can opener wouldn't work right or there was something wrong with the can. Betsy threw the can of peaches in the garbage and took another can down from the cupboard.

"Child, what are you doing?" Florence said, retrieving the can from the garbage pail.

Betsy said, "Florence, I'm too tired, too busy, and too *rich* to put up with crap that doesn't work. Mechanical things get one chance with me and that's it!"

At the radio station, Betsy went into the same studio from which Big 'Un Darly and Dub Cooper's shows emanated. She sat at a table in front of a microphone. Each time, Estill Parch introduced her in a funereal tone of voice, saying:

"This is KVAT, the voice of Claybelle, Texas. We interrupt our regular programming for a special news report. The management regrets any inconvenience this may cause. Here, now, is Betsy Throckmorton, editor-in-chief of the *Times-Standard*."

Betsy read from a prepared statement.

"An exclusive story was published in our newspaper this morning. It is a story about murder for profit. The story is shocking. The story is one of horror. But the story is true. I speak to you now because I believe every law-abiding citizen should be aware of what has been taking place here in Claybelle and the area around us. Here is our story."

Betsy read the piece from the paper, verbally underlining certain words and phrases. She ended both broadcasts by saying, "There can be no doubt that a terrible miscalculation has been made by the Texas Bankers Association. Part of this blood is on their hands. They can only begin to cleanse themselves if they stop these rewards *now*. Thank you for listening."

Ben and Florine went to the *Times-Standard* to help field the phone calls.

Some people wanted to know why they were supposed to think the story was true just because the paper said so. Some people wanted to know if Olin Musgrove was the crook. Some people wanted to know what it was that somebody had said about a story or something on the radio about somebody being killed in Claybelle. Of course, most of the callers wanted to express outrage that *Just Plain Bill* and *Ma Perkins* had been knocked off the air.

Calls came in from reporters on other newspapers and radio stations pleading for more details and the identity of the "cynical, cunning, unscrupulous law enforcement officer." They promised they would keep the information confidential. Sure, they would.

Betsy instructed anyone answering a phone not to divulge Lank Allred's name. When she wasn't on the radio, she was at her typewriter, working on a follow-up story in which she would use Lank's name. She wanted to be the first to use it.

Ben took a call from O. L. Beaton. The banker said, "Your daughter better know what she's talkin' about, Ben! If you want my two cents, I think you're gonna spend the rest of your life in a courthouse defendin' yourself against libel!"

"Why wouldn't she know what she's talkin' about?" Ben said. "She's my daughter, isn't she? It's a genes deal!"

Florine took the call from her ex-husband.

Shady needed to speak to Ben urgently.

Ben would be tied up for a while, Florine said. At the moment, Ben was on the line with a man from NBC News, and there were other calls he was supposed to return—to someone at every tabloid in New York, to a researcher at *Time*, to a researcher at *Newsweek*, to a feature writer at INS, to the Lieutenant Governor, to Amon Carter, to the chairman of the Texas Bankers Association, and to a story developer at Warner Brothers in Hollywood.

"Ask him if he knows a better criminal lawyer than Wild Bill McLean in Fort Worth," Shady said.

"Why?"

"I need me a good criminal lawyer, is why. I'm in bidness with the psycho shitass. I've been drillin' wells with his reward money. Eva Jane says this makes me an accomplice to murder!"

Florine could hear Eva Jane shrieking in the background.

"Did you know where he was getting the money?" Florine asked.

"Fuck, no! What if I did? How am I supposed to know he's killin' innocent people?"

Florine thought she heard a crash. This was followed by the sound of a struggle.

"Shady . . . ?"

"I'm here—barely."

"I don't see where you have a problem. You never told him to commit murder."

"No, but I'm fixin' to!"

Lank Allred's picture was on the front page of the *Times-Standard* the next day and his name was in a big Gothic headline and bells were ringing on the wire machines again, but as he walked across the Claybelle square he was only inconvenienced by autograph seekers.

He signed five autographs on his way to the Fidelity Bank to see O. L. Beaton, one of them for Scooter Pittman to have framed and hang in his pool hall.

Lank wrote on the back of an envelope:

"Dear Scooter: You've still got time to make something of yourself. Capt. Lank Allred, Company C, Texas Rangers."

O. L. Beaton was nauseous, perspiring.

"Newspapers!" O. L. waved his arms and paced. "Radio! Judas Moose of the Fifth Dynasty! How the hell did it ever come to this?"

"Nobody can prove nothin'," Lank said calmly, helping himself to one of the banker's cigars off the desk.

O. L. said, "We were shootin' under par all the way! Never hit one ball out of the fairway! Never three-putted! It was foolproof! Now look at us! Goddamn newspapers! They don't cause nothin' but trouble!"

O. L.'s phone rang. He grabbed it irritably. "Now what?" he said. "If it's cancer, I already got some."

Shady Webster's secretary was calling from Shady's office in the W. T. Waggoner Building in Fort Worth. She said her name was Sandi. A young voice.

"Mr. Beaton, I'm afraid I have some bad news."

"I don't need no bad news," the banker said. "What?"

"It's about the oil well in Possum Kingdom."

"Aw, shit." O. L. turned white.

"Mr. Webster says it sure is a surprise to him, but it looks like a rabbit don't run to the same hole ever time. I think that's what he said."

"It's a dry hole?" O. L. whimpered.

"Same as, I guess. Mr. Webster says you're up to your ass in salt water, but he says he wants you to know he has some real good leases near Mercer's Gap. Let me get this right. He says you couldn't make the ocean over there if you was Magellan."

"Put that lightweight sumbitch on the phone!"

Sandi said, "I would, but he can't talk. His jaw is wired up. He had a bad accident last night."

O. L. hung up.

"Duster?" said Lank.

O. L. made a little noise.

"I figured he'd break his pick again. All that talk about Caddo lime and shit."

"I'm ruint," O. L. said.

Lank stood up to leave. "You ain't ruint, but you got your work cut out for you today. I'll be needin' thirty thousand dollars by tonight. You can bring it to me at the Oasis. If there ain't no oil to wait around for, I think me and Shirley

will be movin' on. Seems like the smart thing to do, what with
the press stirring up all this shit. That thirty thousand dollars
will be for what I lost in them other dry holes."

"Lank, you must be out of your mind. How am I supposed
to do that?"

"I don't know and I don't give a damn, but if you ain't at
the Oasis tonight with my money, you can give your soul to
God, because your ass belongs to *me!*" The Ranger squared
his Stetson over his eyebrows and left.

O. L. Beaton plopped down at his desk. He put his head in
his hands. Maybe it wouldn't be so bad to be dead. He
wouldn't have to pay all of Bernice's doctor bills. He wouldn't
have to pay all of Anna Sue's department store bills. He
wouldn't have to see himself exposed as an embezzler. He
wouldn't have to go to prison. On the other hand, he thought
to himself, dead was the end of the ball game.

He sat awhile longer, and it slowly came to him that there
might be a way out of all this. What if he went to Betsy, the
crusading little bitch, and told her Lank Allred had threatened to kill him if he didn't steal all this money? Why not?
He could say he had been operating all along under a death
threat. He might even come off looking like a hero—a belea-
guered man who had lived with fear long enough and had
decided to come clean and help rid society of a dangerous
lunatic.

O. L. leaned back in his chair and suddenly felt powerful.
By God, Lank Allred better get out of Texas if he knew what
was good for him.

Thirty-one

_____

ON THE Saturday of July 18, 1936, the President of the
United States, Franklin D. Roosevelt, was fishing on a cruiser
off the coast of Maine, but at three-thirty in the afternoon he
pressed a wireless button and electric impulses carried by
Western Union and radio from the ship caused a knife to drop
and cut a lariat that stretched in front of the main gates of
the Texas Frontier Centennial in Fort Worth. Thus, the
showgrounds were officially opened to the public with all of
FDR's good wishes.

The main gates were comprised of ten turnstiles under a
shingled roof on top of which were large letters carved out of
blocks of wood painted dark brown, which said: W-H-E-R-E
T-H-E W-E-S-T B-E-G-I-N-S.

Thousands of people were outside the gates when the knife
sliced the lariat and Amon Carter waved his fleece-white
Stetson in the air, to the East, toward Maine, in gratitude to
his good friend the President.

Betsy was already inside the grounds in an area reserved
for the press and dignitaries. Along with Bob Walker, Ben
and Florine, Shady and Eva Jane, and O. L. and Bernice
Beaton, she stood on the Street of Pinwheels, the major pathway to all of the exhibits and theaters.

She had looked around and been relieved to spot Leland
and Lawton milling around in the crowd.

O. L. Beaton was looking healthier than he had in weeks.
Buoyed by the knowledge that he could rat on Lank Allred at
any given moment and fully explain that all of his own mis-
deeds had been in self-defense, the banker had regained his
old swagger.

He was feeling so good, he had even been nice to Bernice.
He had let her borrow his shooting stick, his golf seat, so she

could rest under shade trees and sort through her four bottles of prescription tablets.

O. L. had not taken any money to Lank at the Oasis two nights earlier, but he had phoned the honky-tonk and left a message with Shirley Watters.

"Tell Lank his messenger boy has suffered a sudden attack of good sense," O. L. had said. "You might also tell him that if he cares to look *down,* he'll see he's standin' in a load of shit up to his knees!"

O.L. had not heard back from Lank.

Shady Webster's jaw was wired into a permanent half-smile, and he wore a neck brace. He could speak but only in slurred words through his teeth. Eva Jane wore a pair of dark glasses to cover her swollen and bloodshot left eye.

The grainy details of their gripping human drama would never be known. Shady's story for public consumption was that he had been struck by a line-drive golf ball at Shadow-lawn Country Club and the blow had knocked him into a ravine, which accounted for the pulled muscle in his neck. It was a believable story to some. Many members at Shadow-lawn had been struck by duck hooks. Eva Jane's explanation for her eye was that she was having the worst sinus attack of her life.

Wonderful things happened after FDR's electric impulses cut the lariat and the gates opened to the Frontier Centennial.

Out of nowhere came dozens of cowboys on horses, firing blank cartridges from their .44s. They rode up and down the Street of Pinwheels, and up and down Sunset Trail, the street that led to the carnival midway and to Casa Mañana, the cafe-theater, and to Pioneer Palace, the dance hall and burlesque-vaudeville house.

A like number of Apaches riding bareback came out of no-where and went galloping about, letting out war whoops and laughing at the U.S. cavalry troops that were chasing them.

Five Wells Fargo stagecoaches, each drawn by four horses, swung this way and that as bathing beauties hung out of the windows tossing out tickets for free drinks—and their phone numbers.

In the midst of all this, music came from everywhere on the

showgrounds. The TCU band played "Stars and Stripes Forever," assisted by the Shrine's Drum & Bugle Corps, as Amon Carter wiggled a baton. Blues, Dixie, and Western swing could also be heard from various musical groups that were performing on huge bales of cotton.

Betsy and Bob Walker planned to do the whole deal this afternoon and tonight, then they wouldn't have to come back. They were going to all of the exhibits, in particular the Pioneer Village, where hundreds of Fort Worth women had worked so hard for so long to round up dolls, china, and frontier furniture. They would have dinner at Casa Mañana at six-thirty and see the opening-night performance of the spectacular revue at eight, giving Anna Sue Beaton the applause she so richly deserved. Afterward, they would move on to the Pioneer Palace to watch Hinda Wassau, "the Frontier's First Lady of Striptease," perform to the music of Booty and Them Others, who had been hired by Billy Rose. They would complete the evening with drinks at Sally Rand's Nude Ranch.

All those who had staying power were invited to come along.

Shady Webster said, "Ah ear Sayer Rin bay dee. Girs air wur guz. Cane zee none."

Eva Jane translated. "He says he hears Sally Rand is a bad deal. The girls wear gauze. You can't see anything."

Betsy was in a mood to celebrate. The Texas Bankers Association had released a statement to the wires saying the organization was going to discontinue the rewards for dead bank robbers. The statement said that while the rewards had been well intended, a careful study conducted over the past several months had proved that they weren't accomplishing what the bankers had hoped. The statement made no mention of Betsy or the *Times-Standard,* or of any pressure that had been applied by Frank Hamer.

"Those jerks," she had said to Ray Fletcher. "Have they forgotten I write a column?"

But the rewards had been stopped. That was the main thing.

The enormous marquee over the entrance to Casa Mañana said:

Billy Rose Presents
THE CASA MAÑANA REVUE
"A Cavalcade of World's Fairs"
Starring

EVERETT MARSHALL - ANN PENNINGTON
Paul Whiteman & His Orchestra
Judy Canova   Joe Venuti
Ramona   The King's Men

FAYE COTTON
"Texas's No. 1 Sweetheart"
Plus
One Hundred of Texas's
Most Beautiful Girls!

Studying the marquee, Eva Jane said, "So much for Anna Sue's big talk. It doesn't say *the* one hundred most beautiful girls in Texas. It says one hundred *of*. There is a big difference, if you ask me."

The Casa Mañana cafe-theater accommodated a modest 3,800 people, in the open air, on seven half-moon tiers. Ben Throckmorton had arranged for an excellent table in the center of the theater, squarely facing the huge revolving stage and looking down on it from the third tier, which meant that the table would be a safe distance from the fountains that were expected to squirt water at irregular intervals.

The group drank for an hour and a half, waiting for their dinner. The fatty roast beef and cold green peas finally were served as the show was starting.

Showgirls dressed in everything from Indian headdresses and panties and high heels to filmy gowns and tiaras came into view from moving staircases and out of the wings. Paul Whiteman's orchestra surfaced in the middle of a pool of water. Spotlights beamed down on a man in a tuxedo and a lady in an evening gown, and Everett Marshall sang to Ann Pennington:

The night is young
And you're so beautiful,

Here among the shadows,
Beautiful lady,
Open your arms.

For the next hour, one production number followed another as the stage revolved. Girls in Army helmets and shorts tap danced around the Eiffel Tower. Girls in cowboy hats and shorts tap danced around the Alamo. Girls in abbreviated togas tap danced around the Roman Forum. Arrayed on pedestals and stairwells, stately girls in bewildering costumes stood motionless, their faces painted into caricatures of smiling young women. Anna Sue may have been one of those. Who could tell?

Betsy had tried to repair her friendship with Anna Sue by putting her picture on the front page of the *Times-Standard.* "Claybelle Beauty Chosen for Casa." Anna Sue had insisted on having a portrait photographer in Dallas shoot the picture. Eva Jane thought Anna Sue had come out looking like Madeleine Carroll's tubercular sister.

"There she is!" Florine exclaimed.

Faye Cotton was parading around the stage in her $5,000 gold-mesh gown, and Anna Sue was clearly one of her six attendants—the one swinging her hips sexily and tossing come-hither looks to the men seated down front.

"Hey, great," Bob Walker said, looking at a page in the elaborate program that had been printed for the Casa Mañana Revue and sold for fifty cents. The names of all the showgirls were listed in the program in alphabetical order.

"Here she is right here," said Bob, handing the program to Betsy. "Anna Sue Beeson, Claybert, Texas."

Betsy spit in her glass.

While the Casa Mañana Revue was in progress, Slop Herster and Tommy Jack Lucas were seated at a remote table in Sally Rand's Nude Ranch, their presence undetected by Lank Allred, who was drinking at the bar with Shirley Watters.

The Nude Ranch was a large barn with a stage at one end, darkly lit by dull blue lights but intentionally so in order to make the waitresses appear to be totally nude, though in fact they were wearing gauze G-strings and gauze pasties.

Slop and Tommy Jack had been tailing Lank since the Ranger had left the Oasis with Shirley. Slop was armed with a .38 revolver, which was tucked in his pants under his shirt. He wasn't sure about what he might do to Lank tonight. He was going to pick his spot and decide when the time came.

The cast on Slop's right hand had been removed and he had been giving his hand plenty of exercise by jacking off three or four times a day. So he told Tommy Jack.

"You can die doin' that," Tommy Jack said. "Drain your spine."

"That's bullshit," Slop said. "Scooter jacked off twelve times in one day and nothin' happened."

Slop and Tommy Jack were studying the G-string on a waitress and didn't see Lank leave the Nude Ranch, but Shirley was still at the bar so they figured the Ranger would return.

Over at the cafe-theater, a waitress wearing a white cowboy hat, white boots, and a Lone Star flag as a dress brought O. L. Beaton a note on a slip of paper. The banker read the note, put it in his pocket, and excused himself from the table.

Judy Canova was now on the stage making animal noises, so Betsy seized the opportunity to go to the powder room.

The restrooms were off the main lobby of the theater, and it was purely by accident that Betsy, out of the corner of her eye, happened to see O. L. Beaton leaving Casa Mañana with Lank Allred.

Betsy wasn't surprised to see Lank at the Frontier Centennial, despite the publicity she had given him. There was no talk of his being arrested. As far as most people were concerned, he hadn't even done anything wrong. Killing worthless hobos? What was wrong with that? Lank Allred, famous Texas Ranger, might sign more autographs tonight than Eddie Foy Jr.

Betsy couldn't resist the temptation. She followed O. L. and Lank out into the Centennial park, keeping out of their sight among the throngs strolling around the lantern-draped pathways.

Lank led O. L. into a concrete-block building around to the

side of the cafe-theater. A dark place. Away from the lights of the Centennial park.

Betsy waited for the men to come out.

And waited.

A stack of wooden crates was piled against the side of the building. She slipped off her shoes and climbed up on the boxes to where she could see inside—and perhaps listen—through a louvered window, a fresh-air vent.

The concrete-block building was an employees' restroom. She could see the men and hear their voices.

O. L. was saying, "Now, God damn it, Lank, what are you gonna do, beat me up? All I've got with me is sixty-five dollars."

"You got a personal check on you."

"I can't write you a check for thirty thousand dollars. You couldn't get it cashed nowhere in the world!"

"Write me one for five thousand dollars. I can get that much cashed."

"Lank, I don't *have* five thousand dollars. My advice to you—"

Lank took out his .45. "Write me that check. I ain't got time to fuck with you."

O. L. pulled out his wallet and produced a blank check. He filled it in with a fountain pen, shaking the pen nervously to make the ink flow.

Lank examined the check, stuck it in his pocket, and put away his .45. But his next move was to clamp a meaty paw around the back of O. L.'s neck. "How long since you've had a dip in the old swimmin' hole?"

"W-what the hell . . . you doin'?" O. L. sputtered.

Lank, with the brute strength of his one hand, dragged the banker to a toilet and forced his face down into the bowl and held it there.

Betsy gagged as she watched O. L. gurgling, his feet kicking, his arms flailing. Christ, he was drowning.

"No!" Betsy hollered through the louvered window.

Lank jerked O. L.'s head out of the toilet and looked around, his eyes blazing. Quickly he took out his .45 and thwacked O. L. across the temple. The banker went sprawling on the floor, unconscious. Just as quickly, Lank flipped off the lights in the restroom and walked outside and looked around.

A voice greeted him out of the darkness. "Lank! It's Tom Leland, Company G."

Betsy was clinging to the louvered window to steady herself on the crates.

"I saw two of you go in there, Lank. Is he comin' out?"

Lank Allred said, "Naw, uh . . . he made a move on me. I didn't have my gun with me. I had to cold-cock him. O. L. Beaton's the mastermind of that ring that's been killin' them hobos. I can furnish the proof. I been workin' on it for three months."

"Call it quits, Lank. Roy Lawton's with me."

Leland and Lawton stepped into Lank's view—and Betsy's.

Roy Lawton said, "You're all done, Lank. You're under arrest. We're gonna have to cuff you."

Leland and Lawton were about twenty-five yards from Lank.

"You've got the wrong man," Lank called out.

"Frank Hamer don't think so," Leland said.

Lank hunched his shoulders over and shuffled his feet, a defeated man, but in a lightning move he whipped out his .45 and fired three shots.

One shot sent Tom Leland spinning to the ground, hit in the shoulder. The other bullets caught Ray Lawton in the thigh and upper arm. He went down like a drunk missing the curb.

An expert marksman, Lank had hit the men exactly where he had aimed. Something in his warped sense of honor made it acceptable to kill a hobo for money but not a fellow Texas Ranger.

The gunfire had not attracted anyone's attention, for it had only blended in with the gunfire coming from inside the arena where "The Last Frontier," a Wild West show, was going on. In there, the U.S. cavalry was slaughtering Apaches.

As Lank pulled the wounded bodies of Leland and Lawton into a less conspicuous place, Betsy chose the moment to jump down off the crates, shoes in her hand. She ran toward the bright lights of the Centennial park.

Lank saw Betsy running away. Glancing back, she saw him coming after *her*.

In this fitful moment, Betsy made a commendable if illogical decision. She chose not to go back to the cafe-theater. Lank was a maniac with a .45, a man who now had nothing to lose. She didn't want to endanger her daddy, Florine, Bob, the others.

The shoes still in her hand, she hurried up a pathway toward Pioneer Palace, the dance hall, thinking she would find a policeman, a security guard, *somebody* to help her.

Pushing through the throngs of Centennial-goers, she reached the entrance to the dance hall and put on her shoes. She grabbed the arm of the man on the door, who, if it hadn't been for his false handlebar mustache, would have looked like an authentic trail-driving cowhand.

"You've got to help me!" Betsy said urgently. "Call the police! Call an ambulance! Two men have been shot! There's a lunatic out here! He's a Texas Ranger! He's coming after me!"

"You part of the show?"

"No, I'm not part of the Goddamn show. Did you *hear* what I said?"

"Lady, if you ain't part of the show, it's a two-dollar cover."

"There's a lunatic out there with a gun!"

"It's still two dollars."

Betsy squandered a second to stare at the man. "You ignorant Texas son of a bitch!" she said, and brushed him aside, wading into the mayhem of the dance hall, which was crammed with customers, music blaring from the stage.

The man called to her. "Lady, if you don't pay up, I'm gonna call a cop!"

"Good!" Betsy yelled back. "Do it! Do it *now!*"

The man only laughed at her and looked up at the stage.

On the stage, Booty and Them Others were providing the musical accompaniment for Hinda Wassau, "the Frontier's First Lady of Striptease."

Betsy threaded her way through the drunks, hoping to get near enough to the stage to yell at Booty, someone she knew, someone who knew *her,* someone who would believe her and find help.

Hinda Wassau was strutting around on the stage in a crimson robe and spike heels, her orange mane swirling. Suddenly she flung the robe into the wings, revealing a stupendous copper body covered only by a red G-string and silver pasties. The crowd howled, and with Booty Pettigrew on vocal, the stripper went into the major part of her act.

A pretty girl . . .

Bump, bump.

Is like a mel-o-dy . . .

Bump, bump.

That haunts you night and day.

Squat, grind, bump.

Betsy was squeezing and gouging her way toward the stage when a hand clutched her arm. It was Sloppy Herster. Not her ideal choice for a friend in need, but a familiar face nonetheless.

"Slop, you've got to help me!" she said. "I can't find a policeman, anybody! Lank Allred's crazy! I saw him shoot two people! He tried to kill O. L. Beaton! I saw it all! He knows it! He's coming after me!"

"Good deal. That'll save me some trouble. I got a score to settle with that old boy."

"What?"

"I'm gonna troll with you, missy."

"He's insane, Slop! He's a killer!"

Betsy gulped as she felt the barrel of Slop's .38 in her ribs.

"You just keep your mouth shut," he said.

"Slop, what in *God's name* do you think you're doing?"

"I said shut the fuck *up.*"

Close behind her, holding her left arm tightly, the gun in her ribs, Slop guided her to a wall that was opposite the dance-hall entrance.

He began to inch her along the wall toward the door that led backstage.

"There's that sucker now," Slop said.

Betsy looked through a corridor of drunks and saw Lank Allred in the doorway of the Pioneer Palace. Lank smiled cordially at the man on the door as he signed an autograph for him.

Now in front of Casa Mañana, Bob Walker, Ben Throckmorton, and Florine, who had been called out of the theater by a Texas Ranger, were frantic. Betsy was missing. Nobody knew where she was. Nobody knew where Lank Allred was, only that he had shot two men. There was madness and confusion all around them.

Captain Frank Hamer was bent over a stretcher talking to Tom Leland.

Roy Lawton, on another stretcher, was being loaded into one of two ambulances that had driven onto the showgrounds and were parked outside the entrance to the theater.

Uniformed cops were shouting at onlookers to stand back and shouting at one another to stand over here, stand over there.

O. L. Beaton, touching the lavender knot on the side of his head, was telling Bernice, Shady, Eva Jane, and Captain A. T. Johnson how he had come this close to being killed by a goofy bastard who was more dangerous than a Goddamn Mexican with a driver's license!

"Yee feckers goan stin ear or goo keshy fecker?" Shady said.

A. T. Johnson looked around for a translation.

O. L. said, "He wants to know if you fuckers are gonna stand here or go catch the fucker."

Two Texas Rangers were guarding Tommy Jack Lucas and Shirley Watters, who were in custody in handcuffs. They had been hauled out of Sally Rand's Nude Ranch, and Shirley wasn't at all happy about it.

"What do you think?" Tommy Jack asked her.

"What do I think about *what?*"

"That phony nude ranch. You can't see no lap moss in there. They got it covered up with biscuits."

Shirley sighed. "All my life I been marchin' in the dumb-shits' parade. I'd like to meet *one man* in Texas who thought about somethin' besides money and pussy."

"*I* do," Tommy Jack said.

"Name somethin'!"

"Football," said Tommy Jack, satisfied that he had exposed in Shirley an obvious lack of sensitivity when it came to men.

Shirley struggled with her handcuffs. "I haven't done nothin' to nobody," she said to one of the lawmen. "Since when is it a felony to fuck a Texas Ranger?"

Frank Hamer came over to Bob, Ben, and Florine. "Tom Leland thinks he saw Betsy goin' up that way. He thinks he saw Lank goin' up that way, too. We have a lot of men out here. We have ways to handle this. You folks stay calm."

"Calm's ass," said Bob Walker, who took off in the direction of the dance hall, an old Claybelle quarterback on a broken-field run.

A stagehand and wardrobe lady did not notice Betsy and Sloppy Herster as Slop, still holding the gun in Betsy's back, moved the two of them through the backstage area and into a storage room.

Slop switched off the lights in the storage room, but the room remained dimly lit by the glow of the Centennial park filtering through a window.

Slop ripped a sash off a costume hanging on a rack and tied Betsy's hands behind her and fastened her to a post, a roof support.

"This is workin' out real good," Slop said. "He's comin' in here after you, but I got a surprise for *his* ass."

"Slop, the window," Betsy said, her lips quivering. "Please let me go."

He put the gun in her face. "Do I have to gag you? You better keep fuckin' still or it's gonna be him *and* you."

Betsy couldn't help thinking about the grotesque novelty of her predicament. There were two psychopaths loose on the world tonight and she would soon be trapped in a room with both of them.

In the dance hall, Frank Hamer and a dozen of his men were circulating as unobtrusively as possible.

Not Bob Walker.

Bob was clawing his way through drunks, asking anyone who looked reasonably intelligent if he or she had seen a person of Betsy's description. Somebody said they thought they had seen her go backstage.

Bob bruised past a beefy truck driver in a baseball cap and work shirt. The truck driver swung Bob around. "Who you pushin', ace?"

"Fuck you," said Bob, dismissing him idly.

The truck driver gave Bob a shove, and Bob angrily floored him—with a left to the stomach and a right to the jaw. Bob didn't have time for this shit. He plowed on toward the backstage door.

Two cowboys looked down at the truck driver, then at Bob. "Must be drinkin' tequila," one of the cowboys grinned.

Up on the stage, Hinda Wassau was doing a lascivious thing to the curtain, as Booty now sang:

> I don't know why
> I love you like I do.
> I don't know why, I just do.

In the storeroom, Slop had found a piece of lead pipe a foot long and an inch thick in a box of tools and plumbing fixtures. With the pipe in one hand and the .38 in the other, he positioned himself by the door, in the dark, where the door would open away from him.

Betsy had been trying to get her hands free and wondering what she would do *then* when she suddenly held her breath, for the door was creaking open.

The first thing Slop—and Betsy—could see coming through the door was Lank Allred's .45. Then his hand. Then his forearm.

Whack!

Slop slammed the lead pipe down on Lank's forearm, knocking the pistol from his hand. A split second later, Slop yanked the Ranger into the room by his shirtfront and just as swiftly kicked him in the nuts.

Lank sucked air and was bent into a crouch. But not for long.

Slop cracked him across the temple with the lead pipe, and this blow put Lank on the floor.

Lank shook his head and came to a sitting position. He looked up at Slop. "Why, you no-count little scum."

Lank started to get up, but Slop, with a slobbering laugh, fired a slug into the Ranger's belly.

Lank's eyes bugged as he was rocked backwards. He now was slumped in a corner, his guts stinging. He was nowhere near death but he was incapacitated, which was how Slop wanted him.

Slop moved nearer Lank and leveled the gun at Lank's face and cocked the hammer.

"No, Slop, no!" Betsy cried out.

Slop snickered as he looked at Lank. "You ain't so tough now, are you?"

Lank muttered, "Use your head, son. You don't want to kill nobody. Kill me and you'll ride Old Toasty—that's a cinch."

Slop looked over at Betsy. "He don't know what I'm gonna do. He ain't for shit without his gun."

Slop turned back to Lank and pointed the .38 in the Ranger's face again. Slop's maniacal gaze told Lank that Slop just might pull the trigger.

Lank Allred was suddenly a person no one had ever seen before. Stark terror had replaced the cold self-assured look that was as much a part of him as his badge.

"Don't kill me," Lank said, cringing, raising his arms in front of his face. "I don't want to die, son. Come on now." He was actually in tears.

Slop snickered again as he slowly lowered the nose of the .38 to Lank's crotch. "April Fool, *motherfucker!*"

Slop fired two shots into Lank's crotch, another into his chest, and finished him off with a bullet between the eyes.

Slop Herster plunked down on a stool, the revolver dangling from his hand.

Bob Walker came bursting into the room an instant later.

Slop alertly pointed the gun at Bob. "Stay where you are, Bobby!"

Bob glanced at Betsy.

"Watch out, Bob, he's crazy!"

"I ain't crazy," Slop said. "I'm just even, is all." Slop let the gun drop to the floor. "Hell, I can count," he said. "It's empty."

Bob quickly kicked the .38 across the floor. Just then,

Frank Hamer, A. T. Johnson, and two other Texas Rangers barged into the room, their weapons drawn.

Johnson and the two Rangers pounced on Slop.

Bob Walker sprang to Betsy and untied her hands. She fell into his arms. He held her and caressed her.

"It's okay, babe. It's all over. You all right?"

"I think so," she said.

Frank Hamer took out a handkerchief and picked up Slop's gun.

In handcuffs and being roughhoused out of the room, Slop said, "Betsy?"

She looked at him.

"I'm sorry," he said. "I'm sorry about . . . ever'thing."

The Rangers shoved Slop out the door.

Examining Slop's gun, Frank Hamer said, "I'll be damned. There's one round left."

To Bob Walker, the Ranger said, "He could have used it on you, son. I guess lettin' you off the hook was his way of tryin' to make it up to the young lady here."

The Ranger's eyes shifted to Betsy. "Sloppy Herster killed your husband, Miss Throckmorton. Slop and Tommy Jack were the ones lining up those 'lookouts' for Lank."

"Jesus," said Betsy quietly.

Frank Hamer said, "That night in the hobo camp, your husband overheard Slop and Tommy Jack talkin' to a young drifter, a kid we tracked down in Lubbock, thanks to a lot of hard work by a lot of good Texas Rangers. Your husband confronted 'em. Slop panicked, and . . . well, that's what happened."

Everything had come to a stop in the dance hall. Police were all over the place. Three of them were annoying the hell out of Ben Throckmorton. Ben and Florine were being restrained from going backstage.

They had seen Slop Herster led away by the Texas Rangers, and A. T. Johnson had told Ben that his daughter and Bob Walker were unharmed, but Ben was taking down the badge numbers of the cops and telling them what the *Claybelle Times-Standard* and the *Fort Worth Star-Telegram* and Mr. Amon G. Carter, his good friend, were going to do to their asses, which weren't worth a shit for anything, anyhow, except for beating up colored folks and giving people a parking ticket!

"And I'll tell you another Goddamn thing," Ben was saying as Betsy and Bob Walker came walking through a cordon of officers. Bob ushered Betsy into her daddy's arms.

"Thank the Lord you're okay, honey."

"Who's got a cigarette?" Betsy asked.

Florine lit a Lucky and gave it to Betsy as she hugged her, and said, "Would it be fair to guess you have a tale to tell?"

Betsy managed a smile for Florine.

Outside the Pioneer Palace, more policemen were keeping the crowd back. Bob Walker and Ben were each holding on to Betsy.

Frank Hamer said, "I won't put you through it tonight, Miss Throckmorton, but I'll need a report of everything you saw. What if I come to Claybelle tomorrow?"

"That'll be fine," Betsy said. "I can tell you it's the longest I've ever gone without a cigarette."

Frank Hamer instructed two Rangers to walk Betsy and the others to Ben's Packard, which was parked in a V.I.P. lot about a hundred yards away, near the main entrance.

Music and revelry resumed inside the dance hall. They could hear Booty Pettigrew's whiskey voice.

Is it true what they say about Dixie?
Does the sun really shine all the time?

They had walked less than ten feet when Betsy's attention was suddenly drawn to a public telephone booth.

"What time is it?" she asked anxiously.

"Eleven-thirty," Bob said, glancing at his wristwatch.

"Who has a nickel? I need some change!"

Ben reached in his pocket. He handed his daughter a fistful of coins.

Betsy raced to the telephone.

Bob Walker and Ben and Florine stood and watched Betsy at the phone, speaking rapidly, thinking hard, now cussing, now laughing, now gesturing with the hand that held the cigarette.

They were looking at her with love, with pride, with awe. None of them had to ask what she was doing. They all knew. If she could dictate fast enough, she could still make the final edition.

PART FIVE

The
Newshen

Epilogue

BETSY THROCKMORTON sat on a bench in the Claybelle square and assured the young reporter that her old hometown had looked better in the days when there weren't so many yellow hamburger arches soaring above the treetops.

This was a fine day in May of 1987.

Betsy was off on another book tour that had brought her through Fort Worth and Dallas, and she was granting an interview to a feature writer on the *Claybelle Times-Standard,* a newspaper that was now being printed in dizzying colors and had become part of a New Jersey–based media chain.

She had rented a car and driven to Claybelle from her hotel in Fort Worth. No bother. It was an easy trip these days. Eight-lane freeways veering off in every conceivable direction now connected the Dallas–Fort Worth "Metroplex" to all of the fast-food ghettos and instant townhouse slums that were devastating North Central Texas.

Before going to meet the reporter, Betsy had stopped for a while at the cemetery, to say hello to Ben and Florine, to Elizabeth, and to Warren and Florence. They were all buried in the same family plot.

She had also stopped for a few moments to gaze at the mall on Wildflower Drive. "Attention, K-Mart shoppers," Betsy said to herself. "My old room was on aisle three."

The reporter, whose name was Sean or Skip, something like that, was a trim young man with a short dark beard. He wore scruffy jeans, sneakers, a faded black polo shirt, and spoke in the flat, indistinguishable accent of someone who had moved to Texas from Cleveland or Seattle or one of those Omahas in between.

"You still smoke?" he said with alarm as Betsy, now seventy-nine, lit a Winston.

Her hair was completely gray now, but full and beautifully coiffured. Betsy was still a handsome, erect, lively woman.

She said, "I smoke as much as I can—for a person with only one mouth."

One of Millie's old lines.

When Millie had passed away in 1985, Betsy had flown to the funeral in England on a private jet owned by Millie's fourth husband, Sir James Corcoran, the conglomerateur, who adored Millie and had given her half of London and an Alp or two over the last twenty years. Like Betsy, Millie had smoked two packs a day, often three, since college, but she had fooled the clean-air zealots and lived a healthy seventy-six years. It had been a freak fall down a long curving staircase in her stately home in Sussex that had done her in. Standing over the closed casket at the funeral, Betsy had said, "You bitch, I told you cigarettes would kill you."

To the reporter, Betsy said, "I hope you're not one of those people who worry about 'passive' smoke."

He wasn't.

"Good," said Betsy. "It's only a cigarette. I'm getting fed up with people who act like I'm wrapping their mouth around the exhaust pipe of a city bus!"

The young man claimed he had made an effort to familiarize himself with Betsy's career as a journalist, war correspondent, and author. He had read two of her books, he said, but only parts of her latest one, *The Newshen,* a memoir. He said he was sure it was a good book, but he couldn't appreciate "all that World War Two stuff." It was a long time ago.

"I can tell you how the book ends," Betsy said. "I elope with my manual typewriter."

Betsy looked around the square and thought of another lovely afternoon in Claybelle, in the spring of '39, the day she and Bob decided to move to New York. Bob had been offered the sports columnist's job on the *Daily Mirror,* so Betsy had accepted a long-standing offer to become a staff writer for *Life,* with the personal guarantee from "Harry" Luce that she could cover the war.

"What war?" Stillwell Padgam-Norris had asked.

The one Hitler was going to start, she had said.

With his unfailing air of *Time-Life* self-confidence, Still

Norris had said, "Oh, I rather imagine the German people are too intelligent to do anything *that* mischievous."

Three months later the Nazis had invaded Poland.

Well, you had to be there, Betsy said to the *Times-Standard* reporter, who had reacted to the anecdote with a blank stare.

The young man wasn't the least bit intrigued by the fact that very few lady journalists had covered World War II; that Betsy had been among the most prominent, along with Margaret Bourke-White, the *Life* photographer, Marguerite Higgins of the *Herald-Tribune,* Barbara Finch of Reuters, and Rebecca West of *The New Yorker.*

"We couldn't get in the locker rooms in those days, you know," Betsy said with a glint.

Another blank expression.

It crossed Betsy's mind that she was once again being interviewed by a person whose sense of history dated all the way back to his first spasm at a rock concert, but she was used to it.

"That war was the Grand Adventure," she said. "I wasn't about to miss it. Journalism is a seductive profession, and it is irresistibly so, I think, when there's big stuff to write about. No other writing compares with it. That's a good quote. You should jot it down."

The reporter scribbled something in his spiral notebook.

Betsy still found it fascinating that some of the lady war correspondents had wound up in the same place at the same time. Amazing when you considered how few of them there were and how global the conflict was.

The two Maggies, for instance. Maggie White was the first woman assigned to cover the U.S. Army Air Force, Betsy explained, and Maggie Higgins traveled with the Seventh Army in France, but both of them had somehow arranged to be on the scene when Patton's Third Army liberated Buchenwald.

Sean or Skip had seen the old movie *Patton* on TV, but he had never heard of Buchenwald.

"It wasn't a ski run," Betsy said.

At that particular time, Betsy recalled, she had moved to the Pacific Theater to cover the Marines' assault on Iwo Jima, and it was on Guam that she had met Barbara Finch and they had become partners in crime. They decided to get a firsthand report of the battle on Iwo Jima. So from Guam they had hopped on a cargo plane and had flown to an island in the Marianas, and from there they had talked their way onto a Navy C-47 hospital plane that was on its way to Iwo Jima to pick up wounded Marines. The plane had landed on Iwo Jima when the fighting was the most furious—the Marines were in the process of having to kill 20,000 Japanese troops to take the island.

The plane had only stayed on the ground for thirty minutes, but Betsy and Barbara Finch had been the first women to set foot on Iwo Jima.

"I'll never forget the name of that plane," Betsy said. "It was called *Peg O' My Heart.*"

"Do you have a favorite story you've written?"

"No. I've never stopped typing long enough to give it any thought. I don't believe in retirement. When you stop competing, you die—and that includes competing with yourself."

"Your D-Day story has appeared in most anthologies."

"I suppose it's because of the event. It was a fairly big regatta."

The reporter read Betsy's lead to her from his spiral notebook.

"From a balcony seat in the sky above, in a combat Marauder piloted by a young Texas boy, I watched the curtain go up on the greatest drama in the history of mankind, the invasion of Hitler's Europe."

"My editor says it would have been a better lead if you hadn't used first person."

"Oh?" said Betsy. "What did *he* do in the war?"

About Ben Throckmorton, the reporter said: Did people really call him Football Silly—to his face?

Betsy said, "I adored my daddy, but he *was* Football Silly. Nineteen Thirty-eight was his silliest year. TCU won the National Championship that season, quite easily, in fact. The Frogs had a wonderful little quarterback, Davey O'Brien. He was an All-American, a great passer, the best player in the country. He won the Heisman Trophy. Daddy was impossible. When we all went down to the Sugar Bowl to watch Davey and the Frogs beat Carnegie Tech, Daddy had a bright purple suit made for the occasion. He looked like the King of Siam. Florine and I wouldn't let him wear it to the game. After the war he became Hogan Silly. When TCU stopped winning National Championships as often as Daddy liked, he and Florine started traveling around the country watching Ben Hogan win golf tournaments."

The reporter seemed puzzled by the name.

"Ben Hogan?" Betsy said. "The famous golfer? From Fort Worth?"

"Sorry. I'm not too up on golf."

Betsy reached for another cigarette.

They talked briefly about her son and daughter and the two grandchildren. Betsy's son, Bob Jr., was a network news producer in New York. Bob Jr.'s two boys, Ben and Jake, were both in college, the smart one at Duke and the "normal" one at Oklahoma. Betsy's daughter, Millicent, was a bond trader in New York who had yet to find time to fall in love.

"I don't quite know how I've happened to produce a bond trader for a daughter," Betsy said. "I blame Stanford for it, frankly. But I must say she's good at what she does, whatever that is. I could have two books on the best-seller list at the same time and my income wouldn't equal her annual bonus. There's still a lot wrong with this country."

"You've written that the Thirties is your favorite decade. Were you serious?"

"Everything was better in the Thirties, young man. Food was better. Movies were better. Automobiles, trains, ships . . . music, songs, *singers*. Newspapers, football games, baseball players, gangsters, tyrants . . . Presidents, it goes without saying. Theater, drugstores, summer nights, rivers, cafes, saloons—everything but air conditioning. It was the longest decade, incidentally. It began with the Wall Street crash in '29 and it wasn't over until Pearl Harbor in '41. Write that down."

"What about the Forties?"

"Great war, good music."

"The Fifties?"

"Boring."

"Sixties?"

"Stoned."

"Seventies?"

"Wired."

"Eighties?"

"Health nuts. In the Nineties, I expect we'll see thousands of people curiously dropping dead from the mesquite-grilled fish and overdone exercise of the Eighties."

Betsy was asked why her husband had never tried to write a novel, or some sort of nonfiction book, of his own.

"He published a collection once," she said. "*No Cheering in the Press Box*. It's still in print. Your sports editor may have read it, if he cares anything about his craft. Bob took pride in being a sports columnist. He worked harder at it than people realized. He always said he had an eight-hundred-word mentality—he couldn't endure any subject longer than eight hundred words. He still says this, but it's not true. I can think of one or two books he's read all the way through within the past year."

Although Betsy had been awarded a Pulitzer Prize in fiction for her novel *The Deadline Muse,* the Pulitzer she treasured the most was her first, the one she received for local reporting back in the Thirties.

The reporter said, "I wanted to look that story up in our files, but we had to throw out all our microfilm prior to 1950."

"Whose idea was *that?*"

"We needed room for another computer terminal."

Betsy looked away, sadly.

"They say you dictated that story over the phone, right on deadline."

"It was the only choice I had."

"Do you remember your lead?"

"Of course."

"What was it?"

Betsy smiled as she said it.

"Lank Allred wept."

Afterword

A LOT OF PEOPLE who consider themselves Dan Jenkins fans don't even know he wrote *Fast Copy*. Published in 1988, it's the one Jenkins novel that pretty much disappeared from reader radar soon after publication. *Semi-Tough's* Billy Clyde Puckett has lived on forever; ditto Juanita Hutchins from *Baja Oklahoma*. Why not Betsy Throckmorton from *Fast Copy*, since she might be the most interesting made-up character Jenkins has ever committed to print?

A lot of it probably has to do with reader expectations. Dan Jenkins only came to fiction in his professional midlife. For a couple of decades, readers knew him as one of the best sports writers around, and probably the best golf writer ever. His articles in *Sports Illustrated* and *Playboy* were classic. Whether he was describing the plight of high-school quarterback Jack Mildren trying to pick a college or why it wasn't as easy as it looked for Arnold Palmer to sink those long putts, Jenkins combined a fine eye for detail with a wonderful ear for dialogue. He let readers see and hear things no other writer could bring before them.

Then, in 1972, Jenkins blew everyone away with *Semi-Tough*, a funny, insightful glimpse into the bawdy, black-and-blue world of professional football. The antics of Billy Clyde Puckett and Shake Tiller kept readers laughing so hard they had trouble turning to the next page. Quicker than you could say, "best seller," Dan Jenkins was semi-famous, semi-wealthy, and everyone was ready for him to write more funny books.

He obliged. *Dead Solid Perfect* in 1974, *Baja Oklahoma* in 1981 and *Life Its Ownself* in 1984 (the latter continuing the Billy Clyde/Shake saga) all delighted readers for the same reasons *Semi-Tough* had. They were racy, obscenity-laden paeans to political incorrectness and the wisdom of people who knew enough to not take themselves too seriously. The good guys always won. Nobody died.

Fast Copy was different. Jenkins meant it to be. He kept some elements from his previous books—the humor and the cussing, especially—but, from the first pages, *Fast Copy* was obviously a book with a purpose. Jenkins wanted readers to laugh and learn a little Texas history at the same time. Some of his subject matter, specifically murders of destitute men during the Depression, was a lot more serious than who won a mythical Super Bowl. And, this time, one of the good guys died.

So readers and critics, who'd been expecting yet another Jenkins 100 percent chucklethon, were surprised by *Fast Copy*. They responded by (a) not buying it and (b) panning it. Some of the criticism—that Jenkins was trying to do too much in one book, that it was a mistake to juxtapose matter-of-fact tragedy with out-and-out slapstick—was probably valid. But anyone who called *Fast Copy* a bad book was mistaken. It still contains some of Dan Jenkins' best-crafted characters, from spunky protagonist Betsy Throckmorton to hilariously inept small-town sportswriter Big 'Un Darly. There are scenes, particularly when Betsy takes over the Claybelle *Times-Standard,* that can stand with any in Jenkins' better-known novels. And *Fast Copy* is, above all else, a glimpse into the real recesses of Dan Jenkins' heart. He loves Texas and Fort Worth and college football and small-town newspapers. That shows on every page. If he tried to do too much in the book, it was because there was so much he wanted his readers to know.

Accordingly, the first chapters of *Fast Copy* are intended to be as much history lessons as they are entertainment. Twenty-seven-year-old Betsy Throckmorton returns to her Texas hometown of Claybelle from New York City, where she has worked at *Time* magazine and married co-worker Ted Winton, a college football star-turned-journalist. Betsy's father, Ben Throckmorton, owns most of Claybelle, a small town some two dozen miles southwest of Fort Worth. The Throckmorton family holdings include the town newspaper and the radio station, which Ted will oversee. Jenkins presents this with the same sense of edgy humor that distinguished his earlier, better-selling novels:

"To start with, she had told her daddy, it might be a slight improvement to run more stories about world affairs than how to put up peach preserves. She was determined to be an aggressive, innovative editor. She understood that most people didn't care for the press in general, but screw the people. The people needed a free press whether they wanted one or not."

But readers lulled into thinking their old pal Dan was spinning another funny yarn were set straight by chapter three. The year 1935 was the very depth of the Depression, and Jenkins' description of a hobo camp outside Fort Worth was anything but humorous:

"One of the hobos, a gaunt unshaven man in his thirties, held up a hand-lettered sign that said, WORK IS WHAT I WANT—NOT CHARITY. An older black man wearing a tattered army jacket over an undershirt and moth-eaten wool trousers on this hot day—he must have owned nothing else—clutched a sign that said, MY CHILDRENS NEED MILK AND WOMAN NEEDS SHOES AND DRESSES. Leaning against the fender of a rusty jalopy, a younger white man pointed to the sign he had made, which said, STARVED, STALLED, AND STRANDED. A frail young woman, Betsy's age maybe, held hands with a little girl of about seven. Both were caked in dirt. They smiled feebly at the passengers on the train."

I suspect that is where too many Dan Jenkins fans decided to put down *Fast Copy* and re-read *Semi-Tough*.

The book goes on to follow two main plots: Betsy taking over the newspaper, and a Texas Ranger blasting his way into headlines by killing a series of bank robbers after the Texas Bankers Association begins paying $5,000 for any miscreants shot dead while committing holdups. Scenes in the *Times-Standard* newsroom are classic Jenkins; just as Billy Clyde Puckett could use page after page describing his eccentric teammates, Betsy has to deal with colorful hick journalists who aren't receptive to writing stories that actually make a whole lot of sense. Reading these scenes, we can laugh and learn at the same time. But the bank shootings are simply horrifying stuff. It's soon evident that local Ranger Lank Allred and a couple less-than-bright associates are setting up gullible transients as profitable, unsuspecting targets. Jenkins presents these passages matter-of-factly. Laughs are non-existent here, as they should be—Jenkins is basing this part of his novel on real-life events. But the effect is jarring for readers who've just finished chuckling over one of Big 'Un Darly's convoluted stories. ("The furor and holy crusade of football is in town again and was in evidence last night at Clay Field, which have a lusteral history to it, like all stadiums buried in a colorful past, which Clay Field harkens to its depths.")

When Jenkins brings these plot elements together, he does so at the expense of reader affection for Betsy. Though Ted has given up a high-profile career in New York City to come back and run a radio station in his wife's tiny hometown, Betsy still finds herself regretting they ever married. She's more impressed by old boyfriend Bob Walker, a sports columnist for a big-time Dallas newspaper. Since Jenkins has made Ted an altogether sympathetic character, it's unnerving to have him unappreciated by Betsy—and even worse when Ted, trying to write a first-person account of life in a transient camp, runs afoul of Lank Allred's minions and is murdered by them. By the time Betsy finally helps justice to be done amid the hoopla of the Texas Frontier Centennial opening in Fort Worth in 1936—Casa Manana and Sally Rand's Nude Ranch, anyone?—there's no laughter left in the story. And laughter is what Dan Jenkins' readers had wanted most. They wouldn't settle for clear-eyed historical fiction instead.

But, thirteen years later, we can. There's so much good about *Fast Copy* that it deserves a second chance. Complete enjoyment is possible just flipping through its pages for glimpses of real-life figures interacting with made-up characters: newspaper publisher/civic hustler Amon Carter is here; so are steely-eyed Ranger Frank Hamer and sportswriting superstar Grantland Rice. Even FDR makes a brief appearance, pushing a button thousands of miles away to officially open the front gates of the Texas Frontier Centennial. Historically speaking, there's something true on every page of this book.

If we can forgive Betsy her irrational lack of appreciation for Ted, we can find much to admire about her—one scene in which she backs down an advertiser who wants control over her paper's editorial content ought to be required reading in every college journalism class. In *Baja Oklahoma*, Juanita's dream of being a country singer instead of a waitress came true through luck as much as anything else. Betsy would flatten Juanita in a catfight. And Lank Allred has an almost Dickensian aura of evil. Oliver

Twist's Bill Sikes would have worked for Lank, not the other way around.

Let's conclude that *Fast Copy's* sins, such as they are, mostly involve Dan Jenkins trying to do two things at the same time. (I personally have never liked the epilogue, where we learn Betsy went on to marry Bob and win a couple of Pulitzers; real life is never that neat. But feel free to disagree.) The book would have worked as a straight comedy and could have worked as flat-out tragedy. I suspect funny writers, like movie comedians, long for a chance to show they can do the serious stuff, too. In *Fast Copy*, Dan Jenkins took a chance he didn't have to, and more or less got his literary wrist slapped for it. He's since written more best-sellers, all in the *Semi-Tough* vein. The man is simply a damned good writer. Being funny in print isn't easy; being consistently funny, which Jenkins can be, is impossible for all but the best of 'em.

Still, if you enjoy reading Dan Jenkins, you'd be depriving yourself if you didn't try *Fast Copy*. The book shows him trying to bring something extra to a formula that was already success-ful. I liken *Fast Copy* to some of the lesser-appreciated jazz exper-iments of Miles Davis. The true masters constantly have to test boundaries, have to try and push themselves out of comfortable patterns now and then. If there are a few off-notes in *Fast Copy*, its overall music will still have meaning for anyone willing to read it with their hearts as well as their minds.

—Jeff Guinn
Fort Worth, Texas
2001

About the Author

Much of the detail in *Fast Copy* comes naturally to Dan Jenkins, who is a Fort Worth native and a product of Paschal and TCU. In his early career, he wrote for the now defunct papers, the Fort Worth *Press* and the Dallas *Times-Herald*, then moved on to New York and *Sports Illustrated* and *Golf Digest*. He is the author of sixteen books, including *Baja Oklahoma, Semi-Tough, Life Its Ownself*, and *You Gotta Play Hurt*. *Fast Copy*, first published in 1988, was his sixth novel, tenth book. His newest novel is *Rude Behavior*.

After living in New York City and Florida, Jenkins and his wife, June, have moved back to Fort Worth to be "closer to barbecue, Tex-Mex, and the TCU stadium."

Sally Jenkins, daughter of Dan and June, is the coauthor, with Lance Armstrong, of the best-selling *It's Not About the Bike*. Jeff Guinn is the book review editor of the Fort Worth *Star-Telegram*.